LAST EXIT TO BROOKLYN

LAST EXIT TO BROOKLYN

HUBERT SELBY JR

BLOOMSBURY

First published in Great Britain by Calder and Boyars 1966

This Bloomsbury edition first published 2000
in arrangement with Marion Boyars Publishing Ltd

This paperback edition published 2004

Bloomsbury Publishing Plc, 38 Soho Square, London W1D 3HB

A CIP catalogue record for this book
is available from the British Library

ISBN 0 7475 7459 6

10 9 8 7 6 5 4 3 2

All papers used by Bloomsbury Publishing are natural,
recyclable products made from wood
grown in well-managed forests.
The manufacturing processes conform to the
environmental regulations of the country of origin.

Typeset by Hewer Text Ltd, Edinburgh
Printed in Great Britain by Clays Ltd, St Ives plc

www.bloomsbury.com

INTRODUCTION

I started writing because I did not want to die having done nothing with my life.

I had gone to sea when I was 15, as a merchant seaman, and at the age of 18 I was taken off a ship in Germany and the doctors said I couldnt live more than a few months. I had TB and both lungs were extremely diseased. I came back to the States and went into the Marine Hospital. This was in October of 1946, and streptomycin was an experimental drug being used to treat TB, but none was available for merchant seaman. My family was able to buy it at an incredibly inflated price and brought it to the hospital, where it was administered. It kept me alive, and healed enough of the disease so I could undergo surgery. The toxic effects of the streptomycin were strong and it impaired my vision, my hearing, my inner ear was almost totally destroyed and I couldnt walk properly and I would fall down in the dark, and all my muscles were petrified from the drug. I also went wacky . . . or perhaps I should say, wackier. But I was alive.

By the time I got out of the hospitals I had spent 3 years in bed, had 10 ribs removed, one lung had been permanently collapsed and a section had been cut out of the other one. And then things got worse. All in all I have spent a lot of time and energy, as well as money, just staying alive. But here I is.

I had been out of the hospital for about 5 or 6 years when I was suddenly back in with asthma. A 'specialist' told me I cant live, I simply do not have enough lungs to survive, so I should just go home and relax. I got a second opinion in the next hospital. I have a rather defiant attitude and refused to die just because a doctor told me I cant live. Actually I started to die 36 hours before I was born, so dying was a way of life for me.

I was married at this time and our daughter was about 2 or 3 years old. We were living behind a barber shop in the Marine Park section of Brooklyn. It was the Christmas Season and my wife had a part-time job at Macys while I stayed home. One day I had an extraordinarily profound experience, one more 'real' than any I had ever had. I experienced the fact that some day I was going to die, not almost, as had been happening, and managing to survive, but I was really going to die, and just before I died two things would happen: One, I would regret my entire life; Two, I would want to live my life over again, and then I would die. This experience terrified me. The thought that I would live whatever number of years and look back on it and see I hadnt done anything with my life, had wasted it, was something I just could not live with. So I decided to write.

As I recall my reasoning at the time, all these years later, I wanted to be a composer, but knew I could never go to school long enough to learn how, but I did know the alphabet so I figured I/d be a writer. I had to do something!

It seems to me I was less equipped to be an artist than any other artist who has ever lived. I only had 9 years of schooling, and when I was a kid I was completely physically oriented. I never read, never studied, never thought of writing. Actually, I have no natural talent in any area, including mechanics, electronics, or any thing else. I was a pretty good football and hockey player in my early teens, but was not an exceptionally talented athlete either. The one thing I have always had is determination and a hard head. At times these attributes have caused me great pain, but they have also saved my life.

Actually I started reading shoot-em-ups in the hospital, reading everything from S. S. Van Dine to Mickey Spillane. Then eventually I started reading novels. When I got out of the hospital I started hanging out with a few guys in my neighborhood who were going to Brooklyn College and had been reading since they were very young. One of them is Gil Sorrentino, who became my literary mentor. Hes one of those nuts who read *The Iliad* when he was 6 years old, and had been writing poetry since he was a kid. I would listen to these guys talk about books and writers and try to remember as many of the names as possible. The next day I would sneak, literally, over to the library and get the books. I was hooked.

Having made the decision I got a portable Remington typewriter and looked at it. I had no idea for a story, or anything else. So I looked at it for a few weeks, then wrote a letter to someone. They answered and I wrote again. I think my first piece of fiction was a suicide note in which I attacked every institution I could think of. Eventually I started to write a story. I would read what I had written each day to my wife and we got a lot of laughs out of it. After about 12 pages I realized I had no idea what I was doing. So I threw everything away and thought about it for a few days and became aware of the foundation of my life as a writer.

I realized that everything, for me, is in the story, the people, but I had to do more than just tell a story. If you want to hear a great story, go to any candy store in NYC, or poolroom, or street corner, and youll hear stories that will knock your socks off. But I had to do more than that. I was aware that we all have a million stories, so why was a particular one in my mind? It seemed to me simple enough: that was the one I was supposed to write. I realized that for me I had to understand the essence of the story given me to write, and for me that meant to get to the heart of the matter, the true dynamic, and from that essence create a work of art. Obviously this required me to go as deep into the darkness as possible and bring it back to the light. Just as obviously, there is always the chance that you will go too deeply into the darkness and not come back. So far I have, but there is no guarantee I will continue to do so.

I was also aware that the primary responsibility of the artist is to get free of the human ego. I have no right to impose myself, in any way, between the reader and the people in the story. It is my job, as a writer, to fulfill the responsibility to the story that has been given me to write. So often I will see these people making decisions, and taking actions, that will lead to a disaster and want to change the story, but I do not have the right to do that. I must simply honor their lives and allow them to follow their own path, and not interfere in the natural evolution of their lives.

I also knew that I was a frustrated teacher, and a frustrated preacher, and had to work very hard to get them, as well as all my opinions, out of the work. If there is a message in the work it is in the lives of the people, their story, and how they live it. Who cares what I think about such matters. I/ll leave that to the experts and professionals, they always do a much better job of telling people how to live.

So I sat with this typewriter and started teaching myself how to write. I quickly discovered that thinking of a story is not the same as getting a line of prose to say exactly, and simply, what needs to be said. How do you get Harry from the living room to the bathroom? Seems simple, but can be impossible. You can end up either forgetting about it or having him wet his pants. So I came face to face with the biggest terror a writer faces, a blank piece of paper, but, thank God, we do have a wastepaper basket!

I read so many different writers at the same time I did not have to work off any influences. Also, never having gone to school I didnt have to unlearn all the lies a person can learn in school about how you should write. I was unaware of the 'rules of writing' as proclaimed by individuals who had never written an original line in their lives. Fortunately, I had no recourse but to find my own way.

I was influenced by many writers, certainly Melville, Joyce, and Babel, but the only 'conscious' influence I had as a writer was Beethoven. I dont mean I was trying to put his music into words, but the power of his music really inspired me. He has the ability to make everything so simple it becomes profound. He knows, to perfection, how to hammer a phrase into your mind, repeating it over and over, yet always stopping at precisely the right time. And his work is beautifully inevitable, yet never predictable, no matter how many times you hear it. And there are times when his music is so exquisitely lyrical it makes you cry. He really stirs up the emotions and makes it possible for you to make sense of what you are feeling.

The gestation of a story may start years before Im aware of it, but when it starts to come to the surface of my mind I can feel it. Then I have an image of it, and can hear it. Then I sit down and try to find the word that perfectly describes what I see, hear and feel.

It took me 6 years to write *Last Exit* because I had to learn how to write. First I had to become aware of myself as a writer, and I realized that I wanted to put the reader through an emotional experience. I wanted the reader to 'feel' what the people were experiencing even if they were unaware of it. I did not want to limit the readers imagination, but to give them room so they could experience the story from their own POV, from their own lifes experiences. So again, I had to get out of the way.

Because I write by ear, I had to develop a typography that would work as musical notation. I believe all the senses are involved in our experiences, so the way a story 'looks' on the page is important. Forcing the eye to move an extra space will provide the ear with the necessary musical effect.

Dialog was another difficult task. I have always been enamored with the music of speech, and the streets of NYC are certainly rich with this music. But if I were to simply put the speech down as spoken it would be incomprehensible. Profanity was the foundation of much of the speech I was dealing with and would be a bore if simply transcribed. Also, every area, at times every street corner, has its own vernacular, all of which would be unintelligible to the reader. Yet I had to be true to the people in the story. So I had to find a way to edit the speech so the same flavor was there as well as reflecting the psychodynamics of the people, and to make the various idioms self-explanatory. Not easy.

I also had to create the natural flow of the conversations, which meant I had to eliminate all the conventional 'he saids' so I could create the feelings of the streets and people of the streets. This meant concentrating on the specific vocabularies and rhythms of speech of individuals so the reader doesnt get bogged down in trying to figure out whose talking . . . they will either know or it wont make any difference to them.

This also had to be reflected in the narrative; e.g., when Vinnie is the subject the language and rhythms reflect him with their harshness; and with Georgette the sounds and rhythms are sibilant, soft, feminine, a lot of alliteration, the images romantic.

I came to realize that I did not know how to sit and think these things out, that my thinking was deceptive. I could believe I had found an answer, believing I had gone from A to D, when in reality I was still stuck in A. Ultimately the only way I could figure things out was by writing; i.e., thinking out loud. I ended up throwing away a lot of paper. What I was doing was struggling to find what the problem that needed solving was in a particular work. I believe we do not just learn everything at once, that at various times we are learning different aspects of writing. One time it may be structure, or dialog, or narrative, or balance or anything else. But once I could see clearly what it was I had to understand, the story usually flowed. 'Tralala,' which is about 20 pages long, took 2½ years to get to that point. The story starts with a very short, flat line, then starts to open and flow as she does, until eventually the line never ends as she starts to disintegrate and the final line is a couple of pages long, having the feeling of utter chaos, and never really ends, but stops.

A few weeks, or months, after starting to write, I had to go back to work, so I wrote at night for as long as I could. I would come home and take off my suit and tie, try to act like a husband and father for a while, then go to the typewriter and be a writer. It was impossible, but I guess the only way we can transcend the human limitations we establish is by being in an inhuman situation and are forced to exceed ourselves. There were times when I would sit there for a couple of hours and get one or two words. The end of 'The Queen Is Dead' was like this. Because Georgie was dying of an OD I initially thought I would have to be under the influence of some drug to do it. I took some Demerol I had for pain, but it didnt work. Next I tried sipping beer, but that was a failure. So I just sat there and did it one word at a time. It took a very long time to write the last couple of pages of that story.

Actually Georgies death was responsible for my writing *Last Exit*. I had written the first part of 'The Queen Is Dead,' the part up to where he gets stabbed in the leg and they take him home. It was called 'Loves Labors Lost.' About a year and a half later I found out that Georgie had been found dead in the street, the gutter, of an OD, and it moved me very much. He was probably still in his teens when he died, or not much older. Somehow it just didnt seem right for a life, any life, to be dismissed like that, so I felt I had to honor his life by completing his story, he deserved no less than that. Certainly not romanticize or sentimentalize it, but to allow him to live it as he lived it. With the completion of his story the book started to take shape.

I always liked Georgie, and in retrospect (which is the only way I know anything), I can see why. I always felt alienated, apart from, separated, on the outside looking in, never belonging and trying desperately to be a part of something. Obviously Georgie felt the same way. A teenage, screaming, hysterical, drag queen, living near the waterfront in Brooklyn, padded T-shirts and glitter on his eyes, in the late 40s and early 50s. This is alienation. Today I see that I identified with his sense of alienation and so, in a way, writing his story I was writing my story.

In my need to put the reader through an emotional experience I obviously had to experience the feelings, the emotions, I was attempting to project. This really took its toll. I was new at this and didn't know how to do it without falling apart. Also, it would take me so long to finish a piece I spent a long time 'emotionally involved' with the people. When I finally finished 'Tralala' I was in bed for 2 weeks. The same with Georgie, and the others, until I learned how to write, and not be devastated by my peoples pain.

When I was writing *Last Exit* I was only aware of the

rage and anger within me. I see, now, how necessary that was. I was attempting to do the impossible (just the act of writing was impossible, no less to accomplish what I was attempting), and so I needed that energy, that madness, to keep going on. During this time I was working full time, supporting 3, then 4, of us on $60 and $70 a week. I had great difficulty breathing, and the medication I was taking for that added a horrifying dimension to my madness, for me and my family. I recently found out that the word 'violent' comes from a Latin word that means 'Life Force,' so I can see how the anger was what was keeping me alive, it animated my Life Force.

Twenty-five years after finishing *Last Exit* a movie was made from the book, and I was involved and on the set every day. It was then I started to see how I really felt about these people. We were screening the dailies of Harry/s crucifixion and when we were finished, and the lights went on, Uli, the director, asked me what I thought. It was just he, myself, Bernd, the producer, and Desmond, the screenwriter. I started to answer him and I ended up crying and sobbing so intensely I could not speak for many minutes. I was totally shattered. I remember so clearly hearing myself say, That poor son of a bitch, he only wanted to be happy. My involvement with the film made it possible for me to see how much I love these people.

In looking back I can see where the seeds for writing may have been planted. My mother was an avid reader. My father used to tell stories of when he was a merchant seaman during the 20s. I went to sea when I was a kid, like him, sailed in the Black Gang, like him and started reading in the hospital. This background could also lead to being an accountant. I/ll let the shrinks and psychobiographers, if any, play around with these things. For me the first step in uncovering the love, and the writer, within me happened in the hospital when I was about 19 years old. I was asked to write a letter to the family of a young Greek boy who died. I wrote about this in an unpublished story called 'Lost & Found.' I did not know how to write a letter, but said yes, and wrote it. The family lived in Egypt, but in time, a relatively short time, they replied and thanked me for the letter, saying it brought them much joy. Today I believe that was where the writing started, though it was another 10 years before I sat in front of that typewriter.

One of the major things I had to learn was how to allow the writer to take over. I guess I thought writing took place in the head. Of course the mind is important for many things, but ultimately I have to get out of the way and allow the writer within me, that my thinking gives the information to, to take over. I must learn to trust it and surrender to it and not encumber it with my ideas, opinions or desires, other than the desire to write the very best story I can write.

There is always so much in a work that we are unaware of having put there. I learned very early to re-read my work and look for these elements. The first thing I noticed, after having written a couple of stories, is that the people were having troubles not because they were illegal, or immoral from some one elses POV, but because they lost control, and then I started using this consciously in my work. Also its obvious to me that they were really unaware of themselves and what they were doing and the possible results for, and to, themselves.

It seems to me that when these elements, known and unknown, conscious and unconscious, mesh perfectly an overtone is produced, a synchronicity created, that sings off the page and becomes a 'work of art' rather than simply 'authorship.'

Often I am asked which of my books is my favorite, my answer is, none. However, there is one aspect of *The*

Room I love: I can see so clearly that in writing *Last Exit* I truly did learn how to write. Today I am able to simply accept the fact that I am, indeed, a good writer. I have contributed something of value to this life.

One of the great advantages I had was living in NYC during the 50s and early 60s. Everything was happening there then. It had been the 'Art Capital' of the world since the end of the war. A bunch of us writers, painters, poets, musicians, hustlers, hangers-on would hang out at Amiri Baraka's (LeRoi Jones then) on the week ends. Anyone from Edward Dahlberg to Cecil Taylor might be there. Its not so much that we discussed 'Art,' which we sometimes did, it was the joy and stimulation of being with your peers. For me it was extraordinary because most of these people had been involved in their art for many, many years, and I, as a newcomer, was deriving the benefit of their experience. We talked mostly about sports, movies, women, broken romances and hearts, gossiped, ranted, raved, but everyone could tell a good story, always putting a new skin on it. Hearing someone describe a favorite scene from a film was better than seeing it. For me it was inspiring and Ive come to believe that that is one, if not the, most important things we can do for each other, getting us *in spirit*, awakening the gift of God within us.

I have always thought of Gil Sorrentino as *THE* man of letters of my generation. He has the remarkable ability to read your work from your POV. He and I would go over everything I wrote, especially in the first few years. It seems there were times when we would spend an hour discussing one word. He was absolutely invaluable to me in helping me learn how to write. Because of these detailed discussions, by the time I had finished *Last Exit* I knew why every word was where it was, every comma, every space, every dropped line. Each and every word was engraved in stone, I struggled so hard to find exactly the right one. Yet

I also had to make the book sound as if it came off the top of my head, as if no thought had gone into it. This was essential to achieve the desired effect of being true to the people, and make all elements organic. I believe I have succeeded because some critics say Im not a writer, just a typist. Of course they are unaware of it, but thats the greatest compliment they could pay me.

In the process of trying to do something with my life before I died, I have abandoned myself to my art. This has filled my life with a purpose I could not have imagined. The process has been extremely painful, but such is the nature of life. I have given up everything to be a writer, but it has been worth it. Today I have a sense of dignity and integrity that I cherish, and I can look back on my life, without any regrets, and say, 'Right on Cubby, you've done a good job. You may have felt like the Alchemists Crucible, but the lead and dross have been burned away and been transformed into gold.' My life is full and rich and I know I have accomplished much with it. If I die today I know I shall leave a valuable legacy, thanks to my commitment, and the love of friends. I have experienced, in all my Being, the fulfillment of the Vision in my Heart.

Hubert Selby, Jr.
June 1994

FOREWORD TO THE POST-TRIAL EDITION

Last Exit to Brooklyn was first published in Great Britain on 24th January 1966. It had already been available in an American edition for over a year and had had exceptionally favourable reviews in the U.S.A. It had come to the notice of Marion Boyars who, with the enthusiastic approval of John Calder, negotiated the British rights and acquired it for publication by Calder and Boyars. They both felt that it was a book which a serious publisher could not afford to ignore.

Because *Last Exit to Brooklyn* contains controversial material – many descriptions of violence, detailed descriptions of the activities of homosexuals, precise descriptions of the sexual act and of what is going on in the minds of the characters at such times – it was decided to submit the book to the Director of Public Prosecutions in advance, so that if objection was taken to the book, no bookseller would be involved. The Director's office gave an inconclusive reply, which ended with the words: 'If you find – as I am afraid you will – that this is a most unhelpful letter, it is not because I wish to be unhelpful, but because I get no help from the Acts.' The book was accordingly published and received a highly favourable press which, while making it clear that this was not a suitable present for Aunt Edna, established the book as a possible masterpiece, certainly a remarkable first novel by a writer with a

Zolaesque passion for truth and morality – not the morality that consists of not noticing or pretending not to notice the unpleasant side of life, but a morality that sees evil where it exists, seeks out the causes of that evil, and commits itself to eradicating those causes. Anthony Burgess said in *The Listener*: 'No book could well be less obscene . . . We are spared nothing of the snarls and tribulations of pimps, queens and "hip queers", but the tone is wholly compassionate although sometimes whipped by the kinesis of anger.' Kenneth Allsop in *The Spectator* also emphasised Hubert Selby's ability to create compassion out of sordidness. He said: 'Mr Selby's stream of reality, an urgent ticker-tape from hell, works stunningly . . . The taste of this stew of callousness, savagery and hatred, and the pitiful, blind gropings towards substitute tenderness, is one of compassion for the subterraneans and rage at the averted eye.'

On 2nd March 1966 Sir Charles Taylor MP first asked in the House of Commons for an unnamed book to be prosecuted. The book had, as the publishers were later to learn, been brought to his attention by Richard Blackwell, a director of the Oxford bookselling firm, whose father, Sir Basil Blackwell, was to be a key prosecution witness in both trials. It was soon an open secret that the unnamed book was *Last Exit to Brooklyn*. Several times, with the backing of some thirty-odd MPs of similar views, Sir Charles Taylor pressed the Attorney-General to order that proceedings be taken, while a similar number of Members, of more liberal views, opposed the request. Finally Mr Tom Driberg told the House – and the world – the name of the book. The Attorney-General at last broke the deadlock by announcing in the House that the Director of Public Prosecutions had taken advice from a professor of literature, who had given a high opinion of the book, and from a psychiatrist, and that both had advised against prosecution.

Then Sir Cyril Black, MP for Wimbledon, a highly successful property dealer, lay preacher and campaigner against liberal causes, brought a private prosecution against the book. The case was heard by Mr Leo Gradwell at Marlborough Street Magistrates' Court who, after hearing witnesses for both sides, found the book obscene. The witnesses for the prosecution were H. Montgomery Hyde, Robert Pitman, Sir Basil Blackwell, Dr Ernest Claxton, Robert Maxwell MP, Professor George Catlin, Fielden Hughes and David Holloway. The defence witnesses were Marion Boyars, Dr Lindsay Neustatter, Edward Lucie-Smith, Dr Lionel Tiger, Bryan Magee, Robert Baldick, Goronwy Rees, Timothy O'Keefe, Anthony Burgess, Peter Fryer and John Calder.

Calder and Boyars then wrote to the Director of Public Prosecutions advising him that, notwithstanding the magistrates' court decision, which was not binding outside the district in which the court was situated, they intended to continue to publish the book. They had now sold two impressions totalling 13,872 copies and were about to order a reprint when the Director of Public Prosecutions, reversing his earlier decision, informed the company of his intention to prosecute under Section 2 of the Obscene Publications Act (a criminal charge), which entitled the defendants to be heard by a judge and jury. The previous conviction had been under Section 3 and the only penalty the seizure and destruction of three copies of the book.

On 3rd April 1967 the publishers returned to the Marlborough Street Magistrates' Court where they pleaded 'Not Guilty' and were committed for trial at the Central Criminal Court – the Old Bailey. The case began on 13th November and lasted nine days. Senior counsel for the defence was Mr Patrick Neill QC, and he was assisted by Lord Lloyd of Hampstead and Mr Cyril Salmon. The prosecution counsel were Mr John Mathew

QC assisted by Mr Corkery. Mr Montgomerie, a partner in the firm of Goodman, Derrick and Co., prepared the case for the defence.

The Old Bailey trial was conducted in courteous terms; everybody, with the exception of one of the witnesses for the prosecution, seemed concerned to keep the temperature low. There was some initial argument between opposing counsel about the order in which the witnesses should appear, and the admissibility of evidence as to obscenity. Judge Rogers ruled that the defence must produce their witnesses first, and that evidence of the book's obscenity was inadmissible, it being a matter for the jury alone to decide. He also ruled that there should be no women on the jury, and twelve male jurors were sworn in. Mr Mathew explained the law to them: a book was obscene if it had a tendency to deprave and corrupt those into whose hands it was likely to fall. He defined 'to deprave' as 'to make people do wrong acts', and he explained that under Section 4 of the Act, even if the book was found to be obscene, it must nevertheless be allowed if publication could be proved to be 'in the interests of science, literature, art or learning, or other objects of general concern'. Mr Mathew's opening was very fair, leaving it for the jury to decide for themselves after hearing the evidence, although it was perhaps unfortunate that he several times referred to the case as not being a very 'serious' one, which might have given some of the jurors the impression that they were wasting their time. Mr Neill, on the other hand, stressed the seriousness of the case, and went on to explain that the jury might find the book shocking, and even perhaps disgusting, but that that was a very different matter from finding it 'liable to deprave and corrupt'. The jury was sent out at 2.15 on the first afternoon to read the book. At 4.15 they were asked by the judge how long they would need to finish it, and to the consternation of the defence some members of the jury claimed to have already done so. One man said, 'You'd need an interpreter to read this' and others said they would need another hour or so to finish it.

The following morning Mr Neill asked for the jury to be dismissed on the grounds that they were obviously not reading the book properly. This was refused, but it was emphasised to the jury that they must read the book as a whole, and except for one man who insisted he had read it and was excused for the day they spent the Tuesday reading. One man took it home with him to finish that night.

The first defence witness, Professor Frank Kermode, Lord Northcliffe Professor of English Literature at the University of London, spent the greater part of the next day in the witness box, expounding the book chapter by chapter. He was followed by Eric Mottram and A. Alvarez, who concentrated on the literary merits of the book, placing it in the tradition of American naturalistic literature which, as Professor Kermode had already pointed out, had developed from writers like Zola and Dickens. Many other literary experts were called, as well as experts to support the defence's contention that, in addition to its literary merits, the book's sociological and ethical merits also gave grounds for a verdict of 'Not Guilty' under Section 4 of the Act.

The thirty witnesses for the defence were, in order of appearance: Professor Frank Kermode (professor of English literature), Eric Mottram (lecturer in American literature), A. Alvarez (poet and critic), Professor Barbara Hardy (professor of English literature), John Calder, Professor Dan Miller (professor of sociology), Dr Michael Schofield (sociologist), Professor Ronald Atkinson (professor of philosophy), Quentin Crewe (journalist and critic), Marion Boyars, Jocelyn Baines (publisher), Jeffrey

Simmonds (publisher), Kenneth Allsop (writer and television commentator), Anthony Storey (psychologist and writer), Martin Goff (writer and bookseller), Edward Lucie-Smith (poet and critic), Eric Blau (writer), Philip French (critic), Lyman Andrews (lecturer in American literature and poet), Professor Bernard Williams (professor of philosophy), Olwen Wymark (playwright), Dr David Downes (sociologist), Judith Piepé (social worker), Alan Burns (writer), John Arden (playwright), Dr David Galloway (lecturer in American literature), Professor Gorham Davis (professor of English literature), Stuart Hood (writer, TV producer, former comptroller of BBC TV), Robert Baldick (lecturer in French literature) and the Rev. Kenneth Leach (curate of St Anne's, Soho).

The first prosecution witness was Professor Catlin, an elderly sociologist, who was admitted exceptionally between two defence witnesses as he had to return to America. Catlin insisted on talking through Mr Neill, proclaiming among other things that 'if this book is not obscene then no book is obscene'. While admitting that what happened in the book happened in life, he announced that he did not object to it in life but he did object to it in literature. The other prosecution witnesses were David Holloway (critic), Sir Basil Blackwell (bookseller and publisher), H. Montgomery Hyde (writer), Dr Dennis Leigh (psychiatrist) and the Rev. David Sheppard (priest and social worker). Sir Basil claimed that the book had depraved him, but it transpired that he had only read it because he had been asked to appear as a witness for the prosecution. The most telling of the prosecution witnesses was the last, the Rev. David Sheppard, who emerged as a naïve and well-meaning man, sympathetic to the jury. He said he felt the book pandered to all that was worst in him, and had left him 'not unscathed'. He was not cross-examined as to what he meant by this, but the assumption is that he found the book erotically stimulating.

Mr Mathew stressed in his cross-examinations and in his final speech the great difference between the way an intellectual would read this book and the way it would be read by what he called 'the normal average reader'. He suggested to the jury, for example, that an unhappily married man reading 'Strike' might be tempted to conclude that his way to happiness lay in homosexuality. His closing speech was full of insinuating time-bombs designed to go off later in the jury room. Mr Neill stressed again that to shock was not to deprave, and that the jury must not think of the book's possible effect on some extremely disturbed or abnormal person but on the average reader. The defence, he repeated, claimed that the book was not obscene, but even if the jury found it so, that obscenity was over-weighed by the book's merits, to which thirty highly qualified witnesses had testified. The judge reviewed the evidence briefly and fairly and gave the impression that he was sympathetic to the defence. However, there were certain vital omissions in his summing-up which were later to change the whole case.

The jury was out for five and a half hours in all. At one point, when they had already been deliberating for some considerable time, they returned to ask the judge whether they had to decide the question of obscenity before going on to consider the book's merits. The judge's answer was 'an emphatic yes'. At 4.15 on 23rd November they returned a verdict of 'Guilty'.

Calder and Boyars were fined £100 and ordered to pay £500 prosecution costs. Their own legal bill for the trial was £8,600, with a further expenditure of about £2,000 on defending the private prosecution brought by Sir Cyril Black the year before. And this does not include the myriad other costs incurred in connection with the two cases, such as witnesses' fares and accommodation, transcripts, and special expenses, not to mention the time put in by the publishers and their staff and the very serious damage done to their business, which was already trying to cope with the difficulties of steering a small firm through the credit squeeze and the commercial disadvantages of publishing an intellectual list in a country traditionally middle-brow in its reading tastes. Without resources of their own they nevertheless decided to appeal to the public and to go on. At the time of the verdict they had already raised nearly £3,000 from other publishers, sympathisers in the Arts, and from the general public. They now helped to found *The Defence of Literature and the Arts Society*, which became active in fighting the case, and which now intends to continue to defend literature and the other Arts – probably including the Theatre too, now that the Lord Chamberlain's censorship is removed – from repressive litigation. After lengthy and serious deliberation by the publishers and their legal advisers, the case went on to the Court of Criminal Appeal.

The hearing of the appeal began on 22nd July 1968 before Lord Justice Salmon, Mr Justice Geoffrey Lane and Mr Justice Fisher. This time Mr John Mortimer QC, himself an eminent playwright, led for the defence, assisted by Mr Salmon. The appeal was made on eleven points, two of which the judges found to be sufficient to overturn the verdict. The first was that the judge had not put to the jury in his summing-up the defence case against the alleged obscenity of the book, and the second was that the judge had not given the jury any guidance as to how they were to balance the defence case under Section 4, which deals with the book's merits, against the obscenity, if proved. The meaning of the word 'obscenity' in law is very different from its meaning in everyday usage, and it is perhaps the definition that Mr Mortimer gave in the Appeal Court that will now become standard: that 'to deprave and corrupt' means to make a person behave worse than he or she otherwise would behave, or to blur a person's sense of discrimination between right and wrong.

The success of this Appeal was an event of the utmost importance, not simply for one publisher, one author and one book, but for the future interpretation of the 1959 Obscene Publications Act, the intentions of which had manifestly been frustrated by the verdict given at the Old Bailey. The very carefully worded judgement delivered by Lord Justice Salmon clarifies many issues and will, it is hoped, prevent the prosecution of books of recognised value and make it easier for publishers to defend works of merit. Whether or not the Act needs further reform, or whether we should do away with legal censorship altogether, are matters which must and will continue to be debated.

The publishers wish to express their deep gratitude to all those who have supported them, morally and financially, through these last two difficult years; to the witnesses who appeared for them and to those who were prepared to appear, to their solicitors and barristers, whose brilliant preparation of the case was finally rewarded by the success of the Appeal, and to those members of the public who donated money towards the costs and who it is hoped will continue to support *The Defence of Literature and the Arts Society* so that this fight may not have been won in vain.

The Publishers
September 1968

This book is dedicated,
with love, to Gil.

Part I

Another Day Another Dollar

> For that which befalleth the sons of men
> befalleth beasts; even one thing befalleth them:
> as the one dieth, so dieth the other; yea, they
> have all one breath; so that a man hath no
> preeminence above a beast: for all is vanity.
>
> Ecclesiastes 3:19

T HEY sprawled along the counter and on the chairs. Another night. Another drag of a night in the Greeks, a beatup all night diner near the Brooklyn Armybase. Once in a while a doggie or seaman came in for a hamburger and played the jukebox. But they usually played some goddam hillbilly record. They tried to get the Greek to take those records off, but hed tell them no. They come in and spend money. You sit all night and buy notting. Are yakiddin me Alex? Ya could retire on the money we spend in here. Scatah. You dont pay my carfare . . .

24 records on the jukebox. They could have any 12 they wanted, but the others were for the customers from the Base. If somebody played a Lefty Frazell record or some other shitkicker they moaned, made motions with their hands (man! what a fuckin square) and walked out to the street. 2 jokers were throwing quarters in so they leaned against the lamppost and carfenders. A warm clear night and they walked in small circles, dragging the right foot slowly in the hip Cocksakie shuffle, cigarettes hanging from mouths, collars of sport-shirts turned up in the back, down and rolled in front. Squinting. Spitting. Watching cars roll by. Identifying them. Make. Model. Year. Horse power. Overhead valve. V-8. 6, 8, a hundred cylinders. Lots a horses. Lots a chrome. Red and Amber grill lights. Yasee the grill on the new Pontiac? Man, thats real sharp. Yeah, but a lousy pickup. Cant beat a Plymouth fora pickup. Shit. Cant hold the road like a Buick. Outrun any cop in the city with a Roadmaster. If ya get started. Straightaways. Turns. Outrun the law. Dynaflows. Hydramatics. Cant get started. Theyd be all overya before ya

got a block. Not in the new 88. Ya hit the gas and it throwsya outta the seat. Great car. Aint stealin nothin else anymore. Greatest for a job. Still like the Pontiac. If I was *buyin* a car. Put fender skirts on it, grill lights, a set a Caddy hubcaps and a bigass aerial in the rear . . . shit, thats the sharpest job on the road. Your ass. Nothin can touch the 47 Continental convertible. Theyre the end. We saw one uptown the other day. What-a-fuckin-load. Man!!! The shitkickers still wailed and they talked and walked, talked and walked, adjusting their shirts and slacks, cigarettes flipped into the street – ya shoulda seen this load. Chartreuse with white walls. Cruise around in a load like that with the top down and a pair of shades and some sharp clothes and ya haveta beat the snatch off witha club – spitting after every other word, aiming for a crack in the sidewalk; smoothing their hair lightly with the palms of their hands, pushing their D A's gently and patting them in place, feeling with their fingertips for a stray hair that may be out of place and not hanging with the proper effect – ya should see the sharp shirts they got in Obies. That real great gabadine. Hey, did yadig that sharp silverblue shark-skin suit in the window? Yeah, yeah. The onebutton single breasted job with the big lapels – and whats to do on a night like this. Just a few drops of gas in the tank and no loot to fill it up. And anyway, wheres to go – but yagotta have a onebutton lounge. Ya wardrobe aint complete without one. Yeah, but I dig that new shawl job. Its real sharp even as a sports jacket – the con rolled on and no one noticed that the same guys were saying the same things and somebody found a new tailor who could make the greatest pants for 14 skins; and how about the shock-absorbers in the Lincoln; and they watched the cars pass, giving hardlooks and spitting; and who laid this broad and who laid that one; and someone took a small brush from his pocket and cleaned his suede shoes then rubbed his

4

hands and adjusted his clothing and someone else flipped a coin and when it dropped a foot stamped on it before it could be picked up and as he moved the leg from the coin his hair was mussed and he called him a fuck and whipped out his comb and when his hair was once more neatly in place it was mussed again and he got salty as hell and the other guys laughed and someone elses hair was mussed and they shoved each other and someone else shoved and then someone suggested a game of mum and said Vinnie should start and they yelled yeah and Vinnie said what-thefuck, hed start, and they formed a circle around him and he turned slowly jerking his head quickly trying to catch the one punching him so he would replace him in the center and he was hit in the side and when he turned he got hit again and as he spun around 2 fists hit him in the back then another in the kidney and he buckled and they laughed and he jerked around and caught a shot in the stomach and fell but he pointed and he left the center and just stood for a minute in the circle catching his wind then started punching and felt better when he hit Tony a good shot in the kidney without being seen and Tony slowed down and got pelted for a few minutes then finally pointed and Harry said he was fullashit, he didnt really see him hitim. But he was thrown in the center anyway and Tony waited and hooked him hard in the ribs and the game continued for another 5 minutes or so and Harry was still in the center, panting and almost on his knees and they were rapping him pretty much as they pleased, but they got bored and the game broke up and they went back in the Greeks, Harry still bent and panting, the others laughing, and went to the lavatory to wash.

They washed and threw cold water on their necks and hair then fought for a clean spot on the dirty apron that served as a towel, yelling through the door that Alex was a no good fuck for not havin a towel forem, then jockeyed for a place in front of the mirror. Eventually they went to the large mirror at the front of the diner and finished combing their hair and fixing their clothes, laughing and still kidding Harry, then sprawled and leaned.

The shitkickers left and they yelled to Alex to get some music on the radio. Why dont you put money in the jukebox? Then you hear what you want. Comeon man. Dont be a drag. Why dont you get a job. Then you have money. Hey, watch ya language. Yeah, no cursin Alex. Go get a job you no good bums. Whos a bum? Yeah, who? They laughed and yelled at Alex and he sat, smiling, on a small stool at the end of the counter and someone leaned over the counter and turned the radio on and spun the dial until a sax wailed and someone yelled for service and Alex told him to go to hell, and he pounded on the counter for service and Alex asked if he wanted ham and eggs and he told Alex he wouldnt eat an egg here unless he saw it hatched and Alex laughed, Scatah, and walked slowly to the coffee urn and filled a cup and asked if he was going to buy everybody coffee and they laughed and Alex told them to get a job, you all the time hang around like bums. Someday you be sorry. You get caught and you wont be able to drink this good coffee. COFFEE!!! Man this is worse than piss. The dishwater upstate tastes betteran this. Pretty soon maybe you be drinking it again. Yourass I will. I should report you. Then Id have some peace and quiet. Youd die without us Alex. Whod protect ya from the drunks? Look at all the trouble we saveya. You boys are going to get in trouble. You see. All the time fuck-around. Ah Alex. Dont talk like that. Ya make us feel bad. Yeah man. Ya hurt our feelings . . .

Alex sat on his stool smoking and smiling and they smoked and laughed. Cars passed and some tried to identify them by the sound of the motor then looked to see if they were right, raising their shoulders and swaggering back to their seats if they were. Occasionally a drunk came in and they would yell to Alex to get up off his ass and serve the customer or tell the guy to getthehell out before he was poisoned with Alexs horsemeat and coffee and Alex would pick up the dirty rag and wipe off the spot in front of the drunk and say yes sir, what you want, and theyd want to know why he didnt call them sir and Alex would smile and sit on his stool until the drunk finished and then walk slowly back, take the money, ring it up then back to his stool and tell them they should be quiet, you want to scare good customers away, and Alex would laugh with them and spit the cigarette butt out of his mouth and turn his shoe on it; and the cars still passed and the drunks still passed and the sky was clear and bright with stars and moon and a light breeze was blowing and you could hear the tugs in the harbor chugging and the deep 00000 from their whistles floated across the bay and rolled down 2nd avenue and even the ferrys mooring winch could be heard, when it was quiet and still, clanging a ferry into the slip . . . and it was a drag of a night, beat for loot and they flipped their cigarettes out the doors and walked to the mirror and adjusted and combed and some-one turned up the volume of the radio and a few of the girls came in and the guys smoothed the waist of their shirts as they walked over to their table and Rosie grabbed Freddy, a girl he laid occasionally, and asked him for a halfabuck and he told her to go fuckerself and walked away and sat on a stool. She sat beside him. He talked with the guys and every few minutes she would say something, but he ignored her. When he moved slightly on his stool she started to get up and when he sat down she sat. Freddy stood, adjusted his pants, put his hands in his pockets and slowly walked out the door and strolled to the corner. Rosie walked 6 inches to his right and 6 inches to his rear. He leaned against the lampost and spit past her face.

Youre worse than a leech. A leech yacan get rid of. You dont go for nothin. Dont bullshit me ya bastard. I know yascored for a few bucks last night. Whats that to you? and anyway its gone. I aint even got a pack o cigarettes. Dont tell me. I aint ya father. Ya cheap motherfucka! Go tell ya troubles to jesus and stop breakin my balls. I'll break ya balls ya rotten bastard, trying to kick him in the groin, but Freddy turned and lifted his leg then slapped her across the face.

Three drunken rebel soldiers were going back to the Base after buying drinks for a couple of whores in a neighbourhood bar and were thrown out when they started a fight after the whores left them for a couple of seamen. They stopped when they heard Rosie shout and watched as she staggered back from the slap, Freddy grabbing her by the neck. Go giter little boy. Hey, dont chuall know youre not to fuck girls on the street . . . They laughed and yelled and Freddy let go of Rosie and turned and looked at them for a second then yelled at them to go fuck their mothers, ya cottonpickin bastards. I hear shes good hump. The soldiers stopped laughing and started crossing the street toward Freddy. We'll cut yur niggerlovin heart out. Freddy yelled and the others ran out of the Greeks. When the doggies saw them they stopped then turned and ran toward the gate to the Base. Freddy ran to his car and the others jumped in and on the fenders or held on to the open doors, and Freddy chased the doggies down the street. Two of them continued running toward the gate, but the third panicked and tried to climb over the fence and Freddy tried to squash him against it with the car but the doggie pulled his legs up just before the car bumped the fence. The guys jumped off the fender and leaped on the doggies back and yanked him down and he fell on the edge of the hood and then to the ground. They formed a circle and kicked. He tried to roll over on his stomach and cover his face with his arms, but as he got to his side he was kicked in the groin and stomped on the ear and he screamed, cried, started pleading then just cried as a foot cracked his mouth, Ya fuckin cottonpickin punk, and a hard kick in the ribs turned him slightly and he tried to raise himself on one knee and someone took a short step forward and kicked him in the solarplexus and he fell on his side, his knees up, arms folded across his abdomen, gasping for air and the blood in his mouth gurgled as he tried to scream, rolled down his chin then spumed forth as he vomited violently and someone stomped his face into the pool of vomit and the blood whirled slightly in arcs and a few bubbles gurgled in the puke as he panted and gasped and their shoes thudded into the shiteatinbastards kidneys and ribs and he groaned and his head rolled in the puke breaking the arching patters of blood and he gasped as a kick broke his nose then coughed and retched as his gasping sucked some of the vomit back in his mouth and he cried and tried to yell but it was muffled by the pool and the guys yells and Freddy kicked him in the temple and the yellowbastards eyes rolled back and his head lolled for a moment and he passed out and his head splashed and thumped to the ground and someone yelled the cops and they jammed back into and on the car and Freddy started to turn but the prowl car stopped in front of them and the cops got out with their guns drawn so Freddy stopped the car and the guys got out and off the car and slowly walked across the street. The cops lined them against the wall. The guys stood with their hands in their pockets, their shoulders rounded and heads slumped forward, straightening up and raising their arms while being frisked, then resuming their previous positions and attitudes.

Heads popped from windows, people occurred in doorways and from bars asking what happened and the cops yelled for everybody to shutup then asked what was going on. The guys shrugged and murmured. One of the cops started yelling the question again when an MP and the 2 doggies who had continued running, holding the third one suspended between them, head hanging limply, his toes dragging along the ground, came up to them. The cop turned to them and asked what this was all about. Those goddam yankees like takill our buddy heuh, nodding to the soldier between them, his head rolling from side to side, face and front of his uniform covered with blood and puke, blood dribbling from his head. Freddy pointed at him and stepped toward the cop and told him theres nothin wrong with him. Hes only foolin. The guys raised their heads slightly and looked at Freddy and chuckled and someone murmured hes got some pair of balls. The cop looked at the soldier and told Freddy if hes fooling hes one hell of an actor. The chuckling grew louder and a few in the crowd of onlookers laughed. The cops told them to shut up. Now, what in the hell is this all about. The doggies started to speak but Freddy outshouted them. They insulted my wife. Someone said o jesus and Freddy stared at the doggies waiting for them to say something so he could call them a goddam liar. The cop asked him where his wife was and he told him right over there. Hey Rosie! Comere! She wentover, her blouse hanging out, her hair hanging in lumps, lipstick smeared from Freddys slap, her eyelashes matter and the heads of pimples shining through many layers of old dirty makeup. We was standin on the corner talkin when these three creeps started making obscene remarks to my wife and when I toldem ta shutup they came after me. Aint that right? Yeah. They insulted me, the god – Yuh dirty hoarrr. How could yawl be insulted??? Freddy started toward him but the cop rapped him in the gut with his club and told him to take it easy. And youd better watch your mouth soldier. All

10

yuhgoddamn yankees are the same. A buncha no good niggerlovin bastards. Thats all yuare. The cop stepped over to the soldier and told him if he didnt shut up right now hed lock him up, and your friend along with you. He stared at the soldier until the doggie lowered his eyes, then turned to the crowd and asked if anyone had seen what had happened and they yelled that they saw the whole thing that the drunken rebels had started it, they insulted the boys wife and tried to beat him up and the cop told them ok, ok, shut up. He turned back to the soldiers and told them to get back to the base and have someone look after their friend, then turned to Freddy and the others and told them to beat it and if I see any of you punks in a fight again I'll personally split your skulls and – Hey wait a minute. The cop turned as the MP walked up to him. This aint going to be the end of this officer. These men have rights and its my duty to remind them of them. They might want to prefer charges against these hoodlums. What in hell are you? a Philadelphia lawyer? No sir. Im just doing my duty and reminding these men of their rights. Alright, you reminded them now go back to the base and leave well enough alone. You know these neighbourhood bars are off limits. Yes sir, thats true, but – but nothing. The MP started stammering something, then looked to the three soldiers for support, but they had already started back to the Base, the two dragging the third, blood splattering on the street as it fell from his head.

The bodies went back in the doors and bars and the heads in the windows. The cops drove away and Freddy and the guys went back into the Greeks and the street was quiet, just the sound of a tug and an occasional car; and even the blood couldnt be seen from a few feet away.

They slammed around the lavatory washing, laughing, nudging each other, roaring at Freddy, splashing water, inspecting their shoes for scratches, ripping the dirty apron, pulling the toiletpaper off by the yard, throwing the wet wads at each other, slapping each other on the back, smoothing their shirts, going to the mirror up front, combing their hair, turning their collars up in the back and rolling them down in front, adjusting their slacks on their hips. Hey, didya see the look on the bastards face when we threwim off the fence? Yeah. The sonofabitch was scared shitless. A buncha punks. Hey Freddy, hows ya gut. That was some rap that bastard giveya. Shit. I fuck cops where they eat . . .

Someday you boys going to get in trouble. All the time fighting. Whatayamean Alex. We was just defendin Freddys wife. Yeah, they insulted Rosie. They roared, stamped, and banged their fists on the counter and tables. Alex grinned and said Scatah. Someday you be sorry. You should get a job. Hey, watch yalanguage Alex. Yeah. No cursin in fronna married women. They laughed and sprawled along the counter and on the chairs. All the time fuckaround. Someday you get in trouble. Ah Alex, dont talk like that. Ya makus feel bad. Yeah, man, ya hurt our feelings . . .

Part II

The Queen Is Dead

*So God created man in his own image, in the
image of God created he him; male and female
created he them.*

Genesis 1:27

G EORGETTE was a hip queer. She (he) didnt try to disguise or conceal it with marriage and mans talk, satisfying her homosexuality with the keeping of a secret scrapbook of pictures of favourite male actors or athletes or by supervising the activities of young boys or visiting turkish baths or mens locker rooms, leering sidely while seeking protection behind a carefully guarded guise of virility (fearing that moment at a cocktail party or in a bar when this front may start crumbling from alcohol and be completely disintegrated with an attempted kiss or groping of an attractive young man and being repelled with a punch and – rotten fairy – followed with hysteria and incoherent apologies and excuses and running from the room) but, took a pride in being a homosexual by feeling intellectually and esthetically superior to those (especially women) who werent gay (look at all the great artists who were fairies!); and with the wearing of womens panties, lipstick, eye makeup (this including occasionally gold and silver – stardust – on the lids), long marcelled hair, manicured and polished fingernails, the wearing of womens clothes complete with padded bra, high heels and wig (one of her biggest thrills was going to BOP CITY dressed as a tall stately blond (she was 6′ 4″ in heels) in the company of a negro (He was a big beautiful black bastard and when he floated in all the cats in the place jumped and the squares bugged. We were at a crazy pad before going and were blasting like crazy and were up so high that I just didnt give a shit for anyone honey, let me tell you!); and the occasional wearing of a menstrual napkin.

She was in love with Vinnie and rarely came home while he was in jail, but stayed uptown with her girl friends, high most of the time on benzedrine and marijuana. She had come home one morning with one of her friends after a three day tea party with her makeup still on and her older brother slapped her across the face and told her that if he ever came home like that again hed kill him. She and her friend ran screaming from the house calling her brother a dirty fairy. After that she always called to see if her brother was in before going home.

Her life didnt revolve, but spun centrifugally, around stimulants, opiates, johns (who paid her to dance for them in womens panties then ripped them off her; bisexuals who told their wives they were going out with the boys and spent the night with Georgette (she trying to imagine they were Vinnie)), the freakish precipitate coming to the top.

When she heard that Vinnie had been paroled she went to Brooklyn (first buying 10 dozen benzedrine tablets) and sat in the Greeks all night following Vinnie everywhere and trying to get him alone. She bought him coffee and sat on his lap and asked him to go for a walk. He would refuse and tell her theres plenty of time sweetheart. Maybe later. Georgette would wiggle on his lap, play with his earlobes feeling like a young girl on her first date. She looked at him coquettishly. Let me do you Vinnie, forcing herself to refrain from trying to kiss him, from embracing him, from caressing his thighs, dreaming of the warmth of his groin, seeing him nude, holding her head (not too gently), pressing close to him, watching his muscles contract, running her fingertips gently along the tightened thigh muscles (he might even groan at the climax); the feel, taste, smell . . . Please Vinnie, the dream almost carrying over to consciousness, the benzedrine making it even more difficult not to try to animate the dream *now*.

It wasnt fear of being rebuked or hit by him (that could be developed in her mind into a lovers quarrel ending in a beautiful reconciliation) that restrained her, but she knew if done in the presence of his friends (who tolerated more than accepted her, or used her as a means to get high when broke or for amusement when bored) his pride would force him to abjure her completely and then there would not only be no hope, but, perhaps no dream. She put her hand tentatively on the back of his neck twisting the short hairs. She jumped up as he pushed her, and giggled as he patted her on the buttox. She strutted over to the counter. May I please have another cup of coffee Alex? you big Greek fairy. She put another benzedrine tablet in her mouth and swallowed it with the coffee; put a nickel in the jukebox and started wiggling as a tenor sax wailed a blues number. Some of the others in the Greeks clapped in time to the music and yelled, Go Georgette, Go! She put her hands behind her head, ellipsed her pelvis slowly and – bumped – up to one of the girls who was laughing *at* her and *threw* her hip in her face. Heres one for you, you big bitch. When the music stopped she sat on a stool at the counter, finished her coffee, spun around a few times on the stool, stopped, stood up holding her hands delicately in front of her in the dramatic manner of a concert singer and sang *un bel di* in a wavering falsetto. Someone laughed and said she should go on the stage. You have a nice voice Georgie. Yeah, from the same girl, fa callin hogs. Georgette turned, put her hands on her hips, leaned her head to one side and looked at her disdainfully. What would you know about opera Miss Cocksucker? She *threw* her head back and sauntered out to the street in her finest regal fashion.

Vinnie was 12 the first time he was arrested. He had stolen a hearse. He was so short that he had to slide down in the seat so far to reach the pedals that a cop standing on a corner looking at the hearse, stopped for a redlight, thought the cab was empty. The cop was so surprised when he opened the door and saw Vinnie behind the wheel that he had almost shifted the gears and started moving before the cop realised what was happening and pulled him out. The judge was just as surprised as the arresting officer and had some difficulty suppressing a laugh while reprimanding Vinnie and making him promise never to do such a bad thing again. Go home and be a good boy.

Two days later he stole another car. This time with friends who were older and better able to drive a car without attracting too much attention. They would keep a car, driving to school when they went, until it ran out of gas then leave it and steal another. They were caught many times, but Vinnie was always released after promising not to do it again. He was so young, looking even younger, and innocent looking that it was impossible for a judge to think of him as a criminal and they were hesitant about sending him to an institution where he might learn to be a thief rather than just a mischievous boy. When he was 15 and arrested for the 11th time he was sent to a correctional institution for boys. When he was released a representative of a social organisation talked with him and asked him to visit their boys club in the neighbourhood. Vinnie had grown during the last year and took great pride in his ability to fight better than other kids his age and better than most who were older. After starting a few fights at the boys club for kicks he stopped going and another invitation was never extended.

He was sent up for his first real bit when he was 16. He had stolen a car and was speeding along Ocean Parkway (he wanted to see how fast the car could go in case he had to outrun the law) and crackedup. His only injury was a gash in his head. An ambulance and the police were called. The ambulance attendant bandaged his head and told the policemen he was well enough to be taken to the police station. Vinnie still wasnt fully aware of what had happened as the 2 policemen helped him up the steps of the stationhouse, but he knew they were cops. He pushed one down the steps, punched the other knocking him down, and ran. Possibly he might have gotten away, but he went to the Greeks and displayed the gash in his head to his friends telling them how he dumped the two cops.

He was permitted to plead guilty to a misdemeanour and was sentenced to 1 to 3 years.

He seemed to enjoy the time he spent in jail. While there he tattooed his number on his wrist with a pin and ink and displayed it to everyone when he came home. He went straight to the Greeks when he was paroled, sitting there all night telling stories about the things he did while doing time. Many of the others in the Greeks had been in the same prison and they talked about the guards, the work, the yard and their cells. The day after his release 3 gunmen were shot attempting to stickup a store. One died instantly the other 2 were in the hospital in critical condition. When he heard about it he bought a paper, cut the story and pictures out and carried them with him for days, until they finally fell apart from handling, telling everyone that they were friends of his. I did time with them guys. Yaknow this guy Steve who got killed? He was my boy. He was on the same bench with me. Me and him was real tight man. We ran the yard up there. We was the *gees* on the first bench and what we said was law. We even got sent to the hole tagether. A couplea creeps wouldnt giveus the packages they got from home so we dumpedem. Im tellinya, we was real tight man.

The glory of having known someone killed by the police during a stickup was the greatest event of his life and a memory he cherished as would an aging invalid, at the end of a disappointing life, a winning touchdown made at the end of the final game of the season.

Vinnie got kicks from refusing Georgette when she tried to get him to take a walk with her, and from patting her on the ass and telling her not now sweetheart. Maybe later. He felt good having someone hot forim like that. Even if it is a fag. He followed her over to the counter where she was sitting and, wetting his finger and sticking it in her ear, laughed as she squirmed and giggled. Too bad I didnt haveya upstate. I had a couple a sweet kids but they didnt have chips like this, patting her again on the ass and looking at the others, smiling, and waiting for them to smile in appreciation of his witticisms. It cost loot ta do me now sweetchips, turning once more to the others wanting to be certain that they understood that Georgette was in love with him and that he could have her anytime he wanted to, but, he was playing it cool, waiting for her to give him loot before he condescended to allow her to do him; feeling superior to the others because he knew Steve who had been killed by the bulls, and because Georgette was smart and could snow them under with words (at the same time hating anyone else who might use polysyllabic words and thinking anyone who went to school was a creep), but (mistaking in his dull, never to be matured mind, her loneliness for respect of his strength and virility) she would never try that with him.

He followed Georgette out to the street turning to laugh at the girl Georgette had insulted, sitting, trying desperately to think of something to say, her rage manifest on her face and thickening her tongue. She spat and called him a goddam faggot bastard. Georgette turned, holding a cigarette between middle and forefinger of the right hand, hand inverted and outstretched, left hand on her hip and looking disdainfully at the flushed face, Whats your excuse churl? did you leave your nature in the outter ring or in a cesspool?

Vinnie laughed trying to give the impression he dug Georgettes remark (only vaguely aware that there *may* be something in the remark he didnt understand) and pushed the girl back into her chair as she started toward the door, and walked out and pinched Georgette on the cheek, then took a cigarette from her pocket. Whattayasay we take a walk? I might even letya do me. Oh aren't you the one though, hoping he was serious, trying in her finest effeminate manner to act coy. I'll only chargeya a fin, leaning against the fender of a parked car looking through the open door into the Greeks at the others, wanting to be certain they saw and heard. Your generosity overwhelms me Vincent, smiling at his, My name is Vinnie and can that Vincent shit, and wanting to have him even if she did have to pay, but not wanting him on a business basis. She would give him money if he wanted it, but not at *that* time; if she did it would not only kill, or at least blur, the dream, but it would make her his john and that would be unbearable, especially after having waited so long. She knew he wouldnt go with her while the others were there, fearing the jeers of queerbait, so was forced to wait and hope the others might leave. Reasoning thus, yet hoping, in her benzedrined mind, that she may be wrong and he would take her by the arm and walk away with her, she continued the little game. I'll have you know that I have dozens of johns who pay me, and not a paltry five dollars either.

I wont charge ya nothin Georgie, grabbing one of her ears. Dont touch me Harry, you big freak, pushing his hand away and slapping at it. Im not about to have sex with *you*. Harry took his pushbutton knife from his pocket, opened it, locked the blade in the open position, felt the blade and tip and walked toward Georgette as she backed away shaking limp wristed hands at him. Stand still and I'll makeya a real woman without goin ta Denmark. He and Vinnie laughed as Georgette continued to back away, her hands limply extended. You dont want that big sazeech gettin in yaway Georgie boy. Let me cut it off. It is *not* big Miss *Pinky*, trying to suppress her fears by thinking herself a heroine, and get away from me.

Harry flipped the knife underhand at her and yelled think fast! She lifted her left leg slightly, covered her face with her hands, turned away and shrilled an OOOOOOO as the knife hit the sidewalk, bouncing off the wall behind her and skipping a few feet away. Harry and Vinnie were laughing, Vinnie walking over to the knife and picking it up, Georgette walking away still screeching at Harry. You big freak! You Neanderthal fairy! You – Vinnie threw the knife yelling think fast. Georgette leaping, pirouetting away from the knife screaming at them to stop (only the benzedrine preventing hysteria now), but they laughed, their daring growing with her fear; throwing the knife harder and closer to her feet; the knife skipping and billiarding away, picked up and thrown again at the dancing feet (the scene resembling one in a grade B western); the laughing, leaping and pirouetting stopping suddenly as the blade of the knife stuck in the calf of her leg (had it been a board, not flesh, the blade would have vibrated and twanged). Georgette looked quizzically at the small portion of the blade visible, and handle sticking from her leg, too surprised to feel the blood rolling down her leg to think of the wound or the danger, but just staring at the knife trying to understand what had happened. Vinnie and Harry just looked. Harry muttered something about that being a good shot and Vinnie smiled. Georgette looked up, saw Vinnie smiling at her, looked back at the knife and screamed that her new slacks were ruined. The others, watching from the Greeks, laughed and Harry asked her what she was growin from her leg. Georgette simply called him a fuck and hopped over to the step leading to the side door of the Greeks and sat down slowly, carefully keeping the leg stiff and extended in front of her. Harry asked her if she wanted him to yank the knife out and she screamed at him to go to hell. Leaning down and gently holding the handle in her fingertips and closing her eyes she tugged tentatively, then slowly pulled the knife from her leg. She sighed and dropped the knife, then leaned back against the door jamb, flexed her leg slightly and reached down and pulled her shoe off. It was filled with blood. The effects of the benzedrine were almost completely worn off and she shivered as she poured the blood from her shoe, the blood splattering as it hit the sidewalk, the small puddle flowing off in rills into cracks in the pavement, mixing with the dirt in the cracks and disappearing . . . She screamed and cursed Harry.

Whats the matta Georgie? Has the poor little girl got a Booboo? She screeched. You brought me down! You rotten freaks, you brought me down! She looked at Vinnie with pleading in her eyes trying to regain her composure (the effects of the benzedrine completely gone now and panic starting to take its place), hoping to gain his sympathy, looking tenderly as a lover taking irrevocable leave, and Vinnie laughed thinking how much she looked like a dog beggin for a bone. Whats the matta? Ya hurt or somethin?

She almost fainted from fear and anger as the others roared with laughter. She looked at the blur of faces wanting to kick them, spit into them, slap them, scratch them, but, when she tried to move the pain in her leg stopped her and she leaned back against the jamb, now fully conscious of her leg and, for the first time, thinking of the wound. She lifted her pant leg up to her knee and trembled as she felt the blood soaked pant leg and looked at the wound, blood still oozing out, her blood soaked sock and the small pool of blood under her foot, trying to ignore the whistles and, Atta girl, take it off.

Vinnie had gone into the Greeks and got a bottle of iodine from Alex and came out and told Georgette not taworry about it. I'll fix it up. He lifted her leg and poured the iodine into the wound and laughed, with the others, when Georgette screamed and jumped up, holding the injured leg with both hands, hopping up and down on the other. They whistled, clapped their hands and someone started singing, Dance Ballerina Dance. Georgette fell to the ground, still clutching her leg frantically, and sat in the middle of the sidewalk spotted by the light from the Greeks, one leg curved under her, the other up and bent at the knee, her head bowed and between her legs, like a clown imitating a dancer.

When the pain subsided she got up and hopped back to the step, sat down and asked for a handkerchief to wrap around her leg. Whatta yacrazy? I dont want my handkerchief all messed up. The laughter again. Vinnie stepped gallantly forward and pulled the handkerchief from her pocket and helped her tie it around her leg. There yaare Georgie. All fixed up. She said nothing but stared at the blood; the wound growing larger and larger; blood poisoning streaking her leg, the streak widening and almost to her heart; the stench of gangrene from her rotting leg . . .

Well, comeon, give. What? What did you say Vinnie? I said give me some loot and I'll getya a cab so ya can go home. I cant go home Vinnie. Why not? My brothers home. Well, whereya gonna go? Ya cant sit here all night. I'll go to the hospital. They can fix my leg and then I'll go uptown to Marys. Areya crazy or somethin. Ya cant go to the hospital. When they see that leg of yours theyll wanna know what happened and the next thing yaknow the lawll be knockin on my door and I'll be back in the can. I wont tell them anything Vinnie. You know that. Honestly. Inna pigs ass. They getya up there and shoot somethin inya and youll talk ya ass off, vague memories of radio programs heard and movies seen. I'll getya a cab and takeya home. No Vinnie, please! I wont tell them anything. I promise. I'll tell them some spick kids did it, holding her leg tightly with both hands, rocking back and forth with a steady hypnotical rhythm and trying with desperation not to get hysterical and to ignore the throbbing pain in her leg. Please! My brothers home. I cant go home now! Look, I dont know what yabrother will do and I dont give a shit, but I know what Im gonna do if ya dont shut thehellup.

Georgette called to him as he walked toward the avenue to hail a cab, pleading and promising anything. She didnt want to argue with Vinnie; she didnt want him to dislike her; she didnt want to provoke him; but she knew what would happen when she got home. Her Mother would cry and call the doctor; and if her brother didnt find the bennie (she couldnt throw them away and there was too much to take at once) the doctor would know she had been taking something and tell them. She knew they would take her clothes off and see the red spangled G string she was wearing. Her brother might ignore the makeup (when he saw her leg and all the blood; and when her Mother started worrying about her and telling the brother to leave him alone) but, he would never ignore the bennie and the G string.

Yet this was not what she really feared; it wasnt being slapped by her brother that brought back the fear that almost caused her to faint; that made her think (only briefly) of praying; that pushed from her mind the smell of gangrene. It was knowing that she would have to stay in the house for a few days, maybe even a week. The doctor would tell her to stay off the leg until it healed properly and her Mother and brother would enforce the doctors order; and she knew they wouldnt allow any of her girl friends to visit her and she had nothing except the benzedrine which would probably be found and thrown away. There was nothing hidden in the house; no way she could get it. In the house a week or more with nothing. I'd crack.

I cant stay down that long. Theyll bug me. Bug me. O jesus
jesus jesus . . .

A cab stopped in front of the Greeks and Vinnie got out
and he and Harry helped (forced) Georgette into the rear
of the cab. She continued to plead, to beg; she told them
she had a john who was a Wallstreet Broker and she was
going to see him this weekend and he was good for 20,
maybe more. I'll give it to you. I'll give you more. I know
where you can get hundreds without any trouble at all.
I know a few fairies who own an Arts & Crafts Shop in
the Village. You can stick them up. They always have a lot
of money around; it wont be any trouble – Vinnie slapped
her face and told her ta shut the hell up, trying to see if the
cab driver was paying any attention to what she was
saying and telling him something, almost incoherently,
about his friend just having a accident and was still kindda
shook.

It took less than 3 minutes to drive the few blocks to
Georgettes house. When the cab stopped in front of her
house Vinnie took the change from her pocket and the 3
singles from her wallet. Is that all yagot? I'll give you more
in a few days if you take me to the hospital. Look, if ya
dont walk in, we'll carryya in and tell ya brother ya tried ta
pick up a couplea sailors and they dumpedya. Will you
come over to the house tomorrow and see me, alone?
Yeah, sure. I'll seeya tomorrow, winking at Harry. Georgette tried to believe him and for a moment forgot her
previous fears and the old dream flashed briefly across her
mind and she could see her room, the bed, Vinnie . . .

She limped toward the door and stopped in the vesti-
bule, put a handful of bennie in her mouth, chewed then
swallowed them. Before knocking on her door she turned
and yelled to Vinnie not to forget about tomorrow. Vinnie
laughed at her.

Vinnie and Harry waited in the cab until they saw the

door open and Georgette go inside, her Mother closing the door behind her, before they paid the driver. They left the cab, walked down the street to the avenue, turned the corner and walked back to the Greeks.

The door closed. A hundred times. Closed. Even as it swung open she heard it bang shut. Closed. Closed. Dozens of doors like many pictures jerkily animated by a thumb, tumbling mistily like shadows . . . and the click, click, the goddamn click click click of the latch and it banged shut. SHUT. Again and again and again it BANGED SHUT. A thousand miserable times. BANG BANG. BANG. Always banging shut. Never a knock. Think it. Force it. A knock. A knock. Please, please. O Jesus a knock. Make it a knock. Make it someone knocking. To come in. Why cant it be a knock. Goldie with bennie. Anything. Anybody. Closed. Closed. Bang. BANG. BANG! SHUT!!! O Jesus SHUT! And I cant get out. Only roll in bed. This dirty freak of a bed (VINNIE!!!) and that rotten fairy of a doctor wouldnt give me anything. Not even a little codeine. And it throbs. It does. It does. It throbs and pains. I can feel it squeezing up my leg and it hurts. It hurts dreadfully. It does. It really does. I need something for the pain. O Jesus I cant stay down. And I cant get out. Not even Soakie. She might have *something*. Let her in. I cant get out. Out. Up – (the door banged and her Mother looked up and noticed first the strange look on her sons face, the staring eyes; then the blood on his slacks and as she ran to him she collapsed on Mothers shoulder, crying, wanting to cry on Mothers shoulder and have her listen and stroke her hair (I love him Mother. I love him and want him.); and knowing that she must scare her Mother so she would be protected by her sympathy, and perhaps Mother would get her to bed (she wanted to run to the bed, but she knew she had to

27

hobble to impress her), get her to bed before her brother came in the room. She might be able to hide the bennie. She had to try! Her Mother staggered and they hobbled toward the bed (mustnt run), wanting her Mother near, wanting the comfort; and feeling calmer, safer, as her Mothers face paled and her hands shook; yet calculating just how far she could go with the scene so Mother would be properly concerned yet still capable of protecting her from Arthur . . . and she may yet be able to hide the bennie) . . .

Why couldnt he be out. Why did he have to be home. If only he were dead. You sonofabitch die. DIE (Whats the matter with mommys little girl. Did ooo stub oo little toesywoesy Georgieworgit? Dont touch me you fairy. Dont touch me. Look whos calling someone a fairy. Aint that a laugh. Ha! You freak. Freak FREAK FREAK FREAK! Why you rotten punk – Georgette leaned more heavily upon Mother and swung the injured leg from side to side, groaning. Please Arthur. Please. Leave your brother alone. Hes hurt. Hes passing out from loss of blood. Brother? Thats a goodone. Please – Georgette groaned louder and started sliding from Mothers neck (if only she could get to the bed and hide the bennie. Hide the bennie. Hide the bennie); please, not again. Not now. Just call the doctor. For me. Please.) If he had stayed out. Or had just gone to the kitchen . . . Georgie porgie puddin n pie . . . Why do they do this to me? Why wont they leave me alone??? (Arthur looked at his brother and grunted with disgust then went to the phone and Georgette tried frantically to get the bennie out of her pocket but her slacks were so tight she couldnt get her hand in and she was afraid to move away from her Mother so she could get her hand in her pocket. She fell on the bed and rolled on her side and tried to get them out and under the mattress or even the pillow (yes, the pillow) but her Mother thought she was rolling with pain and held her hands trying to comfort and soothe her son, telling him to try to relax, the doctor will be here soon and you will be alright. Dont worry darling. Youll see. Everything will be alright . . . and then her brother came back, looked at his Mother then the ripped slacks and blood and said they had better take the pants off and put a little mercurochrome on the leg and Georgette tried to yank her hands free, but her Mother gripped tighter, trying to absorb her sons pain, and Georgette fought furiously, trying to hold her slacks and keep her brother from pulling them off. She screamed and kicked, but when she did the pain really throbbed through her leg, and she tried biting her Mothers hands but her brother pushed her head down (the G string! The bennie!!!). Stop. Stop! Go away. Dont let him. Please dont let him. It will be alright son. The doctor will be here soon. Nobody wants to hurt you. You rotten fairy, stop. Stop! You queer sonofabitch. STOP, but brother loosened the belt and grabbed her pants by the cuffs and Georgette screeched and her Mothers tears fell on her face, begging Arthur to be careful; and Arthur pulled them slowly yet still tore loose the clot from the wound and blood started oozing, then flowing down the leg and Georgette fell back crying and screaming, and Arthur let the pants fall to the floor and stared at his brother . . . watching the blood roll to the sheet, the leg jerk . . . listening to his brother crying and wanting to laugh with satisfaction, and even happy to see the misery on his Mothers face as she looked at Georgette and lifted his head in her arms and stroked his head, humming, shaking tears from her face . . . Arthur wanting to lean over and punch his face, that goddamn face covered with makeup, wanting to tear at the leg and listen to his fairy brother wail . . . He straightened up and stood silently at the foot of the bed for a moment half-hearing the sobs and his thoughts, then stepped around to the side and started yanking at the Red Spangled G String. You disgusting degenerate. In front of my Mother you have the nerve to lay here with this thing on. He yanked, and slapped Georgette across the face, Mother pleading, crying, soothing, and Georgette rolled and clawed as the tight G String scraped along her leg, and Mother begged Arthur to leave his brother alone – BROTHER? – but he tugged and yanked, yelling above them until it was off and he flung it from him into another room. How can you hold him like that. Hes nothing but a filthy homosexual. You should throw him out in the street. Hes your brother son. You should help him. Hes my son (hes my baby. My baby) and I love him and you should love him. She rocked with Georgettes head cradled in her arms and Arthur stormed out of the house and Georgette rolled over on her back trying to reach the slacks and the bennie, but her Mother held her, continuing to tell her son that it would be alright. Everything will be alright.)

O please, please, please, please . . . why are you torturing me? The bitches. The dirty bitches. O let me out. Let someone come in. I dont want to be alone. Please let them come. Anything. Im down. Let them come. For christs sake. Im down. DOWN! I cant stay in this room. This dirty room. Let Vinnie in. Let him take me away. Vinnie. O Vinnie, my darling. Take me away. Its ugly in here. Ugly. And I loved the carousel. Puddin n pie. Vinnie – (the doctor looked at her eyes, said nothing, then examined her leg. He washed the wound, probed gently, and Georgette groaned, hoping hed write a prescription, and rolled on the bed trying to hang over the side and reach the slacks and the doctor mumbled; her Mother watched, shaking, and Georgette looked pleadingly at her, wanting her caresses and protection, but she couldnt reach the slacks. Jesus, why cant I reach them? She stopped rolling and cried. Her Mother stroked her forehead and the doctor bandaged the leg and told her to stay off it for a few days and come in to see him when she felt better. He closed his bag (shut. Shut. It banged Shut!), smiled and told Mrs. Hanson it would be better if George didnt have any visitors for a few days. She nodded (Georgette leaned slowly to the edge of the bed – when they go to the door) and thanked him. Dont bother to walk me to the door. I can find my way out – not even a little codeine. Nothing. If that fucking Harry wasnt there. That freak. And those rotten bitches. Two cent cunt. Not even a nebbie. He could have given me one at least. Not much of a cut. Just stay in bed a few days. Days. Days. Days . . . DAYS. DAYS!!! The walls will fall. Theyll crush me. Mother? O Mother. Mother? Give me something. Please. Anything. Try to relax son. Your leg will be better soon. My leg? – (Stop. Arthur, for the love of God stop. Stop? You see these? You see them? More of those goddamn dopepills. Thats what they are. Dopepills. Well, you will never see these again dear sweet *brother!* Give them to me. Give me them. Mother, make him give them to me. Shut up or I ll kill you. Do you hear me? I swear I will kill you. Always crying. Mommy this and Mommy that. Everytime you get a little scratch – Arthur. Stop! He stood shaking, clutching the end of the bed watching brother crawl and squirm on the bed, hiding behind his Mommy, wanting Mommys love and kisses . . . then shoved the pills in his pocket, spun around and dragged out the boxes in the back of the closet and dumped them on the floor – Mommy this and Mommy that – ripping and tearing Georgettes drag clothes, her lovely dresses and silks, stamping on her shoes . . . You see these Mother? You see them? Look. Look at these disgusting pictures. O Arthur – Look at them. Just LOOK! Men making love to each other. It isnt pretty is it? Arthur, please. Well? is it? Are they? ARE THEY??? Filth. Thats what they are. FILTH!!! Why dont you die Georg*ie!* Why

31

dont you go away and die. Stop. STOP! For the love of god Arthur, stop. I cant stand it anymore. Well, neither can I. You saw those pictures. Now you should know what he *really* is. A degenerate. A filthy degenerate! Arthur, please, for my sake. I know. I know. Leave your brother alone. Please. *Brother???*) – O god, theyll bug me. They know I cant stay down. They know it. Nothing to see. To look at. Why me? Why wont somebody help me. I dont want to be alone. I cant stand it. Please help me. At least Goldie has bennie. I cant stay down. Always alone. O jesus, jesus jesus . . . why me??? Mommy? Mommy? O god I need something. Those sick johns. Always? I dont want to be straight. I just need something. I ll go crazy. Theyre keeping me down. Down. Why do they want to kill me? and the near shadowless room continued shrinking and she looked for dark corners, but there were none, just a penumbra as the closet door partially blocked the light from the living room. Georgette called . . . looked around the room. At the bed. Sat up and called again . . . then slowly swung her legs over the side and tentatively touched the floor . . . stood . . . hobbled to the door and looked at Mother sleeping in a chair. She dressed, took money from Mothers pocketbook and left. When she stood on the stoop she realised she didnt know the day or time. But the sun had set. Leaning against parked cars she limped to the corner and hailed a cab, praying that Goldie was home. She gave the driver the address and thought of Goldies and bennie.

When she got to Goldies one of the girls helped her upstairs and to a chair. She asked for someone to light her a cigarette and leaned back in the chair, closed her eyes, allowing her hand and body to shake, extending her leg stiffly in front of her and groaning. The girls stood around, asking, wondering, thrilling to the scene and exulting over the sudden breaking of the monotony; the monotony of the last few days that dragged them even with bennie and pot and forced them to sit, just sit, and bitch about the heat like tired johns, and remember beatings by punks, and stares of squares; but Georgette twisted her face with pain, not too much though, and they wondered and thrilled. Goldie handed her half a dozen bennie and she swallowed them, gulped hot coffee and sat silent . . . trying to think the bennie into her mind (and her room and the past few days out); not wanting to wait for it to dissolve and be absorbed by the blood and pumped through her body; wanting her heart to pound *now*; wanting the chills *now*; wanting the lie *now*; Now!!! The others jabbered and squealed as she opened her eyes, shaking her head tragically, her arms hanging limply . . . speaking in whispers and shaking away questions, nodding and slowly raising her cigarette to her lips and taking shallow asthmatic puffs. They gave her more coffee and then the tingle, the pounding of the heart and she lit another cigarette and straightened slightly in the chair. Goldie asked her if she was feeling better and she said yes. A little thanks. Would you like some pot? O, do you have any? Of course honey. Goldie gave her a stick and Georgette sucked the smoke refusing, absolutely refusing, to cough; and they watched and waited until Georgette had chewed the roach and put her makeup on before bubbling forth with their questions. Well, I must say you look much better now. You looked simply frightful when you came in. I have been down for days. Days? What happened. Yes, dishus honey. Do you have another stick Goldie. Of course. Well for gods sake, you just going to sit there all night or are you going to tell us what happened. O really Miss Lee. Cant you see the poor girl is overwrought. You dont have to yell Miss Thing. Im simply dying to know what happened, thats all. Thats alright honey – O thank you Goldie – I understand. Just let me get myself together and I'll tell you the whole story. She smoked the second stick and told them how she was stabbed; how the freak Harry started the whole thing; how the doctor wouldnt give her anything, not even one little nebbie; and how they kept her locked in her room not allowing her to have one visitor, and I heard Vinnie at the door a couple of times and they wouldnt let him in; and how she defied her brother, the freak, and how she laid him out and walked right out of the house. And I mean right past him honey, right past him, and you should have seen his face! he was agog, simply agog. O I laid him out but good. O how wonderful. How simply wonderful. O how I wish I had been there. I would have adored seeing you lay that big freak out. I'll never forget that atrocious scene he pulled on us. Never. All those straight creeps are like that. They clapped their hands, twittered and aaad and decided to have a party in honour of Georgette and the laying out of Arthur.

Goldie sent Rosie, a demented female who acted as sortofa housemaid, for gin, cigarettes and another gross of bennie. They made a small pot of bouillon and danced around it dropping tablets in and chanting *bennie* in the *bouil*lon, *ben*nie in the *bouil*lon, whirling away the fear and boredom, giggling, popping bennie, drinking gin, toasting Georgette: Long Live THE QUEEN, and the laying out of Arthur. He should be laid out, but I mean really, the freak, each in her mind and turn laying out every rough or straight sonofabitch that ever hit them or pointed and laughed; dancing through the apartment until they fell into chairs trying to catch their breath, fanning themselves; and Rosie brought bouillon, ice and gin and they spoke more quietly, still laughing, asking Georgette again and again to tell them how she laid her brother out . . . then gradually they quieted, too spent to shout, stretching in their seats, getting higher and higher as they sat quietly and becoming conscious of the absence of men, their high spirits and overflowing joy making the absence of love known. So her subjects petitioned the Queen to summon forth her dashing husband and his rough trade friends, for tonight they were daring and even Camille, a frail queen from a small town in Jersey, longed for rough arms, there being no room, but absolutely no room, for johns. So Georgette, flying in her world of junk, called the Greeks and flushed (O, my libido is twitching) when she heard Vinnies voice and fluttered her lids when he said hello sweetchips, whereya been? O, Ive been balling it loverman, smiling at her friends and too high to be bothered by, Ive got ya loverman shit. Itll still costya. She asked him to come over with some of the boys, giggling yes when he asked if she was high, telling him they had loads of gin and not to worry about gold for gas to get back, and Vinnie said maybe they would (for kicks) and Georgette continued to talk after Vinnie hungup, rolling her hips as she sighed, O Vinnie baby, and sighing as she slowly lowered the phone. They asked her if they were coming, how many, when – and Georgette played it cool and to the hilt; regally walking back to her throne, telling the girls to be quiet. Really! One would think it was years since you had a real man. They may be here in an hour or so, if they dont pull a job, so just keep your legs crossed, flaunting her arms, smiling graciously and secretly. They drank more bouillon, popped more bennie and dished the dirt. Camille was nervous, never having met an excon before. You just never meet that sort back home. As a matter of fact Goldie was the first hip queen she had ever met. All the fairies in her town were closet queens or pinkteas, so she was all a dither, jumping up, jerking around the room, asking question after question, Georgette telling her stories about broken noses, cut throats and Camille ooood and squealed, loving the tightness in her stomach and the apprehension in her bowels.

She said she felt faint and that she simply must take a bath. The others laughed and chided, Georgette waving off the how could you's as Camille filled one of the tubs in the kitchen and laid out her brushes: One for her back, one for her stomach, one for her chest, one for her arms, one for her legs, one for her feet, one for her toe-nails, one for her hands, one for her fingernails, and a special jar of cream for her face. She lined them up, handles facing her, and started from the left with the back brush. They told her to hurry or she would be attacked while bathing and O she was frightened, they should know better than to talk of such things. She was so upset she almost broke wind.

Camille had finished her bath, collected her brushes and was primping in the bathroom when the bell rang. Georgette almost jumped to the door, but contained herself, sat back, leaning her head to one side hoping the light was falling on her face properly, and waited for someone to open the door. She held her cigarette daintily and tried to hide her excitement. Over an hour since the call and though Miss Camille, while in the tub, had afforded Georgette an opportunity to appear relaxed and carefree, during the time that elapsed since Camille finished Georgette was forced to retain her position, and the center of attraction, by amusing the others with stories, laying this one and that one out, the girls laughing at her wit; continually talking and hoping the bell would ring before too many seconds of silence forced her to think of what to say next or allowed the others to become conscious of time and ask about Vinnie (VINNIE!!! Vinnie had to come) or allowed her fears to come back to the surface . . . but the bell rang and she swallowed another bennie, finished her bouillon and once again adjusted herself on her throne.

Goldie opened the door and the boys strolled in, looked around, stood in the kitchen, looking, until Vinnie led the way into the living room. Whatayasay Georgie? Hows the leg? O, just fine, thank you, tilting her head to the side just a wee bit more and taking a quick Bette Davis like drag on her cigarette. The other guys strolled around the room, eventually flopping here and there. Harrys eyes bugged when he saw Lee. She looked like one of the show girls you see in some of the magazines (her hair was shoulder length and golden blond and she was always smartly in drag), a real doll. Harry kept staring, not digging the score. He had never been to Goldies before and he thought maybe she was Rosie the freak he had heard the guys talk about, but man, she didnt look like no freak. She looked like a real fine piecea ass. Goldie prepared drinks, putting a bennie in each, and stepped lightly through the rooms dispensing them, smiling and simply brimming over with joy. Lee told Rosie to bring her another pack of cigarettes and when Rosie simpered and said no Lee pointed a finger at her and told her to bring them here at once or you will be out on the street with the other freaks, Miss Cocksucker. (Harry looked at Lee, still puzzled, then figured she must be one of the queens. But shes still a fine piecea ass.) Rosie threw the cigarettes to Lee and ran to the bathroom and pounded on the door until Camille unlocked it, then stepped around her and sat on the floor between the sink and the toilet-bowl. O really Rosie. I mean! Camille sniffed, primped her hair again, peeked out, walked to the kitchen and slowly inched her way to the living room hoping her makeup was on properly (that light over the mirror is simply terrible) and glided into the room and slowly lowered herself beside Goldie and, as did the other girls, surveyed the prospective suitors. Her eyes almost blurred with excitement. They had such hard looks. Why their eyes went right through you as if you were naked. She squirmed slightly. But it is wonderful. But what should she do? Of course she had never even so much as hinted the truth to the other girls, but she was a virgin. She had talked with a few of the queens back home and they told her how to go about *doing* it, always cautioning her never, but never to take it out of her mouth when he was coming because it might just get all over you and in your eyes and you know honey, you can go blind from that, and anyway thats the moment when everything just explodes and you wont want to take it out . . . But how do you start? what do you say??? O, I hope everything will be alright.

Goldie inquired if they were ready for another drink and they said yeah, but not so much of that sodashit. Thats OK for you girls, but I like somethin with a kick, so Goldie swished lightly to the kitchen, lowering her eyes at Malfie, fixed another drink with just a drop of mixer and another bennie, distributed the drinks and asked them if they would like a bennie. Sure, why not. So she passed the box around, telling them to take two, then sat down glancing coyly from time to time, at Malfie.

Georgette no longer tried to control the conversation, but concentrated on Vinnie, trying, of course, to give a disinterested impression, wanting to let her friends see that he was hers. She tried toying with Harry, hoping to arouse a sense of jealousy in Vinnie, but Harry continually grabbed her by the ears and rubbed his crotch and tolder he got a nice fat lob forer to suck, and Georgette sat back on her throne and threw her head to the side and told him she wasnt interested in boys, Miss Pinkie, then leaned toward Vinnie when she saw him staring at Lee. Vinnie was hip to Lee, but she still looked like a lovely doll and he thought of her as a dame. Lee enjoyed the idea of them staring at her, but turned her head and spoke to Goldie or Camille or the room in general. After all, she had worked in some of the best drag joints and had been featured in the professional magazines and it certainly would be beneath her dignity to openly fraternise with roughtrade (admittedly though she did enjoy them within the safety of the

38

apartment). That may be alright for Georgette, and the others, but someone in her position couldnt afford to be seen with scum, and their manners are far too replusive . . . but it might be fun to play with them . . . Camille continued to look, worry and hope.

Goldie asked Malfie if he would like another drink and he said sure sweetheart, fillerup and Goldie filled the glass with gin, just a bit of mixer, no bennie (too much might kill his nature), yelled for Rosie to get more gin like a good girl. Rosie smiled, you like me Goldie? and Goldie patted her head, of course Rosie. Now run along like a good girl and get the gin. When Goldie handed the drink to Malfie she brushed lightly against his leg and smiled. Malfie raised his eyes slightly and Goldie twittered and asked if he would like some pot. Yamean weed? Of course darling. Yeah. She rushed into the bedroom (he didnt move his leg), came out with a small cookie tin and passed the joints around. Georgette blasted with a flourish, letting the ash get long and loose then dragging hard and sucking the ash in with the smoke. She laughed loudly, turning and pointing to be certain that everyone was aware why she was laughing, and watched Harry as he struggled with the stick and ranked him as he covered his nose and mouth trying to suppress a cough. You should have asked us to show you how *Harold*. Theres no sense in wasting good pot on amateurs. Georgette enjoyed the light laughter and sat back sucking hard on her joint, pointing at Harry as he continued to struggle, feeling her eyes cloud slightly . . . She rolled her shoulders and looked at her Vinnie then turned back to Harry as he finally stopped choking and tolder ta shuter mout, ya cocksucker. I am an expert in my field honey. Nobody can suck a cock better than I. But you!!! why youre not even a good thief. Youre just rank, and she sucked the joint down to an eighth of an inch then dropped the roach in her mouth and, smiling disdainfully, leaned over and took the partially smoked stick from Harry. His body was as sluggish as his imagination and he only got partway to his feet then sat down, trying to ignore the smiles of the guys and the twittering of the queens, straining to think of something to say, but only mumbling, fag. Shutup and take your dope pills, ya hophead. Lee burst out with a roar and told Georgette she was surprised that her friends were so square. Not all of them honey, and she flourished her wrist and tapped Vinnie on the knee. Lee continued to rank Harry, but he was getting frightfully nasty and Lee started getting nervous and asked Goldie to turn on the radio and get some music. Goldie tuned in a jazz program and they slowly relaxed with the tea and the music. Harry wanted to open a window, but the guys said nothing and the queens frowned so he sat still, sipping his drink and watching Lee. Goldie watched Malfies eyes fog, then stared at his chest as it swelled with the beating of his heart, told him he may as well take his shirt off as having it hanging open like that, then watched his flesh move and shine with sweat, loving the small mat of hair between his breasts and the sweat rolling down and into the mat. Rosie had been knocking on the door for almost a minute before Lee, annoyed with the manner in which Miss Goldie was ogling Malfie, got up in a huff and opened the door. She took the gin from Rosie, put it on the table in the living room, took four more bennie and a glass of hot bouillon and sat down, disgusted, and tried to withdraw as far as possible from the sordid party. Cant even take a few bennie and a little pot without simply drifting off. How ridiculous. I must say Georgette that I dont think much of these *men* friends of yours. I thought they were hip. Goldie heard, but didnt bother to look at her and continued to stare at Malfie, thinking of how wonderful it was that they *werent* used to bennie (getting kicks too from turning them (him) on), and waiting for the time to fly, as it does when youre up on bennie, and stop with her and Malfie. Georgette went to the kitchen, brought back a bowl of ice and a bottle of mixer, and filled hers and Vinnies glasses. There is no need to worry Miss Lee. They dont want to have anything to do with the likes of you. Vinnie was digging the conversation, but was goofed with the tea and didnt bother to say anything, and just took the drink from Georgette and looked over his glass at Lee, letting the smoke come slowly from his nose, and gave her a *gee* look until Lee turned her head then Vinnie pursed his lips at Camille and smiled, glowing inside at the fear in her eyes. Dont worry chippy, nobodys gonna hurtya. Maybe fuckya a little – Georgette asked him for a cigarette and he told her ta smoke her own and she fumbled for a moment until she was certain he was finished speaking to Camille, then found them.

Rosie sucked at a glass of gin, sitting at Goldies feet, and Georgette worried about Vinnie going with one of the other girls and what they would say if he did . . . then stopped worrying about what they might say but simply about keeping them away from him. She wanted them to think he was her lover, but more than that she wanted him as her lover. Even if only once. If only that. She took another bennie with her gin and listened to the music. The Bird was playing. She tilted her head toward the radio and listened to the hard sounds piling up on each other, yet not touching, wanting to hold Vinnies hand, the strange beautiful sounds (bennie, tea and gin too) moving her to a strange romance where love was born of affection, not sex; wanting to share just this, just these three minutes of the Bird with Vinnie, these three minutes out of space and time and just stand together, perhaps their hands touching, not speaking, yet knowing . . . just stand complete with and for each other not as man and woman or two men, not as friends or lovers, but as two who love . . . these three minutes together in a world of beauty, a world where there wasnt even a memory of johns or punks, butch queens or Arthurs, just the now of love . . . and the strange rhythms of the Bird ripped to her, the piling patterns of sound all falling properly and articulately into place, and there was no wonderment at the Bird blowing love.

Then it was over and the background music came in and Georgette looked up and her eyes cleared as she saw the sick look in Harrys eyes as he looked at Rosies snatch. Her legs were raised and she rested her head on her knees staring at a spot on the rug, waiting, as always, for Goldie to speak and she would jump. Georgette turned her head and tried to think the Bird back into her mind, but she slowly turned her head back, unable to ignore Rosie, or avoid thinking about her. Rosie had always been more than taken for granted – she had never been thought of. Not even as a demented human, but as a scooper: someone to scoop up the empties; to buy the bennie; to meet the connection . . . Georgette looked at the spot on the rug, then back at Rosies face. Who was Rosie? What? Did she think? What did she feel? She must feel something or why would she stay with Goldie? Had she ever loved? Was she ever loved? Could she love? Georgette looked at the leer on Harrys face, the lust breaking through the junk facade. If Rosie were to move Harry would jump up and lay her right there – hold her arms, bend over her with his leering face next to hers (spit dribbling from his mouth) and shove it in if he had to fight for – Georgette lifted her head so she couldnt see his face. If Harry did have sex with her would she enjoy it? Would Rosie feel anything? Did she ever think of it? Did she ever long for love??? An analogy started to form and Georgette had to fight it, she had to fight before it defined itself or she would not be able to ignore or deny it. She popped more bennie and gulped gin. She almost puked from the gin and in panic lit a cigarette and sat still, smoking, until the nausea passed (the analogy becoming fainter) then turned up the radio and concentrated on the music, snapping her fingers, looking at Vinnie and hoping the bennie would soon overtake the tea and Vinnie would get with it.

Camille asked Georgette what the name of the number was that was being played, saying she liked it very much, and Georgette told her, and who was blowing and Camille started moving slightly in time with the music and Lee turned to her and told her not to wiggle like a slut in heat. And I really dont see how you can listen to that trashy music Georgette. You who love Opera so much. O really Miss Thing – Camille moved back and sat still – take the icecube out of your ass. Vinnie laughed and Georgette turned to him, coyly, turning the volume up a little more and marked one up on Lee, took a drink of gin and when the record ended and another came on she asked Camille if she liked it, digging the glance she directed at Lee – well dont look at me honey. Its your bad taste not mine – and Camille wished she new what to say, if she liked it or not (did she like it?), looked at Sal and shivered again. Its alright, I guess (would he be as rough as he looks?).

The phone rang and Goldie tapped Rosie on the head and she jumped up and answered it, then turned to Goldie and said it was Sheila. Goldie listened, said yes and hung up. Shes coming home with an all night John so we will have to go down to Miss Tonys. O that place is loathsome. Well *Lee*, you can always go home, if you have one. Rosie, heat up the bouillon. O I think youre awful, living with a woman. O youre just jealous Lee. Why dont you just go about your own business Georgette. Honestly Goldie, I really dont see how you do it, even if she does support you and keep you in bennie. I think that that is my business Miss Lee. Hey, whats all this bullshit about? Were going downstairs to someone elses apartment. That is if its

43

alright with you Harold. I honestly dont see how you can have sex with her Goldie. Or do you only eat it? O O OOO. Goldie flew from the room and Rosie spat at Lee and ran after her. O for heavens sake, dont be so touchy. The guys started stirring and digging the scene, but didnt know from nothin, so they just shrugged and Georgette looked after Goldie and inquired if she was alright and Camille was much taken aback, after all this is not the way ladies should act. And Lee is supposed to be so elegant. This sort of thing never happened back home. But it is exciting and he is *so* manly; and Lee said she was terribly sorry, I didnt mean to upset you dear. Its just that Tonys place is so dreary, with the electricity turned off and everything, and I guess I just have the rag on tonight anyway, so they kissed and made up, and they all helped finish the bouillon (with a few more bennie) gathered the gin and bennie and went downstairs, the guys stumbling behind, not sure exactly what was happening but having kicks and too high to care, and walked into Tonys apartment.

She was sleeping so Goldie lit a few candles and told her Sheila was turning a trick so they had to come down here and Im sure you dont mind honey, handing her some bennie, and told Rosie to make coffee. Rosie lit the small kerosene stove in the kitchen and put on a pot of coffee. When it was ready she passed out paper cups of coffee then went back to the kitchen and made another pot, continuing to make pot after pot of coffee, coming in inbetween to sit at Goldies feet. The guys slowly snapped out of the tea goof and soon the bennie got to their tongues too and everybody yakked. Goldie said she felt ever so much better. I guess I needed a good cry and she passed around the bennie again and they all popped bennie and sipped hot coffee and Goldie sat next to Malfie and asked him if he was enjoying himself, and he said yeah, Im havin a ball; and Goldie just floated along on a soft purple cloud, feeling luxurious and slightly smug: a handsome piece of trade beside her; wonderful girl friends; and a beautiful bennie connection in the corner drugstore where she could get a dozen 10 grain tables for 50c. O this is divine. I mean the candlelight and everything . . . it brings to mind Genet. Genet? I fail to see how *this* reminds you of her. Whose this junay? A french writer Vinnie. I am certain you would not know about such things – I really dont see how all this gloom reminds you of Genet (Georgette looked at Lee as she talked and glanced at Vinnie and sighed. Vinnie will never have anything to do with her after that remark). I mean she is so beautiful. Well that is exactly what I mean darling. She creates such beauty out of the tortured darkness of our souls – O well, yes. That is true enough – and I feel so beautiful. Hey! wheres the shithouse. Georgette jumped up (Camille was shocked and looked askance) and said it is outside. I will show you. Vinnie walked past her, patted her on the ass. Thats OK sweetchips, I can find it. Georgette whirled slightly and sat down, smiling and chalking another one up. O it will be so wonderful . . . later. Rosie was passing more coffee around and Harry asked her if she blew cock and she fell back spilling some of the coffee. Goldie told her to be more careful, you might have burned someone, and Rosie wailed and buried her head in Goldies lap and Goldie told her it was alright. Nobody was hurt. You can continue serving the coffee, and Rosie smiled a smile of salvation and stepped over the feet and passed out the coffee; and Georgette looked at the tears slowly streaking Rosie's face and glistening in the sepia room; and Harry thought it might be kicks ta sloff it inna weird dame like that. Whattsa matta Rosie? afraida my lob? Rosie backed out of the room and Harry laughed and asked the guys if they saw the look oner face. Man, shes a real weirdy. Whered yapick that up? Goldie said she found her somewhere and Camille went out to the kitchen to see if Rosie was alright, thinking Harry was terribly cruel and Goldie should not let them do that to her. She did not see Rosie immediately and stared at the low blue flame of the kerosene stove, the perking coffee looking like a witches brew. Then she saw Rosie sitting in the corner, her head resting on her knees. Camille was nervous, but felt she should try to comfort her. She called softly, tentatively, then stood silent for a moment listening to the coffee perking, the strong rhythm broken every third or fourth beat with a double beat, then she looked back in the living room and everyone was talking, drinking (Georgette seemed to have been watching her), and when she caught Sals eye she blushed and turned back to Rosie and called her again. Rosie sat in the corner with her head on her knees. Camille walked over to her, carefully avoiding the stove, asked if she was alright. Why dont you come back inside Rosie, lightly touching her shoulder. Rosie jerked her head around, bit Camilles hand, looked at her for a moment then put her head back on her knees. Camille screeched and ran back to the living room clutching her injured hand, extending it before her. She bit me, she bit me, that crazy little thing. She turned in a circle, arms still stiffly extended, jumping up and down. What thefucks wrong wit you? O she bit me. O for heavens sake Camille sit down. Sit down. O she bit me. Shaddup. Harry pushed her and she fell on Lee and they screeched and tried to right themselves, but Camille kept falling down as she tried to push herself up then remembered her hand and halfway up she would try to clutch it and fall again, her arms whirling in the air and she rolled off Lee and Lee fought frantically to keep her skirts down, all the time yelling at Camille to get off her and Camille finally raised herself to her knees and grabbed the elusive hand and searched for the teeth marks. Dont worry little girl, yawont get the rabbyz. Lee sat up and smoothed her skirt and threw Camille a vicious glance, O really Miss Thing, and took a mirror from her pocketbook, examined her face then dove in her pocketbook and extracted her comb, cosmetics and hurriedly fixed her face. Camille finally sat down and continued to examine her finger, completely ignoring the laughter. O it was terrible. All I did was try to speak to her and she bit me. She bit me like—like some kind of animal. O it was terrible. Why didntya biter back? She'd get the crud. Here, dipit in the hot coffee. Goldie was laughing as hard as the rest but managed to lean over and offer solace and bennie. O yes, please. She brought me down something dreadful. O . . . she scooped up the bennie and dropped them in her mouth (with her good hand) then picked up her coffee (with her good hand) and took a few tiny sips until the bennie were down. Hey, what times does the next show start? They were all laughing, except Camille, and Lee only sneered at first, but when she finished putting her face on she too relaxed and joined the party, each new remark bringing forth a loud guffaw and refined laughter; Camille sitting with a peevish look on her face; but the boys were having a ball, not too sure what they were laughing about, but really digging the bennie scene, enjoying the cold chills and the strange feeling in their jaws as they clenched and ground their teeth (Harry wondering if maybe he oughtta go out to the kitchen and straighten Rosie out); Georgette content to relax and laugh (she was 3 up on Lee) yet still watchful for an opportunity to regain the center of attraction; and Goldie was ethereal . . . things were going so well and she was atingle with anticipation; but poor Camille felt ashamed and tried to relax and laugh it off but O it was so terribly embarrassing. She had carried on so; and Lee was determined to maintain her aloofness (yet she did not want to estrange herself from Goldie), the aloofness that her beauty and position demanded. The laughter continued even after they were too breathless from laughing to continue dropping remarks, and Goldie called for more coffee and Rosie made the rounds once more and retired to the kitchen and started a new pot and sat in the corner with her head on her knees. Goldie counted the bennie determining that there would be enough left for a few rounds (and by then the drugstore would be open) and handed more out. Vinnie asked for some gin (spurts of giggling still coming forth) and Georgette offered her glass but Vinnie refused (the code forbids drinking from the same glass as a fag) so she filled a paper cup for him, hoping this would not alter the score and glanced at Lee but she did not seem to notice; and Tony said thank you after taking a bennie and wondered if they would share their trade with her and trying desperately to think of something to say or do that would draw everyones attention to her and make them aware of her presence and perhaps Goldie would be grateful and one of the men would find her attractive. She looked around the room, smiling and rapidly blinking her eyes . . . then jumped up and jerked open a drawer and took out a new candle. She slammed the drawer closed and tripped lightly to the candle that was burned to the bottom, lit the new one and placed it carefully over the old one. There, that is much better, then sat down happily and beaming at Goldie certain she would appreciate the act.

Everyone stared at the new candle and the shadows the jerking flame created, still speaking softly, still smoking, still sipping coffee and gin; watching the top soften and the first little drop of wax seep to the edge and stagger down the side of the candle, the wick glowing brighter and redder in the middle of the flame . . . then another drop rolled to the first; and another started a new stream as the flame bent and the edge sloped away and soon many little drops were rolling down and piling up and flowing down the side of the candle and everyone relaxed even more, calmed by the new flame and slightly enervated by the laughing, and they sat deeper in their seats and the guys stretched their legs even more and the girls became softer and more coy; and their eyes eventually strayed from the flame and everything seemed softer and even Lee felt she was a part of the group and turned in her seat and faced the others and started telling little tidbits about backstage life and soon they all joined in and when someone was not talking they were listening to two or three stories being told at once. Lee told them about how almost all actors are gay (and even most of the church officials – and you know who honey), and how the cast of one of the revues she was starring in were pickedup and the club closed because they were all blasting backstage – and their hands fluttered about and the guys flipped their ashes – and I am telling you it was a scream. Caldonia was just so high – I mean she had been drinking like crazy for hours and she struts around Broadway and 45th st. crowing like a rooster, COCK-adoodledo COCKadoodledo – Im not shittinya, he was caught fuckin a stiff. He was in the El witme. He worked inna hospital, you know, in the morgue, and this nice lookin young head croaks so he throws a hump inner – Rosie refilled all the cups and ran back to the kitchen when Harry lunged for her snatch, and sat in the corner with her head on her knees – well, you think you have weird johns . . . well, I have one that makes me beat him with his belt – O that is just masochism honey – O I know that, but I have to be wearing a bra – ice blue with lace and panties to match, and stockings and a garter belt and he rubs his hands up and down my legs and snaps the garters until I am just black and blue and by the time he comes I can hardly move my arm – we got a weirdy like that in the neighbourhood. He owns a beauty shop in the 80s on third and comes around a couple a nights a week – yeah, yeah, I know the guy. Hes got a new Dodge. Green. Yeah. And he picks up somea the kids and takesem for a ride and paysem a quarter ta fart – Tony kept leaning forward more and more, listening, laughing, making certain that each one was aware that she was listening to their story and enjoying it; trying to think of some little anecdote she could tell, some funny little thing that had happened or she had seen . . . or even something in a movie . . . she refilled her glass with gin, smiling at Goldie; nodded, smiled, laughed, still trying to think of something funny, even slightly humorous, thumbing through years of memories and finding nothing – Well how about Leslie? – O!!! that filthy thing – she goes through Central Park about 5 in the morning looking for used condoms and sucks them. Holy Krist. Well I have a john who makes me throw golfballs – we had a kid upstate who stuck a life magazine up his ass and couldnt get it out. The – O I love the ones who almost cry when they are finished and start telling you about how much they love their wife and kiddies. And when they take out the pic – O I hate those freaks – Hey, how about that guy the Spook met in the Village that night who gaveim 10 bucks for his left shoe. The Spook toldim he could havem both for 10 bucks and his socks too – Goldie kept looking at Malfie and the way his hair waved back into a thick D A; and Georgette leaned closer to Vinnie and everyone seemed so close, as if they belonged to and with each other and everything was wonderful – Did Francene ever tell you about that Arab she met one night? Well honey, he just fucked her until she thought she would turn insideout. O, that must have been divine. – Camille looked nervously at Sal – It is so refreshing to meet a man who will give you a good fucking. Yes honey, but she almost had to have a hysterectomy. O was she – We had this here guy—

The door banged open and a young woman with a

bruised face and an enormous belly stumbled in and called to Tony. Tony looked at the others apologetically then crossed the room to her sister, led her into the kitchen and helped her lie down, took the pot off the stove and turned up the flame. Rosie looked at them, at the pot, but when Goldie said nothing she lowered her head to her knees. Tony knelt beside her sister, embarrassed because she knew Goldie and the others didnt like Mary, and asked her what was wrong. She raised her head slightly then let it fall back and it seemed to bounce on the floor (Goldie and Lee turned their heads, disgusted. Camille stared and shook), then rolled it from side to side, moaning, jerking up with a scream, clutching her moundish abdomen, banging her head and arms on the floor, jerking her legs up then jutting and spreading them out, grabbing Tony by the shoulders as another pain ripped her and Tony clawed at her hands. Let go! Let go! O youre hurting me, and the hands finally fell and she lay still and Tony looked into the other room, hoping they wouldnt hold her responsible for all this; and the queens turned their heads and the guys looked blankly, taking another drag or another drink, a little curious, and Tony asked if she should call the police so they could take her to a hospital. You aint callin no cops. Not with us here – What am I going to do? Why dont you just throw her out, the dirty slut. Shes going to have a baby – O is she? I thought perhaps it was gas. They roared with laughter (Rosie opened her eyes, her head on her knees, then closed them) and Tony almost cried. (O why did she pick now of all times? They would have asked me upstairs and we could have been friends) Why dont you get the slob shes living with? After all, he is the father, not us. I assure you. They roared again – how do you know he is. It could be almost anybody. (Camille still felt a little nauseous but she was determined to ignore it and be one of the girls.) Hey, did she swolla a watermelon seed. Even

Harrys belching brought forth laughter, but everyone was becoming tense, especially the queens. This could ruin a perfectly delightful evening. If this were prolonged much longer it would bring everybody down and all the plans – Mary bolted up! Screaming! Not just one short scream, but one after another after another. Her face darkened and threatened to burst. The welts on her face oozed and she sat as if propped from behind, screaming, screeching, wailing, screaming . . . Tony leaned back and banged into the wall (Rosie still sat with her head on her knees) and Camille covered her face with her hands. The screams scraped through their ears and her eyes bulged, her arms still lifted toward Tony, her face becoming darker . . . then she stopped and fell back, her head smashing on the floor and the screams and the sound of her head hitting the floor resounded through the room and jammed in everyones ear and wouldnt leave like the sound of the sea in a shell . . . O O OOO!!! She broke water. She broke her water. The queens jumped up and Harry stared at the spreading moisture. Get her out of here. Get her out Get her out! Comeon yafuck, geter outta here before the law comes. O shes bringing me down. That dirty slut. That filthy whore. Rosie ROSIE! Get her out. Get her out! Rosie grabbed an arm, but it was wet with perspiration and it slipped from her grip. She pulled Marys skirt up and wiped her hands and Marys arms, then noticing her face wiped it too and told Tony to get the other arm. She tugged and Tony kept falling under the weight and looking pleadingly at Goldie and Rosie screamed at Tony to pull, pull, and Rosie yanked and Marys body jerked with each yank and shuddered with each shock of pain and the sweat burned her eyes and blinded her and all she could do was moan and moan and Harry got up and walked over to them and said hed help. He got behind her and put his hands over her tits, smiling at the guys, and lifted her up and Rosie yanked again almost pulling them over, and they slowly raised the mountainous Mary and dragged her to the door. Harry told Tony to get a cab and he and Rosie would get her to the door. Tony left, and Rosie held on to the arm, watching Harry, and they dragged her along the hallway, water and blood dripping down her legs, to the door. Harry asked Rosie how she was doin and she didnt move. Just held on to the arm and watched Harry. He laughed and dropped Mary on the floor and waited for the cab.

When Harry and Rosie came back everyone was silent, shadows jumping on the walls, and Harry asked what was wrong, this a morgue or somethin, and sat down and lit a cigarette. Man, shes some ton of a dame. She had a nice pair though. Couldnt get my hand aroundem they were so big . . . The others remained silent, not even smoking, and Rosie put the pot back on the stove and waited. Lee was simply repulsed at the entire scene – thats a real drag though man. Whatta yamean Sal? You know, havin a kid and some guy lumps yaup. – Camille still frightfully upset – the others agreed with Sal that it was a real drag to be havin a kid like that and a guy lumps yaup. A guy like that should be dumped, the sonofabitch, even if she is a pig – and Goldie and Georgette were anxious. They had been planning and anticipating all evening and things were going so well that it just wasnt right that everything should crumble now . . . now when it was coming close to the time . . . and Georgette frantically searched for something to say or do . . . something that would not only save the moment and the night, but something that would make it her moment and night . . . something that would once more make her the nucleus of the night. She looked around the room . . . thought . . . then remembered a book and yes, it was still there. She picked it up, opened it, looked at it for a moment then decided to say nothing but to start to read

> *Once upon a midnight dreary, while I pondered,*
> *weak and weary, . . .*

The first few words were low, tentative, but hearing her voice above the breathing of the others, ringing through the room, thrilled her and she read louder, each word clear and true

> *As of some one gently rapping, rapping at my*
> *chamber door.*
> *''Tis some visitor,' I muttered, 'tapping at my*
> *chamber door . . .'*

and the others hushed and Vinnie turned his face toward *her*

> *Ah, distinctly I remember it was in the bleak*
> *December;*
> *And each separate dying ember wrought its ghost*
> *upon the floor.*
> *Eagerly I wished the morrow; – vainly I had*
> *sought to borrow . . .*

they were all watching her now (could Rosie be watching too?). They were all looking at her. At HER!

> *Deep into that darkness peering, long I stood there*
> *wondering, fearing,*
> *Doubting, dreaming dreams no mortal ever dared to*
> *dream before;*
> *But the silence was unbroken, and the stillness gave*
> *no token, . . .*

the drama of the moment swelled her breast and the poem came forth with beauty and feeling and the waves from her mouth caused the candle flames to flicker and she knew that everyone saw a Raven in the shadows

> Let me see, then, what thereat is, and this mystery
>   explore –
> Let my heart be still a moment and this mystery
>   explore; –
>   "Tis the wind and nothing more!' . . .

and she was no longer merely reading a poem, but she was the poem and every word was coming from her soul and all the wonderful shadows whirled around her

> Then this ebony bird beguiling my sad fancy into
>   smiling,
> By the grave and stern decorum of the countenance it
>   wore,
> 'Though thy crest be shorn and shaven, thou,' I said,
>   'art sure no craven,
> Ghastly grim and ancient Raven wandering from the
>   Nightly shore . . .

The guys were staring and Vinnie seemed so close she could feel the sweat on his face and even Lee was listening and watching her read and they all knew she was there; they all knew she was THE QUEEN.

> Nothing farther then he uttered – not a feather then
>   he fluttered –
> Till I scarcely more than muttered, 'Other friends
>   have flown before –
> On the morrow he will leave me, as my hopes have
>   flown before.'
>   Then the bird said 'Nevermore.' . . .

Vinnie was staring at Georgette and the shadows that highlighted her eyes, then her cheeks, then her eyes . . . thinking it was a shame she was gay. Hes a good lookin guy and real great, especially for a queen . . . being honestly moved by Georgettes reading, but even with the bennie stimulating his imagination it was impossible for him to get beyond the weirdness and the kick

Fancy unto fancy, thinking what this ominous bird of
yore –
What this grim, ungainly, ghastly, gaunt, and
ominous bird of yore
Meant in croaking 'Nevermore.'

This I sat engaged in guessing, but no syllable
expressing
To the fowl whose fiery eyes now burned into my
bosom's core;
This and more I sat divining, with my head at ease
reclining
On the cushion's velvet lining that the lamp-light
gloated o'er, . . .
She, shall press, ah, nevermore! . . .

and the Bird was blowing (can you hear him Vinnie? Listen Listen Its the Bird. Can you hear him? Hes blowing love. Blowing love for us) and the incongruent rhythms of the Birds whirled and rang . . . then reconciled and O God it is beautiful

'. . . Quaff, oh quaff this kind nepenthe and forget
this lost Lenore!'
Quoth the Raven 'Nevermore.'

'Prophet!' said I, 'thing of evil! prophet still, if bird or
    devil –
Whether Tempter sent, or whether tempest tossed
    thee here ashore,
Desolate yet all undaunted, on this desert land
    enchanted . . .'

and through a rip in the black shade she saw dancing
points of grey and soon light would streak the sky and the
shadows would soften and dance and the soft early
morning light would seep through the room pushing
the shadows from the now darkened corners and the
candles soon would be out

And the Raven, never flitting, still is sitting, still is
    sitting
On the pallid bust of Pallas just above my chamber
    door;
And his eyes have all the seeming of a demon's that is
    dreaming,
And the lamp-light o'er him streaming throws his
    shadow on the floor;
And my soul from out that shadow that lies floating
    on the floor
            Shall be lifted – nevermore!

and the Bird was blowing a final chorus, high, and the set
wouldnt end, but the Bird would slowly fade and you
would never know when he really stopped and the sounds
would hang and roll in your ear and all would be love –
Quoth the Bird Evermore – and the flames bowed and
licked the edge of the candles and even Harry didnt fight
his lethargy and try to break the spell and Georgette
lowered the book to her lap with full dramatic presence
and the final words still whirled with the light and stayed

in the ear as the sea in a shell and Georgette sat on a wondrous throne in a wondrous land where people loved and kissed and sat silent together, holding hands and walking through magic nights and Goldie got up and kissed the Queen and told her it was beautiful, simply beautiful and the guys mumbled and smiled and Vinnie struggled with the softness he felt, trying honestly, for a second, to understand it, then let it slide and slapped Georgette on her thigh, gently, as one does a friend, and smiled, at her – Georgette almost crying seeing the flash of tenderness in his eyes – he smiled and groped for words, battling with his boundaries then saying, Hey, that was alright Georgie boy, then the knowledge of his friends being there, especially Harry, forced its way through the bennie and the mood and he sat back quickly, took a drink and grubbed a smoke from Harry.

The light forced itself through the many holes in the shades . . . the candles slowly becoming anonymous. Goldie opened the box of bennie slowly and proffered it to Georgette. She took two, just two thank you, smiled and laid them on her tongue and sipped her gin. They spoke quietly, smiling, sipping their drinks, at peace with all and Georgette leaned back in her chair speaking softly with Vinnie, and the others when addressed, all her movements: smoking, drinking, nodding, soft and regal; feeling extremely human; looking upon her world (kingdom) with kindness, softness; waiting, excitedly yet not nervously, for the time, soon, for her to nod to her lover . . . but the sun continued to rise and the room became brighter and the girls became conscious of the perspiration streaks in their makeup, hoping the boys would not notice it before they got upstairs and had a chance to fix their faces. Goldie kept glancing at her watch and listening to hear Sheila and her john leaving, wanting to get out of this ugly room and upstairs with the boys before the light brought them down and they lost what Georgette had given them; afraid if a bennie depression set in that the boys would simply become rough and not trade. She watched the room becoming brighter, too bright, and listened, listened . . .

Then she heard some(one) rushing through the hallway and Tony opened the door – Goldies heart was pounding and she tried to ignore Tony and listen for steps (four) on the stairs – and started apologising, looking hopefully at Goldie, before the door closed and Goldie finally turned to her and told her to shut up. Tony obeyed immediately (she had dropped her sister off at the hospital and stayed in the cab and came right back, wanting to get back before Goldie left; hoping to be invited to join them; she didnt want to sit alone in that evil apartment and she wanted so much to be a friend of Goldies, to get high with them and have other girls to talk with) she obeyed immediately and stopped in the middle of a syllable and looked around the room but they all ignored her – Goldie jumped up and went to the door, listened then opened it slightly – so Tony walked across the room (between them . . . between them. Theyre watching me. I know they are. It wasnt my fault) and sat – Goldie turned and said they left. Rosie, gather our things. They left. Tony sat, then got up and walked around the room (not even a bennie . . . not one); went to the kitchen, poured a cup of coffee (maybe I should have stayed with her. Might just as well have) and walked back to her chair.

Goldie ran to the bathroom to fix her face. Georgette picked up the half filled bottle of Scotch that the john had left and poured Vinnie a drink, on the rocks, then turned on the radio. She could see that Vinnie and the boys were getting higher and higher and by the time the Scotch would be finished (and there was still gin and a fresh supply of bennie forthcoming) they would be searching for the floor when they walked. O what a wonderful day. (She went to the windows and fixed the blinds so too much light would not come in.) Just simply too much. She visited different parts of the room, talking, smiling, fixing drinks, singing (Vinnie, Vinnie), dancing; even laughing with Lee. Camille ran to the bathroom, when Goldie came out, with her hair brush, nail brush, finger brush and hand brush. Goldie gave Rosie money for bennie then called Georgette aside and asked her to be intermediary between she and Malfie and she told her, Of course; and Goldie told her she had a box of syrettes and in a few minutes when things are a little more settled we will go inside and turn on. Georgette kissed her and really started swinging. A little morphine now would be just perfect. O yes, just perfect. O Lordy . . . MS and Vinnie!!! She filled a glass with gin and sat next to Vinnie (should I offer him a shot too?) talking with him and the boys (No. Might ruin him) and even Harry and his absurd remarks were palatable (O God! I hope the bennie didnt kill his nature), but of course she did her utmost to avoid any dissertation with *him* (If only the others would leave we could sit together and he would kiss me and I would caress his neck and kiss the lobe of his ear and we would undress each other and lie on the bed with our arms around each other and I would run the tips of my fingers along his thighs and his muscles would tighten and we would both squirm slightly and I would kiss his chest and feel his back and smell the sweat and put my legs around his hips – Whatta yasay sweetchips? Georgette turned and started opening her arms and Vinnie pinched her cheek, how about taking this inside and ringing it out, standing up slowly his hand clutching his crotch. Georgette lowered one hand (not now . . . later) and let the other one slide along his leg. Wanna help me empty this? wavering slightly then spreading his legs further apart and laughing as he bounced his balls with his hand. She leaned forward slightly (no no no!!! You will ruin everything) and he turned, still laughing, and went to the bathroom (his eyes are bugging out of his head. O Christ he is high. It will be beautiful!!!) and roared as Camille leaped from the bathroom when he goosed her, dropping her brushes then carefully stooping, watching the bathroom door, picking them up and dashing to the living room.

Georgette sat back and sipped her gin for many seconds. Harry got up and chirped at Georgette, stoned out of his head, and plopped down beside Lee. Georgette followed him with her eyes, still sipping gin and still fighting for control of herself. She could not fuck it up now. It wont be long. It wont be long. Vinnie and MS. Yes. She picked up the bottle of gin and refilled Malfies glass and asked him if he would let Goldie do him. Malfie closed his eyes slightly and smiled, took the glass from her hand. Got more bennie? She patted his cheek and got two more for him and went to tell Goldie that everything was arranged. O everything is just so wonderful. Vinnie and his boys are stoned out of their heads and soon she would have Vinnie. Goldie took her into the bedroom and gave her a syrette. Arent you going to take one? Not now honey. I'll wait until after that big cocked guinea has fucked me. So Georgette shot up and waited for the first wave to pass then went back to her throne, next to Vinnie. He was yakking with Malfie and Harry – Lee and Camille joining in, Goldie just watching Malfie and occasionally laughing – and tugged Georgettes ear when she sat down. She smiled and did a rolling bump before sitting down, nodding modestly to the applause. Georgette whirled digging the scene and everybody was swinging. Even Harry and Lee were making it and the sounds came from the radio and Camille was snapping her fingers (a little too demonstratively if you ask me, but its alright because we're (Vinnie and MS – VINNIE) swinging) and everything fell into its proper place, all words fitted; and Goldie sat beside Malfie and he grinned, *aspet . . . una moment*; and Camille felt real bitchy and daring and winked at Sal and he tried to speak but he couldnt stop grinding his teeth and his head just lolled back and forth, droplets of scotch dribbling down his chin, but he was so strong and handsome – O what a marvelous chin – and she giggled thinking of the letter she would write to the pinkteas back home: O honey, do you know from nothing. What a gorgeous way to lose ones virginity! Sal laughed and blurted, I gotit swingin bitch HAARRR; and Malfie emptied his glass, refilled it and followed Goldie into the bedroom and Georgette watched, floating around their heads bopping SALT PEAnuts, SALT PEAnuts – quoth the Diz evermore – Vinnie and MS – VINNie and MS – and Lee moved a few inches and Harry grabbed her by the arm and yanked her back, Where doya think ya goin, queeny, grabbing her wrist and forcing it between his legs. I gotta nice hunka meat forya and Vinnie yelled, Is she tryin ta get fresh witya man? and they both roared and Lee started to panic, trying to free her arm, but Harry squeezed tighter and twisted until she screeched, Stop, Stop! Youre hurting me you vile fairy (wonderful, wonderful. This should teach you a lesson you evil queen. *He* is what you deserve. VINNie and MS – VINNie and MS – cause we're having a party and the people are nice, and the people are nice . . .) and Harrys eyes bugged even more and he stood up and pulled Lee off the couch, comon motherfucka. You wanna look like a broad ya gonna get fucked like one (Camille shoved her fingers in her mouth, rose halfway then fell back onto the couch and inched her way to the other end (but hes not like *that* (?))) – Hey Vinnie, comeon. Lets throw a hump intaer. Shit man, Im down. Letsgo. He grabbed her other arm and they started dragging her to the bedroom, screaming, screeching, crying, pleading and they roared and twisted her arms then Harry grabbed her by her hair, her precious golden shoulder length hair, and slapped her face. Comeon ya cocksucker. Stop theshit. Hey Malfie, open the door. Malfie opened the door and grinned as they dragged Lee in, and Goldie shrieked and ran from the room, the door slamming behind her. She listened to Lee screaming and the guys slapping her and cursing as they ripped her dress off . . . then Goldie swallowed a half dozen bennies; Camille looked at Georgette, who hadnt moved (No, No! No you fucking bitch. VINNie VINNie . . . VINNIE!!! Not with Lee. I love you Vinnie. I love you. He will see my red spangled G string. Please Vinnie. Vinnie . . .), Camille looked at Georgette then at Sal as he wobbled across the room toward her. No room in there. He opened his fly and yanked out his cock (Its so big. And red. Be careful of your eyes. Put your arms around his ass) O???? O . . . Sal? Sal dont. Sal? Please. Ple – I got a big lob forya. Sa – he shoved it in her mouth and grabbed her long-shining-wavy-auburn-hair – Lee stopped squirming as Vinnie and Malfie held her and Harry mounted her. Vaseline. Vaseline! Please, not without vaseline. Vinnie handed her the jar, then Lee said alright then closed her eyes and cringed as Harry lunged viciously then put her arms around him and her legs around his waist. Vinnie and Malfie leaned against the wall and Harrys sweat fell on Lees face and she smiled and sucked his neck and groaned, hoping he would never come, that he would continue to lunge and lunge and lunge . . . – Thats the way Camille. Thats it HAHA OOOOO Hey, take it easy with yatongue, and Camille clutched at his belt hoping she was doing it properly; and Goldie took the syrette from her pocket, calmer now that the screaming had stopped, and though she did not approve of Camille having public sex like that she had to admit that she did not have much choice in the matter, and they did so seem to enjoy each other (I hope Malfie wont be completely useless after this), and turned on. Everything seems to have developed beautifully – He had to help his friends. Of course. Why shouldnt he help Harry fuck her. Cause we're having a party and the people are nice, and the people are nice . . . – Harry took a slip from a drawer and wiped his cock. I bet yaknow youve been fucked! Harry and Malfie laughed and Lee watched Vinnie as he mounted her then closed her eyes and wrapped her legs around his hips – Goldie went back to the living room and sat on the couch, ignoring Camille and Sal, watched the smoke drift from her mouth and the sound waves from the radio; and Sals legs shook and he bent at the knees and Camille grunted and gurgled, moving her head fantastically, digging her nails into his ass, trying to get every inch of his cock in her mouth – Soon. Soon . . . (Quaff, oh, quaff this kind nepenthe); and we will hear tugboat whistles blowing high . . . – Sal put his pants over the back of a chair and stretched out with a new cigarette and drink; Camille went to the bathroom with her nail brush, finger brush, hand brush, hair brush and toothbrush – The guys came out of the bedroom, sweat pouring from their faces, and filled glasses with gin and ice. Lee called to Miss Goldie and asked her if she could borrow a dress, and she told her, Of course. The gorgeous blue number I wore to the DRAG BALL last year is in the closet if you want it. Thank you, but I think it would be better if I wore something simple, an afternoon dress will do. Something I can slip out of easily. Yeah! HAHAHAHARRR The guys took a few more bennie each and sauntered back into the living room. Hey Sal, whatta yadoin? posin fa holy pictures? They all roared and Goldie looked with pride at Malfie. Vinnie sat next to Georgette and stuck a wet finger in her ear. How yadoin Georgie? O Vincent (of course he did not) dont do that, squirming and trying to giggle but she couldnt fight the momentum of the centrifuge and her face only twisted. Whats the matta? got a booboo? You like the Bird? Bird? Hey whats withya sweetchips, pinching her cheek and turning to the others, ya been eatin birdseed? laughing and looking around the room. O snapping his fingers, yamean the Raven thing. Yeah, Yeah, sure. Take me inside Vinnie(?) dropping her hand on his leg. Whatsa matta? ya hungry? rubbing her hand in his crotch. It takes loot tado me sweetchips, looking around the room lifting his glass to his mouth, the gin slobbering down his chin, how much yagot? I have love, I have love – (Camille came back from the bathroom, fresh and clean, her hair so neatly brushed, the highlights gleaming, swishing ever so gaily across the room. O really Miss Thing, one would think it was the first cock you ever sucked. Camille fluttered a few fingers at Goldie and sat beside Sal) – I have love and the Bird. (O god not after *her*. Vinnie. O Vinnie. Please. That was so long ago. So long ago. When? When? It was my brother and the G string) – Lee stepped from the bedroom and hurried to the bathroom. I dont know why she doesnt keep at least a hair brush in there – (Goldies not half as attractive as I) still silent and trying, trying to smile coquettishly, but it wouldnt come, it wouldnt come. And the Bird was gone. Gone! Only a Raven. Nevermore . . . and she whirled and whirled and whirled and sounds whirled and smoke whirled and Vinnie laughed, he laughed. Vinnie laughed and soon he would pick her up and carry her to the bedroom . . . A voice A voice. O God, not his john. I cant. Not now. Not after – Lee clicked into the room wearing a pair of Sheilas stockings and best shoes and sat daintly and looked at Harrys wet, dirty, smug, leering face . . . happy, O so happy that she wasnt a degenerate freak like that pervert; but loving his vicious prick and the next time we will be alone and he can be as freaky as he wants, and suck my tongue, and he will come around many times

. . . if I want him to. She looked at Georgette and lifted an eyebrow. What are you on honey? (bitch! Evil Bitch! Leave me alone!) Well common Georgie. Getup somea those chips. Ya dont want yadinner taget cold, doya?

She rose with dignity – come and get it Sweetchips – and they walked hand in hand through the softness and he gave her a rose and she laid it across her hand like a scepter and gently raised it to her lips and its fragrance was enchantment and she smiled the smile of a rose, so soft, delicate, so lovely and the Bird was there oncemore, blowing, and she placed the rose on its satin cushion and let the robes slip from her body – Whatta yadoin? – and they folded softly at her feet – ya just gonna suckit. Here yaare sweetchips, and make sure ya dont biteit, haha – A rose. Rose! No. It was Harry. Nevermore! Evermore. EVERMORE EVERMORE!!! O Vinnie, Vinnie my love my love – Stop the shit man and start suckin. (my love, love) He flicked his ashes, laughing, and took a drink. Will he groan? Make him groan, and she opened his belt and pulled his pants down and slid her hands along his sweaty ass (love, love) and he grabbed her ears and laughed, and she ran her fingers gently along his tightened thigh muscles (now, brother, now!) felt the hairs on his ass . . . the feeling, the feeling . . . – no. NO. O JESUS NO!!! Its just a smell from the bed – Watch the balls fa chrissake – from Harry. Harry. Its not shit. Please. He didnt fuck her. Dont let it be shit – the feel, taste, smell – SMELL! Vinnie picked up the slip from the floor. Youre alright Georgie, patting the kneeling queen on the head. Yacan do me anytime. Too bad I didnt haveya upstate. We couldda had a ball. She looked up at him and smiled. Vinnie? He looked into her face, bent and patted her cheek gently. Comeon Gerogie, Lets havea drink.

She sat amonsgt her robes and watched him leave. Why didnt he kiss me? If he would only let me kiss him. She looked at her slacks and the small hole in one leg, running her finger tips over the scab on her calf. Dance Ballerina Dance. Dreams? Now? When? When? I had him. I *did* have him. He didnt fuck her. Smell, feel, taste . . . It was on the bed. From Harry. It was right. It is beautiful. It was what I wanted. It is . . . is . . . I had him. Vinnie. Again. She tried to scrape the scab off the wound, sticking her fingernail under the edge, but only a tiny piece broke loose; she felt the slime of puss and tried to tear the scab loose with one quick rip . . . her hand wouldnt move. It hurt. Pained . . . She covered the wound with her hand and took a syrette from the drawer, found a vein in her arm then put her hand back on her leg. And it was now. Now. It wasnt yesterday and it isnt tomorrow . . . but there will be a tomorrow and there will be dreams . . . fulfilled . . . fulfilled . . . no it wasnt . . . It was Harry. Vinnie has me. Anytime . . . yes anytime . . . But Rosie is different . . . its not the same . . . She took another syrette, toyed with it for a few moments, hit a vein in her leg then placed it on the bed and rushed from the apartment. The others watched her leave and Camille asked where she was going. O her libido is probably twitching so madly shes going to run around the block 3 times. Yeah. She wishes she had one.

The door banged shut and she leaned against the banister until the nausea subsided then stumbled down the stairs (Tony watching her) and out to the street. The sun was hot and bright and light rammed and slashed her from windows, windshields, hoods of cars, from tin signs, shirt buttons, bottle caps and slips of paper lying in the street. Her gut glowed and she bumped against parked cars, but she was moving, moving, and everything got brighter, whiter, hotter. She clutched the railing and stumbled down the stairs to the subway, the beautiful dark subway. Only a few people. No one near her. She folded her arms and rested her head on the seat in front of her. Cool. It cooled. Yes, it was cooler and her head was beautifully warm and she would have Vinnie again and the next time, some time, he would kiss her. And they would go out together. A movie and hold hands or go for walks and he would light her cigarette . . . yes, he would cup his hands around the match, his cigarette hanging from the corner of his mouth, and I will put my hands around his and he will blow out the match and toss it away . . . but we dont have to go dancing. I know he doesnt like to dance. I will wear a smart print dress. Something simple. Something trim and neat. Vinnie? It *was* Harry . . . No. No, I wont have to go in drag. We will defy them all, and love . . . Love. And we will be loved. And I will be loved. And the Bird will come in high blowing love and we will fly . . . O that evil bitch. I am a far more convincing woman in drag than Lee. She looks like Chaplin. And I will dance like Melissa. If only I were a little shorter. Well we showed Miss Lee up, didnt we Vincent – (Georgette danced around the room humming tunes, in her silk panties and padded bra, and a john sat naked, on the edge of the bed, sweat sliding down his greasy body, touching the silk as Georgette whirled by, playing with his genitals, licking his lips, spit hanging from his lips; then she stepped out of her panties and he grabbed them, buried his face in them and fell on the bed groaning, groveling . . .) – No. No. Its now. Tomorrow. Vinnie . . . yes, yes. Vincennti. Vincennti d'Amore. *Che gelida mania* . . . yes, yes. Cold, O my beloved. *Si me chiamano Mimi* . . . Sì, A candle. Soft candle light . . . and I will read to you. And we will drink wine. No. Its not cold. Not really. Just the breeze from the Lake. Its so lovely. Peaceful. See, just the slightest ripple on the surface. And willows. Yes. Sì. Majestic bowing willows looking at themselves in the waters; nodding, saying yes to us. Yes, yes, yes . . . O Vincennti, hold me. Tighter. Vincennti. d'Amore. *O soave fanciulla.* – (Georgie is a

friend of mine, he will blow me anytime, for a nickle or a) –
The Lake. The Lake. And a moon . . . Yes . . . Look.
Look. Do you see there? A swan. O how beautiful. How
serene. The moon follows her. See how it lights her. O such
grace. O yes yes yes I do Vinnie, I do . . . Vincennti . . . See.
See, she glides to us. Us. For us. O how white. Yes. She is.
Whiter than the snows on the mountains. And they are but
shadows now. But she glistens, shimmers. The queen of
birds. Yes. O yes, yes, Cellos. Hundred of cellos and we
will glide in the moonlight, pirouetting to THE SWAN and
kiss her head and nod to the Willows and bow to the night
and they will grace us . . . they will grace us and the Lake
will grace us and smile and the moon will grace us and the
mountains will grace us and the breeze will grace us and
the sun will gently rise and its rays will stretch and spread
and even the willows will lift their heads ever so slightly
and the snow will grow whiter and the shadows will rise
from the mountains and it will be warm . . . yes, it will be
warm . . . the shadows will stay, but the moonlight will be
warm (Dance Ballerina Dance) Vinnie??? the moonlight
will be warm. It will get warmer. Hold me Vincennti. Love
me. Just love me. But fields of flowers are so lovely in the
sun. In the bright flooding sunlight. Warm and brilliant.
And the tall grasses flow and part and the colors burst and
small drops of dew glisten and it is all red and violet and
purple and green and white . . . yes white, and gold and
blue and pink, soft pink and see the fireflies . . . like
flowers of night . . . o yes, yes, flowers of night. Soft little
lights. Lovely little lights. O, Im so cold. *La commèdia è
finita*. NO! NO! Vincennti. Yes, yes my darling. *Sì me
chiamano Mimi*. Georgie-porgie puddin n pie. The Bird.
Listen Vinnie. Bird. O yes my darling, I do I do. I love you.
Love you. O Vinnie. Vincennti. Your mouth, lips, are so
warm. d'Amore. O see how the stars soften the sky. Yes,
like jewels. O Vinnie, im so cold. Come, let us walk. *Sone

Andati. Yes my love, I hear him. Yes. He is blowing love. Love Vinnie . . . blowing love . . . no NO! O God no!!! Vinnie loves me. He loves me. It.

Wasn't.

Shit　　　　.

Part III

And Baby Makes Three

Thou shalt know also that thy seed shall be great, and thine offspring as the grass of the earth.

Job 5:25

T HE baby was christened 4 hours after the wedding. Well, whatthehell, they got married first anyway. But I'll tellya man, it was a ball! I mean after. Her old man threw a great party. And Spook with his damn motorcycle. Tommy had a 76 Indian. Hes the guy who got married. He had this Indian – you know, one of those small jobs. Not a onelunger. Nonea the boys would have one a those. They can really move and all that, but theyre too small. Yawant somethin that can be fixed up. Yaknow, made real sharp – streamers and things and a bigass buddyseat with chrome. Man, the snatch really comes runnin. Its real crazy! Anyway, he had this 76 and Tommys long and kinda skinny and he sorta looked like the bike was growin outtaim; like he had a bike between his legs instead of a pecka. And when he kicked it over he just sat there like he was restin or somethin and gave a little push on the peddle and BaR-OOOOM. All the other guysd be standin with their bikes leanin and kickin and kickin and the goddamn bike coughin and fartin and Tommyd sit on this pecka with wheels gunnin the motor and retadin the spark soundin like a gun battle and then hed ride around, slow, in circles and wait forem to get their bikes started.

But Tommy was a great guy. Sorta quiet. Especially compared with the other guys. And he worked. Mosta the time anyway. He used ta go out with Suzy once inawhile. Hed taker ridin on the bike and a few movies (I think) and they usually went to the neighbourhood beerrackets tagether. But we didnt know she was knockedup until she was about 7 months gone. Maybe more. She was a big-hipped Polack and even her oldman didnt know she was knockedup until she was in the hospital, I suppose he didnt look very hard. Yaknow, he was a bit ofa lush anyway. So when the oldlady toldim why Suzy was in the hospital he flipped. But afta stayin juiced for a few days he went sloberin up to the hospital cryin how he was gonna do everythin for his little girl (she was only a inch or 2 shorter than Tommy and outweighedim by 40 pounds); and why didnt she tellim she was in trouble and she just sorta looked and askedim for a smoke and toldim she wasnt in any trouble and a week or so later the oldman was like always studyin the scratchsheet and sippin beer until a liveone came in. But I gotta hand it toim. He really threw a ball after the christenin. It started after the weddin, but things really moved after the christenin. Thats when Spook had a few beers and hadta go ridin. Spook had the hots for a bike for months. 6 months before he even got one he was wearing a motorcycle hat. Of course all the boys with bikes woreem. No boots or jackets with eagles or anya that shit, but yagotta have a hat ta keep ya hair outta ya eyes. Anyway, Spook had this hat and he didnt have no bike. Had sit in the Greeks a 1 nite and wouldnt part with that hat for nothin. Man, you try and get that thing off his head and hed go outta his mind. Well, anyway, once inawhile Tommyd let Spook ride his bike and Spookd be bugged outta his mind. Hed spark the damn thing and bang it and blast it and yell and scream and fix that damn hat of his and go rollin along 2nd avenue making all kindsa goddamn noise. Then Tommyd waveim back and Spookd make a slow turn and come backfirin up to Tommy, gun the motor a few times, push the kick stand down, turn the motor off, and get off real careful and sorta pat the seat and tank and tell him itsa great bike. Real great. And the next day Spookd make the rounds of all the bike shops downtown and stare at the jobs in the window, droolin, and go in and pricem and the guyed tellim its still 1500 dollars just like two days ago and Spookd ask if he got any new second hand jobs and the guyd shake his head and go about his business and Spookd look around at the lights, seats, streamers, windshields and boots and go half out of his mind and hed come back to the Greeks and tellus about the great Harley-Davidson machine he saw – a brand new model and he knew every goddamn strip of chrome and every bolt and nut on the sonofabitch and everbodyd laugh and someone would sneak up behind him through the side door and take his hat off and toss it around and Spookd go ape tryin ta get it back and then someoned plop it on his head and we'd laugh and hed tellus that we didnt know what it was ta want a bike. Fifty times a day the same thing. You dont know what it is ta want a bike. Then somebodyd tellim he could ride withim if he bought coffee and, so Spookd breakdown and part with a dime (it was pretty hard ta getim ta part with anything, especially money. I guess he stashed his loot in a piggybank tryin ta save for a bike.) and hed fix his hat and theyd take off and hed yell GerOOOOnimOOOOO and theyd hit the Belt Parkway and weave between traffic and Spookd be flipped off his ass yellin and screamin and theyd get back ta the Greeks and hed say, Christ! I gotta get a bike. Man, you dont know what it is ta want a bike, and off hed go the next day, downtown.

Well, anyway, when Suzy told Tommy she was on the hill I guess he was a little surprised. I dont know. He didnt say nothin, but I guess he was. So she toldim and they went for a ride along the Belt and on the way back they stopped at Coney Island and had some hotdogs at Nathans and he was workin at the time and I guess he toler hed marryer. Anyway I dont think he said he wouldnt. It really didnt make too much difference. I mean he had his bike. All paid for an fixedup like he wanted it and they could move in with her oldman and oldlady. Downstairs. So whatthehell. And I think she sorta wanted to get married anyway. You know. But I dont know if she even askedim. I mean, she coulda dumped the kid without too much trouble. Theres all kinds of agencies. But Tommy was alright. He never bothered nobody and hed never beaterup or anythin so I guess she wanted ta get married. And like this she wouldnt haveta work. Just feed the kid and that sorta stuff. So actually it worked out pretty good. So anyway, Tommy comes into the Greeks one nite and tellsus hes gonna be a father and Alex givesim a cupa coffee on the house and Tommy lets Spook go for a ride.

So when her oldman dries out a little he tellser (when she comes home from the hospital with the baby and she says, thats grandpa, and the oldman starts slobberin again) that hes gonna giver a real party and he goes and sees Murphy in the bar and tellsim he wants ta rent upstairs for a weddin reception. And when Murphy asks when he says he dont know, but itll be soon and Murphy tellsim that the Raven S.A.C. is goin ta throw a racket soon so the oldman tellsim two weeks and he leaves a deposit and goes home and tellsem and they get a holda Tommy and he says OK and finishes shining his bike so they set the wedding date and make arrangements for the christenin. Of course they lied a little at the christenin, you know, but the oldlady figured it was better forem ta lie a little than not have the poor little tyke christened at all. So they got the papers and a few of the boys went withem and it was over in a few minutes and then we went ta Murphys ta wait until it was time for the christenin and ta figureout who was gonna be godparents. I think they finally got some aunt and uncle, I dont know, but anyway that was when things started swingin. Murphys Hall is a big room above the bar and he had bottles of whisky on a small bar in the corner and kegs abeer and a big long table stacked with all kindsa sandwiches. So we each grabbed a pitcher a beer and started scoffin the sandwiches and Spook comes in and tellsus he got a bike. Ya shoulda seenim. His eyes was bugged outta his head. I thought he was up on tea or somethin, but he was just high with a bike. He picked up a old police bike for a few bucks and fixed it up. You know, threw some paint on it and stole a wildass buddyseat all covered with fur and chrome, and was all fulla piss and vinegar ta go. We toldim ta play it cool and relax and celebrate Tommys marriage. So someone pushed a beer in his hand, but he flipped when someone tried ta get that goddamn hat off his head so we said OK, wed go down stairs and look at his bike. So we looked. Big deal. Yaknow, when the cops is finished with a bike, man, its had it. But it was a bike and it moved. I think that sonofabitch woulda used it even if he had ta push it or pedal it like a kiddy car. So he kicks it over after 5 minutes and we listen to it cough and miss and Spook went puttin off with a shiteatin grin on his face and we went back up stairs and a few minutes later he comes back. Smilin all over the goddamn place and the strap of his hat under his chin. I tellya man, it was a pissa. But whatthehell, we were havin a ball and we didnt know what it was ta want a bike and pretty soon he was talkin ta Suzys old lady about this bike and she was throwin the booze down like crazy and soon she starts weepin about her poor little girl and tellin Spook how she looked when she was born and it seems like only yesterday and now here she is all grownup and married and a mother and Spook kept noddin and said yeah, but all he really has ta do is clean the sparks and maybe giver a carbon job – which he could do himself at nite and it wont cost nothin – and itll run as good as any bike on the road and when ya figure it only cost a yard its a damn good deal . . . and long since Suzy had cut from the oldman and oldlady and was shovin salami sandwiches down likemad and things was really movin. Of course some a the skells from the bar worked their way up and congratulated and grabbed what they could and when the christenin was over and they came back with the kid everybody was tellin the oldman and oldlady that it looked just likem (and man, the old-ladys some dog!) and they sniff and pound backs and tellem ta drinkup and somebody had a camera and flash-bulbs was poppin then smashed against the wall. Of course the kid started yappin but they took care of it and the party really started. They had a phonograph and a lot of real great records like Illinois Jacquet and Kenton; and Roberta, a real hip queer from the neighbourhood, cameup and started dancin and wigglin and somea the boys was stoned and was dancin wither and she was havin a ball! Of course she was up on bennie, like always (unless she got some pot) and onea the guys askeder if she was the bride and she said no, she practices birth-control and then she started dancin with Suzys oldlady and oldman. That was a real gassa! She was still all snots and tears and her big lardass was wigglin and we were pissin in our pants. Man, it was a ball!

Of course Tommy didnt drink much. I mean, not because he got married. That didnt make any difference now. He just never drank much. A couple a beers now and then was about all. Ya know. But he was sorta ballin. For Tommy anyway. The oldlady almost put a drag on the party by diggin up a record with some dame singin Because, and then she goes staggerin over ta Suzy and starts huggin and kissener and Suzys tryin ta stuff a salami sandwich in her mouth and she cant chew because the oldladys all overer. But Roberta really broke usup. She was standin in a corner makin like she was singin and man, it was a gas. You know, flutterin her eyelids (she had that shiny stardust stuff glued to her eyelids) and doin a few bumps and grinds and that sorta stuff. But the oldlady didnt seeer (I dont think she could see much by that time) and she wanted to dance with Suzy and starts waltzin around, stumblin all over and Suzy still holdin that salami sandwich, but the record ended and Roberta threw a Dinah Washington side on real quick and Suzy got ridda the oldlady and we all started ballin again. Pretty soon the oldlady passed out and they stretched her out on a cot in the back and we ended up in a corner jumpin with the music and doin some real juicin and even Spook was a little high. Tony got real stoned and goosed some dame and there was a bit of rumble with her husband, but it didnt amount ta much so we just pushed Tony in the corner and letim sleep. Of course a few of the old Irishmen started throwin blows at each other, but they didnt do any real damage and as long as they didnt get too close ta the bar they letim fight until they passed out.

But Spook couldnt sit still for long. He wanted ta go ridin. Everybody toldim ta go, but he didnt want ta go alone and everybody, but Tommy, was too stoned ta ride a goddamn bike. So Suzy tells Tommy ta go. Whatthehell. Cant do anythin tonite anyway. You know, too soon. And she figured shed look around for the kid and takeim home and go ta bed. She said her ass was draggin anyway. It was only two weeks or so since she had the kid. And it was a pretty good size one. Eight pounds somethin. I dont know exactly, but somethin like that. She said it was like shittin a watermelon. Havin a kid. So she hunted around and found the kid and cutout. So Tommy figured hed take a spin with Spook. It was a real nice nite. Just right for ridin. And probably be in the house all day tomorra fixin things. You know, puttin this here and that there and takin care of the kid and that kinda stuff. So when Roberta sees Tommy gettin ready ta cut she comes hustlin over and starts cooin at Tommy ta takeer for a ride, shes feelin so depressed watchin somebody else with a baby and gettin ready for a honeymoon, and she flutters her lids and everybody cracksup, so Tommy laughs and says OK and Roberta

79

giggles and waves bye bye and Spook is halfway down the stairs his hat all tied under his chin and they cut.

Of course we stayed until they kicked us out the next morning. I mean, whatthehell. The oldman paid good money for the joint and everything. No sense in lettin it go ta waste.

Part IV

Tralala

I will rise now, and go about the city in the streets, and in the broad ways I will seek him whom my soul loveth: I sought him, but I found him not.

The watchmen that go about the city found me: to whom I said, Saw ye him whom my soul loveth?

Song of Solomon 3:2, 3

T RALALA was 15 the first time she was laid. There was no real passion. Just diversion. She hungout in the Greeks with the other neighbourhood kids. Nothin to do. Sit and talk. Listen to the jukebox. Drink coffee. Bum cigarettes. Everything a drag. She said yes. In the park. 3 or 4 couples finding their own tree and grass. Actually she didnt say yes. She said nothing. Tony or Vinnie or whoever it was just continued. They all met later at the exit. They grinned at each other. The guys felt real sharp. The girls walked in front and talked about it. They giggled and alluded. Tralala shrugged her shoulders. Getting laid was getting laid. Why all the bullshit? She went to the park often. She always had her pick. The other girls were as willing, but played games. They liked to tease. And giggle. Tralala didn't fuckaround. Nobody likes a cockteaser. Either you put out or you dont. Thats all. And she had big tits. She was built like a woman. Not like some kid. They preferred her. And even before the first summer was over she played games. Different ones though. She didnt tease the guys. No sense in that. No money either. Some of the girls bugged her and she broke their balls. If a girl liked one of the guys or tried to get him for any reason Tralala cut in. For kicks. The girls hated her. So what. Who needs them. The guys had what she wanted. Especially when they lushed a drunk. Or pulled a job. She always got something out of it. Theyd take her to the movies. Buy cigarettes. Go to a PIZZERIA for a pie. There was no end of drunks. Everybody had money during the war. The waterfront was filled with drunken seamen. And of course the base was filled with doggies. And they were always good for a few bucks at least. Sometimes more. And

Tralala always got her share. No tricks. All very simple. The guys had a ball and she got a few bucks. If there was no room to go to there was always the Wolffe Building cellar. Miles and miles of cellar. One screwed and the others played chick. Sometimes for hours. But she got what she wanted. All she had to do was putout. It was kicks too. Sometimes. If not, so what? It made no difference. Lay on your back. Or bend over a garbage can. Better than working. And its kicks. For a while anyway. But time always passes. They grew older. Werent satisfied with the few bucks they got from drunks. Why wait for a drunk to passout. After theyve spent most of their loot. Drop them on their way back to the Armybase. Every night dozens left Willies, a bar across the street from the Greeks. Theyd get them on their way back to the base or the docks. They usually let the doggies go. They didnt have too much. But the seamen were usually loaded. If they were too big or too sober theyd hit them over the head with a brick. If they looked easy one would hold him and the other(s) would lump him. A few times they got one in the lot on 57th street. That was a ball. It was real dark back by the fence. Theyd hit him until their arms were tired. Good kicks. Then a pie and beer. And Tralala. She was always there. As more time passed they acquired valuable experience. They were more selective. And stronger. They didn't need bricks anymore. Theyd make the rounds of the bars and spot some guy with a roll. When he left theyd lush him. Sometimes Tralala would set him up. Walk him to a doorway. Sometimes through the lot. It worked beautifully. They all had new clothes. Tralala dressed well. She wore a clean sweater every few days. They had no trouble. Just stick to the seamen. They come and go and who knows the difference. Who gives a shit. They have more than they need anyway. And whats a few lumps. They might get killed so whats the difference. They stayed away from doggies. Usually. They played it smart and nobody bothered them. But Tralala wanted more than the small share she was getting. It was about time she got something on her own. If she was going to get laid by a couple of guys for a few bucks she figured it would be smarter to get laid by one guy and get it all. All the drunks gave her the eye. And stared at her tits. It would be a slopeout. Just be sure to pick a live-one. Not some bum with a few lousy bucks. None of that shit. She waited, alone, in the Greeks. A doggie came in and ordered coffee and a hamburger. He asked her if she wanted something. Why not. He smiled. He pulled a bill from a thick roll and dropped it on the counter. She pushed her chest out. He told her about his ribbons. And medals. Bronze Star. And a Purpleheart with 2 Oakleaf Clusters. Been overseas 2 years. Going home. He talked and slobbered and she smiled. She hoped he didnt have all ones. She wanted to get him out before anybody else came. They got in a cab and drove to a down-town hotel. He bought a bottle of whiskey and they sat and drank and he talked. She kept filling his glass. He kept talking. About the war. How he was shot up. About home. What he was going to do. About the months in the hospital and all the operations. She kept pouring but he wouldnt pass out. The bastard. He said he just wanted to be near her for a while. Talk to her and have a few drinks. She waited. Cursed him and his goddamn mother. And who gives a shit about your leg gettin all shotup. She had been there over an hour. If hed fucker maybe she could get the money out of his pocket. But he just talked. The hell with it. She hit him over the head with the bottle. She emptied his pockets and left. She took the money out of his wallet and threw the wallet away. She counted it on the subway. 50 bucks. Not bad. Never had this much at once before. Shouldve gotten more though. Listenin to all that bullshit. Yeah. That sonofabitch. I shoulda hitim again. A lousy 50 bucks and hes talkin like a wheel or somethin. She kept 10 and stashed the rest and hurried back to the Greeks. Tony and Al were there and asked her where she was. Alex says ya cutout with a drunken doggie a couple a hours ago. Yeah. Some creep. I though he was loaded. Didju score? Yeah. How much? 10 bucks. He kept bullshitin how much he had and alls he had was a lousy 10. Yeah? Lets see. She showed them the money. Yasure thats all yagot? Ya wanna search me? Yathink I got somethin stashed up my ass or some-thin? We'll take a look later. Yeah. How about you? Score? We got a few. But you dont have ta worry aboutit. You got enough. She said nothing and shrugged her shoulders. She smiled and offered to buy them coffee. And? Krist. What a bunch of bloodsuckers. OK Hey Alex . . . They were still sitting at the counter when the doggie came in. He was holding a bloodied handkerchief to his head and blood had caked on his wrist and cheek. He grabbed Tralala by the arm and pulled her from the stool. Give me my wallet you goddamn whore. She spit in his face and told him ta go fuck-himself. Al and Tony pushed him against the wall and asked him who he thought he was. Look, I dont know you and you dont know me. I got no call to fight with you boys. All I want is my wallet. I need my ID Card or I cant get back in the Base. You can keep the goddamn money. I dont care. Tralala screamed in his face that he was a no good mothafuckin sonofabitch and then started kicking him, afraid he might say how much she had taken. Ya lousy fuckin hero. Go peddle a couple of medals if yaneed money so fuckin bad. She spit in his face again, no longer afraid he might say something, but mad. Goddamn mad. A lousy 50 bucks and he was cryin. And anyway, he shouldve had more. Ya lousy fuckin creep. She kicked him in the balls. He grabbed her again. He was crying and bent over struggling to

86

breathe from the pain of the kick. If I dont have the pass I cant get in the Base. I have to get back. Theyre going to fly me home tomorrow. I havent been home for almost 3 years. Ive been all shot up. Please, PLEASE. Just the wallet. Thats all I want. Just the ID Card. PLEASE PLEASE!!! The tears streaked the caked blood and he hung on Tonys and Als grip and Tralala swung at his face, spitting, cursing and kicking. Alex yelled to stop and get out. I dont want trouble in here. Tony grabbed the doggie around the neck and Al shoved the bloodied handkerchief in his mouth and they dragged him outside and into a darkened doorway. He was still crying and begging for his ID Card and trying to tell them he wanted to go home when Tony pulled his head up by his hair and Al punched him a few times in the stomach and then in the face, then held him up while Tony hit him a few times; but they soon stopped, not afraid that the cops might come, but they knew he didnt have any money and they were tired from hitting the seaman they had lushed earlier, so they dropped him and he fell to the ground on his back. Before they left Tralala stomped on his face until both eyes were bleeding and his nose was split and broken then kicked him a few times in the balls. Ya rotten scumbag, then they left and walked slowly to 4th avenue and took a subway to Manhattan. Just in case somebody might put up a stink. In a day or two he'll be shipped out and nobodyll know the difference. Just another fuckin doggie. And anyway he deserved it. They ate in a cafeteria and went to an allnight movie. The next day they got a couple of rooms in a hotel on the east side and stayed in Manhattan until the following night. When they went back to the Greeks Alex told them some MPs and a detective were in asking about the guys who beat up a soldier the other night. They said he was in bad shape. Had to operate on him and he may go blind in one eye. Ain't that just too bad. The MPs said if they get ahold of the guys who did it theyd killem. Those fuckin punks. Whad the law say. Nottin. You know. Yeah. Killus! The creeps. We oughtta dumpem on general principles. Tralala laughed. I shoulda pressed charges fa rape. I wont be 18 for a week. He raped me the dirty freaky sonofabitch. They laughed and ordered coffee. When they finished Al and Tony figured theyd better make the rounds of a few of the bars and see what was doin. In one of the bars they noticed the bartender slip an envelope in a tin box behind the bar. It looked like a pile of bills on the bottom of the box. They checked the window in the MENS ROOM and the alley behind it then left the bar and went back to the Greeks. They told Tralala what they were going to do and went to a furnished room they had rented over one of the bars on Ist avenue. When the bars closed they took a heavy duty screwdriver and walked to the bar. Tralala stood outside and watched the street while they broke in. It only took a few minutes to force open the window, drop inside, crawl to the bar, pickup the box and climb out the window and drop to the alley. They pried open the box in the alley and started to count. They almost panicked when they finished counting. They had almost 2 thousand dollars. They stared at it for a moment then jammed it into their pockets. Then Tony took a few hundred and put it into another pocket and told Al theyd tell Tralala that that was all they got. They smiled and almost laughed then calmed themselves before leaving the alley and meeting Tralala. They took the box with them and dropped it into a sewer then walked back to the room. When they stepped from the alley Tralala ran over to them asking them how they made out and how much they got and Tony told her to keep quiet that they got a couple a hundred and to play it cool until they got back to the room. When they got back to the room Al started telling her what a snap it was and how they just climbed in and took the box but Tralala ignored him and kept asking how much they got. Tony took the lump of money from his pocket and they counted it. Not bad eh Tral? 250 clams. Yeah. How about giving me 50 now. What for? You aint going no where now. She shrugged and they went to bed. The next afternoon they went to the Greeks for coffee and two detectives came in and told them to come outside. They searched them, took the money from their pockets and pushed them into their car. The detectives waved the money in front of their faces and shook their heads. Dont you know better than to knock over a bookie drop? Huh? Huh, Huh! Real clever arent you. The detectives laughed and actually felt a professional amazement as they looked at their dumb expressions and realised that they really didnt know who they had robbed. Tony slowly started to come out of the coma and started to protest that they didnt do nothin. One of the detectives slapped his face and told him to shutup. For Christs sake dont give us any of that horseshit. I suppose you just found a couple of grand lying in an empty lot? Tralala screeched, a what? The detectives looked at her briefly then turned back to Tony and Al. You can lush a few drunken seamen now and then and get away with it, but when you start taking money from my pocket youre going too far sonny. What a pair of stupid punks . . . OK sister, beat it. Unless you want to come along for the ride? She automatically backed away from the car, still staring at Tony and Al. The doors slammed shut and they drove away. Tralala went back to the Greeks and sat at the counter cursing Tony and Al and then the bulls for pickinem up before she could get hers. Didnt even spend a penny of it. The goddamn bastards. The rotten stinkin sonsofbitches. Those thievin flatfooted bastards. She sat drinking coffee all afternoon then left and went across the street to Willies. She walked to the end of the bar and started talking with Ruthy, the barmaid, telling her what happened, stopping every few minutes to curse Tony, Al, the bulls and lousy luck. The bar was slowly filling and Ruthy left her every few minutes to pour a drink and when she came back Tralala would repeat the story from the beginning, yelling about the 2 grand and they never even got a chance to spend a penny. With the repeating of the story she forget about Tony and Al and just cursed the bulls and her luck and an occasional seaman or doggie who passed by and asked her if she wanted a drink or just looked at her. Ruthy kept filling Tralalas glass as soon as she emptied it and told her to forget about it. Thats the breaks. No sense in beatin yahead against the wall about it. Theres plenty more. Maybe not that much, but enough. Tralala snarled, finished her drink and told Ruthy to fill it up. Eventually she absorbed her anger and quieted down and when a young seaman staggered over to her she glanced at him and said yes. Ruthy brought them two drinks and smiled. Tralala watched him take the money out of his pocket and figured it might be worthwhile. She told him there were better places to drink than this crummy dump. Well, lez go baby. He gulped his drink and Tralala left hers on the bar and they left. They got into a cab and the seaman asked her whereto and she said she didnt care, anywhere. OK. Takeus to Times Square. He offered her a cigarette and started telling her about everything. His name was Harry. He came from Idaho. He just got back from Italy. He was going to – she didnt bother smiling but watched him, trying to figure out how soon he would pass out. Sometimes they last allnight. Cant really tell. She relaxed and gave it thought. Cant konkim here. Just have ta wait until he passes out or maybe just ask for some money. The way they throw it around. Just gotta getim in a room alone. If he dont pass out I'll just rapim with somethin – and you should see what we did to that little ol . . . He talked on and Tralala smoked and the lampposts flicked by and the meter ticked. He stopped talking when the cab stopped in front of the Crossroads. They got out and tried to get in the Crossroads but the bartender looked at the drunken seaman and shook his head no. So they crossed the street and went to another bar. The bar was jammed, but they found a small table in the rear and sat down. They ordered drinks and Tralala sipped hers then pushed her unfinished drink across the table to him when he finished his. He started talking again but the lights and the music slowly affected him and the subject matter was changed and he started telling Tralala what a good lookin girl she was and what a good time he was going to show her; and she told him that she would show him the time of his life and didnt bother to hide a yawn. He beamed and drank faster and Tralala asked him if he would give her some money. She was broke and had to have some money or she'd be locked out of her room. He told her not to worry that hed find a place for her to stay tonight and he winked and Tralala wanted to shove her cigarette in his face, the cheap sonofabitch, but figured she'd better wait and get his money before she did anything. He toyed with her hand and she looked around the bar and noticed an Army Officer staring at her. He had a lot of ribbons just like the one she had rolled and she figured hed have more money than Harry. Officers are usually loaded. She got up from the table telling Harry she was going to the ladies room. The Officer swayed slightly as she walked up to him and smiled. He took her arm and asked her where she was going. Nowhere. O, we cant have a pretty girl like you going nowhere. I have a place thats all empty and a sack of whiskey. Well . . . She told him to wait and went back to the table. Harry was almost asleep and she tried to get the money from his pocket and he started to stir. When his eyes opened she started shaking him, taking her hand out of his pocket, and telling him to wakeup. I thought yawere goin to show me a good time. You bet. He nodded his head and it slowly descended toward the table. Hey Harry, wakeup. The waiter wants to know if yahave any money. Showem ya money so I wont have to pay. You bet. He slowly took the crumpled mess of bills from his pocket and Tralala grabbed it from his hand and said I toldya he had money. She picked up the cigarettes from the table, put the money in her pocketbook and walked back to the bar. My friend is sleeping so I dont think he'll mind, but I think we'd better leave. They left the bar and walked to his hotel. Tralala hoped she didnt make a mistake. Harry mightta had more money stashed somewhere. The Officer should have more though and anyway she probably got everything Harry had and she could get more from this jerk if he has any. She looked at him trying to determine how much he could have, but all Officers look the same. Thats the trouble with a goddamn uniform. And then she wondered how much she had gotten from Harry and how long she would have to wait to count it. When they got to his room she went right into the bathroom, smoothed out the bills a little and counted them. 45. Shit. Fuckit. She folded the money, left the bathroom and stuffed the money in a coat pocket. He poured two small drinks and they sat and talked for a few minutes then put the light out. Tralala figured there was no sense in trying anything now so she relaxed and enjoyed herself. They were having a smoke and another drink when he turned and kissed her and told her she had the most beautiful pair of tits he had ever seen. He continued talking for a few minutes, but she didnt pay any attention. She thought about her tits and what he had said and how she could get anybody with her tits and the hell with Willies and those slobs, she'd hang around here for a while and do alright. They put out their cigarettes and for the rest of the night she didnt wonder how much money he had. At breakfast the next morning he tried to remember everything that had happened in the bar, but Harry was only vaguely remembered and he didnt want to ask her. A few times he tried speaking, but when he looked at her he started feeling vaguely guilty. When they had finished eating he lit her cigarette, smiled, and asked her if he could buy her something. A dress or something like that. I mean, well you know . . . Id like to buy you a little present. He tried not to sound maudlin or look sheepish, but he found it hard to say what he felt, now, in the morning, with a slight hangover, and she looked to him pretty and even a little innocent. Primarily he didnt want her to think he was offering to pay her or think he was insulting her by insinuating that she was just another prostitute; but much of his loneliness was gone and he wanted to thank her. You see, I only have a few days leave before I go back and I thought perhaps we could – that is I thought we could spend some more time together . . . he stammered on apologetically hoping she understood what he was trying to say but the words bounced off her and when she noticed that he had finished talking she said sure. What thefuck. This is much better than wresslin with a drunk and she felt good this morning, much better than yesterday (briefly remembering the bulls and the money they took from her) and he might even give her his money before he went back overseas (what could he do with it) and with her tits she could always makeout and whatthe-hell, it was the best screwin she ever had . . . They went shopping and she bought a dress, a couple of sweaters (2 sizes too small), shoes, stockings, a pocketbook and an overnight bag to put her clothes in. She protested slightly when he told her to buy a cosmetic case (not knowing what it was when he handed it to her and she saw no sense in spending money on that when he could as well give her cash), and he enjoyed her modesty in not wanting to spend too much of his money; and he chuckled at her childlike excitement at being in the stores, looking and buying. They took all the packages back to the hotel and Tralala put on her new dress and shoes and they went out to eat and then to a movie. For the next few days they went to movies, restaurants (Tralala trying to make a mental note of the ones where the Officers hungout), a few more stores and back to the hotel. When they woke on the 4th day he told her he had to leave and asked her if she would come with him to the station. She went thinking he might give her his money and she stood awkwardly on the station with him, their bags around them, waiting for him to go on the train and leave. Finally the time came for him to leave and he handed her an envelope and kissed her before boarding the train. She felt the envelope as she lifted her face slightly so he could kiss her. It was thin and she figured it might be a check. She put it in her pocketbook, picked up her bag and went to the waiting room and sat on a bench and opened the envelope. She opened the paper and started reading: Dear Tral: There are many things I would like to say and should have said, but – A letter. A goddamn LETTER. She ripped the envelope apart and turned the letter over a few times. Not a cent. I hope you understand what I mean and am unable to say – she looked at the words – if you do feel as I hope you do Im writing my address at the bottom. I dont know if I'll live through this war, but – Shit. Not vehemently but factually. She dropped the letter and rode the subway to Brooklyn. She went to Willies to display her finery. Ruthy was behind the bar and Waterman Annie was sitting in a booth with a seaman. She stood at the bar talking with Ruthy for a few minutes answering her questions about the clothes and telling her about the rich john she was living with and how much money he gave her and where they went. Ruthy left occasionally to pour a drink and when she came back Tralala continued her story, but soon Ruthy tired of listening to her bullshit as Tralalas short imagination bogged down. Tralala turned and looked at Annie and asked her when they leter out. Annie told her ta go screw herself. Youre the only one who would. Annie laughed and Trala told her ta keep her shiteatin mouth shut. The seaman got up from the booth and staggered toward Tralala. You shouldnt talk to my girl friend like that. That douchebag? You should be able ta do betteran that. She smiled and pushed her chest out. The seaman laughed and leaned on the bar and asked her if she would like a drink. Sure. But not in this crummy place. Lets go ta some place thats not crawlin with stinkin whores. The seaman roared, walked back to the table, finished his drink and left with Tralala. Annie screamed at them and tried to throw a glass at Tralala but someone grabbed her arm. Tralala and Jack (he was an oiler and he . . .) got into a cab and drove downtown. Tralala thought of ditching him rightaway (she only wanted to break Annies balls), but figured she ought to wait and see. She stayed with him and they went to a hotel and when he passedout she took what he had and went back uptown. She went to a bar in Times Square and sat at the bar. It was filled with servicemen and a few drunken sailors smiled at her as she looked around, but she ignored them and the others in the bar ignored her. She wanted to be sure she picked up a liveone. No drunken twobit sailor or doggie for her. O no. Ya bet ya sweetass no. With her clothes and tits? Who inthehell do those punks think they are. I oughtta go spit in their stinkin faces. Shit! They couldnt kiss my ass. She jammed her cigarette out and took a short sip of her drink. She waited. She smiled at a few Officers she thought might have loot, but they were with women. She cursed the dames under her breath, pulled the top of her dress down, looked around and sipped her drink. Even with sipping the drink was soon gone and she had to order another. The bartender refilled her glass and marked her for an amateur. He smiled and was almost tempted to tell her that she was trying the wrong place, but didnt. He just refilled her glass thinking she would be better off in one of the 8th avenue bars. She sipped the new drink and lit another cigarette. Why was she still alone? What was with this joint? Everybody with a few bucks had a dame. Goddamn pigs. Not one ofem had a pair half as big as hers. She could have any sonofabitch in Willies or any bum stumbling into the Greeks. Whats with the creeps in here. They should be all around her. She shouldnt be sitting alone. She'd been there 2 hours already. She felt like standing up and yelling fuck you to everybody in the joint. Youre all a bunch of goddamn creeps. She snarled at the women who passed. She pulled her dress tight and forced her shoulders back. Time still passed. She still ignored the drunks figuring somebody with gelt would popup. She didnt touch her third drink, but sat looking around, cursing every sonofabitch in the joint and growing more defiant and desperate. Soon she was screaming in her mind wishing takrist she had a blade, she'd cut their goddamn balls off. A CPO came up to her and asked her if she wanted a drink and she damn near spit in his face, but just mumbled as she looked at the clock and said shit. Yeah, yeah, lets go. She gulped down her drink and they left. Her mind was still such a fury of screechings (and that sonofabitch gives me nothing but a fuckin letter) that she just lay in bed staring at the ceiling and ignored the sailor as he screwed her and when he finally rolled off for the last time and fell asleep she continued staring and cursing for hours before falling asleep. The next afternoon she demanded that he giver some money and he laughed. She tried to hit him but he grabbed her arm, slapped her across the face and told her she was out of her mind. He laughed and told her to take it easy. He had a few days leave and he had enough money for both of them. They could have a good time. She cursed him and spit and he told her to grab her gear and shove off. She stopped in a cafeteria and went to the ladies room and threw some water on her face and bought a cup of coffee and a bun. She left and went back to the same bar. It was not very crowded being filled mostly with servicemen trying to drink away hangovers, and she sat and sipped a few drinks until the bar started filling. She tried looking for a liveone, but after an hour or so, and a few drinks, she ignored everyone and waited. A couple of sailors asked her if she wanted a drink and she said whatthefuck and left with them. They roamed around for hours drinking and then she went to a room with two of them and they gave her a few bucks in the morning so she stayed with them for a few days, 2 or 3, staying drunk most of the time and going back to the room now and then with them and their friends. And then they left or went somewhere and she went back to the bar to look for another one or a whole damn ship. Whats the difference. She pulled her dress tight but didnt think of washing. She hadnt reached the bar when someone grabbed her arm, walked her to the side door and told her to leave. She stood on the corner of 42nd and Broadway cursing them and wanting to know why they let those scabby whores in but kick a nice young girl out, ya lousy bunch apricks. She turned and crossed the street, still mumbling to herself, and went in another bar. It was jammed and she worked her way to the back near the jukebox and looked. When someone came back to play a number she smiled, threw her shoulders back and pushed the hair from her face. She stood there drinking and smiling and eventually left with a drunken soldier. They screwed most of the night, slept for a short time then awoke and started drinking and screwing again. She stayed with him for a day or two, perhaps longer, she wasnt sure and it didnt make any difference anyway, then he was gone and she was back in a bar looking. She bounced from one bar to another still pulling her dress tight and occasionally throwing some water on her face before leaving a hotel room, slobbering drinks and soon not looking but just saying yeah, yeah, whatthefuck and pushing an empty glass toward the bartender and sometimes never seeing the face of the drunk buying her drinks and rolling on and off her belly and slobbering over her tits; just drinking then pulling off her clothes and spreading her legs and drifting off to sleep or a drunken stupor with the first lunge. Time passed – months, maybe years, who knows, and the dress was gone and just a beatup skirt and sweater and the Broadway bars were 8th avenue bars, but soon even these joints with their hustlers, pushers, pimps, queens and wouldbe thugs kicked her out and the inlaid linoleum turned to wood and then was covered with sawdust and she hung over a beer in a dump on the waterfront, snarling and cursing every sonafabitch who fucked herup and left with anyone who looked at her or had a place to flop. The honeymoon was over and still she pulled the sweater tight but there was no one there to look. When she crawled out of a flophouse she fell in the nearest bar and stayed until another offer of a flop was made. But each night she would shove her tits out and look around for a liveone, not wanting any goddamn wino but the bums only looked at their beers and she waited for the liveone who had an extra 50c he didnt mind spending on beer for a piece of ass and she flopped from one joint to another growing dirtier and scabbier. She was in a South street bar and a seaman bought her a beer and his friends who depended on him for their drinks got panicky fearing he would leave them and spend their beer money on her so when he went to the head they took the beer from her and threw her out into the street. She sat on the curb yelling until a cop came along and kicked her and told her to move. She sprawled to her feet cursing every sonofabitch and his brother and told them they could stick their fuckin beer up their ass. She didnt need any goddamn skell to buy her a drink. She could get anything she wanted in Willies. She had her kicks. She'd go back to Willies where what she said goes. That was the joint. There was always somebody in there with money. No bums like these cruds. Did they think she'd let any goddamn bum in her pants and play with her tits just for a few bucks. Shit! She could get a seamans whole payoff just sittin in Willies. People knew who she was in Willies. You bet yasweet ass they did. She stumbled down the subway and rode to Brooklyn, muttering and cursing, sweat streaking the dirt on her face. She walked up the 3 steps to the door and was briefly disappointed that the door wasnt closed so she could throw it open. She stood for just a second in the doorway looking around then walked to the rear where Waterman Annie, Ruthy and a seaman were sitting. She stood beside the seaman, leaned in front of him and smiled at Annie and Ruthy then ordered a drink. The bartender looked at her and asked if she had any money. She told him it was none of his goddamn business. My friend here is going to pay for it. Wontya honey. The seaman laughed and pushed a bill forward and she got her drink and sneered at the ignorant sonofabitchin bartender. The rotten scumbag. Annie pulled her aside and told her if she tried cuttin her throat she'd dump her guts on the floor. Mean Ruthys gonna leave as soon as Jacks friend comes and if ya screw it up youll be a sorry sonofabitch. Tralala yanked her arm away and went back to the bar and leaned against the seaman and rubbed her tits against his arm. He laughed and told her to drinkup. Ruthy told Annie not ta botha witha, Fredll be here soon and we'll go, and they talked with Jack and Tralala leaned over and interrupted their conversation and snarled at Annie hoping she burns like hell when Jack left with *her* and Jack laughed at everything and pounded the bar and bought drinks and Tralala smiled and drank and the jukebox blared hillbilly songs and an occasional blues song, and the red and blue neon lights around the mirror behind the bar sputtered and winked and the soldiers, seamen and whores in the booths and hanging on the bar yelled and laughed and Tralala lifted her drink and said chugalug and banged her glass on the bar and she rubbed her tits against Jacks arm and he looked at her wondering how many blackheads she had on her face and if that large pimple on her cheek would burst and ooze and he said something to Annie then roared and slapped her leg and Annie smiled and wrote Tralala off and the cash register kachanged and the smoke just hung and Fred came and joined the party and Tralala yelled for another drink and asked Fred how he liked her tits and he poked them with a finger and said I guess theyre real and Jack pounded the bar and laughed and Annie cursed Tralala and tried to get them to leave and they said lets stay for a while, we're having fun and Fred winked and someone rapped a table and roared and a glass fell to the floor and the smoke fell when it reached the door and Tralala opened Jacks fly and smiled and he closed it 5 6 7 times laughing and stared at the pimple and the lights blinked and the cashregister crooned kachang kachang and Tralala told Jack she had big tits and he pounded the bar and laughed and Fred winked and laughed and Ruthy and Annie wanted to leave before something screwed up their deal and wondered how much money they had and hating to see them spend it on Tralala and Tralala gulped her drinks and yelled for more and Fred and Jack laughed and winked and pounded the bar and another glass fell to the floor and someone bemoaned the loss of a beer and two hands fought their way up a skirt under a table and she blew smoke in their faces and someone passedout and his head fell on the table and a beer was grabbed before it fell and Tralala glowed she had it made and she'd shove it up Annies ass or anybody else and she gulped another drink and it spilled down her chin and she hung on Jacks neck and rubbed her chest against his cheek and he reached up and turned them like knobs and roared and Tralala smiled and O she had it made now and piss on all those mothafuckas and someone walked a mile for a smile and someone pulled the drunk out of the booth and dropped him out the back door and Tralala pulled her sweater up and bounced her tits on the palms of her hands and grinned and grinned and grinned and Jack and Fred whooped and roared and the bartender told her to put those goddamn things away and get thehelloutahere and Ruthy and Annie winked and Tralala slowly turned around bouncing them hard on her hands exhibiting her pride to the bar and she smiled and bounced the biggest most beautiful pair of tits in the world on her hands and someone yelled is that for real and Tralala shoved them in his face and everyone laughed and another glass fell from a table and guys stood and looked and the hands came out from under the skirt and beer was poured on Tralalas tits and someone yelled that she had been christened and the beer ran down her stomach and dripped from her nipples and she slapped his face with her tits and someone yelled youll smotherim ta death – what a way to die – hey, whats for desert – I said taput those goddamn things away ya fuckin hippopotamus and Tralala told him she had the prettiest tits in the world and she fell against the jukebox and the needle scraped along the record sounding like a long belch and someone yelled all tits and no cunt and Tralala told him to comeon and find out and a drunken soldier banged out of a booth and said comeon and glasses fell and Jack knocked over his stool and fell on Fred and they hung over the bar nearing hysteria and Ruthy hoped she wouldnt get fired because this was a good deal and Annie closed her eyes and laughed relieved that they wouldnt have to worry about Tralala and they didnt spend too much money and Tralala still bounced her tits on the palms of her hands turning to everyone as she was dragged out the door by the arm by 2 or 3 and she yelled to Jack to comeon ahd she'd fuckim blind not like that fuckin douchebag he was with and someone yelled we're coming and she was dragged down the steps tripping over someones feet and scraping her ankles on the stone steps and yelling but the mob not slowing their pace dragged her by an arm and Jack and Fred still hung on the bar roaring and Ruthy took off her apron getting ready to leave before something happened to louse up their deal and the 10 or 15 drunks dragged Tralala to a wrecked car in the lot on the corner of 57th street and yanked her clothes off and pushed her inside and a few guys fought to see who would be first and finally a sort of line was formed everyone yelling and laughing and someone yelled to the guys on the end to go get some beer and they left and came back with cans of beer which were passed around the daisychain and the guys from the Greeks cameover and some of the other kids from the neighbourhood stood around watching and waiting and Tralala yelled and shoved her tits into the faces as they occurred before her and beers were passed around and the empties dropped or thrown and guys left the car and went back on line and had a few beers and waited their turn again and more guys came from Willies and a phone call to the Armybase brought more seamen and doggies and more beer was brought from Willies and Tralala drank beer while being laid and someone asked if anyone was keeping score and someone yelled who can count that far and Tralalas back was streaked with dirt and sweat and her ankles stung from the sweat and dirt in the scrapes from the steps and sweat and beer dripped from the faces onto hers but she kept yelling she had the biggest goddamn pair of tits in the world and someone answered ya bet ya sweet ass yado and more came 40 maybe 50 and they screwed her and went back on line and had a beer and yelled and laughed and someone yelled that the car stunk of cunt so Tralala and the seat were taken out of the car and laid in the lot and she lay there naked on the seat and their shadows hid her pimples and scabs and she drank flipping her tits with the other hand and somebody shoved the beer can against her mouth and they all laughed and Tralala cursed and spit out a piece of tooth and someone shoved it again and they laughed and yelled and the next one mounted her and her lips were split this time and the blood trickled to her chin and someone mopped her brow with a beer soaked handkerchief and another can of beer was handed to her and she drank and yelled about her tits and another tooth was chipped and the split in her lips was widened and everyone laughed and she laughed and she drank more and more and soon she passedout and they slapped her a few times and she mumbled and turned her head but they couldnt revive her so they continued to fuck her as she lay unconscious on the seat in the lot and soon they tired of the dead piece and the daisychain brokeup and they went back to Willies the Greeks and the base and the kids who were watching and waiting to take a turn took out their disappointment on Tralala and tore her clothes to small scraps put out a few cigarettes on her nipples pissed on her jerkedoff on her jammed a broomstick up her snatch then bored they left her lying amongst the broken bottles rusty cans and rubble of the lot and Jack and Fred and Ruthy and Annie stumbled into a cab still laughing and they leaned toward the window as they passed the lot and got a good look at

Tralala lying naked covered with blood urine and semen and a small blot forming on the seat between her legs as blood seeped from her crotch and Ruth and Annie happy and completely relaxed now that they were on their way downtown and their deal wasnt lousedup and they would have plenty of money and Fred looking through the rear window and Jack pounding his leg and roaring with laughter . . .

Part V

Strike

I went by the field of the slothful, and by the vineyard of the man void of understanding;

And, lo, it was all grown over with thorns, and nettles had covered the face thereof, and the stone wall thereof was broken down.

Proverbs 24: 30, 31

HARRY looked at his son as he lay on the table playing with a diaper. He covered his head with it and giggled. Harry watched him wave the diaper for a few seconds. He looked at his sons penis. He stared at it then touched it. He wondered if an 8 months old kid could feel anything different there. Maybe it felt the same no matter where you touched him. It got hard sometimes when he had to piss, but he didnt think that meant anything. His hand was still on his sons penis when he heard his wife walking into the room. He pulled his hand away. He stood back. Mary took the clean diaper from the babys hand and kissed his stomach. Harry watched her rub the babys stomach with her cheek, her neck brushing his penis occasionally. It looked as if she were going to put it in her mouth. He turned away. His stomach knotted, a slight nausea starting. He went into the living room. Mary dressed the baby and put him in the crib. Harry heard her jostling the crib. Heard the baby sucking on his bottle. The muscles and nerves of Harrys body twisted and vibrated. He wished to krist he could take the sounds and shove them up her ass. Take the goddamn kid and jam it back up her snatch. He picked up the TV guide, looked at his watch, slid his finger down the column of numbers, twice, then turned on the set and twirled the dials. In a few minutes his wife came into the room, stood alongside Harry and rubbed the back of his neck. What show you watchin? I dont know, twisting his head and leaning away from her hand. She walked over to the coffee table, took a cigarette from the pack on the table and sat on the couch. When Harry shook her hand from his neck she felt disappointed for a second, but it passed. She understood.

Harry was funny sometimes. Probably worrying about the job, what with the chance of there being a strike and everything. Thats probably what it is.

Harry tried to ignore the presence of his wife but no matter how he stared at the TV, or covered the side of his head with his hand, he was still conscious of her being there. There! Sitting on the couch. Looking at him. Smiling. For krists sake, what thefuck she smilin at? Got hot fuckin pants again. Always breakin my balls. Wish takrist there was somethin good on TV. Why cant they have fights on Tuesday nights. They think people only wanna look at fights on Fridays? What the fuck ya smilin at?

Harry yawned, turning his head and trying to hide his face with his hand – Mary said nothing, just smiled – trying to interest himself in the show, whatever it was; trying to stay awake until she went to sleep. If only the fuckin bitch would go tabed. Married over a year and you could count the times she went to sleep first. He looked at the TV; smoked, and ignored Mary. He yawned again unable to hide it it came so quickly. He tried to swallow it in the middle, tried to cough or some damn thing, but all he could do was let his mouth hang open and groan. Its gettin kindda late Harry, why dont we go tabed? You go. Im gonna have anotha cigarette. She thought for a moment of having another one too, but figured she'd better not. Harry got very aggravated, when he was like this, if you bothered him too much. She got up, stroking the back of his neck as she passed – Harry jerking his head forward – and went into the bedroom.

Harry knew she would still be awake when he went to bed. The TV was still on but Harry wasnt watching it. Eventually the cigarette was too short to allow him to take another drag. He dropped it in the ashtray.

Mary rolled over onto her back when Harry came into the room. She said nothing, but watched him undress –

Harry turning his back toward her and piling his clothes on the chair by the bed – Mary looking at the hair on the base of his spine, thinking of the dirt ingrained in the callouses on his hands and under his finger nails. Harry sat on the edge of the bed for a moment, but it was inevitable: he would have to lie down next to her. He lowered his head to the pillow then lifted his legs onto the bed, Mary holding the covers up so he could slide his legs under. She pulled the covers up to his chest and leaned on her side facing him. Harry turned on his side facing away from her. Mary rubbed his neck, his shoulders, then his back. Harry wished takrist she'd go to sleep and leave him alone. He felt her hand going lower down his back, hoping nothing would happen; hoping he could fall asleep (he had thought that after he got married he would get used to it); wishing he could turn over and slap her across the goddamn face and tell her to stop – krist, how many times had he thought of smashing her head. He tried thinking of something so he could ignore her and what she was doing and what was happening. He tried to concentrate on the fight he saw on TV last Friday where Pete Laughlin beat the shit out of some fuckin nigga and had him bleedin all over the face and the ref finally stopped the fight in the 6th and Harry was madashell that he stopped it . . . but still he was conscious of her hand on his thigh. He tried remembering how the boss looked last week when he told him off again – he smiled twistedly – that bastard, he cant shove me around. I tellim right to his face. Vice President. Shit. He knows he cant fuck with me. Id have the whole plant shut down in 5 minutes – the caressing hand still there. He could control nothing. The fuckin bitch. Why cant she just leave me alone. Why dont she goaway somewhere with that fuckin kid. Id like ta rip her cunt right the fuck outta her.

He squeezed his eyes shut so hard they pained then suddenly rolled over on Mary, hitting her on the head with his elbow, squeezing her hand between his legs as he turned, almost breaking her wrist – Mary stunned for a moment, hearing more than feeling his elbow hit her; struggling to free her hand; seeing his body on hers; feeling his weight, his hand groping for her crotch . . . then she relaxed and put her arms around him. Harry fumbled at her crotch anxious and clumsy with anger; wanting to pile drive his cock into her, but when he tried he scratched and burned the head and he instinctively stopped for a second, but his anger and hatred started him lunging and lunging until he finally was all the way in – Mary wincing slightly then sighing – and Harry shoved and pounded as hard as he could, wanting to drive the fucking thing out of the top of her head; wishing he could put on a rubber dipped in iron filings or ground glass and rip her guts out – Mary wrapping her legs around his and tightening her arms around his back, biting his neck, rolling from side to side with excitement as she felt all of his cock going in her again and again – Harry physically numb, feeling neither pain nor pleasure, but moving with the force and automation of a machine; unable now to even formulate a vague thought, the attempt at thought being jumbled by his anger and hatred; not even capable of trying to determine if he was hurting her, completely unaware of the pleasure he was giving his wife; his mind not allowing him to reach the quick climax he wanted so he could roll off and over unaware that his brutality in bed was the one thing that kept his wife clinging to him and the harder he tried to drive her away, to split her guts with his cock, the closer and tighter she clung to him – and Mary rolled from side to side half faint with excitement, enjoying one orgasm, another, while Harry continued driving and pounding until eventually the semen flowed, Harry continuing with the same rhythm and force, feeling nothing, until his energy drained with the semen and he stopped suddenly,

suddenly nauseous with disgust. He quickly rolled off his wife and lay on his side, his back toward her, and gripped the pillow with his hands, almost tearing it, his face buried in it, almost crying; his stomach crawling with nausea; his disgust seeming to wrap itself around him as a snake slowly, methodically and painfully squeezing the life from him, but each time it reached the point where just the slightest more pressure would bring an end to everything: life, misery, pain, it stopped tightening, retained the pressure and Harry just hung there his body alive with pain, his mind sick with disgust. He moaned and Mary reached over and touched his shoulder, her body still tingling. She closed her eyes, her body relaxing, and soon went to sleep, her hand slowly sliding from Harrys shoulder.

Harry could do nothing but endure the nausea and slimy disgust. He wanted to smoke a cigarette, but was afraid, afraid that the slightest movement, even the taking of a deep breath, would cause him to heave his guts up; afraid even to swallow. So he just lay there, a sour taste in his throat; his stomach seeming to be pressuring against his palate; his face still buried in the pillow; his eyes tightly squeezed shut; concentrating on his stomach, trying to think the pressure and foul taste away or, if not, at least control it. He knew, after years of fighting it, losing each time and ending up hanging over a bowl or sink if he was lucky enough to make it there, that this was all he could do. Nothing else would help. Except crying. And he was no longer able to cry. He had many times, locked in a bathroom or on the street after running from the woman he had been with, but now the tears no longer rilled from his eyes, even if he tried relaxing and allowing them to, his eyes just ached, feeling swollen and damp, unrelieved, just as the pressure at his throat remained constant and unrelieved. He just lay there . . . if only something would happen. He clutched harder at the pillow; clenched his jaw tighter until a piercing pain in his ear and a spasm in his neck muscles forced him to relax. His body jerked slightly, involuntarily. Nothing broke through or even slightly greyed the darkness; his eyes were shut and his head was jammed in the hemispherical blackness, the boundaries unseen, unfelt, to Harry nonexistent. It was just black.

He tightened the muscles in his toes until they cramped, the pain increasing; trying to concentrate on the pain enough to forget everything else. His toes felt as if they would shatter and his feet started to cramp, then the calves of his legs, and still he didnt relax his muscles until the pain became unbearable and he wanted to scream and only then he relaxed but the muscles remained tightened and he had to direct all his energy to the relaxing of the muscles before the pain killed him. His calves still ached, though they started to loosen slightly, but his feet felt as if they were going to twist and bend back upon themselves and his toes felt as if they were going to snap. His ears and neck started paining again from the clenching of his jaw – one thing though accomplished, he was no longer aware of the nausea and disgust, of the pressure against his throat and the taste of bile – his ears and neck pained though he was only vaguely aware of it. His calves loosened a little more and slowly the muscles relaxed until his feet and then his toes started to straighten and he then became aware of the ache in his jaw, then that too started slowly to lessen and eventually the cramps and pains disappeared and he loosened his grip slightly on the pillow and lay there, enervated, sweating, feeling for a moment nothing but weakness, then slowly aware of his throat and stomach, the disgust and nausea forcing themselves upon his consciousness again. If something would happen . . . tears pounded against his eyes but couldnt force their way through, something . . . anything . . . krist. jesus fuckin krist. He allowed his eyes to open – the tears still pounding behind his eyes. His eyes focused on the bureau:

there were two large knobs, a smaller one above, another large one to the side; a wall. His eyes started to smart from sweat. He wiped his face against the pillow. He turned his head slightly until he could see the ceiling. Now his vision reached to an end. The ceiling was there. The walls were there. No mysteries. Nothing hidden. There was something to be seen. It had an order. His eyes felt better. No longer felt pinched. No longer afraid to look. Now he had to move. The pressure must have gone down. It was still there, but it must have lessened. It must have. Should be able to move. He swallowed . . . again . . . his throat burned with the bitterness. He lay completely immobile. Not breathing. Stomach bubbling, trying to erupt. Throat pulsating. Burning. He swallowed again . . . breathed. Shallowly. Eruption subsiding slightly. Throat quieting. Still burning. Swallowed . . . breathed . . . slowly pulled his legs up . . . let them slide over the side of the bed. Sat up slowly. Not breathing. Contracting his nostrils. Sucking air gently between his teeth . . . he stood. Rubbed his face . . . went slowly to the parlour. Sat down and lit a cigarette and stared out the window. Smoked. Nothing on the street. No one. Car parked across the street, empty. Lit a second cigarette from the first. Throat burned, but stomach relaxing. Nausea no longer critical. Still there though. Foul. Mouth tasted foul. He sat and smoked. Stared. Eyes damp. Aching. No tears. Dropped the cigarette in the ashtray. Rubbed his face. Went back to bed. Stared at the ceiling until his eyes started to close. If something would happen. What? What? What could happen?? For what? About what? His eyes burned and watered. Couldnt keep them open. His body started to loosen. His head rolled slightly to one side. He adjusted his body. Still hadnt looked at Mary. Hadnt thought of *her*. His body twitched. He brushed his face against the pillow. He moaned in his halfsleep. Soon he slept.

The Harpies swooped down on Harry and in the

darkness under their wings he could see nothing but their eyes: small, and filled with hatred, their eyes laughing at him, mocking him as he tried to evade them, knowing he couldnt and that they could toy with him before they slowly destroyed him. He tried turning his head but it wouldnt move. He tried and tried until it rolled back and forth but still the eyes glared and mocked and the gigantic wings beat faster and faster and the wind whirled around Harry and his body chilled and he could sense their large sharp beaks and feel the tips of feathers as they brushed his face. He tried to slide down the rock but no matter how often he did he was still on the top with the wind whirling and the Harpies screeching, screeching and above the roar of the wind and the screeching he could hear his flesh being ripped from his belly, could hear the sharp tearing sound prick its way into his ears and then he heard his screams and the Harpies slowly, very slowly tore bits of flesh from his belly then slowly tugged as the long strips of flesh were pulled from his body and he yelled and rolled over and over and leaped up and ran, tripped and tumbled down the rock yet he was still on top of the rock and the Harpies still mocked him as they tore the flesh from his belly, his chest, and scraped their beaks on his ribs and suddenly thrust their beaks into his eyes and plucked them from their sockets and he heard the plop, plop of his eyes leaving his head and the screeching of the Harpies increased until he no longer could hear his own screams and he kicked and punched at them yet his body refused to move and all he could do was lie still as they once again, and again, over and over started ripping the flesh from his belly and chest, scraping his ribs and once more plucking the eyes from his head.

And he was alone on a street looking, turning slowly around in a circle, looking, looking at nothing. Everything was endless in every direction until there were walls that seemed to be moving on an eccentric rod and the walls came closer together, still rolling in half circles and Harry still turned in a circle and the walls came closer together and Harry yelled and started crying yet it was silent not even the walls making a sound as they approached each other and Harry ran until he hit a wall and was in the middle of the diminishing room and he could feel the slate smoothness of the walls as they touched his arms, the back of his head, his nose, and the wall slowly crushed him.

And his eyes rolled and bounced up the hill and Harry stumbled after them trying to find them, picking up stones, pebbles and burrs and trying to force them in the empty sockets and he spit out the stones and yelled as the burrs tore the already bleeding sockets and he continued to stumble up the hill and occasionally the eyes would stop and they would look at each other with a gigantic stare and wait until Harry almost touched them then continued to roll up the hill and Harry jammed two more burrs into the sockets and screamed as they ripped the lids and he screamed louder and louder as he twisted the burrs trying to get them out, his bloodied hands preventing him from getting a firm grip on them and his screams were louder and louder until he finally did scream and he sprang up in bed and opened his eyes waiting years for the wall and the chest of drawers to be recognised.

Mary stirred slightly and Harry held his head with his hands and moaned. The nightmare wasnt always exactly the same but after it was over it always seemed as if it had been. Year after year Harry would bolt up in bed occasionally, near dead with terror, trying to shove the weight off his chest so he could breathe and then slowly some familiar object would be seen and he would know he was finally awake. Again his eyes swelled but no tears flowed. He sat for many minutes then slowly lowered his head back to the pillow, wiping his face and head with his hand then covering his eyes with his arm.

Harry moved along the few blocks from his house to the factory, punched his time card, changed his clothes and went to his bench. He was the worst lathe operator of the more than 1,000 men working in the factory. He started shortly before the war and remained there all during the war. Soon after the war started the shop steward was drafted and Harry took his place and devoted more time to the activities of the union than he did his job. From the beginning he hounded and haunted the bosses and soon he was part of the outer clique of the union. During the war the company was powerless to fire him and when they tried after the war the union threatened to call a strike so Harry still stood in front of the same lathe.

Harry worked for 30 minutes or so each morning then turned off his lathe and made the rounds of the factory reminding those who were behind in their dues that they had to pay by a certain date; asking others why they hadnt been to the last union meeting; or simply telling others not to work so fast, it aint gonna get ya nothin. Youre only makin money for the company and they got enough. And though he had been doing this for years and the foremen had learned to ignore him, many of the executives, especially cost estimators, production engineers, and the General Manager of the plant who was also a Vice-President of the Company, were still incensed whenever they saw him walking around the factory in defiance of all the rules and regulations. Usually they stormed off in another direction, but occasionally they would demand to know what he was doing and he would tell them he was doin his job, and if they persisted in questioning him he would tell them to go fuckthemselves, and if they did their job as good as he did his everybody would be better off and what the fuck do they know about work, all they do is sit on their fat asses all day breakin balls . . . and he would be sure to walk away smiling his sneering smile, looking at everyone, letting them know by his attitude that he wasnt afraid of any bigass boss, but they damn sure were afraid of him, convinced that what he had said was true and that he was right in doing and saying what he had.

His morning round usually took an hour and a half to 2 hours. Then he would go back to his bench and work until lunch time. Harry never went home for lunch, but went across the street to the bar and ate with the boys. He always started with a couple a quick shots and a beer, then a few beers with a sandwich and a few more after. He talked with some of the men, listening to their jokes, their stories of dames fucked, following each story with one of his own about how he bagged some dame and threw a fuck intoer and how she thought he was so great and wanted to seeim again and the others would listen, tolerating him, relieved when he would finally leave their group to go to another; and Harry would continue making the rounds of the bar, listening briefly then telling his stories or a joke about a queer who had his ears pulled off; occasionally sticking a finger in someones stomach and farting; or asking someone when they were going to buy him a drink, laughing, slapping the guy on the shoulder, and leaving when he said right after you do; or if they were new on the job he would put his empty glass on the bar and wait for the bartender to fill it up and take the money from their change on the bar.

During the middle of the afternoon Harry reached the part of a job that required resetting the lathe and doing a small amount of figuring to set the job up properly so he decided to take a little walk. If he got too far behind in the work the foreman would have to set the job up. He slowly roamed around the factory asking some of the men how it was going, but mostly saying nothing and just smiling his smile, looking and roaming. He was walking around the 6th floor when he suddenly stopped and frowned, thought hard for a few minutes, took the small union booklet from his pocket describing the duties of different classifications, checked it then went over to one of the benches, turned off the lathe and asked the man working there what inthehell he thought he was doin. The man just stood there, trying to understand what had happened and trying to understand what Harry was talking about. Harry stood in front of him waving the booklet in the air, yelling over the noise of the factory. A few of the men near by turned to look and the foreman came running over, yelling at the operator, still standing in front of Harry trying to understand what was going on, and yelled, whys that goddamn machine off? Harry turned to the foreman and asked him if he told him to do this job. Whointhehell do you think toldim to do it. Im the foreman aint I. Well what the fucks the idea of havinim cut heavy stainless, eh? What the fucks the idea? Whattayamean whats the idea? This guys a A man. Hes been cuttin stainless for years. Why shouldnt he cut it. Cause hes a new man thats why. He only been here a couple a months. He doesnt even have a full union book yet. Aint that right, eh? Aint it? yellin in the operators face, waving the booklet. Yeah, but Ive been in the business 20 years. I can cut anything. Harry stepped closer to him, turning his back to the foreman and yelling louder. I dont give a fuck what ya can cut, a ya hear me? The union says ya gotta have a full book or been here 6 months before ya can cut heavy stainless, and ya betta do like I tellya or youll find yaself blackballed, yelling even louder, his face swollen – the operator staring, not understanding, wanting only to do his work and be left alone – ya hear me? The foreman finally forced himself into the line of Harrys vision and yelled at him ta shut up. Fa krists sake, what thefuck ya yellin about? Im yellin cause I wanna yell. And youd betta get this guy off the job or youll find your ass inna sling too. Fa krists sake Harry, this jobs gotta be done and hes the only guy whos not workin a job that can do it. I dont give a fuck if ya havta wait ten fuckin years ta get it done, and I dont giveashit how much it costs the boss. Comeon Harry be reasonable, you – I can cut stainless or any other damn thing you got around here. Look buddy, youd better shut yafuckinmouth or youll be out on your ass. The operators face turned red and he started to reach for a wrench and the foreman quickly stepped in front of him, grabbed him by the shoulders and told him to go take a break, I'll getya when we settle this. He left and the foreman took a deep breath and closed his eyes for a second before turning back to Harry. Look Harry, theres no sense in making a issue of this. You know I never break any union rules, but this jobs gotta be done and he can do it so whats the harm? Dont try and brownnose me Mike. He aint cuttin no stainless. OK, OK, let me call upstairs and see what we can do. He walked back to his desk to call and Harry leaned against the idle lathe. The foreman hung up the phone and came back. Wilsonll be right down and maybe we can get this straightened out. I dont give a fuck whos comin down.

In a few minutes Wilson, a production manager, came rushing across the floor. He smiled, put his arms around Mikes and Harrys shoulders. What seems to be the problem boys, smiling at Harry and giving Mikes shoulder a reassuring and knowing squeeze. Harry scowled, turned slightly so that Wilsons hand fell from his shoulder and barely opened his mouth when he spoke. The man at this machine aint cuttin no stainless. I tried to tellim Mr. Wilson that the job had ta be done – thats OK Mike, patting his shoulder and smiling even broader at both of them, Im sure we can straighten this thing out. Harrys a reasonable man. Nothin ta straighten out. He aint cuttin

119

stainless. Mike started to throw his arms up in disgust, but Wilson put an arm around him and held his arms for a second, smiled then patted him again on the back. Why dont we go into the lounge and have a smoke and talk this over? How about it boys? Mike said OK and started walking toward the smoking room. Harry grunted and stood still as Wilson motioned him on, waiting until Wilson started walking behind Mike before he too followed, a foot or so behind Wilson. When they got to the smoking room Wilson took out a pack of cigarettes and offered them. Mike took one and stuck it in his mouth. Harry said nothing, but took one out of his own pack, ignored Wilsons lighter, lighting his own cigarette. Wilson asked them if they would like a coke and they both declined. The operator, who had been sitting in the corner, came over to Mike and asked him if he could go back to work. Harry started to yell something, but Mike told the man to go out to his bench, but not to turn his machine on. Just wait there. We'll be out in a minute. The man left and Wilson turned immediately to Harry, smiling, trying to appear relaxed and trying to hide his hatred for him.

Wilson looked at Harry and decided that it wouldnt do to try the arm around the shoulder routine again. Now look Harry, I understand and respect your position. I have known and have had the pleasure of working with you for quite a few years now and I know, just as Mike here knows, and everyone in the plant knows, that youre a good and honest worker, and that you always have the interest of the organisation and the men at heart. Isnt that right Mike? Mike nodded automatically. Like I say Harry, we all know you are a good man and that no one else could have done the job you have in keeping the union affairs of this plant functioning as they have been and we all respect and admire you for this. And we all respect and admire your intelligence and ability. And believe me when

I say this, because I say this not as an executive of the organisation, but as a man who works with the other men here, I say this as a fellow worker: I would be the last person in the world to ask anyone to make even the slightest breach in the union rules and regulations. To me a contract is a sacred instrument and I will stand by it come hell or high water . . . but, and I say this as a worker and and executive . . . look, its like this: its just like in the union itself. You have your constitution and bylaws. Right? I am certain you are familiar with them. And I am also certain that you follow them to the letter but there are times when you might have to make a slight exception. Now wait a minute – Harry leaning forward and starting to speak – just hear me out. Now look, suppose the rules say a meeting should start at 8 oclock, but suddenly theres a big snow storm and it takes the men 30 minutes or an hour longer to get to the meeting. Now, you either will have to wait and start the meeting late or you will have to start it on time without the proper number of members present. Wilson smiled, relaxed and took a drag of his cigarette, satisfied with his cleverness, thinking that Harrys position was untenable. Harry took a drag of his cigarette, blew the smoke in Wilsons direction, dropped the butt on the floor and squashed it under his shoe. What we do at the union meetings is none of your business unless we want ta tellya about it. O, I know that Harry, I certainly didnt mean to imply otherwise. All I am trying to say is that this organisation, like your union, is like any other organisation in that it is a team and everyone connected with the organisation from the President to the elevator operators are a member of that team and we all have to pull together. Everyones job is equally important. The Presidents job is no more important than yours in that if you dont co-operate, just as he must co-operate, we can not get the job done. That is what I am trying to say. We all have to get behind the wheel, just like in the union. Now, we have a job that must be done and it must be done now. This new man is the only man available to do it at this time. That is the only reason he is doing it. We certainly had no intention of being instrumental in asking anyone to do anything that might even be considered a breach of union rules, but the job has to be done – look, this guys a new man and aint cuttin no stainless so just stop the shit. If ya put him back on the job I'll call the whole goddamn plant out, Harrys face becoming redder, his eyes glaring, ya get that? I'll stand by that fuckin bench all day if I have ta and if ya try to putim back on that job I swear ta krist the whole fuckin plantll be out on the street in two fuckin seconds and you and no ballbreakin fuck in the jointll stop me. Ya getit? If ya want a strike I'll giveya one. He walked out of the room, slammed the door and walked back to the bench. He said nothing to the man who was leaning impatiently against the bench, but simply stood at the other end.

Mike and Wilson looked at the door for a moment then Mike asked Wilson if he wanted him to put the man back anyway. No Mike, you had better not. I do not want any trouble. You just go back to your desk. I'll see Mr. Harrington.

Wilson was disconcerted about having to see Mr. Harrington, but he didnt know what else to do. He certainly did not want the responsibility of precipitating a strike. Mr. Harrington waved him toward a chair and asked Wilson what was on his mind. Wilson sat down and told him the story. As soon as he heard Harrys name Mr. Harrington frowned, then banged his desk with his fist when Wilson started relating the details. He listened becoming more and more infuriated and insulted not only because Harry had the audacity to defy him, one of the Vice-Presidents, and the Corporation, but also because he knew he would have to compromise and not break Harry as he would like to, but would have to avoid any trouble; that particular job had to be done according to schedule. He could not afford a delay. But there would be a strike soon and then he would get rid of Harry. He had hated Harry for years and had never been able to get rid of him, but he was hopeful he could use the strike to get rid of him. As head of the Corporations negotiating committee he knew he could persuade the other members to continue to reject the unions demands even if those demands became reasonable. He knew the Corporation could let the men stay on strike for the remainder of the year with only a slight loss in net earnings. He assumed that when the strike was 6 months old the union would gladly settle the strike if he gave in to most of their demands on the condition that he could discharge Harry. It was worth a try. He had nothing to lose.

By the time Wilson had finished telling him what had happened he had decided what to do. He stared directly into Wilsons eyes. Well, you certainly made a mess of it didnt you? The corners of Wilsons mouth sagged a little more. He said nothing. It seems as if I have to do everything around here or the entire organisation starts to crumble. I did the – never mind that now. The important thing is to get the job done. Now . . . we simply have to get someone else to do that job. How many men do you have working on the Kearny job? 6. Fine. Take one of the men off that job and have him change with the man working on the Collins job. The Kearny job is all brass if I remember correctly. Yes, it is. But it will take an hour or so to go over the job with the man and I was trying to save all the time I could. Save time! You have already wasted over an hour trying to save time. Now get back and do as I told you.

Wilson got up immediately and left the office. He went directly to the foreman of the Kearny job, and explained the situation. The foreman took one of his men off the job and the man went with Wilson to the 6th floor. Wilson explained to Mike and Harry what was going to be done then told the new man who to report to upstairs. When Harry saw him leave, and Mike and the man who had come down with Wilson go over to the lathe with the stainless steel stock, he left.

When he got back to his own bench his foreman was just finishing setting up the job for Harry. Think you can finish this job by tomorrow morning Harry? Its a rush. Yeah, sure. I wouldve finished it today, but that wise punk Wilson tried to pull a fast one and I had to straightenim out. He thought he could push me around, but I fixed hisass. Harry turned slightly toward his bench and the foreman left. He was a few feet away when Harry noticed he had gone and he sneered and muttered, chickenshit. Afraid the boss might see him with me. Harry jabbed at the button that turned his lathe on and started working. Fuckim.

Harry worked as slowly as possible, moving the cutting tool almost imperceptibly, and when the time came to go home he still had another hours or so work before the job would be finished.

Harry was in high spirits when he got home. As he washed his hands and splashed water on his face he told his wife what had happened and when she would tell him he ought to be careful, he might lose his job, he would laugh his evil laugh and tell her, they wouldn't fire me. If they tried that Id have the whole joint on strike and they know it. They cant fuck me around. When he finished eating he went up to the bar and yelled to the guys at the bar how he told the punk ballbreaker off at work, punctuating his story with his laugh.

Mary had already gone to bed by the time Harry got home, but it didnt make any difference to him one way or the other whether or not she was awake, she wouldnt bother him for awhile anyway. He undressed and plopped into bed and looked at Mary to see if she would wake up, but she uttered a low grunting noise and pulled her knees up closer to her chin. Harry stayed on his side, facing Mary, and fell asleep.

The next morning Harry went up to the 6th floor before going to his own bench. He checked to make sure the new man wasnt working on the stainless job. He smiled when he saw that he wasnt at his bench and stayed around for a while just to be sure they werent trying to pull a fast one; and before he left he went over to the foreman and told him he would see him later. He made his rounds throughout the rest of the plant and when he got back to his bench more than 2 hours had passed. He jabbed the start button and began working. The foreman came over and asked him when the job would be ready, the rest of the job is finished and we're just waiting for this piece. He sneered at the foreman and told him it would be ready when he finished. The foreman took a quick glance at the job, estimating how long it would be before Harry finished, and left. Harry stared at him for a few minutes, wise fuck, then turned back to the job.

When Harry came back from lunch he went back to the 6th floor and checked again, then strolled around the plant. He got back to his bench eventually and finished the job then went back to the 6th floor. The new man was back at his bench, but a piece of brass was in his machine. Harry went over to him. Thats betta. You come close ta losin your book yesterday mac. He just glanced at Harry, wanting to tell him what he thought of him, but said nothing, having been told that morning about Harry and how he had had more than one book pulled, for no reason at all, from more than one guy. Harry sneered and walked away. He went back to his work, still glowing and feeling omnipotent. He didnt particularly care about the new guy, but he was glad he had shoved it up the boss's ass and broke it off. He stayed at his work the rest of the day thinking occasionally of yesterday and of the fact that the union contract with the company expired in two weeks and the negotiating committees had not reached an agreement for a new contract and it was a sure thing that there would be a strike. Harry was so happy about going on strike – of closing down the entire shop, of setting up picket lines and watching the few bosses going into the empty factory and sitting at their desks and thinking and worrying about all the money they were losing while he got his every week from the union – that he laughed every now and then to himself and at times felt like shouting as loud as he could, fuck all you company bastards, all ya ball breakin pricks. We'll showya. We'll makeya get on yaknees and begus ta come back tawork. We'll breakya ya fat fucks.

With each day Harry felt bigger. He walked around the plant waving at the guys, yelling to them above the noise; thinking that soon it would be silent. The whole fuckin shop'd be quiet. And he had cartoon-like images in his mind of dollar bills with wings flying out the window, out of the pocket and pocketbook of a fat baldheaded cigar smoking boss; and punks with white shirts and ties and expensive suits sitting at an empty desk and opening empty pay envelopes. There were images of gigantic concrete buildings crumbling and pieces flying out of the middle and himself suspended in air smashing the buildings to pieces. He could see himself crushing heads and bodies and heaving them from the windows and watching them splatter on the sidewalks below and he roared with laughter as he watched the bodies floating in pools of blood and drifting toward the sewers and he, Harry Black, age 33, shop steward of local 392 watched and roared with laughter.

At night, after supper, he went to the empty store the union was fixing up to use as a strike headquarters. He did little and talked a lot.

Harry slept better, deep and without dreams; but before sleeping he would lie on his side and let the various images of empty shops, crumbling buildings and splattering bodies drift through his mind, more real, more vivid, the features and images more sharply defined, the flesh more pulpy, more flaccid; the cigar tips glowing, the smell of cigar smoke and after shave lotion resented and enjoyed. Then slowly the images would start overlapping each other, become entangled and whirl together in one amorphous multiexposure picture and Harry would smile, the sneer almost disappearing, then he slept.

The last day of the contract Harry whistled as he worked. Not really a whistle, but a flat hissing sound that at times approached a whistle. A new contract had not as yet been signed and there was to be a union meeting that night. When the working day was over Harry walked happily from the shop, slapping many of the men on the back with as deep a feeling of comradeship as he was capable of feeling, telling them not to forget the meeting and he would see them at the hall. Some of the men stopped in the bar before going home and slowly drank a few beers, talking about the strike, wondering how long it would last and what they would get. Harry bought a beer and walked around the bar slapping a back or squeezing a shoulder, not saying much, simply a this is it, or tonights the night. He hung around for half an hour or so then went home.

The officers were already on the platform when Harry got to the hall. He walked away from the steps on the side of the platform and walked around to the front and vaulted up onto the platform. He shook hands with everyone there, smiling his smile, and listened for a few minutes to each group huddling on the platform, continuing to go from one to the other, as the hall slowly filled, until it was

10 minutes past the official time for the meeting to start and the President of the local indicated that he would start the meeting soon and the groups broke up and the men took their seats, Harry sitting in the second row on the end, adjusting his chair so he could be seen between the two men in front of him.

The President sat, taking papers from his attache case, looking them over, occasionally passing one to some one else, a brief and hushed discussion following. Eventually he had the papers sorted as he wanted and he rose, remaining behind the small desk in front of him. The men in the hall quieted and the President called the meeting to order and called on the Secretary to read the minutes of the last meeting. They were read, voted upon and officially accepted by the rank and file. Next the Treasurer read his report consisting of many figures and explanations of expenditures, of how much was in the treasury and how much in the strike fund, the strike fund figure read last, slowly and loudly and the nonofficial members of the clique scattered throughout the hall applauded, as planned, and whistled, many others joining them. This report was voted upon and accepted by the rank and file.

Then the President got down to the business at hand and informed all the members that they knew what they were really here for tonight. More applause and whistles from the clique and others. The President raised his hands, solemnly, for silence. Your negotiating committee has been working hard for a long time trying to get a fair contract and wage for you men. Applause. We're not asking for much, just what we work for. But the company wants you to do all the work while they keep all the money. Boos and the stamping of feet. Let me just read their last offer. He yanked papers from the desk, crumpled the edges in his hand and looked at them scornfully. They want us to keep a 35 hour week – a loud no – give us a lousy 12 holidays – another no – the President continued to read through the noise that followed. No holiday for birthdays, keep time and a half for overtime – another roar – a stinking 25c an hour raise, and only a small increase in their contributions to the welfare plan and they want it to be controlled by a independent trustee – a look of contempt on his face as he looked at the men and read – and a lot of double talk that amounts to nothing and they have the nerve to offer us this – hoots and catcalls. But we showed them, pounding on the table and yelling defiantly, we showed them what kind of stuff union men are made of: we told them to go to hell. He sipped water then wiped his face and lowered his head slightly and waited for the men to quiet down. Now, we all know how hard we work – dont forget I sweated for 20 years myself over a lathe and that was before the union when they was really sweat shops – applause – the President raised his hands. And the company knows how hard you men work but do they care – a NOOOOO from the clique and a few others, then a roar from the men – but we care, dont we – a roaring YEEEEES – youre damn right we do, and by jesus theres not a man one of us whos going to allow them to get away with this – a roar – and you can bet your life they know it. He paused, took a sip of water, cleared his throat. All we're asking for is an honest wage for an honest days work and decent working conditions, and thats something that every American as a free man is entitled to, pounding on the desk emphasizing the words american, free, entitled, and leaning slightly toward the men as they roared and stamped their feet. Now we all know what we're asking for – the men in the hall looked quizzically at each other, trying to remember just what they were asking for – but I'll read them as they were presented to the company. A 30 hour week – cheers – a $1 an hour raise – cheers – a 25% increase in the companys contributions to our welfare plan

129

to be supervised by the union, looking up from the paper, leaning forward and pounding on the table, I said supervised by the union so those goddamn company lawyers and accountants cant cheat you out of what you should get – whistling and stamping of feet – 16 paid holidays, including every members birthday, or double time if he has to work on any of those holidays – applause. He straightened. Now . . . your negotiating committee met with theirs and after 2 weeks of head to head bargaining – and theres not a man one of us who doesnt know that you deserve everything weve asked for – and after 2 weeks the Vice-President told us that the Company couldnt afford to meet our demands – roars and boos . . . We're going to meet with them again but, I want everyman here to understand that we never have and never will have any intention of allowing them to bulldoze us into accepting a contract thats not fair for the rank and file of this union – whistles, roars, stamping – and no matter how many of their slick or conniving tricks they try or no matter how long the strike lasts theyre not going to get away with it – a roar – and if they think theyre dealing with jerks they got another guess coming . . .

The President of Local 392 continued for another 30 minutes, interrupted with cheers, the stamping of feet, whistling, explaining that if they gave in to the company now theyd grind their faces in the mud for the rest of their lives; and how every union member in the country was behind them, pledged to give all assistance and aid – and that means money – as long as the strike lasts; of how the union was completely ready and geared for the strike – an empty store had been rented as a temporary strike headquarters, signs have already been painted and instructions have been printed telling each brother when he has to walk the picket line – denouncing and promising . . .

When he finished he introduced other members of the

board who talked about what they were doing to help the strike and their union brothers. When they finished the President introduced brother Harry Black, shop steward and militant union brother, who was to be in charge of the strike headquarters. Harry tried to look over the heads of the men in the hall as he spoke, but was unable to keep from seeing their faces so he lowered his head and closed his eyes until they were open just enough to see his shoes and the edge of the platform. Like Brother Jones toldya the unions rented a store for a strike headquarters, you all know the place its next ta Willies bar and a free $10 bag of groceries will be given ta everybody every Saturday morning for as long as the strike lasts and the place is big enough for everything so that we dont have ta worry about it and before we're through with this strike the bossesll be on their knees begginus ta come back. Harry turned, opened his eyes and tried to find his seat but was unable to focus his eyes and he shook his head from side to side trying to orient himself and the President came over to him and tapped him on the shoulder and pushed him toward his seat. Harry stumbled, knocked into one of the members sitting near him and finally found his seat and sat down, sweat dripping from his armpits, his shirt stuck to his chest and back. He lowered his head, closed his eyes for a few moments and heard nothing until he finally raised his head and saw the President once more speaking to the men.

Now you have some idea of how hard we have been working for you to get everything in order for the strike and have it setup so we can take care of everything no matter how long the strike lasts. He sipped water then wiped his face with his handkerchief. He just stood there for a few minutes, head slightly bowed, listening to the men roar and when he noticed that it was starting to subside he turned once again toward the men and raised his hands, looking humble and worn, for silence. The men quieted and he looked around the hall, slowly, still keeping the humble expression, then once more started speaking. He reviewed the preparations that had been made; told them that everyman had to put in a couple of hours a week on the picket line and that his book would be stamped after every turn on the line and if anyone didnt have his book stamped that he had better be able to prove he couldnt walk or his book would be yanked, we're not going to allow any scabbing – yells and cheers – and coffee and sandwiches will be given to all the men on the line and explained a few more details of how they would conduct the strike before putting up to the rank and file whether or not they wanted to accept the companys offer or go on strike. Just as he finished speaking one of the nonofficial members of the clique made a motion that they tell the company ta go tahell and go on strike. Another member seconded the motion and the President yelled that a motion has been made and duly seconded. All in favour say aye and a roar went up as some men murmured, a few looked around confused, but almost everyone remained in the current of the evening and added their voice to the roar after the initial aye. The President banged on the desk, the motion has been accepted by acclamation, banged the desk again and another roar went up along with the scraping of chair legs on the floor as the men got up and started pounding each other on the back. The meeting was over. The strike was official.

Although the picketing wouldnt start until 8 oclock, the beginning of the normal working day, Harry was in the strike headquarters at 6:30. It was a small store that had been vacant for many years and a telephone had been installed as well as a small refrigerator, stove and large coffee urn. There were many folding chairs around the room and an old desk in the corner. Against the rear wall were dozens of picket signs. Harry sat behind the desk and looked at the phone for a few minutes hoping it would ring and he could answer it, local 392 strike headquarters, Brother Black, Shop Steward talkin. It probably wouldnt be long before the phoned be ringin all the time and hed be talkin ta the President and all the other officers all the time about how he was runnin the strike. He wished he knew somebody he could call so he could tellem how he was there and what was goin on. It wouldnt be long before the menll be showin up for the picket line. He leaned back in the chair and it moved slightly. He looked down at the legs and noticed they had wheels so he pushed himself back and forth a few times. He stopped and looked at the phone again for a few minutes, then pushed hard against the desk and the chair rolled back to the wall.

The first few men came a little before 8. Harry got up, rolling back his chair, slapped them on the back and told them everything was all set. The signs are over there. Ya can each take one and start picketing the front of the building. Harry rushed over to the pile of signs and selected three, giving one to each man, trying to remember what else there was to do. The men started to leave, then one of them asked when they got their book stamped. Harry stared for a minute, book stamped, stamp. His jaw started to quiver slightly. Ya gonna stampem now or after we finish walking, uuuuuuhhh . . . They gonna be stamped after? A few more men came in and started talking – book, stamp – with the men who were ready to leave with their signs. No one was looking at Harry. He managed to turn and move toward the desk. The books were to be stamped. Yes. He pulled out a few drawers then he knew definitely what it was he was looking for. A rubber stamp and a stamp pad. He pulled the big drawer all the way out. Looked. Yeah, there it was. He took them out. I guess I might as well do it now. Bring your books over here. The men with the signs went over and Harry stamped their books. Any sonofabitch that dont get this stamped is gonna get his ass inna sling. One of the men who had just come in asked what was going on. Ya gotta get ya book stamped before ya go out. He came over to the desk with his book out. Ya gotta get a sign first, and Harry went back to the pile of signs and handed one to each of the men. OK, now I'll stamp ya books. Ya oughta put a sign up so the guysll know. I was just gonna do that, and Harry stamped their books and the men put the signs on and looked at each other, smiling and joking. OK you guys, hit the concrete. Its afta 8. And dont all you guys stay in one spot. Spread out and keep moving. No standin still.

The men left and Harry went back to his desk and stamp pad. He ripped a piece of paper off a pad and printed a sign, get book stamped before going, and stuck it over the pile of signs. Men continued to come in and Harry handed out signs and stamped books; told some of them to go to the rear of the plant, and keep movin, no standin still; and when the men came in or back from picketing they poured themselves cups of coffee and stood around the store, or out in front, and talked and joked. In a few hours Harry started to panic with so many men around. Something inside his arms, his stomach, legs, seemed to be tightening and caused him to grind his teeth. He told one of the men to take over for a while, telling him to make sure he stamped the books, and went to Willies next door. He went to the end of the bar and had a couple of drinks and started to relax. He stayed for a while, drinking, until the tenseness faded. He left the bar and walked over to the picket line to see how things were going. He looked scornfully at the cops who were there in case of trouble and waved to the men as he walked around to the side to see how things were going there. He asked one of the men if anybody was around back and he said he thought so and Harry figured he might just as well take a look anyway. He walked the block to the rear of the factory and spoke to the men for a few minutes, reminding them to keep movin so the fuckin cops couldnt have nothin ta say, then went back to the office. He went back to the desk and resumed stamping.

The office wasnt as crowded now, many of the men standing outside in the warm May sun talking, joking, enjoying having a day off with nothing to do but hang around and drink beer and talk with the boys; and others used the time to wash and polish their cars, a steady stream of men walking through the office to fill buckets with water.

During the day Harry made a few more trips to the bar, staying outside after each trip to talk with the men and tell them how they was gonna show these ball breakers who was boss. During the afternoon one of the Union Officials came in and asked Harry how everything was going. He told him he had everything under control. I keep the guys movin. The cops aint got nothin ta bitch about; and you can bet nobodys gettin in the shop except a few pencil stiffs. Youre a good man Harry. Harry smiled his smile. And dont forget, if you need anything just charge it to the union and put it on your expense voucher. And dont forget to send your voucher in each week. Harry was glowing. He nodded. Dont worry about nothin. We'll break their backs. The official left and Harry stretched out in his chair and smoked for a while, talking occasionally to one of the men, then slowly once more started to feel squeezed. He got up from the chair and walked to the back and stood in the yard for a while and started to feel better, but soon some of the men came back too, some bringing chairs, others cards, and in a few minutes a card game had started and Harry went back into the office. He figured hed go for a drink, then asked one of the men if he knew of a joint that delivered beer around there. Yeah, theres a guy down a ways on 2nd avenue. Harry called and an hour later the truck pulled up and a keg of beer was rolled in, tapped and Harry drew the first glass. Before the end of the day the keg was empty and Harry called to have another one delivered, but was told it couldnt be delivered before 5 so Harry said to bring it the first thing in the morning.

By the time the picketing day ended Harry was relaxed and joking with the men as they came in with their signs. When all the signs had been piled against the wall, and everyone gone, Harry stayed to have one last smoke while sitting in his chair behind his desk. The tension that made him feel as if his body was going to split was forgotten now. All the signs were back; the books were stamped; the big boys liked the way he was handling the strike and he had a nice whisky glow. Everything was going along just fine. The men kept moving like they was supposed to and everybody was really workin ta break the bosses backs. Nothin to it. Alls we gotta do is keep that picket line movin and the shop closed and theyll be on their knees beggin us please come back on our terms. The first day of the strike was over.

Harry flopped at the kitchen table and tried to ignore his wife as she served supper and asked questions about how the strike went and how long would it be . . . She put the food on the plates and sat down and started eating, still asking questions, Harry mumbling answers. He glanced at his wife from time to time and soon his body started to tighten and it continued until his body was once more one gigantic knot. He felt like rapping her across the face. He looked at her. She continued to ask questions. He dropped his fork on the plate and got up from the table. Where you going? Back to the office, I think I forget something. He rushed from the house before she could say anything and went to the bar. He went to the end of the bar and stayed there, alone, drinking, saying nothing. After an hour or so he once more started to feel better and soon became conscious of a few of the neighbourhood guys standing a few feet away. Actually what attracted him to them was a high pitched feminine voice. It took a moment or two for him to realise that one of the guys standing near him was a fairy. He looked at him, trying not to be too obvious, lowering his eyes everytime somebody moved his head toward him, slowly raising them again to stare at the fairy. Harry couldnt hear everything he was saying, but he watched the delicate way in which he emphasised what he said with his hands, and the way his neck seemed to move in a hypnotic slowmotioned manner as he talked and gestured. He seemed to be telling the guys about a party, a drag ball, that had taken place last Thanksgiving at a place called Charlie Blacks. Harry continued to stare and listen fascinated.

They stayed there for more than an hour, Harry listening and ignoring his beer. When they left he watched them leave hoping they were going across the street to the Greeks so he could follow them in a few minutes, but they got into a car and drove away. Harry continued to stare out the door after they drove away and only the sudden blaring of music from the jukebox caused him to blink his eyes and turn back to the bar. He lifted his glass automatically and finished his beer.

He stayed at the bar until about midnight, the image of the fairys face and hands still in his mind, his voice still in his ear. When he finished his last beer and left for home he was unaware of his body: partly from his preoccupation with the image and sound, partly from the beer. The fresh air clouded the image slightly, but it was still there. It was still there when he undressed and fell into bed. He lay on his side away from Mary, but soon Marys groping hand and voice forced the image to dissolve. When she first started caressing him it was still with him and excitement shocked through him. Then he became aware of her and there was nothing but her and anger, the anger keeping alive the excitement. He bolted around immediately and pounded on her trying desperately to evoke the image and sound but it was irrevocably gone for now and Mary groaned and scratched.

He rolled over, lay awake for a while, once more almost crying, the confusion blinding him, but he was so exhausted from all that had happened that day that he soon fell asleep.

The next morning he awoke early and left before Mary had a chance to speak to him. He went to the Greeks and had coffee and cake, glancing at the clock every now and then, but still it wasnt even 6:30 yet. He had another cup of coffee, another cake, gulping them down, still looking at the clock every few minutes feeling a need to rush, no thought from what or to where, but only a vague yet crushing pressure of time, time that seemed to wrap itself around him like a python. He dropped money on the counter and went across the street to his office. He went immediately to his desk and sat down, looking at the desk for many minutes – the serpent not loosening its grip – unable to feel the air around his body. He lit a cigarette and looked around the office. He went over to the beer keg and pumped for a while but nothing came out. Not even a hint of foam. It was empty. Theyll be here with another one soon though.

The python continued to crush him and time seemed motionless. The hands on the clock were stuck. The urgency now was not only for him to move, but for time to move too; for the men to come, to take their signs, to walk, to joke, to drink coffee and beer; for him to stamp books, to listen, to tell, to watch. They had to come soon. A cigarette only takes a certain amount of time to smoke and though this takes time it seems to take less and less with each one and you can only smoke so many, there comes a time when you have to stop, when you just cant light the next one . . . at least not for a while.

He opened the rear door and looked around not really seeing anything. Nothing seemed to really exist. The objects in the office were there, they could be seen each in its place, yet still there was confusion. He knew what each object was, what it was for yet there was no real definition. He sat at his desk for a while, walked around for a while . . . sat . . . walked . . . sat . . . walked . . . looked . . . sat . . . walked . . . the only important thing was that the men get there. They had to. The day had to start. He walked . . . sat . . . smoked . . . the python still there. Were there no hands on the clock? He smoked . . . Drew a cup of coffee . . . It was strong, bitter, yet it passed his mouth and throat without leaving a taste. Only a film. Dont clocks tick anymore? Is even the sun motionless. The water is boiled, poured over the coffee and it drips through and time passes . . . even if it only drips it passes . . . through. How long does it take his chair to get from the desk to the wall a few feet behind him when he pushes and the chair rolls on its little wheels? Even that takes time: time enough for a man to walk from the door to the signs, or from the urn to the door; enough time to stamp three books one right after the other: 1,2,3 . . . and yet there was not a definable thought in his mind. Only a terrifying effort to get from one side of a match box to another . . . the door opened and three men came in. Harry jumped up. The python slithered into the match box. The day had begun.

Whattayasay, bumping into the corner of the desk and stumbling toward the men. Bright and early, eh? Thats the way. Cant be too early for those bastards. Theres some coffee left. Have some new coffee soon. Gonna have some beer soon too. The men stood looking at him for a moment hearing his rambling voice, then started moving toward the urn. Guess I'll order some cake an buns and stuff from some baker. Cant go all day without eatin, eh? and the union wants ta take care of its men. Cant hit the concrete without somethin. The men looked at the coffee, poured it out and started putting on signs. Dont forget to get ya book stamped, adjusting the sign on one of the men then rushing back to his desk, yanking open the drawer and plunging his hand in and bulldozing it back and forth until he found the stamp and ink pad. Gotta get yabook stamped. Anybody who dont have a stamp is gonna get his ass ina sling. The first crew who walked yesterday did a good job. Ya just gotta keep movin or the copsll break ya balls. The men put their books on the table, looking at each other as Harry pounded the books with the stamp, still rambling. The fuckin copsed just love ta try and break the picket line. The men started moving toward the door. Dont stay in a mob, but stay apart and keep movin. You guys can take the front. I'll send the other guys around back and on the sides and if anybody gives ya any trouble just yell, aint nobody gonna break this strike. The men left and started across the street to the factory, Harry yelling after them ta keep movin and make sure only the punk pencil pushers get in. The men shook their heads and continued walking. They had a little time to put in and then the day was theirs. Strikes can be OK sometimes. It was a nice day.

Harry hustled around the office. The beer should be there soon. He looked at the signs. They were OK. A few more men came in and Harry said ta grab a sign and he stamped their books and told them where to walk, and ta keep movin, and more men came in and grabbed signs and the day was really there now and soon the man came with the beer and Harry told him to come back with two more kegs later and Harry called for boxes of cakes and buns and signed all the bills spreading his signature across the bottom of the paper and putting his title, shop steward local 392, under it and Harry kept his glass filled with beer all through the day and the men came and went, took signs, returned them, had their books stamped; washed and polished their cars, played cards or just stood around talking and joking, enjoying the clear sky and warm weather; leaving when they finished their tour of duty and joking about the three day weekend and about this being the first Friday theyve had off since they cant remember when and not many of them took the strike seriously. Theyd have to picket for a while, a few days maybe even a week or two, but in weather like this who cares (if it gets a little warmer we can even go to the beach after walking) and theyll make the money back in no time with the raise and the unions going to give them food next Saturday so theres really nothing to worry about. It was an early vacation.

The keg of beer was empty almost an hour before the other two were delivered and Harry and a few others who had been drinking steadily were slightly drunk. When the two kegs were set up Harry told the guy to bring four more Monday morning. That should lastus, and he laughed his laugh.

During the afternoon Harry sat in the yard, in the back, drinking and talking with some of the men as they played cards or just sat around. When some one took a sign he yelled at them to come in the back and get their book stamped and they kidded him about what a hard job he had and he slapped them on the back and laughed his laugh and the men laughed and put on their signs and walked up and down around the factory, talking with the cops, kidding them about having to be there longer than they did and the cops smiled telling them they wished they could strike and maybe then theyd get a break and that they hoped the men got what they wanted without being out of work too long and occasionally one of the men would stand still for a moment and look at the cops and smile and someone else would yell, laughingly, to keep moving and the teams of pickets changed every hour or so and the conversation would start from the beginning between themselves and the cops, only an occasional word changing and then the cops too got a relief and the ones leaving waved to the men, happy that their day had ended and their weekend started and the new cops stood silent for a while, but they too, soon started talking with the pickets and everyone enjoyed the weather and the novelty and the day moved along as logically as the sun.

Harry was drunk by the time the last sign was piled against the wall. He put his stamp and pad back in the drawer and he and a couple of others stayed and finished the beer, hanging over the keg, pumping and pumping until nothing came out of the tap but a hiss. Harry put his arms around the shoulders of the two near him and told them they would show those sonsofbitches. And especially that punk Wilson. I'll show that fuckin fairy, that queer punk. They all laughed.

Harry went across the street to the Greeks after locking his office. Some of the neighbourhood guys were there, among them the ones who were in the bar last night, and Harry sat at the counter and ordered something to eat and occasionally spoke to the guys about the strike, they asking him how it was going and he telling them they hadem by the balls and they should come over and have a drink. He hung around the Greeks for a few hours until the guys left then he too left and went home.

The next day he slept late and left the house right after eating and went to the Greeks, but it was too early for any of the guys to be there. He sat around for a while then went over to his office and sat at his desk. He smoked a few cigarettes then called the Secretary of local 392 and told him that he was in the office just checkin on things and the Secretary told him he was doing a good job and Harry hung up the phone and tried to think of someone else to call but he couldnt think of another except the beer distributors number. He called them. He told them who he was and said that they might as well send over the four kegs now as wait for Monday. He sat around for a while, filled out his expense sheet then walked around the office until the beer was delivered and the kegs set up then he filled a pitcher and sat at his desk with it and a glass drinking and watching the street.

Sometime in the middle of the afternoon he saw a car park in front of the Greeks and a few of the guys get out so he locked the office and went to the Greeks. He asked the guys how they were doing and they nodded and he sat for a while with them, but no one else came in. Eventually he asked them if they would like some beer, I got four fuckin kegs in the office, and they said yeah, so they left, the guys leaving word with the counterman where they would be and went to the office. Harry got them glasses and he and Vinnie, Sal and Malfie sat around drinking beer. Harry told them how he was in charge of the office and the entire strike, but they didnt pay too much attention to him, figuring him for a creep from the first time he spoke to them, and just yeahd him and drank the beer and looked around the office. Malfie told him he should have a radio so they could listen to some music and Vinnie and Sal agreed and Harry said he didnt have one, but maybe he should get one. Yeah, sure yashould. The union oughtta give yaone so yawont go nuts just sittin around here doin nothin. Yeah. Why not. Harry told them he had a lot to do takin care of the strike. Ya dont know all the – if the unionll pay for the beer they should pay for a radio. Yeah. If you toldem yaneeded one they couldnt say nothin. Yeah. Yeah, they wouldnt say nothin if I got one. Yeah, and afta the strike ya could take it home. Who would know the difference. Yeah, why not? We can gettya a good one for 20, 30 bucks. Krist, thats a lotta money. A lotta money? Whats 30 bucks to the union. They got millions. We'll getya a good radio and yacan giveus the money and get it from the union. Dont worry about it, they wont say nothin. As soon as we see a good one we'll pick it up forya. The guys looked at each other and smiled thinking of the radio in the window of the new store on 5th avenue. We should be able ta get yaone by tomorrow. Yeah, a real nice job.

They continued drinking and talking, Harry telling them about the union and what he was doing. From time to time he picked up the empty pitcher and refilled it and set it on his desk, being sure to push his chair back and let it roll to the wall before getting up. After a few hours a few more of the guys came in and by the time the sun set Harry was getting drunk and entertaining about a dozen of the neighbourhood guys, feeling like a patriarch because he was in charge of the strike. The guys drank the beer and ignored Harry, talking to him only when necessary; yet Harry was happy, enjoying having them around him and excited with anticipation. He asked Vinnie, laughing and slapping him on the shoulder, who that fruit was that was with them the othernight and Vinnie told him she was just one of the queens from uptown, onea Georgettes friends. Why, ya wanna meeter? Naw, slapping Vinnies knee, what the fuck I wanna meet a fuckin fruit for. I dont know, maybe ya go for that stuff, laughing and peering at Harry. Haha, leaning back in his chair, pushing with his hands against the desk, the chair rolling back to the wall. I was just wonderin what ya guys were doing with a fruit. I didnt think yahung around with those kindda fucks. Theyre OK sometimes. Theyre always good for loot when they got it and they getya high when yawanna. Stick around. She may be around later, smiling. Hahaha, rolling the chair back to the desk. I dont go for that shit. Im strickly a cunt man myself. I was just wonderin how come he hung around with you guys is all. I got more cunt than ya could fuck in a year. Shit, last night I had ta chase one away, a good looking bitch too, but I promised the old lady Id throw a fuck inner, you know how it is. Ya gotta – Vinnie turned his head and started talking to Sal and some of the other guys, but Harry couldnt stop: he soliloquised about the babe who picked him up a few weeks ago and took him home and she had a new car and the blond and how many more women who damned near fucked the ass offim, but they couldnt do that, he could out fuck any woman around and he never did like queers, everytime he saw one he wanted ta rapim in his mouth and whenever he throws a fuck inta the old lady she creams all over the place and Vinnie and the guys got up and walked away and Harry leaned toward a few of the other guys near by, his voice still working, the words still spilling, his laugh blurting out occasionally and he stopped for a second, drank his beer, filled the glass again and continued talking, lower, walking around telling the guys he could fixem up anytime they wanted ta get a good piece a tail and a few nodded, one or two even smiled, and soon Harry was able to stop talking and he went back to his desk and drank beer, more rapidly, keeping all the pitchers full, telling the guys ta drinkup, theres plenty more, the unions gonna keep the beer flowin, hahaha, and he emptied another glass, refilled it and soon was unable to move without staggering and he sat at his desk, pushing his chair back and forth from time to time, spilled a glass of beer on his desk and laughed as it trickled off the edge, someone yelling that it was a good strike and a few others yelled, yeah, and Harry laughed his laugh and pushed the beer off the desk with the palm of his hand and said theres plenty more and the guys laughed and soon tired of hanging around with Harry and told him goodbye, we'll seeya, keep the beer cold, and Harry asked them not to go, hang around a while. We'll getus some pussy later, but the guys said they had business and left.

Harry looked at his desk, the glass and pitcher of beer. Haha. No work tomorrow. Gotta piss. He stood, bumped against the desk, shoved his chair back and laughed when it banged against the wall, leaned on the desk looking at the beer then staggered to the yard and pissed, sighing. Thats what I needed. A good piss, haha. Nothin like a good piss. Maybe the guysll come back tomorrow, ahh . . . thats betta. He turned off the lights and went home.

He left the house the next morning as soon as he dressed and went to his office. He filled a pitcher with beer and sat at his desk. He leaned back and put his feet on the desk. It was kindda nice to sit alone and drink beer for a while. He could use the relaxation. Hed been working hard on the strike and tomorrow would be another busy day. It was kindda nice to sit alone in his office. He really liked it. It really wasnt so bad. He picked up the pitcher to refill his glass. It was empty. Didnt think hed been there that long, but I guess maybe I have. He laughed and got up and refilled the pitcher and then his glass. Somea the guys should be around soon. Must be late enough. He sat back and put his feet back up on the desk. It wasnt bad being alone though. For a while.

A car stopped in front of the Greeks and he got up from his desk and went to the door and yelled across to the guys going into the Greeks. They looked and strolled across the street, Vinnie carrying a package. Harry stood at the door as they walked in and the guys flopped around after filling glasses with beer. Vinnie put the package on the desk and tore the paper off. Here yaare Harry. We toldya we'd getya a radio. Hows this? pretty good, eh? If we wasnt so desperate for loot youd never get it. Harry walked over to the desk and looked at the radio, turned the knobs and watched the needle move along the dial. Youre lucky we're beat man or we'd never giveit toya for a lousy 30 skins. Now at least we can have some music around here. This joints like a morgue, unwinding the cord and plugging it in. It even has short wave man, turning the dial and stopping when a voice singing in a foreign language came from the radio. See. I wish ta fuck I could keep the thing. Yeah, it sounds pretty good, turning the dial again, stopping as the sound of different languages reached them. Hey Vin, get some music, yeah? Vinnie switched it back to the standard band and Harry reached over and started toying with the dial. He watched the needle move slowly across the lighted numbers and when a screeching sax wailed someone yelled, thats it man, and a hand pushed Harrys from the knob and tuned in the sax. The volume was turned up and someone told Harry ta fill up the pichas and someone slapped him on the back, great set, eh man? and Harry nodded and picked up a pitcher and refilled it and he watched and listened to the guys snap their fingers and yell with the music and Harry felt their friendship and felt too, again, spasms of expectation and everything seemed sortofright and Harry felt comfortable.

When Vinnie told him to give him the money now Harry took the thirty dollars from his wallet and handed it to him and told the guys ta drink up, the brewery needs the barrels and laughed and toldem theres plenty more and once more started blithering and babbling about the union and women and the guys just ignored him and continued to drink until they got bored and left Harry with his beer and radio. Harry sat alone for a while listening to his radio, toying with the dials, drinking the beer, laughing his laugh, gripping the knobs tighter and twirling them fast then slow, moving the dial where and as he pleased, listening to a station for a few minutes, changing it, tuning in shortwave and feeling that he could drag the foreign countries in as he pleased.

He stayed at his desk drinking beer and listening to his radio until his head started to hang toward his chest. He emptied his glass, unplugged the radio, put it under his desk, put out the lights, locked the door and started walking the few blocks, which would only take a few minutes and was only a short distance away, home.

Harry was sick the next morning but dragged himself from the house to his office. His entire body was twitching and Harry forced down a few beers to straighten himself out before the men came. He got a couple of glasses down and a half dozen aspirin, his headache slowly leaving and the turmoil in his stomach subsiding, yet he still felt a tension, an apprehension, and he cursed the bars for not being open yet so he could get a shot and get rid of his hangover. When the men started coming, a little before 8, their joking and laughter, as they grabbed signs and had their books stamped, annoyed Harry. When all the signs had been distributed and fresh coffee made, Harry went to the bar for a couple of fast shots and came back convinced he felt better. When he got back to the office he turned the radio on and sat behind his desk drinking beer and joking with the men. When one of the officials called Harry told him he had bought a radio for the office, figured the men'd like a little music or maybe hear a ballgame when they come off the line, and the official told him to send a bill to the union and he would be reimbursed. Harry hung up the phone and sat back in his chair feeling very official and important; and although the morning passed slowly for Harry until he got over his hangover, the afternoon passed rapidly, especially after his phone conversation (strike headquarters, local 392, Brother Black talkin) with the union official.

When the last of the men left that night Harry sat at his desk drinking for a while then went across the street to the

Greeks. He ate slowly until a few of the guys came in and then ate rapidly, talking and laughing. When he finished they went back to the office and drank and listened to the radio, the guys ignoring Harry as usual, just nodding or mumbling an occasional answer. A few more of the guys came in but they didnt stay too long and once again Harry was sitting behind his desk alone with a pitcher of beer and a glass. The sun had set and the street was quiet and cool and though Harry had been drinking beer all day, and had been feeling relaxed for hours, the butterflies in his stomach started again as he walked home.

The baby was asleep when he got there and Mary was watching TV, waiting for him. She called him in the living room and Harry sat in a chair, Mary leaning over to rub his ear, Harry too confused and not drunk enough to shove her hand away. After rubbing his ear for a few minutes without Harry twisting his head away Mary sat on the arm of the chair and put an arm around his neck. A short time later she coaxed him into the bedroom and Harry undressed and lay beside her until she pulled him on her. Harry continued to drift, as he had through the day, only silently and lethargically, still experiencing the sharp depression that overcame him when the guys left and he was alone with his radio, beer, desk and chair, the depression of disappointment after a long wait. When Mary pulled him over on her he allowed his body to move in the directed direction and she put her arms around him, breathing on his neck, rolling under him. Harry just lay on her until he became conscious of her voice then rolled off, lit a cigarette and lay on his side smoking. Mary rubbed his back, kissed his neck and Harry continued to smoke, still immobile, still silent and Mary rubbed his ear and rubbed his arms until Harry eventually shook her hands off. Mary lay on her back for a while, mumbling and rolling slightly from side to side, Harry still silent, until Harry finally put his cigarette out and adjusted himself to go to sleep. Mary looked at his back for a while then rolled over on her side, pulled her knees up toward her chin and eventually fell asleep.

Mary told Harry tagotahell when he told her to fix breakfast. He told her again to fix breakfast or hed break her fuckin head. Do it yourself and dont botha me. Harry called her a fuckin slut and left the house. Harry couldnt remember how he had felt the night before, but he did know he felt different this morning, the usual resentment against Mary filling his thoughts. She was once more responsible for his misery as were the bosses for the fact that he didnt make much money. Between them they tried to make his life miserable; they tried ta fuckim everytime he moved; if it wasnt for them things would be different.

Harry slowed down in his bustling around the office as the days passed until, after a few weeks, he just sat, most of the time, behind his desk except for an occasional walk to the line to relieve the tension of just sitting in the small office. The men too slowed and while on the picket line moved just enough not to be standing still. When they spoke with each other it was with comparatively quiet voices and when they spoke with the police it was just a word or two, or, more usually, a nod. There was no desperation in their appearance or action, but the novelty of being on strike was over and now it was just like a job like any other job only they werent getting paid for this. What little lightheartedness remained after the first full week of picketing slowly vanished with the forming of each Saturday food line and when the men went home with $10 worth of groceries. They had to report to the meeting hall and before the food was distributed the President gave a speech and the first Saturday he told them what a fine job they were doing on the line and especially praised brother Harry Black for the way in which he carried out his duties as organiser and administrator of the strike field office. He told the men that they had met with the companies negotiating committee each day the past week, but they were offering starvation wages and that their committee refused to give in to them even if they had to stay on strike a year. When he finished speaking the clique stamped, cheered and whistled and soon most of the men were applauding the President as he jumped from the platform and walked among the men slapping them on their backs and shaking their hands. Then the men lined up for their food bags. There were many comments, jokes and laughter as the lines slowly moved forward and each man was handed his bag, but when they were alone the bag looked small. The second Saturday the Presidents speech was even shorter, the applause quieter, the men more silent as they stood on line. Only a few could think of something funny to say. And so each week ended.

When the men first started picketing the plant they would make jokes about the few executives who were going to work, greeting them occasionally with jeers and boos, but soon they cursed them each morning and each night, the police telling them to shut up and keep moving. After the first few weeks had passed the men stood still as the executives entered the building and started threatening them, the police waving their clubs in their faces and telling them to be quiet and keep the lines moving or they would pull them in. Each day the voices, curses and threats of the men were more vehement and after a few weeks more police were stationed at the entrance of the building in the morning and evening; and when they told the men to watch themselves and keep moving the men spit in front of the cops or mumbled something about goons; and each day the routine was the same except that it grew more intense and the men were continually looking for an excuse to hit someone, anyone; and the police were just waiting for someone to start something so they too could find relief from the boredom by cracking someones skull. And as the boredom increased so did the resentment: the resentment of the men toward the cops for being there and trying to prevent them from winning the strike; and the police toward the strikers for making it necessary for them to stand around like this for hours each day when they werent even allowed to go on strike if they wanted more money. The men moved as slowly as possible, sneering at the police when they passed them; and the police stood facing them all day swinging their clubs by the leather thong and telling the men to keep moving if they stopped even for a second; and the men would stand still for a moment, staring, hoping someone would say fuckyou to one of the cops so they could wrap their signs around their heads, but no one said anything and as a cop took a step forward the men started moving again and the strike and the game continued.

When the men came back to the office now they dropped their signs on the floor, Harry telling them at first to take it easy then, after being told to go fuckhimself a few times, said nothing and picked the signs up when they left. Soon new signs had to be painted and each time the men saw newly painted signs they became more bitter and cursed the fucks in the company who were keeping them out of work, and cursed the cops for helping those fuckin-bellyrobbers.

The company had been preparing for the strike many months before it started and so, when the first pickets donned their signs and started parading jubilantly up and down in front of the factory, the existing orders had been filled and work transferred to other plants throughout the country or subcontracted to other firms and the primary, and almost only, concern of the executives in the Brooklyn factory was coordinating the transferring and shipping of work and finished products between the various plants and subcontractors. The first few days of the strike were hectic and, at times, slightly chaotic for those executives responsible for co-ordinating work between the various firms, but after that everything proceeded routinely with only an occasional emergency that would be met with long distance calls and soon enough the situation would once more be under control.

When the strike was months old a call came from one of the factories located in the northern part of New York State where the final assembling of large units was being done. The contract was a time penalising one and if all the units werent delivered by the specified date a $1,000 per day, for each day over the time, would have to be defaulted by the company. The work had already been delayed for three days because of various failures and breakdowns, but the assembly line had finally been set up and half the factory and personnel were geared to complete the work by the specified time. The work had proceeded smoothly, and it was determined that the work would be completed on time, when it was discovered that one of the final elements, made in the Brooklyn plant, was missing. A call went in immediately to the Brooklyn plant and a quick check of the records indicated that the entire lot had been finished the day before the strike started but, for some reason, had never been shipped. The shipping department was almost empty so the creates containing the needed parts were found quickly. A call was made to the upstate plant and the information relayed along with a promise that they would go out tonight.

Mr. Harrington cursed the men with him, but only for a moment, then started calling small neighbourhood trucking firms to find one that would cross the picket line and deliver the material. He finally found one who said he would do it and quoted a fantastic price, but the manager had no choice but to agree and made out a cheque for half the amount, the other half to be paid when the delivery was made.

The men on the picket line were startled when the trucks turned into the runway leading to the loading platform, but only for a second. They yelled at the drivers of the trucks that they were on strike and the drivers yelled fuck you. A few of the men tried to jump on the hoods of the trucks, but fell; a few others picked up stones and tin cans and threw them at the drivers but they just bounced off the cabs. When the men tried to follow the trucks to the platform the police grabbed them and held them back. The yelling of the men on the picket line was heard by the others hanging around the office and they came running; and a call was made from one of the police cars for additional men. Some of the police formed a line across the runway while the others pushed the men back. Soon there were hundreds of men yelling and pushing; those in the rear shouting to shove the fuckin cops outta the way and get those fuckinscabs; the men in front screaming in the faces of the cops and being shoved by the mob behind them into the line of police that was slowly weakening. For many minutes the amoeba like mass flowed forward, backward and around, arms and signs bobbing up and down over heads, clubs raised; red infuriated faces almost pressed together, words and spit bouncing off faces; anger clouding and watering eyes. Then more police arrived by the carsfull. Then a firetruck. Men leaped from the cars and were assimilated by the mass. A fire hose was quickly unravelled and connected; a loudspeaker screeched and told the men to breakitup. FUCKYOU FLATFOOT GO AND FUCKYASELF YASONOFABITCH IF YOU MEN DONT BREAKITUP WE'LL RUN YOU ALL IN NOW GET BACK FROM THAT RUNWAY YEAH, SURE, AFTA WE BREAK THOSE FUCKINSCABSHEADS DERE TA-

KIN THE BREAD FROM OUR MOUTHS IM TELL-
ING YOU FOR THE LAST TIME, BREAKITUP OR
I'LL TURN THE HOSE ON YOU WHO PAID YAOFF
YASONOFABITCH. The line of police had been extended and was pushing as hard as it could against the
mob, but the men became more incensed as more cops
fought them and the voice threatened them and they felt
the power of their numbers and the frustration and lost
hope of fruitless months on the picket and food lines
finally found the release it had been looking for. Now
there was something tangible to strike at. And the police
who had been standing, bored, for months as the men
walked up and down, telling them to keep moving,
envying them because they at least could do something
tangible to get more money while all they could do was
put in a request to the mayor and be turned down by the
rotten politicians, finally found the outlet they too had
been waiting for and soon the line became absorbed by
the mass and two and three went down to their knees and
then others too, strikers and cops, and a sign swooped
through the air and thudded against a head and a white
gloved hand went up and then a club thudded and hands,
clubs, signs, rocks, bottles were lifted and thrown as if
governed by a runaway eccentric rod and the mass spread
out, some falling over others and heads popped out of
windows and doorways and peered and a few cars
parked cautiously or slowed and observed for a moment
and the mass continued to wallow along and across 2nd
avenue as a galaxy through the heavens with the swoosh-
ing of comets and meteors and the voice that screeched
now directed itself to the firemen and they walked slowly
toward the grinding mass and a white glove clutched at a
head and the glove turned red and occasionally a bloody
body would be exuded from the mass and roll a foot or
two and just lie there or perhaps wriggle slightly and four

or five beaten and bloodied cops managed to work their way free from the gravity of the mass and stood side by side and walked back to the mass swinging their clubs and screaming and a sign was broken over one of their heads but the cop only screamed louder and continued to swing, still walking, until his club was broken over a head and he picked up the broken sign without breaking rank and continued and the thudding of the clubs on heads was only slightly audible and the sound not at all unpleasant as it was muted by the screams and curses and they stepped over a few bodies until a line of strikers was somehow formed and they charged the cops not stopping as the clubs were methodically pounded on their heads and the two lines formed a whirling heated nebula that spun off from the galaxy to disintegrate as the strikes overwhelmed them and kicked the cops as they tried to regain their feet or roll away and sirens screeched but were unheard and more police jumped from cars and trucks and another fire hose was unraveled and aimed the order given to open the hydrants and not wait until the police who were whirling with the strikers could extricate themselves and a few of the strikers noticed the second hose being readied and then noticed the first hose and charged the firemen but the water leaped forth in an overpowering gush and one of the men took the full force in his abdomen and his mouth jutted open but if a sound came out it was unheard and he doubled over and spun like a gyroscope runamuck bouncing off the men behind him and bouncing to the curb and those who were behind him were knocked and spun and a few policemen ran frantically to the various street corners trying to direct and divert traffic but all of the cars moved slowly no matter how urgently the police waved them on not wanting to miss any of the excitement and the voice screeched again giving directions and the two powered battering rams were directed with knowledge and precision and soon the mass was a chaos of colliding particles that bounced tumbled and whirled around against and over each other and soon it was quiet enough to hear the ambulance sirens and the louder moans that spewed from the mass and soon too the street was clear of the smaller debris and even the blood had been washed away.

The fire hoses were shut off and those who were injured too seriously to move unaided were helped to the sidewalk where they sat down and leaned against the buildings or were helped into one of the waiting ambulances or patrol cars and taken to the hospital. The street was still congested with men, cars, trucks, ambulances and onlookers. There were still hundreds of strikers standing in small groups talking, helping injured strikers, looking at the cops and waiting for the trucks to come out. Harry, who had carefully avoided the fight, moved from group to group, his shirt hanging out, hair mussed and face dirtied, cursing the bosses, the cops and those fuckin scabs, asking the men how they were and slapping them on the back.

The police too were concerned about the trucks. Additional men had arrived and a barricade was setup to keep the strikers away from the runway and the hoses were placed in strategic positions. Again the voice told the strikers to breakitup and again the men said FUCKYOU and remained where they were: eyeing the cops, who stood behind the barricade, and the firemen with their hoses. The voice told them they didnt want to use force but, if they didnt disperse immediately, that force would be used. The men yelled and cursed and started spreading out getting ready to charge the barricade as soon as the trucks came up the runway. The voice told them they had exactly 60 seconds before the hoses would be turned on again and started counting. There were still 30 seconds left when the first truck was heard coming up the runway. The counting was stopped and the hoses were ordered turned on. The men had yet to take their first forward step when the water hit them. The hoses were used expertly and none of the strikers reached the barricade until the trucks were almost a block away and then they just stood yelling and cursing.

When the trucks were out of sight the men backed away from the barricade, stood looking at the cops for a few minutes then slowly walked away, going home or back to the office. The police and firemen slowly gathered up their equipment and went back to their various stationhouses. 83 men were hospitalised.

Some of the strikers going back to the office carried the remnants of signs, some helped others still bleeding or still dazed from the fight. The injured men were driven home, Harry telling them hed see that their books were marked that they got hurt; the others crowded into the office or hung around outside.

The men in the office were still yelling and cursing, Harry passing out beer, telling them how he clobbered a cop – hoping no one had noticed he avoided the fight – or how he just missed getting hit with a club, but everyone was too angry to pay any attention to him just as they had been too busy to remember who was where during the fight. Harry eventually worked his way over to his desk and sat down with a beer, extremely conscious of the noise and wondering if there was something he could do. He leaned on the desk, sipped his beer, wishing a thought would pop into his head. It wasnt until he saw the President and a few other officials forcing their way through the crowd that he realised he should have called the union office. He leaped up and stumbled around his desk shouting that he had been trying to reach the office and everyone was yelling and crowding around the officials and they stood still and yelled for the men to be quiet, for krists sake. How can we find out what happened with everybody yelling. They all started yelling again and the officials waved their hands and the men started to quiet and Harry tried to force his way forward but one of the men placed himself in front of the President and told him hed tellem what happened. I was on the line when the trucks came in. What trucks? All the men started answering and yelling and the officials waved their arms again and the man who had started talking yelled ta shuttup. I'll tellem what happened. We was on the line when all ofasudden these 4 trucks come down 2nd avenue and turned down the runway to the loadin platform . . . When the entire story had been told the President asked if anyone saw the name of the trucking company and one of the men said he knewem. Ive seen those trucks in the neighborhood, and he gave the officials the name and told them where they were usually parked. Then the President told the men that everything would be taken care of and that no more trucks would pass the line and that they should go home and take it easy and that from now on there would be someone watching the street at all times and when anything, I mean anything and I dont give a fuck what it is, tries to pass the line that everybody was to haulass over to the line and block the joint. The men yelled, yeah, we'll show the fucks. But dont hang around the plant or the copsll only start again. The law says you can only have so many men on the picket line and theyll use any excuse they can to split your skulls so dont givem the chance. Try and stay off the street as much as possible when youre not on the line and they cant do a thing.

The President went over to the desk and made a phone call while the other officials shook hands with the men and patted them on the back as they walked them toward the door. The President was on the phone for some time, making arrangements to have more signs printed and making certain that they would definitely be in the strike office by 8 oclock in the morning; then spoke to a few other people in the union office and by the time he finished the office was empty except for the other officials and Harry, who had been standing behind him ever since he first picked up the phone.

Harry offered him a cigarette then fumbled for a match, the President finally taking one out of his own pocket. Harry tried to tell him how he had tried to stop the trucks, but was interrupted by the other officials who started talking to the President. They formed a small huddle, talking low, Harry standing on the fringe, and Vinnie and Sal came in. Whattayasay Harry? I hear yahad a little trouble. Yeah man, I hear we missed a good rumble. They filled a couple of glasses with beer then rejoined Harry. Ya not gonna letem getaway with that shit, areya? Yabet yasweet ass we're not. Dont worry, itll never happen again. If it wasnt for the fuckin cops they never wouldve got pastus. Shitman, theres other ways ta stopem. Yeah, smiling at each other and drinking their beer. Whattaya-mean? Shit, all yagotta do – the President came over and asked Harry who they were. Harry told him their names and said they were a couple of the guys from the neigh-borhood. This is the President of the union. Whattayasay. Had a little trouble, eh? Not too much. You boys have something on your minds? Just a little business proposi-tion, eh Sal? Yeah. Like what? Like gettin ridda the trucks. Is it worth 200 taya ta get riddathem? Do you think you can do it without any trouble? Yeah. If theyre parked where that guy says they are itll be a slopeout. The President turned his back to the others, gave them $200, said goodbye to Harry and left with the other officials. Sal and Vinnie split the money, finished their beers and left. Another day of the strike had ended.

The next day there were hundreds of men at the office by a few minutes after 8. By 8:30 they were spread throughout the office and the street drinking coffee, eating cake and drinking beer. The signs had been delivered a few minutes after Harry opened the office and the men rushed with firstdayofthestrike eagerness to grab them and set up the picket line. They joked, laughed and slapped each other on the back energetically, as they did that first day, but they werent relaxed as they were then, but were tensed and hopeful, hopeful of another fight but this time they would be expecting it and would be ready and each man could animate the dreams and thoughts of the night before where they stopped the trucks, pulled the drivers from the cabs and beat their skulls in, each man doing it singlehandedly or, at the most, with the help of a few friends; and when the cops tried to stop them they took their clubs from them and bashed their fuckinskullstoapulp then took the fire hoses and washed the rotten bastards down the fuckin sewer. They drank beer and coffee, continually looking toward the factory, slapping each other on the shoulder but, as they did they tensed their muscles wishing, and hoping takrist, that it was the face of one of the shiteatin cops or one of the scabbastard drivers that they were shovin their fist in . . . or maybe one of the punk executives would givem some shit and they could beat his ass.

But no one came to work that day and no trucks came within two blocks of the factory. Mr. Harrington told the others to stay home, it was Friday and one day would not do any harm. The shipment went out and there was nothing left that they had to do; and by Monday the strikers would have gotten over their anger and everything would settle back into the routine of the days, months, preceding the fight. The men stayed all day, greeting each newcomer loudly, slapping briskly, but as the day moved and nothing happened they became tired of commenting on all the cops they had there now, must be over a hundred ofem, and how theyd like to break their fuckin skulls; and as the day slowly passed so did their enthusiasm, their frustration and anger increasing. Their cursing was more vehement but it not only lacked organisation it also lacked direction. The cops were just standing there, saying nothing; there were no trucks trying to break the line and no wiseyoungpunkofapencilpusher trying to take the bread from their mouths.

The sky remained cloudless all day and the sun bright. It was hot. Very hot. A perfect day for the beach, but none of them were in a mood to enjoy the beach yet they cursed those bastards, if it wasnt for them they could be down the beach now or sittin home with a can of beer watching the ballgame on TV. And they cursed those bastards to each other and by mid afternoon the 4 kegs of beer were empty and Harry ordered a few more and they were delivered rightaway, but some of the men were tired of drinking beer and they drifted, in small groups, into the bar next door to get something stronger, something more satisfying and by the time 5 oclock came, and the sun still had a few hours before it set, their anger was simply anger, no longer even attempting to direct it but just letting it grow until they went home and passed out or got in a fight in a neighborhood bar. When the men left Harry told them to be back bright and bright and early Monday.

Harry felt good sitting at his desk drinking beer and smoking. He had spent the day telling the men how the union wouldnt let them get away with that kindda shit, and wishing he could tell them what he had planned to do to the trucks. If only he could tell them. Then theyd really know how important he is. But whatthefuck, theyd know how important he was anyway. Yeah. He put his feet up on the desk and emptied his glass and leaned back thinking of how soon all the men would nod and say hello when he came by and hed really be respected and maybe he could get rid of that bitchofawife who was always breakin his balls and gettinhim so nervous he could hardly work sometimes and then that fuckinpencilpushinpunk wilson would shit when Harry Black came around and his smile almost became a smile and he refilled his glass, lit a cigarette, closed his eyes and watched wilson and some of the other punks cowering in fear.

Sal and Vinnie left the Greeks a little after 11, stole a car, got a few cans of gasoline and drove to the small lot where the trucks were parked. They stopped for a moment, looked around, then drove around the block a few times, then the neighborhood for about 10 minutes or so making sure there were no streets closed for any reason or cops in the vicinity, then drove back to the lot and parked the car. The trucks were old models with gas tanks on the side. They tossed gasoline over the trucks, opened the gas tanks, soaked rags in gasoline and put them in the tank openings letting them hang to the ground, then poured a line of gasoline from one rag to the other, all the lines connecting and leading toward the exit. They put the empty gas cans back in the car then lit the stream of gas and ran to the car. They waited until they saw the first trucks catch fire then drove away, turning left on 3rd avenue and speeding as fast as they could for a few blocks then turned down to 2nd avenue which was completely deserted. About a minute after they left the lot they heard an explosion and saw a red glow in the sky. There goes the first one Vin. Looks kindda pretty, eh? Yeah. Itll look even better when the others go too. Yeah, and they laughed. They were half way back to the Greeks when they heard more explosions, muffled but still identifiable, and the glow in the sky was brighter. Pretty good job, eh? Yeah. I guess we gavem their moneys worth. You know Sal, we could go in business if the strike lasts long enough. Yeah, laughing. They ditched the car, first dumping the gas cans, and went back to the Greeks.

Harry was standing on the sidewalk looking down 2nd avenue toward the glow in the sky. Harry laughed his laugh when he saw Sal and Vinnie. Whaddayause a hand grenade? hahaha. Whattayasay Harry? Whattayadoin here? I came ta watch the fireworks, haha. Ya guys sure know how ta blow things up, haha. Take it easy, eh man. Yeah, dont talk so fuckin loud. Dont worry. We're not, but youd betta get home. If the law comes around they'll drag yaass in. Yeah, turning away from the creep and going into the Greeks. I'll seeya, laughing his laugh and going home.

Harry had a long lovely sleep. When he awoke, late in the morning, he lit a cigarette and looked at the ceiling, closing his eyes from time to time, hearing, but not paying attention to, the sounds Mary made, as she walked around the apartment, and his son, as he played on the living room floor. He thought of that lovely red glow in the sky and how hed like to go up to wilson and the boss and tell them ta watch out or theyd get their asses blown up too, just like those fuckin scab trucks ya sent out. Ya may think youre a big wheel or somethin, but dont fuck with me or youll be sorry, yahear? Dont fuck with Harry Black, Shop Steward of Local 392 so watch it buddy, youre not fuckin with a nobody. Im on the union payroll now and dontya forget it because I pull weight around here and I get my money every week no matter how long the strike lasts and what Mary dont know wont hurt her, I could use the extra money myself anyway, Im the fuckin boss around here and she'd betta not fuck with me either or I'll throw her ass out in the street. Id be betta off withouter the way shes always breakin my balls . . .

Harry stayed in bed for a couple of hours, looking at the ceiling, closing his eyes smoking, his face twisting occasionally into an almost smile. When he got up he dressed and went up to the Greeks. He had a couple of cups of coffee and something to eat and sat around for a while then told the counterman to tell Sal and Vinnie, or any of the guys that come in, that he was across the street in his office.

He filled a pitcher with beer, grabbed a glass and sat at his desk, rolling the chair back and forth a few times. He sat at the desk for a few minutes then jumped up and went next door to the bar and asked the bartender if he had todays paper. Yeah, theres one on the table in the back. Take it if yawant. Harry took the paper and left the bar waving to the bartender. Seeya lateta. He spread the paper out on his desk, after looking at the front page, and looked at the centrefold. There was a small picture of a few trucks burning. The caption said that the trucks were parked in the lot for the night and had mysteriously burst into flames and exploded. No one was injured. Harry guzzled some beer, licked his lips and stared at the picture, almost smiling, for many minutes, then called the union office. I see in the paper that a couplea trucks got burned last night, hahaha. Yes, the police have been here already. No shit? what happened? Nothing. They asked some questions and we told them that we knew nothing about it. Fuckem, the pricks. Right, and the conversation was ended.

Harry had almost finished his second pitcher of beer when Sal, Vinnie, a few of the other guys and the fairy that had been in the bar, came in. Harry got up and waved to the guys, whattayasay, looking at the fairy, watching her walk daintily across the floor toward him. The guys grabbed glasses. Howd yalike that little job we did? Not bad, eh? and someone handed the fairy a glass. She eyed it disdainfully, I hope you dont expect me to drink from this filthy thing . . . really! Theres a sink in the back. Go washit. What the fuck ya bitchin about? youve had worse than that in ya mouth, and the guys laughed.

Any meat I put in my mouth honey has the government stamp of approval, and she sauntered to the sink and carefully washed the glass, Harry watching her until she came back then he turned to Vinnie. Yeah, that was a good job. Theres a picha in the paper. Here. They looked at the picture and laughed. Man, whatta night. What a fuckin ball. Yeah. Were been gobblin bennies all night man and we're highern a motherfucka. Hey, how about some music, and the radio was turned on. Hey, this kegs almost empty man. That one over theres full. Tapit. Hey Harry, this heres Ginger, a real sweet kid, chuckling, but dont fuck witer man. She use ta be a brick layer. Yeah, now shes a prick layer. The guys laughed and Harry leered at her. Hey, dont yaknow how ta tap a fuckin keg? the fuckin beers goin all over. Whattaya want from me? its warm as piss. Harry said hello and Ginger curtsied. Go next door and get some ice from Al. Its too fuckin hot ta drink warm beer. No shitman, she really use ta be a bricklayer. Yeah, shoim ya muscle Ginger. She smiled and rolled up her sleeve and exhibited a large appleshaped muscle. Aint that some shit? But she got some lovely chips, snapping his fingers and making a chirping sound. You can look but dont touch. Thats it man, pack the sonofabitch with ice. I like cold beer. Tell me Harold, are you in charge of this establishment. Hey, watch yalanguage. Harry sat down, pushed his chair back and drank some beer. Yeah. Im in charge a the strike, wiping his mouth with his hand, still staring. Ginger smiled and almost told him he looked ludicrous, but could not be bothered putting the freak down. My, that must be quite a task. Yeah, its a bitch of a job, but I get it done. Im pretty big in the union yaknow. Yes, I can well imagine, her stomach twitching from swallowed giggles. Whattayamean its not cold enough yet. Im dyin a thirst. How inthefuck can yadrink warm beer. Wit my mouth, what thefuck yathink. You know,

I'm hungry. Why dont one of you gentlemen get me something to eat. Here, I got ya suppa, swingin, and they laughed. Im sorry honey, but I dont like moldy worm eaten meat. Save it for your Mother . . . if you have one. Hahaha, youre my motha, come an getit. Hey Harry, how about callin up some joint and havin some food sent down here. Ya can sign the bill. O, can you do that Harold? Sure. I can get anythin yawant. I just send the bills to the union. I got a expense sheet. Id just love a barbecued chicken. How the fuck canya eat afta all those bennies. I couldnt go near any food. All I wanna do is drink. Im driernhell. O you novices. Really! Order me a barbecued chicken Harold and get a chocolate layer cake, waving her hand majestically and nodding her head to indicate that she had given an irrevocable order. Yeah, get some chickens, a couplea cakes – and a gallon a ice cream. Man could I go for some ice cream. And how about some potato salad and pickles? Yeah, and – call up Kramers delicatessen on 5th avenue. They got all that shit up there. Harry got on the phone and they continued to shout orders at him and he relayed them to Mr. Kramer. When he finished ordering he sat back and took another gulp of beer and watched Ginger as she danced lightly around the room, the excitement that had started when he awoke and increased as he looked at the picture and continued to grow when he called the union office and when the guys and Ginger came in, continued to increase and he leaned forward in his chair slightly as Ginger whirled around the room shaking the tight cheeks of her ass and Harry caressed his beer glass and licked his lips not knowing exactly what he was doing, his body reacting and tingling, aware of nothing but a lightness, almost a giddiness, and a fascination. And a feeling of power and strength. Things would be different now. He was Harry Black. On the payroll of local 392.

When the food came Ginger accepted Harrys gracious

offer and sat in his chair and well mannerdly ate a chicken, a few helpings of potato salad and cole slaw and cake, then, tired of drinking unladylike beer, told Harry he should get a few bottles of gin, some tonic water and a few limes which Harry did, adding the bills to the pile in the drawer, and the party continued. Harry was getting very drunk and Ginger, who was in an even more bitchy mood than usual, thought it would be fun to toy with him. She got up from the chair and told Harry to sit then sat on his lap, put her finger in his ear and played with his hair. Harry leered, his eyes rolling slightly. He was drunk but still able to feel the tingling in his thighs yet unaware of the spasmodic jerking of his fingers, the moisture in his mouth. Ginger leaned her face closer to Harrys, tenderly caressing his neck and she watched Harrys lips quiver, felt the trembling in his legs and saw his eyes unfocusing and rolling back. Ginger roared hysterically inside herself and leaned closer to Harry, smiling, until she could feel his slimy breath on her cheek, then jumped up and tapped him playfully on the nose. Oh you naughty man, getting a nice young girl like me all excited, posing provocatively in front of him. She took a few short dainty steps backward, smiling at him coquettishly, and wriggled in time to the music from the radio, glancing over her shoulder at Harry occasionally, leaning her head to one side and winking. Harry continued to lean forward until he fell from the chair, spilling his drink, and kneeling on the floor behind his desk. He dropped the glass and pulled himself up, tiny droplets of saliva hanging from his lips and chin. He pulled himself up and leaned forward. Comeon, lets dansh. Ginger put her hands on her hips and watched him lumber toward her, feeling the power she had over him and despising him. She put her arms around him and started dragging him around the floor, stamping heavily on his toes and lifting her knee up into his groin from time to time, Harry wincing but still trying to smile and drunkenly trying to get closer to her. Ginger pinched his neck fiercely with her fingernails and laughed as Harrys eyes closed, then patted him on the cheek and rubbed his head. Thats a good dog. Do you know how to beg for a bone, lifting her knee into his crotch, Harrys face twisting. Its a shame we're not in Marys now. You could buy me drinks and we would have a wonderful time, pinching him again. Harrys eyes closed again. Watch Marys? O, a lovely club I know on 72nd street thats just filled with freaks like you. Youd love it, stepping on his foot and grinding her heel into it. Harrys eyes watered. Letsgo, sliding his hand down Gingers arm, Ginger flexing her hard muscle, bending her arm and squeezing Harrys hand in the crotch of her elbow until he stopped dancing and tugged to loosen it, Ginger squeezing harder, her face set in a smile, putting all her strength, hatred and loathing into the squeezing of Harrys hand, wallowing in the joy of holding Harry immobile with the bending of her arm, feeling like David, not killing Goliath with one stone from his sling, but slowly twisting him down and down and down with the simple twisting of one massive finger with her small dainty ladylike hand. Ginger applied as much pressure as she could, the pressure now hurting her too, but she continued to squeeze Harrys hand as he tugged to loosen it, his face becoming whiter, his eyes bulging, too startled and in too much pain to yell, his mouth hanging open, saliva dripping, spreading his legs for balance and leverage, pushing her arm with his other hand, looking at her in complete bewilderment, not understanding what was happening, too drunk to comprehend the incongruity of the situation: the little faggot conquering the giant with the crotch of her arm; his eyes asking why but no question formed in his mind, just instinctively trying to free himself of the pain. Ginger stared directly into his face, smiling still, wanting to crush him, to force him to his knees. He bent his arm to one side, still not using his other hand against Harry, his face stiffening as Harrys body started to lean with the pressure, Ginger wanting to yell IM MORE OF A MAN THAN YOU, then suddenly she opened her arm, spun around and left Harry standing there, looking after her as she mixed herself another drink, holding his hand and rubbing it.

Ginger strolled around the room, gulping at her drink, talking with the guys and looking at Harry occasionally and smiling. Harry made his way back to his chair, filled his glass and sat, rubbing his hand, wondering just what had happened, slowly becoming conscious of the noise from the guys and the radio. Somebody slapped him on the back, whattayasay Harry, laughed and staggered away, Harry looking at him dumbly and nodding. Ginger came up behind him and twirled his hair with her fingers and slowly moved around in front of him and leaned against the desk. I like your party. I hope the strike lasts for a while, we can have a ball. Harry nodded his head as he weaved back and forth in his chair, almost falling off again. Ginger patted his cheek, Youre cute. I like you, smiling and giggling inside as Harrys eyes once more showed his bewilderment. Its too bad we cant be alone, we would have such fun. Harry put his hand on her leg and Ginger lifted it gently. Fresh. My, but you get a girl all aquiver, crossing her arms against her breast. Harry leaned toward her, licking his lips, mumbling something, and Ginger patted his cheek, then turned away, tired of her little game, turned the radio off and announced that they should go back uptown. I find staying in Brooklyn too long very oppressive. Yeah, letsgo. Maybe therell be some action tanight. Harry tried to grab Gingers arm as she picked up the gin bottle, but she twirled away from him and strutted out of the office. Harry leaned forward in his chair holding onto the edge of the desk and watched her leave, not noticing the guys as they picked up the other gin bottles and food and left.

Harry leaned against the desk staring at the door in a semicatatonic state, his head slowly drooping to one side until his head finally bumped against the desk. He jerked it up, blinked his eyes then stared again at the door, slowly sliding from his chair until he was on the floor. Harry curled up under the desk and slept.

Harry slept, curled cosily under his desk, until late morning. The sun was bright and shone through the office window, lighting the entire office except for Harrys snug little cove. Harry sat in the darkness under his desk with his knees under his chin fighting to squint his eyes open, peering up at his chair, and its barred shadow on the wall, conscious only of the pain in his eyes. He attempted nothing, not even closing his eyes against the brightness of the sun shining on the wall, a brightness that reflected only on his eyes and not into the darkness of his cubicle. He sat there for hours not thinking of challenging his lethargy until the demand to urinate became so intense he was forced to crawl from his niche. After he urinated he leaned over the sink and let cold water pour on his head for many minutes then found his way back to his chair and sat smoking and staring until the pain in his head prodded him from his chair and he locked the office and went next door to the bar. He sat alone and silent at the end of the bar drinking, not thinking or glowing over the fact that he could spend as much as he wanted then get it back from the union as he had been doing since the strike started; not even aware that his head stopped aching after an hour or so. For a short time, after drinking for a few hours, he started thinking of the previous day and he felt an excitement in his body but he could not fight through the haze that obscured the night and soon he was just drunk. It was still early evening when he left the bar and stumbled home and into bed, still fully clothed, and curled up in a corner and slept.

Monday morning the men had regained some of their former enthusiasm with the possibility of another truck trying to cross the picket line, a truck that they would be prepared to stop. The incident of the trucks took on added importance to the men during the weekend. They had talked about it continually on Friday and by the time they drank their last beer Sunday night they were convinced that the fact that the company had to break the line with trucks meant that they were hardup to fill orders and that soon they couldnt afford to keep the shop closed. Some even thought, briefly, of going down to the office Sunday night or early Monday morning to see if the company would try to sneak trucks in before the men started picketing, but soon convinced themselves that it wasnt necessary. So, Monday they were slightly elated as they knew the strike would soon be over and they could stop haggling with the wife about money. They were convinced too that the company would try again to break the line before giving in to the strikers and so everyone, even those who stayed in the office drinking, were ready to run down 2nd avenue when the word was given that more trucks were coming and when they did and were stopped, then the company would have to accept the unions demands. And so they waited and hoped.

Everytime Harry stamped a book during the morning he asked the men if they saw the picture in the paper of the trucks burning, and intimated in every way that he was completely responsible for burning the trucks. By late morning even Harry was a little tired of hearing the same thing for hours so he stopped talking about the trucks and soon, after a pitcher of beer or so, a few memories and images of Saturday night returned and he remembered the guys coming in the office, he remembered the music, the gin and Ginger dancing. He had felt good Saturday night, that he definitely remembered, and too he remembered how the guys seemed to respect him because of his position in the union and because he could order any thing he wanted and have the union pay for it; and he remembered how Ginger admired him for his strength and how she liked to talk with him and feel the muscles in his arms and legs. There were still a few things he could not remember, but they must have been unimportant and soon the thought that they existed was absorbed and they had never happened.

The men rejuvenated their hope through the day, but as the picketing day approached an end, the effect of all the hopeful efforts was almost negligible. The trucks that were to prelude the ending of the strike never arrived and though they tried at first to think that they would not come until later and that it was natural that the company should wait a day or so before trying again, the men could not accept these explanations no matter how hard they tried. They had started the day expecting a deus ex machina and with its appearance their troubles and the strike would be over; and though they tried to convince themselves, and each other, with many arguments, that the company would have to give in soon they found it impossible to maintain any optimism and when the day came to an end they put their signs away quietly, nodded to each other and left. The day had been long and hot. It had been many hours since anyone had looked up at the clear blue sky. It was still summertime and there were many more hot days to come.

The union and management met regularly to arbitrate their dispute. Each side was more arrogant and noisy than usual the first meeting after the incident of the trucks, but the result of the meeting was the same as all the previous ones. The union could not allow anyone to administer the welfare plan but, even if their books had been in order it was far too late now for them to concede to the companys demands. After being on strike this long they could not settle for the same contract that had been offered before they started the strike. There was still ample money in the strike fund, enough to continue to give the men their 10 dollars bag of food each week, to last a year if necessary; and other unions throughout the country had pledged assistance any time it was needed. The union officials were indignant about the companys attitude in being so rigid and in sending trucks through the line and left Mondays meeting declaring they would not meet with them for a few weeks, not until the company reconsidered its arbitrary stand and realised that the men were willing to stay on strike for a year if necessary in order to get a decent contract. The recording secretary remained in the city and the other officials went to Canada for a rest. They needed a rest from the pressures of the strike and the oppressive heat.

Mr. Harrington told the other company representatives that they had to remain firm. Except for the oversight that necessitated their hiring a freight forwarding firm to cross the picket line and deliver the much needed parts to the upstate plant, everything had been running smoothly. Their other plants, and subcontractors, throughout the country had been geared in ample time to handle all existing orders and any that might come in during the immediate future. All their government contracts were being fulfilled and no new ones would be forthcoming before February of the following year. At least none of any quantity. And too, the manner in which the contracts had been distributed to other plants, and the manner in which the transfers had been noted on the books, meant a substantial tax saving would be effected. Of course a few of the younger executives had a burdensome amount of work to do because of the strike, but a substantial bonus at Christmas and a pat on the back would not only satisfy them but would encourage them to work even harder in the future. And the cost of the bonuses would only amount to a minute percentage of the money saved in unpaid wages. Perhaps they would be prevented from taking a vacation now, but Mr. Harrington did not care if no one went on vacation for years, he was determined to try and get rid of Harry Black. After all, what did he have to lose.

Harry did not notice the change in the men as they carefully leaned their signs against the wall and left. A few minutes after five he was the only one in the office so he just hung around for a while, drinking beer, his mind wandering over what had happened lately, and he remembered Ginger mentioning Marys on 72nd street. He thought about it for a while then decided to go. He got a cab and when they got to 72nd street he told the driver to go down the street and when he saw Marys he told the driver to stop at the next corner and he walked back.

It wasnt until he approached the door that he started to feel uneasy, that he became conscious of being in a strange neighbourhood, outside a strange bar. He went in and moved immediately to the side and tried to melt in with the others standing at the bar. There were so many people in Marys and so much noise – the jukebox in the rear clashing with the one at the bar – that Harry was able to lose himself in the chaos and his selfconsciousness faded before he finished his first drink. Eventually he was able to work his way into a spot at the bar where he could see the rest of the bar and most of the back room. At first he was surprised at the way in which the women acted, but after listening to them talk and watching them move he eventually realised that most of them were men dressed as women. He stared at everyone as they moved and talked, never certain of their sex, but enjoying watching them and enjoying too the thrill and excitement he felt at being in such a weird place. The people in the back room fascinated him more than the others as he imagined what they were doing with their hands under the table, and was particularly amazed when he saw a big, muscled, truckdriver-looking guy lean over and kiss the guy sitting next to him. The kiss seemed to last for many minutes and Harry could almost feel their tongues touching. He stared. He noticed the tattoos on the big guys arms. He looked quickly at his own dirty fingernails then back at the lovers in the booth. Their mouths slowly separated and they looked at each other for a moment then reached for their drinks, the big guys arms still around his lovers shoulder. Harry continued to stare until his uneasiness forced him to lower his eyes and he picked up his drink and gulped it down. He ordered another, sipped at it, lit a cigarette and continued to lookaround.

Occasionally someone smiled at Harry, brushed against him or spoke to him and a few times he smiled his smile but it ended the scene rather than continued it, so Harry stayed alone drinking and looking until he noticed Ginger come in. She walked quickly to the back and was out of sight before Harry could move. He stared after her for a moment wanting to go after her, but he knew if he did that the guys from the Greeks would find out so he finally decided to finish his drink and leave before she saw him.

The next morning Mary wanted to know where Harry went last night and where he was last Saturday night and if he was going to be home tonight and if he thought this was a flophouse and he could come home any fuckin time he felt like it and ever since the strike started he was goin around like he thought who he was and she wasnt gonna stand for any shit like this . . .

Harry continued to throw water on his face as she talked and ignored her as he walked past her into the bedroom and got dressed and when he finished and was ready to leave he told her ta shutthefuckup or hed raper in the mouth. Mary stared at him determined not to tolerate his complete indifference. She looked Harry in the eye, expecting, waiting, for him to lower his eyes or turn his head and told him she wasnt going to stand for any more of his shit. Harry stood where he was, still staring at her, but becoming more and more conscious of her eyes, of her, and starting to waver inside, starting to think of spitting in her face, of walking out of the house, becoming more conscious of his thoughts and indecision and almost starting to fear her when her voice pushed these things down in his mind. It wasnt what she said – her words undefined, only one long penetrating sound heard – but just the movement of her lips and the sound providing something tangible to stop his faltering. She had just stopped talking and was still staring at him when he slapped her across the face. Go fuck yaself. Mary continued staring at Harry, her mouth open, touching her cheek with the tips of her fingers. Harry left the house and walked quickly, smiling his smile, to the office ready to start another day of the strike.

The men picked up their signs and gave their books to Harry to be stamped; or filled a cup with coffee, a glass with beer, with a certain amount of resignation and a large degree of silence. They were not completely humourless, but were in no mood for jokes. Harry felt good, free, but was in an introverted mood thinking about Marys and so he sat quietly, nodding, speaking occasionally, and not slapping backs and roaring, but seeming to share the uneasiness and concern of the men.

Harry did not go back to Marys until Friday night. He filled out his expense voucher as usual, talked to the guys who had come over from the Greeks as usual to drink beer, stayed in the office for a while after they left, then went to Marys. He walked right in and went to the corner of the bar, looked around to see if Ginger was there, then ordered a drink. Marys was even more crowded than it had been the other night and there was so much noise from the jukeboxes and people screeching that he could not hear the bartender when he asked him if he wanted his drink mixed. He leaned over the bar to hear, nodded, then jerked his head back when he heard a whistle. A pretty young fairy was looking at him, smiling and shaking his head, saying something, but Harry could not hear him. Harry turned his head but glanced occasionally at him from the corner of his eye. He leaned a little more heavily against the bar, looking around the bar, into the backroom, occasionally at the pretty young one still standing in the same place at the bar. Harry tried to imagine what was being done with hands under the tables in the backroom, and what was being done at the tables out of his sight.

He finished each drink in two swallows and the swallows were closer together. He felt good when the strike started. He was nervous when he had to talk to the men at the meeting when they started the strike, but he felt good then too; and he felt good a couple a times since then when the guys came around and they talked and drank and that sort of thing; and he felt real great when the trucks got blown up, yeah . . . yeah, he felt real good that night and the next day with the picture in the paper . . . yeah, thats when they started to know who he really was. They knew he was something before, but after that they really knew. Yeah, it was great gettin more money and spending all ya wanted and just fillinin a slip, just like those pricks in the company and that punk wilson who think theyre such hot shit walkin around in a white shirt and all that shit, but he was just as good as any ofem, he knew a few things and could throw a buck on the bar. Fuck them, the ball-breakers. They couldnt shove him around anymore . . . yeah, and fuck Mary too. Aint breakin my balls anymore . . . thats right, aint had that dream since the strike started. Blow a couple more trucks up and I'll never have it. Fuckit. Anyway its gone . . . and thingsll be different after the strikes over too. Ya bet yasweetass – he glanced again at the pretty fairy and when he looked back at Harry. Harry didnt turn his head. He continued to look and his face unfolded slightly and fell into his smile, but this time it came a little closer to being a real smile and the pretty one smiled and winked – yeah, thingsve been good since the strike. He wished ta krist he could see that fuck wilson and that ballbreaker harrington – Mr. Bigshit – sweatin it out. They mustta shit their pants when the trucks were bombed. Bet he knows what he'll get if he fucks with me too much – the pretty one was standing next to him. Harry smiled down at him. She wiggled slightly. Can I buy you a drink? Yeah. Harry gulped the last swallow of his drink and let her buy him one. Harry rocked a little on his feet. Guess Im a little drunk. Ive really been throwinem down. You look like the sort of man who can drink a great deal of hard liquor, touching his forearm and leaning closer. I mustta put a quart away already, not countin what I had this afternoon, holding on to the edge of the bar and twisting his arm slightly so his muscles would tighten. Isnt this place simply marvellous? Yeah, trying to stand taller and straighter. I just love men who work hard, I mean who work with their hands. Yeah, I hate pencil pushers. Me, Im a machinist. Ist class journeyman. But I really work for the union. O, are you an union officer too, smiling. All her johns and trade were the same. They were all some kind of big shot. Yeah, Im pretty big in the union. Im takin care a the strike. O, that must be interesting, not minding a certain amount of this sort of conversation, but hoping it wouldnt go too far. It really is rather crowded and noisy in here, isnt it, smiling and tilting her head back gracefully. Yeah, but it aint bad though. Would you care to leave? we could go to my apartment and have a few quiet drinks. Harry stared for a moment then nodded.

When they got to the apartment Harry sprawled on the couch. He felt drunk. Everything was alright. My name is Alberta, handing him a drink. Whats yours? Harry. She sat next to him. Why dont you take your shirt off. Its rather warm in here. Yeah, sure, fumbling with the buttons. Here, let me help you, leaning over and slowly unbuttoning Harrys shirt, glancing up at Harry pulling the shirt out of his trousers then sliding it off the shoulders and arms and letting it fall behind the couch. Harry watched her as she unbuttoned his shirt, felt the slight pressure of her fingers. He almost thought about the guys and what they would say if they saw him now, but the thought was easily absorbed by the alcohol before it formed and he closed his eyes and enjoyed the closeness of Alberta.

She stayed close to him, resting one hand gently on his shoulder, looking up at him, sliding her hand along his shoulder to his neck, watching his face, his eyes, for any reaction; feeling a little uneasy with Harry, not absolutely certain how he would react. Usually she knew how rough trade would react before she attempted anything, but with Harry she wasnt too certain; there was something strange in his eyes. She thought she understood what was behind them, but she still preferred a little caution to recklessness. And too, this was exciting. Occasionally she just had to cruise and bring home trade that looked dangerous; but, slowly, as she caressed his neck and back and looked into his face, she realised that she didnt have to fear Harry; and she understood too that this was new a experience to Harry. The puzzled expectant look on his face excited her.

She had a cherry. She tingled. She rubbed his chest with the palm of her other hand. Your chest is so strong and hairy, the tip of her tongue showing between her lips; rubbing his back, touching gently the pimples and pockmarks. Youre so strong, moving closer, touching his neck with her lips, her hand moving from his chest to his stomach, to his belt, his fly; her mouth on his chest, then his stomach. Harry raised himself slightly as she tugged at his pants then relaxed, then tensed as she kissed his thighs and put his cock in her mouth. Harry pushed against the back of the couch, squirmed with pleasure; almost screamed with pleasure at the image of his wife being split in two with a large cock that turned into an enormous barbed pole, then he was there smashing her face with his fist and laughing, laughing and spitting and punching until the face was just a blob that oozed and then she became an old man and he stopped punching and then once more it was Mary, or it almost looked like Mary but it was a woman and she screamed as a burning white hot cock was shoved and hammered into her cunt then slowly pulled out, pulling with it her entrails and Harry sat watching, laughing his laugh and groaning, groaning with pleasure and then he heard the groan, heard it not only from inside, but heard it enter his ear from outside and he opened his eyes and saw Albertas head moving furiously and Harry moaned and squirmed frantically.

Alberta kept her head still for many minutes before getting up and going to the bathroom. Harry watched her walk away then looked at his prick hanging half rigidly between his legs. It hypnotised him and he stared at it for a moment knowing it was his yet not recognising it, as if he had never seen it before yet knowing he had. How many times had he held it in his hands as he pissed; why did it seem new to him? Why did it suddenly fascinate him so? He blinked his eyes and heard the water running in the bathroom. He looked at his penis again and the strangeness disappeared. He wondered briefly about his thoughts of a moment ago. He couldnt remember them. He felt good. He looked toward the bathroom waiting to see Albertas face.

Her face had a polished wax glow and her long hair was neatly combed. She wiggled toward him, smiling. She laughed, lightly, at Harrys surprised look when he noticed she was wearing nothing but a pair of womans lace panties. She poured two more drinks and sat beside him. Harry took a gulp of his drink and touched her panties. Do you like my silks? Harrys hand jerked back. He felt Albertas hand on the back of his neck. She gently guided his hand to her leg. I love them. They're so smooth, holding his hand on her leg and kissing his neck, his mouth, sliding her tongue into his mouth, searching for his, feeling the bottom of it as Harry curled his tongue back in his mouth, caressing the base of his tongue with hers, Harrys tongue slowly unfolding and lapping against hers, his hand grabbing her cock. Alberta moving his hand away and back on her leg, letting her saliva drip from the tip of her tongue onto Harrys, squirming as her clutched her leg tightly, almost feeling the drops of spit being absorbed by Harrys mouth, feeling his tongue lunging into her mouth as if he were trying to choke her; she sucked on his tongue then let him suck on hers, rolling her head with his, moving her hand over his lumpy back; slowly moving her head back and away from his. Lets go into the bedroom, darling. Harry pulled her toward him and sucked on her lips. She slowly separated her mouth from his and tugged him from the back of his neck. Lets go to bed, slowly standing, still tugging. Harry stood, staggering slightly. Alberta looked down and laughed. You still have your shoes and socks on. Harry blinked. He was standing with legs spread, penis standing straight before him, naked except for his black socks and shoes. Alberta giggled then took his shoes and socks off. Come on lover. She grabbed him by the prick and led him to the bedroom.

Harry flopped onto the bed and rolled over and kissed her, missing her mouth and kissing her chin. She laughed and guided him to her mouth. He pushed at her side and at first Alberta was puzzled, trying to understand what he was trying to do, then realised that he was trying to turn her over. She giggled again. You silly you. You never have fucked a fairy before, have you? Harry grumbled, still fumbling and kissing her neck and chest. We make love just like anybody else honey, a little peeved at first then once more relishing the charm of having a cherry. Just relax, rolling over on her side and kissing him, whispering in his ear. When she finished the preparations she rolled back onto her back, Harry rolling over on her, and moved rhythmically with Harry, her legs and arms wrapped around him, rolling, squirming, groaning.

Harry lunged at first, then, looking at Alberta, slowed to an exciting movement; and as he moved he was conscious of his movements, of his excitement and enjoyment and not wanting it to end; and though he clenched his teeth from lust and pinched her back and bit her neck there was a comparative relaxing, the tautness and spasms being caused by pleasure and desire to be where he was and to do what he was doing. Harry could hear hers and his moans blending, could feel her under him, could feel her flesh in his mouth; there were many tangible things and yet there was still a confusion, but it stemmed from inexperience, from the sudden overpowering sensations of pleasure, a pleasure he had never known, a pleasure that he, with its excitement and tenderness, had never experienced – he wanted to grab and squeeze the flesh he felt in his hands, he wanted to bite it, yet he didnt want to destroy it; he wanted it to be there, he wanted to come back to it.

Harry continued to move with the same satisfying rhythm; continued to blend his moans with hers through the whirlygig of confusion; bewildered but not distracted or disturbed by these new emotions giving birth to each other in his mind, but just concentrating on the pleasure and allowing it to guide him as Alberta had. When he stopped moving he lay still for a moment hearing their heavy breathing then kissed her, caressed her arms then rolled slowly and gently onto the bed, stretched out and soon slept. Harry was happy.

Harry didnt open his eyes immediately when he awoke, but lay thinking then opened them suddenly, very wide, and turned and looked at Alberta. Harry sat up. The entire evening jammed itself into Harrys mind and his eyes clouded from his terrible anxiety and confusion. For the briefest moment he hid behind alcohol and overlapping images hung in front of him, then passed. He dropped back on the bed and fell asleep once more. When he awoke again later he no longer wanted to run. The frightening clarity felt for the moment when he first awoke assimilated itself with the usual confusion of Harrys mind and he was now able to look at Alberta and remember the night, in a general penumbrous way, and not be afraid to be there – though still fearing the consequences of having someone find out – but the fears and confusion were overshadowed by his feeling of happiness.

Actually it was this feeling of happiness that bothered Harry more than anything else at the immediate moment he sat in the bed and looked at Alberta and remembered, with pleasure, the night before. He knew he felt good, yet he couldnt define his feeling. He couldnt say, Im happy. He had nothing with which to compare his feeling. He felt good when he was telling wilson off; he felt good when he was with the guys having a drink; at those times he told himself he was happy, but his feeling now went so much beyond that that it was incomprehensible. He didnt realise that he had never been happy, this happy, before.

He looked at Alberta again, then got out of bed and poured himself a drink. Too many things were starting to run through his mind. He couldnt take the chance of sitting there, sober, and allowing them to free themselves upon him. He lit a cigarette and drank the drink as fast as he could, then poured another. He took a little longer drinking this, then went back to the bedroom and sat on the edge of the bed with his 3rd drink.

He wanted to wake Alberta up. He didnt want to sit there alone and vulnerable; he wanted to talk with her, but he didnt know if he should call her or shake her or perhaps just bounce up and down on the bed. He took a drink, a drag of his cigarette, then put the cigarette out, rattling the ashtray on the table. Alberta moved and Harry quickly moved his head so he wouldnt be looking at her and yawned loudly. Alberta rolled over and mumbled something and Harry quickly turned, bouncing the bed as much as possible, whatdidyasay? Alberta mumbled again and opened her eyes. Harry smiled his smile and took another drink. Another day had started.

It took Alberta a while to wake up completely, though she did get out of bed and wash and go about her usual morning routine, and so it was quite a while before she became conscious of what Harry was saying and the fact that he was following her around the apartment. He wasnt hanging over her shoulder, but he was always within a few feet of her and whenever she turned Harry was there, smiling his smile. The first word she was aware of, while they drank coffee, was strike and though she still wasnt awake enough to understand each word she understood that he was telling her how he was running a strike, or some such thing, and how he was gonna shove it up somebodys ass. She hoped that he would either stop or slow down or that she would get enough energy to say something that would at least change the subject; but after a few more drinks Harry slowed down and they enjoyed each others company. They went to a movie in the afternoon; ate when they came out; then sat for a few hours in a bar. When they got home Harry made love to Alberta then they sat drinking and listening to music. Alberta found Harry amusing and enjoyed being with him, except when he tried to convince her he was a big shot – though she didnt mind his throwing money on the bar or taking a cab when they only had a few blocks to go – but when he did she changed the subject; and, too, she liked the way Harry kissed her. Not that he kissed any better or was less freaky than the others, but she could feel his excitement from the newness of the experience. They sat for hours on the couch, drinking, vaguely aware of the music from the radio, holding hands and kissing. Alberta leaned her head on Harrys shoulder, her eyes half closed, humming, turning from time to time to glance at Harry. Harry smiled his smile and there was a slight softness about it, and even his eyes had a slight tenderness in them. He touched her hair lightly and his hand tightened on her shoulder. They spoke infrequently and when they did their voices were low, Harrys even losing some of its roughness. They just sat, cuddled on the couch, for hours, Alberta moving a foot in time to the music; Harry loving having his arm around her and feeling her close to him. When Alberta asked Harry if he would like to go to bed he nodded and they got up and, still holding hands, walked slowly to the bedroom.

When Harry left Alberta Sunday afternoon he was in a daze. He hadnt thought of leaving. If she hadnt told him that she had to see someone that afternoon and that he had better leave he would have remained unaware of time and the fact that tomorrow was Monday and there were books to be stamped. He remembered the weekend and everything that happened, but he couldnt believe it was Sunday. Time just couldnt have passed that fast. The bouncing of the cab and the noises of the streets forced reality upon him and he knew he was going back to Brooklyn. He had wanted to ask her if he could see her again, but he didnt know how, no words came from his mouth, they hadnt even completely formed in his mind. He tried to think of how to ask her and to get the question out, but then the door was closed and he was walking down the street and now he was on his way to Brooklyn. Who was she going to see? Hed probably see her again in Marys. Hed be going there again.

He didnt go right home but went to the bar for a few hours. When he got home Mary was watching TV. He said nothing, but undressed and went to bed, smoked and thought of Alberta, remembering many times the last kiss in the doorway. Before he fell asleep the baby awoke and started crying and Mary eventually came in and talked to him and bounced him in the crib. The sound of their voices seemed to come from a dream and didnt interfere with his thoughts or the memory of the kiss.

The next morning Harry washed and dressed without saying a word. Mary watched determined to say something. She was nervous, but even a slap on the face was better than nothing. As Harry was about to leave she asked him if he was coming home that night. Harry shrugged. Where wereya Friday and Satu – Harry swung his arm in a stiff arc, fist clenched, and hit her in the corner of her mouth with the back of his fist. He hadnt looked or thought, but had simply closed his fist and swung. He paid no attention to the biting sensation he felt as his hand hit her teeth nor later did he think of the fact that it was the first time he had punched her – thousands of times he had thought of it, dreamed of it, had tried – or turn to look at her after hitting her. He just swung and turned and left the house.

He rubbed his hand as he walked. He felt good. Relieved. It had been a long time since he had had his nightmare. It was not even a memory.

Harry stamped books with accuracy, retaining the silent introspective mood he had recently acquired. The men were quieter and more solemn as they picked up their signs and had their books stamped, Harrys still quiet mood allowing them to ignore him, and they walked the picket line in the same despondent way they did everything else. Most of them had lately tried to get another job, but because they were on strike it was impossible to get one, the companies thinking they would leave as soon as the strike was settled, and so they walked around the plant, nodded to each other, took out their book, poured a cup of coffee or a glass of beer, put away their signs, said goodbye and left with the same air of hopelessness. Since the incident of the trucks the police guard had been increased and the men rotated so one officer was never there more than 3 hours a week, the department thinking this would prevent any personal disputes, caused by the boredom of having to be there, doing nothing, from erupting into a major incident; and so the policemen stood their posts, chatted with each other, and watched the strikers in an officially alert and disinterested manner.

At the first meeting between the company and the union after vacations they spoke for a while, said nothing, then decided to meet again in two days. At that meeting a few of the problems were discussed before the meeting was adjourned with a decision to meet in two days. Three, and sometimes four, times a week they met, put their briefcases on the large conference table, sat opposite each other, took their papers out of the briefcases and started talking. Slowly, by almost infinitesimal degrees, they seriously discussed a few of the issues that were preventing a settlement of the strike. Summer was almost over. Harrington was under no pressure to end the strike, having convinced the other officers of the corporation and negotiating committee that the company could afford to allow the strike to continue for many more months without an appreciable loss in net income, and he did not think there was enough pressure on the union to attempt to dispose of Harry, and he was determined not to agree to any settlement until he had tried everything possible to rid himself of Harry Black.

The union would have liked to have the strike settled as soon as possible, but only on their terms: They had to have complete control of the Welfare Plan. Though the strike had been in effect for many months the union officials felt no pressure on them. Everything was going smoothly and though their personal incomes had been cut because there had been no contributions to the Welfare Plan since the strike had started, there were ample funds coming in from other unions throughout the country to take the extra money they needed from these contributions. And the men were getting their bag of groceries each week. Some of them might be getting a little short of money, which was unfortunate, but the strike would continue, for months if necessary, until it was agreed that they would retain control of the Welfare Plan. And so no urgency was felt by either side.

The President, or another member of the committee, gave a short speech each Saturday before the food was distributed. They assured the men they were doing everything they could to settle the strike – they knew the men wanted to get back to work; that they couldnt afford to stay out of work for ever; that their bank accounts were running low; and that, in many cases, their wives had to go to work – but, they also told them, they knew the men wouldnt settle for anything less than a decent contract with a decent wage and that they were going to see that the men got that. They werent going to sign any sweetheart contract and let the company continue to take the bread out of their mouths . . . and the clique whistled and yelled and a few of the others joined in and the orator descended from the platform and mingled with the men, slapping them on the back, encouraging them, and nodding to each one as he accepted his bag of groceries.

Harry went to Marys every weekend and, after the first few weeks, during the week occasionally. The first time he went there after meeting Alberta she introduced him to some of her friends and during the months that followed Harry met some lovely young boys at Marys and the parties he went to with them. When he went to Marys he no longer slid to a place at the bar near the door, but walked around looking to see who was there, nodding and sitting at tables, wondering who was standing at the bar envying him as he put his arm around a young shoulder. Most of the fairies he met liked him – he was a good fuck and he spent money – but didnt like to be with him too long too often. It wasnt just his talking about the strike that caused them to shy away, though he was a boor, but a strangeness and a feeling of uncertainty that eventually made them uncomfortable. They had all seen, kissed, sucked and fucked freaks of all varieties from men who had spent most of their lives in prisons and could be satisfied only by a boy, men who were capable of cutting a throat not only without feeling, but without reason, to men who locked themselves in the bathroom when their wives went out and dressed in their wives clothes, occasionally going to a place like Marys when they had a night out. But these men were completely obvious to the fairies and they knew just how far they could go in any direction with them. Harry was different, or at least they felt he was.

There was some little something that they couldnt sense, that they were uncertain about, that eventually made them nervous. It might simply be that Harry would like to dress up as a woman and go to a drag ball, or parade down Broadway; or perhaps some day he would flip and kill one of them. They didnt know.

As summer passed, and the pleasant autumn weather followed, Harry joined his new friends when they went for a drive in the country. They would jam into a car with a few bottles of gin and benzedrine, turn the radio up and slap the side of the car in rhythm to a jazz or blues song and sing along with it, snapping their fingers, wiggling in their seats – O honey, what I couldnt do to this number – passing the bottle back and forth – taking an occasional bennie – flirting with men in other cars; or, if in the mood, they would listen to an Italian opera, sighing rapturously after each aria; telling anecdotes about the gorgeous tenor or the temperamental diva, their heads moving gently with the music; taking small sips from the bottle; squealing and pointing at trees whose leaves reminded them of a Renoir and they jumped in their seats to see a new combination of colours, each one, almost by turn, pointing to a grove that was thrilling with reds, browns, orange or gold and at ones where all the colours blended and the leaves seemed to toy with the sunlight their colours were so brilliant; and in between were the greens of pines and blues of spruces and a few times they stopped by a lake or pond and giggled as they scampered around picking up acorns or chestnuts and took off their shoes and splashed their feet in the water and giggled as they watched squirrels peek at them for a moment before dashing away; and they would sit by the water or under a tree and sip the gin, take more bennie, then fill the car trunk with leaves, keeping some out to hold on their laps, to look at, to smell, to rub with a handkerchief, continually talking of how beautiful it was

. . . and Harry sat in the back, saying little, not minding the music or their screeching over a bunch of leaves, not noticing much of anything, but happy to be with them.

Walking the picket line was less tiring now that the cooler weather had arrived. When the men finished their time on the line and handed their signs to their relief, or put them away at night, they werent sweaty or fatigued as they had been during the summer, yet they still started and ended each day a little more despondent than the day before. Though a few, while not on the picket line, sat around the office drinking beer, most of them sat or stood in small groups talking. The two kegs of beer that used to be ordered each day now lasted 3 or 4 days – Harry adding the extra money that had been spent on beer to his expense sheet – and were drunk mostly by Harry and the guys from the Greeks. And, as it got darker earlier each day, more of the men left after their tour of duty and went home to watch TV or cook supper and wait for the wife to come home from work; and some went to a bar, going home late to avoid the argument about who was going to cook and clean now that the wife was working.

The men no longer looked down 2nd avenue expecting to see trucks. The incident wasnt forgotten, but the hope that it had aroused – and the hatred that had revived their enthusiasm – was irrevocably lost and they performed their duties as strikers listlessly and hopelessly. A few of the men were able to get new jobs and their books were voided. When this was announced at a Saturday meeting boos and catcalls came from the clique, but the men were silent, some envying them, others no longer capable of anything but lethargy; and the men whose books have been voided were only thought of, if at all, when the strikers joined the hundreds of workers from the Army Base at five oclock walking up 58th street to the subway.

Daylight saving time was in its last week when the company made the long awaited concession: They finally agreed to consider allowing the union to continue the administration of the Welfare Fund. But there were conditions. A few were with respect to the amount of the companys contribution, certain aspects of supervision in the factory, and a few other items that they both knew could be negotiated easily; but they also wanted the right to discharge Harry Black. The union representatives immediately leaped to their feet and declared the demand unreasonable and unthinkable. It was more than just a case of Harry being a member in good standing and an able worker, but to even suggest that they would or could violate the trust and welfare of the membership was an insult to their integrity. Not only that, it was an insult to every union member and officer in the country. They slammed their briefcases shut and the two forces stood opposite each other haggling for many minutes before the union representatives walked out.

The company and the union had had over a hundred meetings since the beginning of the strike and had been meeting every day, for many gruelling hours, for over a month now. Although neither side was, as yet, in a desperate position, pressure was mounting. The union officials knew they couldnt allow the strike to continue too much longer without a good, tangible, palatable reason to give the men. There was too much grumbling; the men were obviously dissatisfied and pressure had been slowly building up from government agencies who might, eventually, investigate the reasons for the prolonging of the strike; but now they had their reason.

Harrington recognised and realised that the men with whom he was negotiating would see the plant remain closed for a year rather than relinquish their control of the Welfare Fund and he was perfectly willing, now, to buy them off – to offer a concession – by allowing them to continue to administer it, but they had to make concessions too. The pressure on the company was increasing, but Harrington was determined to try to get rid of Harry Black and he was willing to keep the plant closed for many more months in order to accomplish this. The company could go to the end of the year without losing too much, that had been definitely established by their accountants and tax experts. Pressure was building up on the company, but Harrington knew it was building up on the union too and so he decided it was time to barter. He felt they would gladly concede Harry for the fund which they obviously could not afford to have checked. Even after the union officials had walked out of the meeting he still retained this hope, knowing that they could not possibly concede immediately, but would have to take at least a month, or perhaps even longer, to devise a method to accomplish this within the legal framework of the union.

Of course each of the union officials thought, at first to himself, of a way they could get rid of Harry without making themselves open to criticism: They could dump him easily enough and give as an excuse that he was defrauding the union of money by submitting fraudulent expense vouchers, or any number of other reasons. Actually they could tell the membership anything and it wouldnt be noticed if they told them just before that the company gave in and signed the new contract. Nobody would miss Harry.

They tossed a few more ideas around, evaluated the whole setup, and decided the best thing to do was to maintain their present position: Harry was a good man and stays on the job. Harry was a nut, but that was what made him so valuable. He continually overstepped the limits of the contract with regard to working, but this, in its own little way, helped prevent the company from trying the same thing. Harry forced the company to fight so hard, and spend so much time, getting what they were allowed under the contract that they didnt have time to infringe on the limitations the contract set on them. They recognised that Harry was the best diversionary action they had. And too, this made dealing with the company easier for the officials. Although most, if not all, of the men they had to deal with at the company hated the union, so much of their hatred was personal and directed against Harry that the union officials had a much easier time talking and, under ordinary circumstances, dealing with them. Harry, in addition to all the other functions he served, was their builtin patsy. They could never find another shop steward for local 392 as willing and as capable as Harry Black. He was irreplaceable.

But of course the real reason they didnt want to allow the firing of Harry was that if they did they would be conceding a point, no matter how meaningless, to the company; and, most important of all, if they ever allowed the company the authority and privilege to fire someone they would be forfeiting a right that was theirs and theirs alone; and if they allowed it once they might somehow, be forced to allow it again. Yet even if they were reasonably certain that the company would not try to exercise this right again they could not allow it even once. Someone might get ideas about them. It had been a long time since anyone tried to take their local away from them (that attempt being stopped easily with a few killings) and if they allowed this there would bound to be someone who thought they were too weak to keep their local. They didnt believe that anyone could actually take it away from them, but they didnt want to be forced to spend the time and money to keep what was theirs, especially now that they had, in addition to many other things, the Welfare Fund functioning so nicely for themselves. Each of them had made long term loans based on their cut from the fund and keeping the books in order required time and attention and then sometimes when theres trouble things get out of hand and there are investigations and more time and money are lost.

All these things were considered and smoked and drunk over and, now that the company obviously wasnt going to fight against their administering the fund any longer, they had no need to worry. Pressure was building up, but the company must be feeling it even more to have made the offer. And now they had something to relieve the pressure, slightly, for a while. Next Saturday, before the men received their bag of groceries, they would tell the rank and file that those sonsofbitches, those bellyrobbinbastards, were willing to concede a few points if we allowed them to fire men. And, of course, they would remind the men of this each Saturday and it should prove enough to get their hatred directed actively and completely against the company. The officials looked at each other. No one had anything to add. They agreed that that was about the size of the situation. Nothing more need be said. They would not give up their power.

The guys from the Greeks still came over almost every night after the picketers had left and sat around with Harry drinking beer and, if in the mood, ordering food. Harry putting the cost on his expense sheet. Harry gave them his usual rundown on the strike and, as usual, the guys ignored him and played the radio and drank and, as usual, Harry continued his narration.

During the week when Harry didnt go up to Marys he would lock up the office after the guys left and go home. He hadnt said more than a few words to Mary, nor she to him, since the morning he punched her. She left for a few days with the baby after that – Harry didnt notice that she was gone – but it was even worse being with her parents so, after a few days, she came back where she could at least watch TV. Harry would go right to bed and lie on his back thinking – not noticing Mary when she got into bed, thinking of her seldom, usually only when he dropped some money on the table for her to buy food. He would lie in bed thinking not only of all his friends at Marys, but hoping, as he had so many times, that tomorrow night he might meet someone who would not only ask him to take her home that night but every night; hoping he might meet someone who would want to live with him and they could make love everynight or just sit and hold hands and feel her small, soft and weak in his arms . . . not all slimy like a ballbreakin cunt.

Saturday the President spoke to the men before they were given their packages. The men, for the last few months, stayed on the side of the hall near the doors where the packages were handed out and half of the hall was empty while they jammed and shoved each other to retain or take a place near the doors; and each week the shoving and yelling increased. The officials tried to get the men to sit, but they absolutely refused to give up their places near the doors and so more than 1,000 men shoved and jostled each other as the President spoke.

Men . . . Men, we're beating them! Theyre starting to COLLAPSE! The men quieted a little and most of them were looking at the President. Its been a long time – and krist knows weve suffered with you – but theyre coming around. They havent given in down the line yet, but its only a matter of time. Theyve agreed to most of the terms and it wont be long before they agree to the rest. The men started to move uneasily at hearing the same words again and the noises started increasing. The President raised his hands and yelled louder. We could have settled the strike this week if we wanted to, but we didnt. You want to know why? The men quieted again and stared. Because we like talking to those stuffedshirtbastards? because we like to argue with men who are trying to take the bread out of our families mouths? because we like workin 16 and 18 hours a day??? No! I'll tell you why. Because they wanted the right to fire anybody they want, thats why. If they get a bug up their ass and decide they dont like the looks of some guy they want to be able to fire him right there and then. No questions asked, no answers given. Just kick him out on his ass and let him and his family starve. Thats why we have been fighting those bastards so hard; thats why we have been out of work so long. The men were silent, still. More than 1,000 men huddled near the doors staring at the speaker. More than once since we have been negotiating with them they have tried to buy us off in one way or another if we would let them throw men out in the cold any time they wanted to. And you know what we told them. You know what we said when they tried that shit on us. I'll tell you what we said. We stood up and looked those bastards right in the eye and told them, right to their fat faces, FUCK YOU! The clique roared approval – thats what we told them – others joined in the yelling and whistling – thats what the elected officials of your union said and we walked out – more yelling and stamping of feet – we left those bastards standing. And you can bet your sweet ass those sonsofbitches know theres no weak link in this union – almost all the men roared and whistled – and we'll see them dead and buried and piss on their graves before we let them throw one of our brothers to the wolves – the men continued to shout and the President leaned over the edge of the platform and yelled over and between their shouts – we let those bellyrobbinbastards know that all we want is an honest dollar for an honest days work . . . we dont want any handouts, we want to work for our money, but by krist we're not going to let them get fat from our sweat. We're the men who break our backs while they sit their fat asses on soft chairs in an air conditioned office and rake in the money for our work. And you know what they say? They say that the average pay for you men is $8,000 a year plus another $1,000 in fringe benefits. They say this is enough. They say that they cant afford to pay more without firing as many as they want. You know what we said? We told them to let us have all over $50,000 a year that they were getting and they shut their goddamn mouths fast enough – the men roared so loud he had to stop speaking for a moment – thats just what we told them. He stood with his head bowed then slowly raised it, his voice lower, husky with dedication. I tell you men now that no matter what happens – even if it should cost me my life – you will not have to worry about whether or not you will have a job tomorrow or the next day or the next, speaking slowly, each word seeming to be forced separately from his over-worked and weakened body, this I tell you now and guarantee that when we sign a contract you will be able to go home from work each night and know that there will be a job waiting for you tomorrow. There will be no sleepless nights or empty bellies. He backed away from the edge of the platform and sat with the rest of the officials, his head bowed slightly. The men roared, slapped each other and laughed as they lined up for their $10 bag of groceries. There would be no trouble from them for a few weeks.

The next Monday the mens spirits were still raised. There wasnt the picnic atmosphere of the first days of the strike when they joked, played ball, shot crap and washed and polished their cars; but the despondency and hope-lessness of the past few months had been relieved, tem-porarily at least. Now, as with the incident of the trucks, they had a tangible reason for hating and this allowed them to ignore the reality of the strike, of their lack of money, of the fact that they had been out of work for 6 months and did not know how much longer the strike would last; the daily arguments with the wife, and that they had to scrimp to make the payments on the house and car and, in some cases, that there no longer was a car. Now their hatred and anger was no longer spread over and around everything and everyone they came in contact with, but was directed, with energy at the company and the men who were trying to break their union. There was even a little buoyancy in their stride as they walked the picket line and a hint of optimism in their voices as they spoke to each other and occasionally laughed.

Harry walked around with the men too, patting them on the backside and telling them that theyd break those ballbreakers. Theyll find out they cant fuckus, and he would smile his smile and stamp books.

Only a slight reminder was needed the following Saturday to keep the men comparatively content, but soon the grins once more faded into scowls and the scowls into blankness and though the President gave an exuberant and loud speech before they received their $10 bag of groceries, and told them in as fatherly a manner as he could, that Thanksgiving morning they would each receive, in addition to their regular bag of groceries, a 4lb. chicken – the clique applauding – they lined up, walked and spoke with the same sullenness and hopelessness they had not too many weeks before. And then it was Thanksgiving day. At least the wife would be home today to cook.

That night Harry went to the dragball. Hundreds of fairies were there dressed as women, some having rented expensive gowns, jewelry and fur wraps. They pranced about the huge ballroom calling to each other, hugging each other, admiring each other, sneering disdainfully as a hated queen passed. O, just look at the rags shes wearing. She looks like a bowery whore. Well, lets face it, its not the clothes. She would look simply ugly in a Dior original, and they would stare contemptuously and continue prancing.

There were, too, hundreds not dressed as women: a few of them fairies who walked about with the others, but the majority were johns, trade, and bisexuals. They sat around the perimeter of the ballroom on folding chairs or stood leaning against the wall, dimly visible in the shadows of the barely lighted ballroom, squinting and leering at the queens. The entire ballroom was lit by four medium sized spotlights, one in each corner, and the light was filtered through multi-coloured discs so spots of coloured light crawled along the ceiling and walls, fell to the floor then crawled along the floor, over a leg or back and back into the corner. The queens standing or walking around the floor were continually brushed with the coloured spots and their smooth bared arms would be pocked with green, purple, red, violet, yellow, or combinations as the colours crossed each other, and flesh would be covered with brownish or bluish cores with various coloured ellipses wiggling from them; or a cheek would be pink or white or tan with makeup then suddenly mottled with a large gangrenous spot, the rest of the face shaded with yellow and violet and then the cheek would turn purple, then red; and an occasional light scratched across the faces of the stag line along the sides of the grand ballroom, a wide staring eye or green wet lips briefly visible in the shadows; the lights crawling down the wall, rushing across their faces, then crawling along the floor to their corner and starting the journey again. A few of the shadows spoke, some even smiled, but most sat still and silent, hunched forward slightly following the movements of the lights and queens. Occasionally a flame would appear as a cigarette was lit and an orange face would be thrust forward then be completely invisible for many seconds before coming slowly from the shadows again, the eyes never once, not for a second, looking anywhere but at the queens and the roving lights.

Harry stood at the entrance to the grand ballroom looking around then slid to the side and leaned against the wall trying to recognise his friends. He know almost everyone from Marys would be there, but he could not recognize them in drag. When his eyes became accustomed to the light he looked more closely at the queens on the floor. He was surprised, though he knew they were men, how much they looked like women. Beautiful women. He had never in his life seen women look more beautiful or feminine than the queens strolling about the floor of the ballroom. Yet, when his surprise passed, he felt a little disappointed and looked at the fairies not in drag. He spotted a few he knew and walked over to them. At first he felt conspicuous leaving the shadowed edge of the room and walking across the floor with the lights bobbing around, but as he stood and talked with his friends he wished the lights were brighter. Occasionally one of their friends, who was in drag, would join them and though Harry was still surprised at how beautiful they were he was impatient for them to leave.

Later in the evening a small band played dance music and couples glided, bumped and twisted across the dance floor. From time to time a couple would stand almost immobile, arms tight around each other, kissing and an evil queen would dance by and tap the queen on the shoulder and tell her to take it easy. You might get a hardon honey and rip that dress all up, and laugh and dance away; and people walked back and forth to the bar and others stood on the stairs in the hallway gulping at a bottle; and couples sprawled up and down the stairs, some looking desperately for a dark corner; and the band played a Charleston and the queens and their johns and lovers shuffled and kicked and a few queens lifted their dresses, squealing and screaming, each trying to kick higher than the other, the coloured spots crawling up their legs and across their genitals; and the walls and corners were empty now except for embracing couples; and Harry went out and bought a couple of pints of gin and he and his properly dressed fairy friends made frequent trips to the hall and Harry, for the only time during the evening, watched the queens, but when the Charleston was over he once more ignored the couples on the dance floor of the grand ballroom.

All the queens were high now on gin and bennie and the dance floor was a chaos of giggling, flitting queens, the drooling bodies from the shadows tracking them. All during the night queens came over to Harry and his friends and talked with them and many asked Harry to dance or take a walk and he always refused and when they left he would turn and start talking to Regina, a fairy he had met many times in Marys, but, for some reason, had never taken home or thought of; and soon he was always at Reginas side, talking, drinking, smoking or just standing, and wherever she went Harry followed. She was wearing a pair of tight slacks and a sportshirt and all the whirling of skirts seemed to force Harry to her side. After the Charleston ended Harry put his arm around her and she smiled and kissed him. Harry smiled his smile and rubbed the back of her neck and they went out of the hall with the others, finished what was left of the gin, stood talking with their friends for a while then, when the others went back to the ballroom, they left and Harry took Regina home.

The weeks following Thanksgiving were lovely and exciting for Harry. He saw Regina often and though, if he thought about it, he might have wished he were with Alberta or one of the other fairies he had made love with, he liked being with her, making love with her and calling her on the phone and making a date to meet in Marys. She was a little different than the others and her attitude toward Harry was not the same as the others. She wasnt nervous with him at all. She had no doubts as to what Harry would do. She was more like Ginger when she danced with him at the office and almost crushed his hand. And Harry loved going up to Marys and walking to the tables in the rear knowing someone was waiting specifically for him. He still hung around the office after five drinking beer with the guys from the Greeks, but left shortly after they did and took a cab uptown. He went out more often with Regina than he had with any of the others and occasionally he would buy her a shirt or some little something she asked for. And so he added a few more dollars each week to his expense sheet.

For the other strikers the weeks following Thanksgiving were the beginning of winter. There were days of cold drizzling rain when the men were so cold after walking the picket line, from the weather and dejection, that the coffee, no matter how hot, did not warm them, nor did they feel alive enough to shiver. They just walked the line or waited in the office, only a few of them bothering to curse the weather and then only under their breath. And each Saturday they lined up, after being reassured by one of the officials, and collected their $10 bag of groceries, no longer interested in what was said at the last meeting of the negotiating committees, or the fact that every union in the country was sending money each week to their local so they could continue to provide their men with the staples of life.

Harry loved sitting in the back of Marys with his arm around Regina, waving to his friends, ordering drinks, inviting people to his table, even waving to Ginger one night when she walked in and keeping her at the table until he left with Regina. One night Harry took Regina home and early the next morning he was slowly awakened by something tickling his face. He opened his eyes and Regina was kneeling beside him rubbing her cock against his mouth. He stared then sat up. Whatthefuck yadoin, unable to look her in the eye for more than a second, looking at her cock and the hand around it, the manicured and redpolished nails. Regina laughed then Harry laughed too and they fell back on the bed laughing until Regina finally rolled over and kissed him.

On Xmas Eve the men reported to the hall for their bags of groceries. The hall was strung with decorations and over the platform was a huge sign stretched from wall to wall: MERRY XMAS AND A HAPPY NEW YEAR. Recorded Xmas carols were played and the officials wished each man, individually, a merry Xmas. Each man got an additional $5.00 worth of groceries, another 4 lb. chicken and an Xmas stocking filled with hard candy.

At the first meeting after the Xmas holidays the strike was settled. New government contracts were awarded the company and work would have to begin by the middle of January so Harrington was forced to settle the strike. He was certain that if they prolonged the strike another month he would be able to rid himself of Harry Black, but the Board of Directors informed him that the plant must be in full operation by the middle of January and so an agreement was reached.

Although the union officials had realised thousands of dollars from the strike fund and there was more money coming in every day from unions throughout the country, it was not as much as their income from the Welfare Fund and so the agreement reached was satisfying. And too, after so many years of leisure, the strain of working a few hours every few days that had been necessitated by the long strike enervated them and they were looking forward to the end of the strike and a rest. And, of course, the deposits to the Welfare Fund had been increased and its administration remained in their control.

On December 29th, at 1:30 pm, the men once again assembled in the hall and though they knew that the strike was over they remained huddled by the doors while the President made the announcement. Well men its all over. They gave in to us one-hundredpercent-right-down-the-line. The clique cheered. A few others joined in. Its been a long hard fight but we showed them what a strong union can do. A few more cheers. The President of local 392 told how hard he and the other members of the negotiating committee worked; reminded them what ratbastards the company men were; expressed his thanks and the appreciation of all the men for the fine job done by Brother Harry Black; and told them that the real credit goes to them, the rank and file of the union, the heart of the organisation, who walked the picket line in fair weather and foul, who gave their time and blood that the union could win and help secure an honourable contract. He then told them about the contract and the additional monies to the Welfare Fund and how their jobs were secure; avoiding telling them that they would be assessed $10 each month for the next year – about half of their increase in pay – to build up the now depleted strike fund. When he finished he asked for a vote on the new contract, announced the ayes had it and so the contract was ratified. The clique hootedandhollered. A few others joined them. They were to start work the next day. As the men ambled out of the hall, the officials walking among them, slapping backs and smiling, a recording of auld lang syne was played.

When the meeting was over Harry called Regina then hopped in a cab and went up to her apartment. When he paid the cabdriver and started up the stairs he realised that he could no longer afford to take cabs back and forth, that he could not spend money the way he had while there was a strike. He would no longer be on the union payroll and have an expense sheet. He realised he would not have much money for himself after the rent was paid and he gave Mary a few bucks for food. Regina opened the door and he went in. You know you awakened me from a simply *delightful* sleep. I dont know why you had to call so *early*. I just came from a meetin. The strikes over. O you and that strike. Im going to shower, dress and put a face on then we can go to Marys for a few drinks and after that you can take me to dinner and perhaps the cinema if I should happen to be in the mood. I–I . . . a dont know if I can go ta Marys – Regina strode briskly to the bathroom. The water splashed suddenly against the side of the shower stall – maybe we could just hanground here – I cant hear a *word* youre saying – Harry still standing in the middle of the room – I thought maybe we could eat here, huh? – Regina was singing – Harry stopped talking yet remained standing in the middle of the room. 20 minutes later Regina turned the water off, opened the bathroom door and started arranging her hair. Yalook pretty Regina. She continued combing her hair, humming and occasionally singing a line or two. Be a dear and get my brush in the bedroom. Harry moved from his spot, picked up the brush from the dresser, walked to the bathroom door and handed the brush to Regina. She grabbed it and started brushing. Harry stayed in the doorway watching. O Harry, for *heavens* sake, dont stand there like that. Go away. Go on. Go. Shoo. He backed away and sat on the couch, the couch he had sat on with her many times. I know what. You can take me to Stewarts for a seafood dinner. I adore the place and they have the most divine shrimp and lobster. She went to the bedroom and Harry got up and followed her. I dont have enough money for

Stewarts. What do you mean you dont have enough money. Go get some. And please dont hang over me like that. You bug me. Harry backed away and sat on the bed. I cant get anymore. I only got a few bucks. O dont be silly Harry. Of course you can get some more. Go get my kerchief from the bathroom. Harry got it. He stood behind her for a second then grabbed her and started kissing her neck. Regina squirmed and pushed him away. Dont be such a bore. Cant we stay here tonight. I'll go get a couple a bottles a beer. O what are you talking about. We dont have ta go out. We could stay here, huh? O, Harry sometimes you are just *too much*. I have no intention of staying here tonight or any night. Now will you please leave me alone. But I dont have enough money ta go out and Id like ta stay here and we could have a few beers and nobodyd botha us and I aint so hungry and anyway we could get some sandwiches and – O for gods sake will you please stop babbling like a baby. Im going out this evening. If you have money you can meet me at Marys, if not please do not annoy me any further. Now please leave so I can dress. But we dont have ta – she shoved him in front of her toward the door. *Really* Harry. You are getting hysterical. She opened the door and shoved him out into the hall. The door slammed shut. Harry stood for a long time, feeling a swelling behind his eyes – how long since he had felt it? It almost felt new yet he knew it was not – then left the building and rode the subway to Marys.

He stood by the door for a moment looking around then walked to the back and sat at a table. The others at the table spoke to him occasionally but Harry just nodded or grunted. He ordered a drink and when the others asked if he wasnt going to buy them one he told them he didnt have much money. They kidded him, but when they realised he was serious they ignored him and Harry sat nursing his drink and watching the door. Harry still had a few drops of melted ice in his glass when Regina finally arrived. She sat and dished with the girls for a few minutes then asked Harry if he was going to take her to Stewarts. Harry mumbled and stuttered and Regina jerked her head around and disdainfully told him to forget about it. She would get someone else to escort her. Why dontya have a drink and we could talk, caressing his glass with his finger tips and hunching over the table. Theres a empty booth in the back. We could be alone and talk. And just what would we discuss? High finance? sneering at Harry then looking at the other girls who giggled. Comeon Regina. O really, getting up with many shrugs of her shoulders and going to the phone booth. When she came back she looked down at Harry, you still here? How long are you going to sit there jerking that glass off? You know its really a terrible habit. Harry looked up at her then lowered his head, his hand tightening around the glass. Harry stayed at the table glancing at Regina from time to time, but Regina and the others ignored him completely and continued to talk among themselves until Regina stood up, adjusted her clothing, my date just arrived. I am sure you girls will excuse me, and walked to the bar. The fairies laughed and Harry stared at Regina until she left with her date. Harry looked at his empty glass for many minutes then left and rode the subway back to Brooklyn. It had been a long time since Harry had ridden the subway and it seemed to be exceptionally cold and stuffy and every turn and bump seemed to be directed against his comfort and he had to fight to keep himself on the seat and not be tossed up against the roof or thrown on the floor or against the opposite side. When he got out of the subway he took a cab the 2 blocks to the bar next to the strike office then regretted it when he paid the driver, debating whether or not to tip him, finally giving him a nickel. He sat at the bar and brooded for an hour over the 35c he spent for the cab. Whatever it was that had happened happened too suddenly. He just couldnt figure it out. But things seemed to be all loused up again. He could have taken Regina to Stewarts. He still had a little money. They could have had a good time. He looked in his wallet. A couple of bucks. Fuckit. An hour later he called Regina. The phone rang and rang and he finally hung up and went back to the bar. An hour or so later he called again. Hello. Regina? Harry. Can I seeya tomorra night we could go ta Stewarts if yalike or som – O really Harry – we could go anywhere youd wanna I – O dont bother me. I am very busy. She hung up and Harry stared at the mouthpiece. Regina? Regina?

He let the phone drop from his hand and left the bar and staggered home. Mary was in bed and he stood over her. Slowly he started leaning toward the bed. The covers were held tightly around her neck with a hand. Her hair was spread over the pillow. Ya ballbreakin cunt ya no good sonofabitch – Mary stirred then rolled over on her back and opened her eyes – Yeah, you bitch, grabbing an arm, twisting it and yanking her up to a sitting position, ya fuckin cunt. Whats the matta with you? ya gone crazy or somethin? trying to pull her arm lose. Yeah, Im crazy, crazy fa lettin ya break my fuckin balls – the baby rolled over and started whimpering then crying. Ya better let me go or I'll killya. Ya aint pushin me around ya drunken slob. Drunken slob, eh? I'll showya. I'll showya, twisting harder and slapping her face. Drunkin slob, eh? howya like that, eh? howya likeit, twisting and shaking, slapping her face. YA FILTY BASTAD. I'LL KILLYA. YA CANT SLAP ME AROUND LIKE THAT, scratching his hand. YA LOUSY CUNT, IF IT WASNT FOR YOU ITD BE DIFFERENT. ITS ALL YAFAULT – Mary bit his hand and he let go of her arm shaking his hand and still yelling – the baby banged against the side of the crib still crying. Harry went out to the bathroom and Mary sat in bed yelling after him and cursing him then lay down and covered her head with the pillow to drown out the noise of the kid crying. Harry let water run on his hand then sat at the kitchen table, rested his head on his arms and still muttering, soon fell asleep. After a while the baby started to fall into an exhausted sleep, still whimpering.

The men felt strange and uneasy the first day back on the job. They had been on strike so long they almost got lost trying to find their machines. The first day of the strike was a warm spring day and the men had joked, cleaned their cars, drunk beer . . . now there was snow on the ground and it was a new year. It had been months since they were even capable of hoping. The executives and foremen were rushing about distributing jobs, getting them set up, getting the proper tools and supplies to the right places; and the men stood by their machines, waiting until they had everything necessary to start a job, then worked without enthusiasm, stopping occasionally as the reality of being back on the job startled them.

Harry fumbled around his machine doing little, looking around at the men rushing from one bench to another, one floor to another, watching Wilson, thinking of Harrington, hearing the noise of the machinery, the piece of stock in his lathe and the prints on his bench annoying him. The foreman set up the job for Harry and turned the lathe on. Harry watched the thin spiralling strip of metal unwind from the stock. He watched the fuckin stock spin and the shavings twirl. He thought may be he should take a look around, make his rounds, but didnt feel like moving. When one cut had been made on the stock he didnt reset the machine, but just stood there until the foreman came over, reset it and left. Eventually Harry left. He didnt turn his machine off or tell anyone he was leaving. He just turned, took a step, then continued walking.

He sat in the bar all afternoon drinking whisky; called Regina a few more times, but she either didnt answer or hung up when she heard his voice. Coulda been uptown. Ballbreakinbastards.

He left the bar a little after 8. He leaned against the wall as he walked, unable to stand, slipping on the icy ground. He leaned against the window of the empty store that had been used as the strike office. He lit a few matches trying to see inside, but he still couldnt see anything. There was nothing to see anyway. He had already taken the radio home. It was once again an empty store with a for rent sign on the door.

He walked to the corner, slipping several times, finally having to crawl to the lamppost to help himself stand. He clutched the post for a few minutes catching his breath. A kid, about 10 years old, from his block walked over to him and laughed. Youre drunk Mr. Black, Harry touched him on the head, then stuck his hand down under the large collar of the kids jacket and rubbed the back of his neck. It was very warm. Even slightly moist. The kid laughed again. Hey, your hands cold. Quit it. Harry smiled his smile and pulled him closer. Where yagoin Joey? Up the corner to see the fellas. Harrys hand was warm now and Joey stopped squirming. Howya like a soda. You buyin? Yeah. OK. They started slowly up 57th street, Harrys hands still on the back of Joeys neck. When they had walked a few feet Harry stopped. They stood still a second then Harry started walking into the empty lot. Hey, where yagoin. Over there. Comeon, I wanna show yasomethin. What yawant ta show me? Comeon. They crossed the lot and went behind the large advertising sign. Whats here? Harry leaned against the billboard for a moment then lowered himself to his knees. Joey watched him, his hands in his jacket pockets. Harry reached up and opened Joeys fly and pulled out his cock. Hey, whatta yadoin, trying to back away. Harry clutched Joey by the legs and put Joeys small warm cock in his mouth, his head being tossed from side to side by Joeys attempts to free himself, but he clung to Joeys legs, keeping his cock in his mouth and muttering please . . . please. Joey pounded him on the head and tried to kick him with his knee. LETME GO! LETME GO YA FUCKIN FREAK! Harry felt the fists on his head, the cold ground under his knees; felt the legs squirming and his hands starting to cramp from holding them so tight; and he felt the warm prick in his mouth and the spittle dribbling down his chin; and Joey continued to scream, squirm and pound his head until he finally broke loose and ran from the lot, still screaming, to the Greeks. When Joey broke loose Harry fell on his face, his eyes swelling and tears starting to ooze out and roll down his cheeks. He tried to stand but kept falling to his knees then flat on his face, still muttering please. A minute later Joey, Vinnie and Sal and the rest of the guys from the Greeks came running down 2nd avenue to the lot. Harry was almost standing, holding on to the billboard, when they reached him. THERE HE IS. THERE HEIS. THE SONOFABITCH TRIED TA SUCK ME OFF. Harry let go the billboard and started to extend his arms when Vinnie hit him on the cheek. Ya fuckin freak. Someone else hit him on the back of the neck and Harry fell to the ground and they kicked and stomped him, Joey squeezing in between to kick him too, and Harry barely moved, barely made a sound beyond a whimpering. A couple of the guys picked him up and stretched his arms across and around one of the crossbars of the sign and hung on his arms with all their weight and strength until Harrys arms were straining at the shoulder sockets, threatening to snap, and they took turns punching his stomach and chest and face until both eyes were drowned with blood, then a few of the guys joined the two pulling on his arms and they all tugged until they heard a snap and then they twisted his arms behind him almost trying them in a knot and when they let go he continued to hang from the bar then slowly started to slide down and to one side until one arm jerked around the bar and flopped back and forth like a snapped twig held only by a thin piece of bark and his shoulder jerked up until it was almost on a level with the top of his head and the guys watched Harry Black as he slowly descended from the billboard, his arms flapping back and forth until his jacket got caught on a splinter and the other arm spun around and he hung, impaled, and they hit and kicked him until the splinter snapped and Harry descended to the ground.

Harry lay still, sobbing. He cried then screamed a long loud AAAAAAAAAAAAAAAAAAAAAAAAAAAAAAAAAAAAAAAA that was muffled as his face fell back into the dirt of the lot.

He tried to raise his head but could not. He could only turn it slightly so he rested on a cheek. He was able to open his eyes slightly, but was blinded by the blood. He yelled again. He heard the sound loud inside his head, GOD O GOD, he yelled but no sound came from his mouth. He heard his voice loud in his head but only a slight gurgle came from his lips. GOD   GOD
          YOU SUCK COCK

The moon neither noticed nor ignored Harry as he lay at the foot of the billboard, but continued on its unalterable journey. The guys washed up in the Greeks, drying their hands with toilet paper and tossing the wet wads at each other, laughing. It was the first real kick since blowing up the trucks. The first good rumble since they dumped that doggy. They sprawled at the counter and at the tables and ordered coffeand.

Coda

Landsend

How much less in them that dwell in houses of clay, whose foundation is in the dust, which are crushed before the moth?
They are destroyed from morning to evening: they perish for ever without any regarding it. Doth not their excellency which is in them go away? They die, even without wisdom.

Job 4: 19–21

MIKE KELLY told his wife ta go tahell and rolled over, covering his head with the blanket. Comeon, gut-up. We need milk and bread. He said nothing. Comeon Mike, I'll be late for work. Still silent. Aw please get up Mike, sitting on the edge of the bed and gently pushing his shoulder. Wont yago to the store while I get dressed. Comeon. Mike turned over, knocking her hand from his shoulder, and leaned on his elbow. Look, go tawork and dont bother me, willya? turning back and falling on the bed, pulling the covers back over his head. Irene jerked up and noisily walked to the chair, yanked her clothing off it and started dressing. Youre a bastard Mike. Yahear me? a bastard, slamming down into the chair and putting her socks on. Get lost bitch before I break yahead. Irene continued to mumble as she dressed then stomped off to the bathroom and banged the door shut. Ya better stop the shit Irene or I'll rapya. She faced the closed door and stuck her tongue out then turned both water faucets on quickly, the water splashing out of the basin. She jammed the stopper into the hole, still cursing Mike (the bastard), wrenched the faucets closed and threw the face cloth into the sink. She scrubbed her face, still muttering and Helen, her 3 year old daughter, knocked on the door. Irene jerked the door open. What do *you* want? Helen put her thumb in her mouth and stared at her mother. Well? Have to go peepee Mommy. Well, go ahead. Helen went to the bath-room and Irene rinsed then dried her face. Im going to be late. I just know it. She attacked her hair with a brush and Arthur, almost 18 months old, started crying. O god-DAMNit. She threw the hair brush into the tub (Helens thumb was still in her mouth and she waited until Irene left the bathroom before sliding off the seat, flushing the toilet and running in to the living room) and raged into the bedroom. The least yacan do is take care of the baby. Mike jerked up and shouted for her to get thehellout and leave him alone. Youre his mother you take care of him. Irene stamped her foot and her face flushed. If youd go out and get a job I could take care of him. He pulled the covers back over his head. Dont bother me. You bastard you. You – she yanked a jacket off a hanger, Arthur still wailing for a bottle, Helen sitting in the corner of the living room waiting for the argument to stop. Irene thrust her arms into the sleeves of the jacket. Give me some money for breakfast. He threw the covers off and reached over to his pants and took a dollar out of his wallet. Here. Now get thehell outtahere and stop breakin my balls. She snatched the dollar from his hand and stomped out of the apartment, hoping Arthur would cry louder and make Mike get up, the bastard. Every morning the same thing. Never gives me a hand. Wont even fix the baby a bottle. I come home from work and *I* have to fix supper and *I* have to wash the dishes and *I* have to wash the clothes and *I* have to take care of the kids!!! O, the dirty bastard!!! – rushing along the street to the store. She went in, ignoring the clerks good morning Irene, and picked up a dozen eggs then put them back and took a half dozen as she needed cigarettes, a quart of milk and 2 rolls. She took the cigarettes out of the bag and put them in her pocket so she wouldnt forget them and leave them for Mike (the bastard). When she got back to the apartment she kicked open the door then slammed it shut. Arthur was still crying, Helen standing alongside the crib talking to him, and Mike yelled out ta shut the kid up. Why dontya take care of the kid before yago to the store, truly and honestly indignant at the manner in which she neglected the children. If youre so concerned why dontya get up and take care of him, bastard? He sat up in bed and turned toward the open door. Youd better watch your mouth or I'll shove a fist init, falling back on the bed and covering his head with the blanket. Irene shook but all she could do was stamp a foot, still holding the bag of groceries, and OOOOOOOOOOOOOOOOOO . . . Then she noticed the time and put the bag on the table, put on a pot of water, ran to the kids room and grabbed Arthurs bottle, filled it with milk, heated it enough to take the chill off; poured some corn flakes and milk in a bowl while the bottle was heating, rushed back to the crib with the bottle, Arthur taking it and stopping his crying (Mike moaning a thank krist); then Irene called Helen to eat her corn flakes and made herself a cup of instant coffee, buttered a roll, dunked it, ate it and rushed to the bedroom. Give me some money. O for krists sake, you still here? Hurry Mike. I'll be late. He threw her half a dollar. Hey, how about the change from the dollar? There isnt any (at least she got an extra dime and a pack of cigarettes). Irene gulped the last of her coffee and rushed out. She ran to the bus stop hoping she wouldnt have to wait too long and still cursing Mike, the bastard. If he doesnt clean the house today I'll quit the job. Thats what I'll do. Let him get a job. She saw a bus coming and ran faster, just getting to the bus stop in time. The bastard.

* * * * * * * * * * * *

Ada opened the window. The air was still and warm. She smiled and looked at the trees; the old ones, tall, big and strong; the young ones small, springy, hopeful; sunshine lighting the new leaves and buds. Even the budding leaves on the hedges and the young thin grass and dandelion sprouts were alive with sunshine. O, it is so lovely. And Ada praised god, the being and creator of the universe who brought forth the spring with the warmth of his sun.

She leaned out the window, her favourite window. From it the factory and the empty lots and junkyards were not visible; she could see only the landscaping and the playground. And everything was coming to life and it was warm with sunshine. There were dozens of shades of green and now that spring was *really* here it would get greener and life would multiply on the earth and the birds would be more plentiful and their song would wake her in the mornings. All would be beautiful. She watched the birds hopping on the ground, flying to the tree limbs still thin but soon to be thick and heavy with green leaves. Yes, the first warm day of the year. She breathed deeply. Yes, it is warm. The first warm day of the year. There were a few other days when the sun had shone and the air had been warm, but there was always the last of the winter winds to chill it or rain to wet it. But not so today. The long winter was over. The long cold bitter winter when all you could do was walk to the store and back to the apartment . . . back to the apartment to sit and stare out the window and wait . . . wait for a day such as this. There were a few days – yes a few, not many – when she had been able to sit on the bench, but even though the winds were still and the sun bright she could only sit downstairs for a few minutes and then, though she had bundled herself well in sweaters, gloves, scarf, and coat and sat where the sun was shining brightest, a chill would seep through her clothing and she would have to go upstairs. And even with the sun bright you couldnt really feel it, not *really* feel it as you should, as the sun is supposed to light your body and warm it through right to your heart. No, you could feel it only a little on your face. And, there was never anyone to talk to in the winter. No one came and sat. Not even for a few minutes. And too, the winters are so long. And lonely. All alone in her 3 rooms filled with furniture, the relics saved from the old days, sitting by the window watching the bare tree limbs shiver in the wind; the birds searching the frozen, bare ground; people walking with their backs turned to the wind and the whole world with their backs to her. In the winter everyones hate was bare if you looked. She saw hate in the icicles that hung from her window; she saw it in the dirty slush on the streets; she heard it in the hail that scratched her window and bit her face; she could see it in the lowered heads hurrying to warm homes . . . yes their heads were lowered away from Ada and Ada beat her breast and pulled her hair yelling to the Lord God Jehovah to have pity and be merciful and she scratched her face until her fingernails filled with flesh and blood dribbled down her cheeks, beating her head against her window until her head was bruised and small droplets of thin blood smeared with the moisture on her wailing wall, her arms still raised in supplication to Jehovah asking why she was being punished, begging mercy, asking why the people turned against her, beating her breast and begging mercy from her God who delivered the Tablets unto Moses and guided *his* children across the burning desert; the wrathful God who parted the Red Sea for the chosen people and drowned the pursuing armies in its turbulent waters; pleading with the revengeful God who delivered a pestilence unto the Pharaoh and the children of Israel when they turned their backs to *him* . . . O God have mercy . . . and Ada stood in front of her wailing wall looking at heaven through the frost covered glass smeared with her blood, praying to the Father as did the trees with their bared limbs raised to heaven; and she beat her breast and pulled her hair and tore the flesh from her cheeks and banged her head, and she would fall against her window weeping, sobbing, slowly sinking, sinking to her knees muttering . . . and Ada would lie on the floor sobbing, crying, bleeding . . . then, after a time, sleep. When she awoke she fasted for 24 hours, sitting among her relics, reciting ancient prayers aloud, rocking back and forth in her chair as she prayed. At the end of the 24 hours she fixed a cup of broth and stood in front of her window looking at the leafless trees and frozen earth, ignoring the concrete, the cars that passed, hearing only the voice of God and thinking only of the warm days to come. For 2 more days, 3 days in all, her face remained unwashed and she stayed within her apartment, drinking only 1 cup of broth each day, praying, looking out the window, walking through her rooms, back and forth, conscious of the stiffness of the dried wounds on her face, looking in the mirror at the scabs and gently touching them with the tips of her fingers. Then at the end of the third day she would wash her face and eat a meal and go to the store and buy the few things she needed, smiling at the people, asking the clerk how he was and telling him to keep well and take care.

But winter was over and now she could sit on a bench and feel the sun, watch the birds, the children playing, and perhaps someone would sit and talk with her.

*　　*　　*　　*　　*　　*　　*　　*　　*　　*　　*

Vinnie and Mary would still be unmarried if they hadnt met. But they finally did, when he was 40 and she was 35, and were married and both families were joyous. As soon as they were alone the first night Vinnie dragged Mary to bed and pounced on her, shaking the bed, the chest of drawers, the picture of the Blessed Mother over the bed, until her stomach was so sore she couldnt move, but could only lie on her back groaning and SCREAMING AT HIM TO STOP. But Vinnie continued to bangaway, slobbering at the mouth and YELLING THAT SHE WAS HIS WIFE AND THEY CONTINUED TO BOUNCE ON THE BED (the Blessed Mother shaking) BANGING, BANGING,

BANGING AND YELLING. 5 years later they had two kids and were still yelling. The kids had been sitting up in the crib yelling for half an hour before Vinnie and Mary got up. Mary rolled to the side of the bed and YELLED TO THE KIDS TO SHATUUUUUP! WHATS THEMATTA? VINNIE SLAPPED HER BACK AND TOLD HER TA FIX A BOTTLE AND STOP YELLIN, then sat on the side of the bed scratching his head. They both got up and stood facing each other, scratching, THE KIDS STILL YELLING. GO ON. FIX THE BOTTLE. IYAM. IYAM. WHATS THE MATTA YOU GOTTA YELL? WHATTAYAMEAN YELL? FIX THE BOTTLE. AW SHATUP. Mary stepped into her slippers and slopped out to the kitchen and fixed the bottle, standing over the stove waiting for it to heat, scratching her belly and armpits. She went back to the bedroom to get dressed after giving the baby the bottle, but when she took her nightgown off Vinnie came over and slapped her tits back and forth. DEY HANG TA YAKNEES. She pushed him away. GOWAY STUPID. He reached down and pulled her pubic hair, WHATTA BUSH. She shoved him away, YA CRAZY. YA NO GOOD, and grabbed her clothes and went to the bathroom to dress, closing and locking the door. Vinnie dressed and went to see the kids. He looked down at them and smiled and pinched their cheeks. YA DRINK THE BOTTLE, EH? THATS GOOD. They blinked, the baby continuing to suck on the nipple of his bottle. THATS A GOOD KIDS, pinching them again before leaving the room. HEY, HURRY-UP, EH? I GOTTA GO THE BATHROOM. WHATTZAMATTA, YAIN A HURRY? SHADUP AND HURRY, YEAH? Vinnie paced up and down, going out to the kitchen, back to the kids room, then pounded on the bathroom door. COMEON, COMEON. HURRYUP, YEAH? WHATS YAHURRY? WAIT, slowly putting her clothes on then slowly filling the sink with water. Vinnie banged with both fists on the door. FA KRISTS SAKE OPEN THE DOOR. I GOTTA PISS. GAWAY. WHY DONTYA DRESS IN THE BEDROOM? CAUSE YA BODDA ME. GOWAY, YEAH? Vinnie punched and kicked the door. YA DIRTY BITCH. He turned from the door and started pacing again, holding his crotch, walking faster and faster, jumping up and down. I CANT WAIT. OPEN THE DOOR. GO WAY. He punched the door again. I'LL KILLYA WHEN YA COME OUT, turning once more from the door and going to the bedroom. He opened the window and urinated, the stream hitting the open window of the bedroom below, splashing off the open window and onto the baby in the crib. Mrs. Jones stared for a moment, then called her husband and told him about the water coming from upstairs and splashing on the baby. I'll go see about it. It must be those crazy ones upstairs. Nobody elsed do that. He marched out of the apartment and up the stairs. Mary finally opened the door and walked slowly from the bathroom. IM FINISHED. GO ON. I TOUGHT YA WAS IN A HURRY. GO AHEAD, PISS. Vinnie slapped her on the head. WHATZAMATTA, YA CRAZY BITCH. YA STUPID A SOMETHIN? EH? She slapped him back. WHO YA TINK YA HITTIN YA MOUNTIN WOP. He swung and missed and SCREAMED AT HER and Mr. Jones pounded on the door and Mary YELLED TO VINNIE TA SHADUUUUUUP and she opened the door and Mr. Jones wanted to know what was the idea of pouring water out the window, it went all over his baby, and Mary shrugged her shoulders and said WHAAAA? WHA WATTA? WHA YA TALKIN ABOUT? and Mr. Jones said you know what Im talking about, and the baby finished his bottle and threw it out of the crib and both kids started yelling again and MARY YELLED TO VINNIE TA SHAD THE KIDS UP AND VINNIE YELLED

HE WAS GETTIN DRESSED, and Mary turned back to Mr. Jones when he tapped her on the shoulder and said, well? and she said WHAAA? AND YELLED AT THE KIDS TA SHADUUUUUP and Vinnie went to the kids room, WHATZAMATTA? WHY YA CRY, EH? and picked the kids up and Mary told Mr. Jones SHE DIDNT KNOW NOTHIN ABOUT NO WATTA OUT THE WINDOW and he threw his arms up in the air and Mary turned and told the kids JUST A MINUTE, YEAH? and Mr Jones said dont let it happen again or hed get the cops and Mary shrugged and let the door close and the kids still YELLED AND VINNIE TOLD THEM TO BE QUIET. MARY, TAKE CAREA THE KIDS, YEAH? and she changed them and Vinnie went to the bathroom to wash and YELLED OUT TO MARY TA FIX BREAKFAST AND SHE SAID TA HOLD HIS WATTA and she finished with the kids and they ran back to their room to get some toys and Vinnie splashed water on his face and Mary SLAMMED THE COFFEE POT ON THE STOVE AND VINNIE CAME OUT AND POURED HIMSELF A GLASS OF JUICE AND SHE SAID HOW ABOUT ME? AND HE TOLD HER TA POUR HER OWN JUICE AND SHE SAID TA FIX HIS OWN BREAKFAST AND HE SLAPPED HER HEAD AND SHE KICKED HIS LEG AND HE KICKED HER BACK AND TOLD HER TA FIX BREAKFAST AND GET THE KIDS READY SO THEY COULD GET SOME FRESH AIR AND SHE SAID PISS ONYA AND BANGED A FRYING PAN ON THE STOVE AND FRIED TWO EGGS FOR HERSELF AND WHEN SHE FINISHED HE FRIED HIS AND TOLD HER SHE BETTA FEED THE KIDS OR HED THROWER OUT THE WINDDA AND SHE SAID DONT WORRY ABOUT IT, YEAH? AND HE DUMPED HIS EGGS ONTO A PLATE AND BANGED THE PLATE ON THE TABLE AND BOTH KIDS

WANTED THE SAME TOY AND THEY TUGGED AT
IT AND THEY SCREAMED AT EACH OTHER AND
CRIED AND MARY SAID SHADUUUUP AND VINNIE
TOLD HER TASEE WHAT WAS WRONG AND
SLURRPED AN EGG INTO HIS MOUTH AND MARY
WENT INTO THEIR ROOM AND TOOK THE TOY
AWAY FROM THEM AND TOLD THEM TA GO
OUTSIDE AND SHE FIXED THEM BREAKFAST
AND VINNIE SAT IN THE LIVING ROOM YELLING
OUT TO MARY AND MARY YELLED BACK AND
EVERY NOW AND THEN THE KIDS WOULD YELL
AND THE BOTH OF THEM WOULD YELL AT THE
KIDS AND THE KIDS WOULD YELL LOUDER AND
VINNIE AND MARY WOULD SCREAM AND FINAL-
LY BREAKFAST WAS FINISHED AND EVERYONE
CONTINUED TO YELL AS THE KIDS RAN TO THEIR
ROOM AND MARY STARTED WASHING THE
DISHES AND THE NEIGHBORS TURNED UP THEIR
RADIOS.

*　　*　　*　　*　　*　　*　　*　　*　　*　　*　　*

PROJECT NEWSLETTER

AIRMAIL

Throwing garbage out of windows is referred to
as AIRMAIL. We do not want any AIRMAIL
from this Project. There have been many com-
plaints lately of garbage on the street, in the
halls, and even a few cases of people being hit
with garbage being thrown from windows.
AIRMAIL is a violation of the Health Code
and a violation of the Housing Authority Regulations. Any tenant found guilty of throwing

garbage from there windows will be immediately evicted. We want this Project to be a safe and clean place to live. It is up to you to keep it this way.

*   *   *   *   *   *   *   *   *   *   *

Lucy got out of bed slowly and went to the childrens room, changed and dressed Robert, her youngest son, took him out of the crib, then dressed Johnny. She told them to play quietly (she certainly wasnt going to allow her children to run around like indians), Daddys sleeping, and went to the kitchen to fix breakfast. She filled 3 glasses with juice and softly called the children. They came running out and she hushed them and told them to be quiet, nice little boys dont run around the house making a lot of noise. They drank their juice and went back to their room to play. A few minutes later they were yelling BANG, BANG and Lucy ran to their room and told them to hush. But we're playing guns Mommy. Johnny, how many times have I told you that nice young boys dont play guns in the house. I dont know Mommy. Lucy looked at him for a second. Well, never mind, just be quiet. OK. Then see that you do, and Lucy went back to the kitchen, listening for noise from the childrens room, relieved that the children were quiet and not acting like a bunch of roughnecks. She was just about to call them when someone knocked on the door. She adjusted her bathrobe, smoothed down her hair then opened the door. The nice young white girl from downstairs smiled at her. I think there may be something wrong in your bathroom Lucy. Water is leaking down through my ceiling. Lucy OOOOO'd and rushed to the bathroom. She opened the door and the children spun around, Johnny frantically trying to turn off the faucets. She glared at them, the water on the floor – Robert starting to whine

and Johnny still turning the faucets and saying Im sorry—
the water still pouring over the sides of the basin. She
reached over and slapped Johnnys hands off the faucets
and turned off the water. Johnny started to cry and she
opened her mouth to scold him when she remembered the
girl was still at the door. She rushed back to the door and
told her she was terribly sorry, the kids were playing and
she hoped no damage had been done. Im really awfully
sorry about this Jean. No, its alright. No harm done. They
smiled at each other and the girl left. Lucy almost slammed
the door, but caught it in time and closed it quietly not
wanting the girl to think she was angry with her. She
leaned against the door mortified. Of all the people in the
Project it had to be that nice white girl. Such a nice quiet
family and now she probably thinks we're just like the rest.
She rushed back to the bathroom. Johnny was still standing by the sink staring at the doorway, but Robert had left
and gone to their room leaving wet foot prints. Lucy
grabbed Johnny by the arm and dragged him from the
bathroom. O youre going to get it. Dont you know better
than to do a thing like that, DONT YOU? slapping him on
the backside, still dragging him to his room. Johnny crying
and yelling Im sorry Mommy. Youre sorry. YOURE
SORRY, slapping him again and pushing him onto his
bed. Johnny continued crying and pleading – Robert
standing in the corner afraid he too would be spanked
– and Lucy yelling at Johnny that he would be punished
for this . . . then she realised she was yelling and perhaps
the people downstairs could hear her, or others may have
heard her . . . she listened for a moment and then quickly
closed the door, telling Johnny to be quiet. Her teeth were
clenched and she snarled at him. If youve wakened your
daddy youll be sorry, shaking with anger and frustration,
exasperated by what had happened and with the fear that
someone had heard her yelling. She listened to hear if

Louis had awakened, but no sound came from the bedroom. She turned back to Johnny, who was trying to stop crying (we didnt make any noise in the bathroom), but tears still rolled down his cheeks and his breath was caught with sobs. Robert started whimpering and Lucy told him to hush, her voice quieter and more controlled. Johnny could see that the worst was over, so he started to control his sobbing, still looking pleadingly at his mother. I-I-Im su-su-sorry Mom-Mommy. Just be quiet and calm down and – THE OATMEAL! She rushed to the kitchen and snatched the pot off the stove. O thank goodness its not ruined. She put the oatmeal on the childrens plates and called them. They sat quietly at the table and started eating. Lucy went back to her now cold cup of coffee. She poured another cup and sat at the table with the children. She could hear Vinnie and Mary screaming at each other. Lucy shook her head and cursed the Project. She finished her coffee then remembered the water on the bathroom floor and grabbed the mop from the closet and rushed to the bathroom and mopped the floor, just waiting for Johnny to make a sound and she would give it to him good. She wrung out the mop, put it away and sat back at the table. Johnny had finished his cereal and sat quietly looking at his Mother as she fed Robert then cleared the table. She told the children to go to their room and play quietly then went to the bedroom and dressed. After dressing she got the clothes ready for the laundromat. She washed, then brushed her hair, put the laundry in the laundry cart and hustled the children from the apartment. She hurried to the elevator, opened the door and was about to step in when she noticed a pile (actually noticing the smell first) of human shit on the elevator floor. Again! She stopped and grabbed Robert as he was about to step in it, then quickly turned away before someone saw her there. Picking up Robert she started down the stairs (O

God, now I'll have to walk up two flights of stairs with the cart). Lucy flushed with embarrassment, wanting to get as far away from the elevator as possible before someone else opened the door, Johnny yelling at his Mother to wait for him. Lucy waited for Johnny at the door (already convincing herself that a spick had done it) then rushed from the building, Johnny running to keep up.

*　*　*　*　*　*　*　*　*　*　*

Abraham got up late. He stayed in bed as long as he could, but the noise the 5 kids made was too much for him. Even the closed door didnt help so he got up. He sat on the side of the bed and carefully took the hairnet off his konked and marcelled hair, lit a cigarette and started thinking about the fine, I mean *real* fine brownskinned gal that was in MELS last night. Her skin was light and real smooth and her hair was long and wavy. Not all tight and stiff, but smooth man, and long. Yeah . . . And she had on this real tight dress and when she walked her big ol ass just quivered and shook like crazy and when she danced the slop you could see the muscles of that fine ass just rollin all ovuh. Yeah . . . that was some fine stuff. Man, he shuh would like to bag that bitch and really lay it oner. Sheeeit . . . Id fuck the ass right offen that bitch man. I mean right *off*. Man when I finish screwin that ol broad she'd know she'd been laid and she'd damn sure know who tu call daddyo. Ghuddamn . . . I'll put on some fine rags tunight and make all those cats look like bums man. I mean this stud is gonna be the sharpest motherfucka that chick ever seed. Sheeit. This is ol Abe. Ol honest Abe Washington, hehhehheh . . . and aint nobody, man I mean nobody caint put no shit ovuh on *me*. This cats hip man, and when I lay it on that chick I mean shes gonna knowit . . . Yeah . . . He stood up and stretched, put out his cigarette and dressed. He opened the bedroom door and yelled to the kids tu shut up as he walked to the bathroom. They quieted for a moment then continued running, yelling and shooting. Abe worked the soap up to a lather then worked the lather thoroughly into his face, rinsing first with warm water then cold. He patted his face dry with the towel then inspected his face in the mirror, going over every square centimeter very carefully, pushing his nose first to one side then the other, stretching the skin of his neck. After 5 minutes he was happy to find only one pimple. This he carefully squeezed then wet the corner of the towel with cold water and patted the infected area. He brushed his teeth, which were naturally white, but he had to be certain he got off the yellow smoking stains. Then he gargled. Next he rubbed skin cream into his face – leaning out of the door to yell at the Ghuddamn kids tu shut up – then inspected his face once more. He was satisfied. He rubbed some hair grease between the palms of his hands then patted it on his hair. Then he picked up the comb and gently, tentatively at first, combed his hair, laying down the comb from time to time and using the soft brush, pushing each wave in place, touching here and there, working up this wave a little more than the other, being careful a hair wasnt sticking up or out of place – why dont chuall shutup – stepping back from the mirror to admire the way his hair sparkled, adjusting a wave a little more, then picking up the small hand mirror and turning his back to the large mirror over the sink and holding the small mirror in front of him he inspected the back of his head, pushing a little here and there, then, smiling and thinking of her fine ass, wiped his hands off on the towel and went out to the kitchen. He told his wife to fix him some eggs and sat down and cleaned his nails, scrapping the funk off on the edge of the table. He filed away at his nails and asked his wife why she didnt get the kids dressed

and send them out. They make too ghuddamn much noise
running all ovuh. She told him she was too busy to fret
about the kids. The kids had stopped for a moment again,
but started running and shooting and one stepped on Abes
foot and he yelled and swung his arm. The kid darted
away, but knocked into his mother as she was taking the
eggs from the refrigerator. She put the eggs down and
yelled that she was gonna get a strap toem and then maybe
theyd stop runnin around like crazy mens. The kid started
whimpering that he was sorry and she took the strap from
around her waist and waved it at him and he cringed and
backed away until his mother relented, then he sat quietly
and his sister, the oldest, scolded him for being naughty
and he wanted to kick her like he usually did, but was
afraid. Hed wait until they got outside. Abe wanted to
know what was holdin up his eggs, he had some things to
do today. She brought the eggs and he ate, Nancy telling
him about how the doctor at the clinic say the kids got the
maltrition and they giver some cod*liver*oil, but he say they
should have some vitamins and Abe dipped his bread in
the yoke and caught the yoke with his tongue as it dribbled
from the bread and tolder not tu wurry him about no
vitamins and she say she need some money forem and he
tolder he giver 20 dollars every week and she can get the
vitamins with that. But ah caint. He shrugged and tolder to
givem more collard greens and he slopped up the stringy
uncooked white of the egg with his bread and tolder to
givem his coffee and she poured it and said Ghuddamnit, I
need some more money and he said sheeit, he worked his
ass off on the docks fur his money and he be Ghudamned if
hed let her throw it away, and the kids still sat in silence
waiting for the father to go so they could be dressed and
get out where it was safe, and Nancy cursed Abes black ass
and he tolder tu shut up those blubber lips and he counted
out 20 dollars and threw it on the table and said she was

lucky to have all that, that he had a whole mess a bills tu pay and all she had tu do was buy food and Ghudamnit if yu caint buy enough with that and the Ghuddamn vitamins then shame onyu. She snatched the money off the table and yelled at the kids to get dressed and get the hell out and the two older boys scampered to their room, the daughter saying, yes Mommy and walking; and Abe gulped down his coffee and left the kitchen. He put on a jacket, inspected his face and hair once more, adjusting the frontmost wave, then left the house.

*   *   *   *   *   *   *   *   *   *   *

THE CHASE

A group of kids, about 5 and 6 years old, stood on the steps of the entrance to one of the buildings. Another group stood huddled about a hundred feet away. The 2 groups eyed each other, spitting, cursing, staring. Some of the kids on the steps wanted to get the mothafuckas now and killem, the others wanted to wait for Jimmy. Jimmy was the biggest guy they had. When he come we'll get the bastards. He run fasteran any ofem. Sheeit man, we'll catchem all and killem. Yeah man, we'll burn the mothafuckas alive. They paced on the steps impatiently, spitting and glaring at the other group. Then they heard someone running down the stairs and Jimmy came out. Jimmy yelled to them and took out a gun and said, comeon, lets kill those fuckinbastards. They all screeched wildly and followed Jimmy as he ran at the other gang. They screeched too and started running. The game of cowboys and indians had started. They ran along the streets shooting, yelling, bang, bang, yur dead motherfucka. I gotya. Yo aiss yo did. I gotya. Bang. Bang. In, out and between the people walking, standing, sitting on the benches;

running around the trees, bang, bang, looking behind and shooting at the pursuer; knocking into someone and spinning them around – Why dontya look where ya goin ya stupid bastard – or if they were small they simply knocked them down the pursuer jumping over the fallen kid who was now crying and yelling for his mommy. Bang, bang, through the hedges and spinning around the young trees; knocking over the shrubs, bang, bang. Jimmy got one cornered by the steps. He stood just in front of Jimmy on the other side of a baby carriage. The kid feinted to one side then the other. Finally Jimmy committed himself to one side and the kid whirled around the opposite side pulling over the carriage, the baby falling out and rolling along the ground, stopping as it hit the hedge. The 2 kids looked at it for a moment, listening to it scream, then a head popped out a window and wanted to know what the fuck they was doin, and the kids hauledass and Jimmy ran through the hedge after the other kid, bang, bang, and they ran around the building out of sight. The game of cowboys and indians continued.

*   *   *   *   *   *   *   *   *   *   *

Ada hummed as she washed the dishes. She scoured the sink then made her bed, first opening the windows so the bed clothes should air out, then carefully tucking in the sheets and blanket, fluffing up the pillows (Hymie always liked his pillow thick and fluffy), then hanging up her nightgown and the pajamas she laid out on Hymies side of the bed each night. (Hymie had always liked a clean pair of pajamas every night and though he had been dead these 5 years, 6 in October, October the 23rd, she still laid out a pair of pajamas every night, though now she used the same pair each night, washing them once a month, ironing them and putting them back on the bed.) Then she tidied up the apartment, sweeping the kitchen floor and adjusting the furniture, before wiping the dishes and putting them away with the other dairy dishes. The humming evolved into light singing as she put on her sweater and coat and readied herself to go downstairs. She looked around the apartment, making certain the stove was off and all the lights out, before closing the door and going out. Near the entrance to the building was a small area bordered with benches and a few young trees. Here Ada sat whenever the weather permitted. She sat on a bench on the near side as she knew it would be in the sun longer than any of the others. This was *her* bench and here she sat and watched the children, the people passing or sitting, and enjoying the warmth of the sunshine. She closed her eyes and faced the sun, lifting her face, and sat thus for many minutes feeling the heat on her forehead, her eyelids, her cheeks, feeling the suns rays penetrating her chest, warming her heart, making her feel almost happy. She breathed deeply, sighing inaudibly, and lowered her head and opened her eyes, then raised her feet slightly and wiggled her toes in her shoes. Her poor feet had such a burden to carry and they suffered so in the winter, but now even they were alive and relieved. It would be many, many wonderfully warm and sunny months before her feet would have to be tortured with thick heavy socks and forced to feel the cold. Soon she could go one day to Coney Island and sit on the Boardwalk and watch the swimmers or maybe she could even walk in the surf, but she wasnt sure if she should. She might slip, or someone might knock her over. Anyway, the beach was nice even just sitting on a bench getting the sun. She watched a small child ride by on his tricycle then watched a group of children running after each other and yelling. Occasionally she would be able to distinguish the words they were yelling and she blushed and immediately pushed it from her mind (this too would be remembered next winter) then turned abruptly as she heard a baby crying, seeing the overturned carriage, hearing the voice from a window, seeing a blur as 2 children ran away; trying to locate the baby, getting up from the bench when she finally saw it lying on the ground, but sitting down when she saw a woman coming out of the building. Those children really should be more careful. She watched the mother pick up the child and drop him in the carriage and shove a bottle in his mouth and go upstairs. I hope it wasnt hurt. The baby eventually stopped crying and Ada turned away and once more watched the child circling the benches on its tricycle. She saw a woman passing with her children and shopping cart. The woman smiled, nodded and said Hello. Ada returned her greeting but didnt smile. She was a nice lady but her husband was a no good. He always looked at Ada funny like he was going to hurt her. Not like her Hymie. Her Hymie was always friendly. Such a good man. They would have been married 43 years this summer, July 29th, if he was still alive. Hymie used to help her all the time. And he too loved the beach. But so seldom they could go. Only on Mondays when they closed the store and then sometimes it wouldnt be so nice. But many times they would go and she would make sandwiches and a thermos of a cold drink and Hymie always got for her a beach chair and umbrella. He always insisted. I want you should be comfortable and enjoy yourself. Thats what he said. She would always say no, dont bother. Who needs it? and they would laugh. But always Hymie insisted she should have the umbrella in case she might want to sit in the shade, but she never did and they would sit on the beach chairs getting the sun and once, maybe twice, during the day they would go down to the surf and splash around. He was so good her Hymie. And sometimes when her Ira got older he would tell them to go to the beach, he would mind the store and they would go an extra day to the beach. Her Ira was the best boy any Mother could have. (Everynight before going to bed she kissed their pictures.) Still only a boy already when they killed him. Just a boy. Not even married. Not even married when the Army took him. And he was such a good boy. When he was still just a little one he would come home from school and tell her to take a nap, hed help papa in the store and Hymie would smile so big and rub little Iras head and say yes, take a nap. Iras a big boy now and he will help me and Ira would smile up at his father and Ada would go back to the small rooms behind the candy store and lie down. And sometimes, when maybe it wasnt too busy, Hymie would fix the supper while Ira watched the store and then Ira would come back and wake her up and say suppers ready Mommy. See? And everything would be on the table and they would eat and she would go out and take care of the store while Hymie ate. And Hymie worked so hard. Opening the store at 6 in the morning and going out and getting the papers off the street, and sometimes it would be cold and raining, and he would carry in the big bundles of papers all by himself (he would never let her help him with that) and cut the cords and arrange them on the stand and she would lie in bed, pretending to be asleep, and all the years they were married Hymie got out of bed so quietly so she should sleeplonger and every morning she would wake up but she never let him know she was awake so he wouldnt worry about her. Then he would come back at 8 oclock and she would pretend to wake up when he touched her, and she would get up and fix the breakfast. For 20 years they had that store and they were so happy – the child ran his tricycle into a tree and toppled off, but got right up and started riding again – maybe they didnt always have so much, but they were happy and she could still smell the soda fountain; the sweet smell of ice cream, syrups, mixed fruits, hot fudge, marshmallow, whipped cream and the fudgicles, popsicles and ices and the candy and chewing gum on the counter and the candy shelves on the opposite side of the store, the sliding glass doors smeared by the smudgy hands of thousands of children. She used to lean on the counter and watch them look at the candies pointing with their fingers pressed against the glass. Many times each day this would happen and Ada would wonder why they had to lean against the glass with their hands and why it took them so long to make up their minds what candy they wanted. And then when Ira came, late in her life, it didnt annoy her as much. They were young like her Ira. But when they get older they werent so nice and said bad things to you. But Ira was always such a good boy. And they had to kill him. And they didnt even see his body. Just a telegram and many years later a sealed coffin. My poor Ira. So young. Not even a father and now dead. Dead already 15 years – a few other children joined the one with the tricycle and they took turns riding it, laughing and running around in circles. Ada smiled as she watched them. Dead 15 years and not even children to remember you. I dont know why they did this to me. Even dead before Hymie, his father. And even Hymie left me. Such a good man. Worked so hard his back bent – someone passed and Ada smiled, but they just walked past not noticing Ada and Ada almost yelled at them, but stopped as she noticed that now women were coming down and people were going to the store and children were running and laughing and the sun was getting brighter and warmer and a few men straddled a bench with a checker board between them and maybe someone would sit down next to her and they would talk.

*　　*　　*　　*　　*　　*　　*　　*　　*　　*　　*

The housewives were on a bench. They looked at Ada and laughed. Everything comes out in this weather. Even Ada. I guess shes airing out her clothes. Laughter. Same shitty coat. She wears it all winter. Why dont she take it off? She got nothin on underneath. Whattaya mean? I bet shes wearing scabs. Laughter. Shes a filthy slob. I bet even the fumigator is afraid ta go up her house. I bet her crotch smells like limburger cheese. Laughter. (One picked her nose, exploring each nostril first with the pinky, locating the choice deposits, then with the forefinger broke loose the nights accumulations, scraping with the thumb and plucking forth, with thumb and forefinger, a choice meaty snot, long and green, spotted with yellows, waving it about, then rolling it in a ball, caressing it between her fingers, trying to flip it off but it clung tenanciously, adhesively to the finger until it was finally rubbed off on the bench.) And that fuckin Lucy. I saw her goin to the laundromat with another bunch of clothes. Aaaaa, who the fuck she think she is. Always washin clothes. Yeah, whos she tryin ta kid. You know her husbands goin ta school. Yeah. I guess he thinks hes gonna be somethin. Maybe hes gonna learn ta be a pimp. What for. Aint nobody gonna want ta fuck Lucy. I bet she thinks its ta piss through. Me, I wash my clothes when they need it, but I dont act like that. (One lifted a cheek of her ass, let go a loud gurgling fart and sighed.) Laughter. Looka Ada smilin. I think shes nuts the way she smiles all the time like that. She is. Shes got people talkin to'er in her head. Somebody oughtta call up Kings County and turner in. Laughter. Yeah, it aint safe with nuts runnin around. All she needs is a good fuckin. Maybe I should send Henry ova, hed do a good job. Laughter. I bet she got money put away somewhere. You know those kind. Yeah. Her husband was in business for himself and you cant tell me shes gotta go on Relief. Look after sittin alone and smilin. If I had her money you wouldnt catch me sittin here. (A scab is picked off a leg, examined from various angles then flicked away.)

*   *   *   *   *   *   *   *   *   *   *

PROJECT NEWSLETTER

It has been brought to the attention of the Management of this Project that certain Adolescent children are taking money from younger children, threatening to beat them up if they do not give up the money they have. They are also stopping the smaller children on there way to the store with deposit bottles and taking them away from them along with any money they might have. Any child caught taking money from younger children will be handed over to the Police Department for prosecution and the families of the children will be immediately evicted. The management recommends that mothers refrain from sending young children to the store with money or deposit bottles. We want this Project to be a safe place for everyone to live. It is up to everyone to cooperate.

*   *   *   *   *   *   *   *   *   *   *

Mike finally got up. The babys crying was faint, but he knew that as soon as he opened the door the crying would be louder and Helen would come over to him and bother him about something, wanting to eat or get dressed or ask some damn stupid questions. He got dressed and sat back on the edge of the bed and smoked a cigarette, then stretched out on the bed hoping he would feel sleepy. He covered his eyes with his arm, but it didnt help. He put out the cigarette and rolled over on his side – Helen heard the movement and turned from the window, where she had been watching the kids, and waited for the door to open – but he just didnt feel tired. Still he lay there hoping he might drowse off and maybe sleep for a few more hours. At least there would be that much more time passed. I wonder what time it is? Cant be 12 yet, didnt hear the whistle. If the kids would just shut up maybe I could get ta sleep. But the sun was bright and even with the shade drawn there was plenty of light in the room and goddamnit, he might just as well get up. Might just as well. He rolled back to the edge of the bed and slowly stood. The goddamn kid was probably wet. Krist can he make noise. He went to the window and peered out, keeping the shade down. Most of the windows of the apartments were open and he looked in each one, not shifting to the next one until he was fully accustomed to the changes of light and was certain there was nothing to be seen. Once he had seen a woman, not a bad lookin head either, leaning out the window, talking to someone downstairs, and one of her tits fell out of her robe. She didnt know he was watching so she didnt hurry to stick it back. And it was a good size tit too. Things like that might happen anytime, especially when the weather was warm. That was a good day. He had felt good the whole day. It was almost as good as gettin a strange piece. He had a gigantic hardon all day and when Irene came home from work he walked her right into the bedroom and they fucked like crazy. He had her sit on it and her tits stuck way out and he buried his face in them and all the time Irene wiggled her ass and Krist did his cock twitch. Yeah, that was some day. He wished ta Krist somethin like that would happen again. A couple a times hed seen a nigga bitch walkin around with her tits hanging out, but that was different. It gotim horny, but not the way it did when he saw a white broads tits with big rosy nipples. Thats what he needed. A strange piece. Been a long time since he fucked anybody but Irene . . . Except, of course, for a couplea gangbangs at beer rackets, but that was different. Its not like really makin a broad. Its not that Irene aint a good piece – shes built real nice and got a great pair of tits – but he was gettin tired of the same old shit all the time. And lately she'd been breakin his balls about getting a job again. Fuck her. Why should he work? He dont get nothin outta it. Why should he get up in the mornin and break his balls? They was doin alright like this with Irene workin. – The baby was still crying, but he was completely accustomed to the noise now and with his mind preoccupied he didnt hear him. He continued looking carefully into each window. A young jew girl lived across from him and he watched her window for a long time. She had a nice pair of boobs and hed like ta catch her sometime. If only he could see in the bathroom window and watch her come outta the tub, man that would be somethin. Nice young stuff. Shit. Shes probably outta the house by now. He passed on to the next window. Why in the hell should I work? Break yaballs for what? Ya dont get nothin anyway. Shit. Almost 26 and whatave I got? Nothin. Why should I break my balls for some jew for a lousy couple a bucks a week and they get all the gravy. Fuckem. If I had a couple a bucks I could see somea the boys tonight and maybe we'd pick somethin up. Thats what I need ta straighten me out. Been feelin kindda crummy lately. Need ta go out with the boys is all. If I dont wanna work its my business. He finished making the rounds of the windows, but went over them again, quickly, but still there was nothing to be seen. Balls. He left the room. He ignored the now loud crying of the baby and went out to the kitchen, Helen walking behind him. I hope ta Krist Irene made a good pot of coffee this morning. He looked at the jar of instant coffee on the table and cursed Irenes lazy ass for not making a pot of coffee. He

242

heated some water and made a cup of coffee, shaking his head yes, no, at Helen who hadnt stopped talking since he came out, agreeing, disagreeing, telling her OK, wait a minute; not today, maybe tomorrow. He lit a cigarette, turned on the radio – Helen still talking – and finally told Helen to stop bothering him. I want to go out Daddy. OK, OK, let me finish my coffee, willya? He drank his coffee and smoked a cigarette then started to dress her, tearing clothes out of drawers, looking for an undershirt, and where the hell areya pants, cursing Irene for not laying out the kids clothes before she left. How inthehell did she expect him ta know where she kept everything and all the time Arthur was crying and Helen stood away, her thumb in her mouth, and Mike was goddamn mad because there was no reason why the things couldnt be where he could find them and why the hell didnt she dress the kid before she left and he finally said the hell with it and Helen started crying and he yelled ta shut up and shoved her in her room. He made himself another cup of coffee and lit another cigarette, trying to ignore Arthur, but he couldnt and knew that sooner or later he would have to change him just as he knew each morning when he awoke that eventually he would have to get up and he would reach this same point when he could no longer ignore the yellin brat and hed have ta change the pissy diaper. Krist, how he hated ta change the kid in the morning. He didnt mind so much in the afternoon, the other time he changed him (when he did), but in the morning it was disgusting. The goddamn diaper was soaked with piss and they stunk like hell. And usually there was a pile of shit and it was smeared all over the kids ass. He finished the coffee and cigarette, but didnt move from the table. Maybe he should go out and get a few bottles of beer first. Yeah, that was a good idea. He bought a few quarts of beer and came back feeling better. He poured a glass and went into the kids room, looked at Arthur, why doya have ta make so goddamn much noise. Krist, ya stink. He yanked the rubber diaper off, then carefully took out the pins and turned his head slightly as he slowly pulled the diaper off. O Jesus, what a fuckin mess! He clamped his teeth together and was so goddamn mad he wanted to slap the kid. Arthur finally stopped crying as the wet diaper was removed and Mike looked at him and told him hed better shut up or hed wrap the diaper around his goddamn head. He dumped the shit in the toilet bowl and dropped the diaper in a bucket. The bucket was filled with dirty diapers and he cursed Irene for not cleaning them yesterday like he told her. She knows she should wash diapers everyday, the sonofabitch. Shit. He went back to Arthur, put a clean diaper on him, pulled up the rubber pants, then dropped a few toys in the crib before going back to the kitchen and his beer. At least that much was over and now he could at least sit and have a beer and listen to the radio and maybe think of something to do.

* * * * * * * * * * * *

The laundromat was crowded and Lucy sat on a bench waiting. She sat the children beside her and told them to sit still, but Robert started kicking his feet and Johnny was sliding off the bench, Lucy grabbing his arm and pulling him back and telling him to sit still and be quiet. I dont want you running around like those other kids. Lucy glanced at the machines that had been assigned her by the woman in charge, trying to determine how much longer it would be before she could use them. She wished she had a magazine to look at to pass the time, but if she did she knew she wouldnt be able to concentrate because Johnny was sure to play with some other kid if she didnt watch him. She pulled him back to the bench and told Robert to keep his legs still. O, how she hated waiting in this place. Nothing to do but sit, and listen to those stupid women giggling and talking to each other and hehehehe-heing all over the place. Always laughing. O, she hated this place. Johnny had slid down again and was standing leaning against the bench watching his Mother to see if she would pull him back. She checked the machines again. Wont be too much longer. Johnny took a step – she hadnt done anything yet and maybe he could walk around now. Lucy pulled him back by the arm and sat him down. He would have to wait. Finally the machines stopped and the woman took her clothes out, Lucy eyeing them. They were still a little dingy. She got her clothes ready for the machines. Johnny, who had slid down again from the bench, was moping around. Robert watched his brother for a moment, then he too slid down and stood, holding on to the bench. Lucy put the soap in the machines, and saw Robert pick something up from the floor and quickly took it from him, then looked around for Johnny as she put Robert back on the bench. He was playing with a little boy at the other end of the laundromat and Lucy almost yelled, but controlled herself and calmly walked over to get him. Johnny was playing with a spick boy wearing dirty dun-garees and filthy ripped sneakers. Lucy wanted to yank Johnny away, but she calmly took his hand and took him back to where they were sitting. Johnny whined and wanted to know why he couldnt play with the other kid and Lucy told him that he must sit down, that he might get hurt by one of the washing machines. Johnny argued, but Lucy was firm. She smiled at him and told him to sit quietly. Then she looked at her machines and frowned as she saw that suds were above the indicated level and were actually visible on the edge of the funnel on the top of the machine where the soap was poured in. She stared at the rising mound of suds, her hand still on Johnnys leg, and watched it foam over the sides and run down the sides of the machine. She didnt know what to do and was too embarrassed to call the woman who worked there. The suds continued to billow over and a stream of water ran down between the machines. Finally someone called it to the attention of the woman and she came over, tinkered with something in the rear of the machines and the suds went down and then she asked who had the machine. Lucy got up and started apologising and the woman told her she should be careful of how much soap powder she put in the machine then told her where she could find the mop. Lucy got it and wiped up the water self-consciously avoiding everyones eyes. She replaced the mop and started feeling a resentment and at the same time incapable of keeping from wondering if the woman thought she was no better than the spick at the other end. She went back to the bench and saw that Johnny was not there, but had once again gone to play with the little boy. She yelled at him roughly and Johnny came running and jumped up on the bench, not daring to look at her (remembering the morning), but knowing she was glaring at him. The children sat still and Lucy said nothing, but stared at the machines, burning with embarrassment and resentment. The machines, finally stopped and she told the children to sit right there and she emptied the machines then sat back on the bench and waited to use the extractor. While she waited a woman came in with a cart of clothes and asked if she could use the extractor, the one in her laundromat across the way broke down. The woman in charge told her she would have to wait until all *her* people were finished, that she couldnt let people from other buildings come in here and use her extractor until her people were finished and she didnt know if theyd be finished in time, it was getting late and there were a awful lot of people waiting and she had to close soon. The woman was annoyed at having waited for an hour in the other laundromat and then the ghuddamn thing went and broke down and she was ghuddamned if shed take any lip from anybody. She said she just wanted to use the *ex*tractor and she'd wait ghuddamnit, but she was gonna use it and she didnt want no argument, glaring at the white-woman and ghuddamn mad at her for talking like that at her. Well, youll just wait until all my people are finished and *if* theres still time you can use it and dont be so damn snotty. Look, ah didnt come here to take any of yo shit, ahm just gonna use the *ex*tractor and thats all, yo hear? The woman wanted to tell her to get her black ass the hell outta her laundromat, but she didnt dare. She turned her back on her, suddenly deciding to help a woman (coloured) take her clothes out of the machine, then told the intruder (the nigga bastard) that this laundromat was only for the people in this building, and anyway, the woman in the other laundromat never lets any of my people use her extractor. The other woman walked over to her and told her not to give her any of her shit, that if she wanted to use the mothafuckan *ex*tractor that she'd use it ghuddamn it. The operator stood straight, put her hands on her hips and beamed. You can just get the hell outta here sister. We have ladies here who arent used to that kind of language (you filthy nigga whore). Dont chuall tell me what to do mothafucka. This heres for usall to use an ghuddamnit Im gonna use this mothafucka if ah gotta break yo fuckin haid. Dont you swear at me you sonofa (black) bitchen scum – Lucy grabbed Robert and the cart, and rushed from the laundromat, up the ramp and out into the air, rushing from the laundromat as she did from the elevator, Johnny running to keep up with her.

*   *   *   *   *   *   *   *   *   *   *

Abraham opened the door of his bigass Cadillac and looked smugly around at the people sitting, the people passing and the people washing their cars, children running back and forth with clean buckets of water, before getting in and closing the door with a flourish. He stretched his legs, pushing back against the seat, and smiled. It was his. Ghuddamn right. All his. He looked at the dashboard with all its knobs and patted it. Every ghuddamn hunk of chrome belonged to him, Abe. He started the motor and let it idle, then turned on the radio and opened the window on his side. He tuned in the station he wanted, tapping his foot as a sax screeched and wailed, took a cigarette out of the pack, placed it slowly and carefully between his lips, pushed in the dashboard lighter, leaned back, still tapping his foot and smiling, until the lighter popped out then pulled it from the socket and lit his cigarette, blowing the smoke at the windshield, watching it drift out the window. He looked again at the poor studs washing their cars by hand and sneered. You didnt catch this cat washing his own car Not ol Abe. He rested his elbow on the door, stretched his legs again and adjusted his genitals I ll fuck the lightskinned ass ofener). Ol Abe always felt relaxed and great in his Cadillac and today he felt betteranever. Ghuddamn if this wasnt a real fine day and he looked at the back seat, at the floor (seems to be a little messy, but the boys always clean it out after theys finished washin), rubbed his hand along the fine upholstery, patted the dashboard again (ghuddamn if it didnt shine like a babys ass), turned up the radio and once more dug the cats washin their cars with buckets of water, soap and sponges. Ghuddamn if it dont look like every ass in the Projects is out today washing his car. Thats not fo me. Ah *pays* to have that shit done. Ah, it was great, real great man, to just sit and dig the radio and smell the car, that special CADILLAC smell and not have those ghuddamn houserats arunnin all ovu-hya, and that ghuddamn bitch yellin. Abe inhaled deeply and flipped his cigarette out the window. Betta get mah ass movin. He threw the car into reverse and backed out, made a screeching u-turn (haha, looka those cats diggin me) and drove to Blackies garage. He stepped forth from his Cadillac and Blackie came over to greet him. How yodoin man? Great Blackie. Hows mah man? OK pops. Want the usual job? Youknow me, ah knows how to treat a Cadillac. Ahll be back afta awhile for it. Abe strolled down the block to the barber shop and when he opened the door everyone greeted him and he smiled and walked to a vacant seat, beaming at everyone and waving his hand, his popularity making him feel great, real great cause everyone knew he was a great guy, a real swingin cat, and everyone dug him the most. As soon as he sat down the bootblack came over and started shining his shoes. He wisht that chick could see him now and how everyone knew he was a great guy, but she'd know that tonight. Man, would she know it. She'd know she wasnt messin with no farm boy fresh from the south, but Ol Abe, and he was one stud who really knew the score (caressing his genitals) and she'd damn sure know it soon enough. The radio was playing and Abe sang along with the vocalist, singing much louder, and he knew he was a damn sight better than the cat on the radio, although he was good enough. The bootblack finished with Abes shoes and he flipped him a half dollar. Before Abe sat in the chair to have his hair cut he carefully combed it again, adjusting each wave until it was in precisely the proper position, then he sat down and said, the usual. He crossed his legs and checked the barber in the mirror as he cut. He supervised the cutting of each and every hair, having the barber lift a mirror to the back of his head every few minutes, making certain the back was absolutely straight across and not too short, checking the length of his sideburns, watching how he shaved around the ears and telling him to cut the tips of the few hairs that were sticking out on the left side just behind the second wave. The chair was levelled and Abe was shaved, the barber working carefully so there wouldnt be any irritation or danger of a slight rash, and Abe told him which way to go as he shaved the different parts of his face, telling him to be careful of that pimple. When he was finished the barber wiped his face with a towel, not too hot but just the way Ol Abe liked it, then carefully rubbed in skin cream and a special after shave lotion. Then Abe had his moustache trimmed and the hair in his nose cut. He stepped out of the chair and looked at himself in the mirror, combing his hair and adjusting the waves, and flashed a couple of bills into the barbers hands. He stayed for a while with the boys, listening to and singing along with the music, telling the boys about the fine chicks hes got after him and the cool brown-skinned chick that was givin him the eye last night and how he dumped some big mothafucka on his ass a few weeks ago in MELS, and ah mean he was big Jim, and he had a blade that long, but ah laid one onim and pow, he went down jus lake that, and showed them his fist and smiled and they all laughed and he waved again as he sauntered out the door. Yeah, they all liked Ol Abe. He looked at his watch, but it was still too early to pick up the Cadillac. Itll takem a few more hours to do a good job. Too bad, cause this was the kindda day you lake to take a ride and just cruise around and dig the music on the radio and maybe pick somethin up. Too bad that chick wasnt around now. They could go for a little drive . . . yeah, man, a little drive, hehehe . . . well, maybe we do a little drivin tonight . . . He snapped his fingers, sheeeit . . . He stopped outside the movie and studied the signs advertising the movies being shown. Two cowboy pictures were playing so Ol Abe decided hed kill the afternoon in the movie and sheeit, he always did dig cowboy pictures and when he got out the Cadillac would be ready.

*　　*　　*　　*　　*　　*　　*　　*　　*　　*　　*

THE PLAYGROUND

Most of the kids were out now, running around, knocking or being knocked down, depending upon their size. Some picked up a few bags of garbage that were lying around the halls and started a fire, running around it yelling, picking up pieces of burning garbage and throwing it at each other until a few doors opened and they were told ta get the fuck outta there ya little mothafuckas and they kicked the fire around the hall, yelled fuck you, and ran down the stairs, screaming, and out of the building. Others put strips of paper in the mail boxes with mail, then lit the paper and jumped up and down gleefully as the mail burned and the flames blackened the wall. When all the mail had been burned they rang as many bells as they could reach then ran screaming from the building. Heads popped out of windows and the kids were told theyd get their goddamn asses kicked if they didnt stop that shit and a bag of garbage and an empty bottle were thrown at them and the kids laughed and said up yur ass and ran to the playground where the smaller ones climbed up the sliding pond, knocking off the even younger kids, stamping on the hands of those who tried to climb the ladder, yanking another one off, kicking another in the face; then they made the rounds of the seesaws, flipping kids off, banging one in the face with the seesaw, the younger kids lying on the ground crying until a few parents, sitting in the sun, looked over and yelled, then the kids ran away to another part of the playground; and some of the bigger kids took a basketball away from the kids on the court and when the owner of the ball started crying for his ball they finally hurled it at him smashing his nose and making it bleed and one of his friends yelled at the fleeing kids calling them black bastards and they came back and told him he was blackeran shit and the other kids said they had black bedbugs and the other kid said his mother fucks for spicks and the kid pulled out a nailfile and slashed the other kid across the cheek and then ran, his friends running with him; and in the far corner of the playground a small group of kids huddled quietly, keeping to themselves, ignoring the fighting and screaming, their arms of comradeship around each others shoulders, laughing and smoking marijuana.

* * * * * * * * * * *

HURRYUP AND DRESS THE KID. I WANNA TAKE JOEY FOR A HAIRCUT. WHATAYA MEAN HAIR-CUT? SHAKING HER HAND IN HIS FACE. WHATS THE MATTA HE GOTTA TAKE A HAIRCUT? SOME-THING WRONG WITH HIS HAIR, EH? WHATZA MATTA YOU WANNA CUT IT OFF? ITS TOO LONG, THATS WHATZA MATTA. LOOK, HES GOT CURLS LIKEA GURL, PULLING JOEY BY HIS HAIR, ALMOST LIFTING HIM OFF HIS FEET, THE KID YELLING AND KICKING AT VINNIE. ITS TOO LONG, THATS WHATZA MATTA. MARY GRABBED A HANDFUL OF HAIR AND SAID WHATZA MATTA WITH THE CURLS? YOU DONT LIKE CURLS SO THE KID GOT-TA TAKE A HAIRCUT? NO, I DONT LIKE ALL THOSE CURLS, VIOLENTLY SHAKING THE HAND HOLDING JOEYS HAIR. I DONT WANIM LOOKIN LIKE NO GURL. HES GONNA TAKE A HAIRCUT. YURAZ HES GONNA TAKE A HAIRCUT. I LIKE HIS HAIR LONG AND CURLY AND ITS GONNA STAY LIKE DAT, PULLING SO HARD ON JOEYS HAIR SHE LIFTED HIM FROM THE FLOOR AND HE SCREECHED AND SCRATCHED HER HAND SO HARD SHE OPENED IT AND HE TURNED AND KICKED HIS FATHER AND SCRATCHED HIS HAND AND VINNIE LET GO OF HIS HAIR AND SLAPPED

HIM ON THE BACK OF HIS HEAD AND MARY KICKED HIS ASS AND THEY YELLED AT HIM, BUT JOEY DIDNT MIND, HE JUST KEPT RUNNING AND THEY TURNED BACK TO EACH OTHER. VINNIE YELLED AGAIN TA GET THE KID DRESSED SO HE COULD TAKEIM FOR A HAIRCUT AND MARY SAID HE DONT NEED ONE. MEEEEEE, WHAT A FUCKIN JERK. THE KIDS HAIRS DOWN TA HISZASS AND SHE SAYS HE DONT NEED NO HAIRCUT. YEAH. I SAY. I SAY. IT LOOKS NICE. I LIKE IT. HE AINT SUPPOSEDTA LOOK LIKE A GURL. WHO SAYS, EH? WHO SEZ. AND ANYWAY HE DONT LOOK LIKE NO GURL. HE LOOKS CUTE. VINNIE SLAPPED HIS HEAD AND GROANED. MEEEEEE, HE LOOKS CUTE. WHAT KINDDA CUTE WITH ALL DOZE CURLS. WHATSAMATTA WITH CURLS, EH? WHATSAMATTA? DIDNT YA BRODDA AUGIES KID HAVE CURLS AND DIDNT ROSIE MAKE IT STAY LONG, EH? EH? SO WHAT THE FUCK YAYELLIN ABOUT? YEAH. YEAH. AND YA SEE HOW CREEPY THE KID IS. LONG HAIR MAKES A KID CREEPY. THATS WHAT IT DOES. GODFABID MY KID GROWS UP LIKE THAT. ID GIVEM A SHOT IN THE HEAD. joey peeked at them from his room. WHO YA GONNA GIVE A SHOT IN THE HEAD, EH? WHO? WHATTAYAMEAN WHO? ILL GIVE YAONE TOO. YA THINK SO, EH? YEAH. GOAHEAD. GOAHEAD. ILL SPLIT YA FUCKIN SKULL. WHOSE SKULL YA GONNA SPLIT. EH? YOU MAKEIM TAKE A HAIRCUT. GOAHEAD, MAKEIM. YOULL SEE. I SAY HES GOTTA TAKE A HAIRCUT SO SHUT UP, YEAH? WAVING HIS HAND IN HER FACE AND MARY HIT HIM ON THE FOREHEAD AND YELLED SHE DIDNT WANT JOEY TA TAKE A HAIRCUT AND VINNIE SHOVED HER, GO WAAAAAAY, AND

WENT TO JOEYS ROOM. JOEY WAS SITTING IN
THE CORNER WATCHING THE DOOR AND
STARTED TO SCREAM WHEN VINNIE PICKED
HIM UP AND CARRIED HIM TO THE CLOSET
AND STARTED YANKING CLOTHES OFF THE
HANGERS. HE SAT THE KID ON THE BED AND
STARTED DRESSING HIM WHEN MARY CAME IN
AND SHOVED HIM AWAY FROM JOEY AND TOLD
HIM TA LAY OFF, HE DIDNT HAVE TA TAKE A
HAIRCUT, AND VINNIE SHOVED HER AGAINST
THE WALL AND TOLD HER TA LEAVEIM ALONE,
YEAH? AND CONTINUED DRESSING JOEY AND
MARY CAME BACK AND SCREECHED IN HIS FACE
AND STARTED SHOVING AND HE SHOVED BACK
WITH ONE HAND WHILE TRYING TO DRESS JOEY
WITH THE OTHER AND JOEY SAT ON THE BED
KICKING HIS FEET AND YELLING AND THE
YOUNGER KID CRAWLED IN FROM THE LIVING
ROOM AND SAT BY THE BED FOR A MOMENT
THEN HE TOO STARTED YELLING AND VINNIE
SHOVED MARY HARDER AND SHE FELL BACK,
TRIPPING OVER THE BABY, FALLING ON THE
FLOOR AND SHE JUMPED BACK UP AND STARTED
KICKING VINNIE AND HE BACKHANDED HER
HARD ACROSS THE FACE AND JOEY TWISTED
AWAY FROM VINNIE AND LAY ON HIS STOMACH
CRYING AND KICKING AND THE BABY WAS SI-
LENT FOR A SECOND AS MARY FELL OVER HIM
THEN STARTED WAILING EVEN LOUDER AND
MARY SAID TA LEAVE THE FUCKIN KID ALONE
AND VINNIE GRABBED HER BY THE SHOULDERS
AND SHOOK HER AND ASKED WHATZAMATTA
YA CRAZY AND SHOVED HER AGAINST THE
WALL AGAIN AND JOEY FELL FROM THE BED
ONTO THE FLOOR AND HE KICKED THE FLOOR

SCREAMING, HIS HANDS POUNDING THE FLOOR AND VINNIE LEANED OVER THE BED AND PICKED HIM UP AND STARTED DRESSING HIM AGAIN AND MARY PUMMELLED HIM OVER THE HEAD WITH HER FISTS AND VINNIE KEPT SHOVING HER AWAY AND DRAGGING CLOTHES OVER THE KIDS ARMS AND LEGS AND WHEN HIS SHIRT RIPPED AND VINNIE PULLED HIS ARM TOO FAR HE LET GO OF THE KID FOR A MINUTE AND PUNCHED MARY ON THE JAW AND SHE WENT STAGGERING THROUGH THE DOORWAY, BOUNCED OFF A WALL AND FELL TO THE FLOOR AND THE BABY WATCHED, STILL WAILING AND JOEY STOPPED KICKING FOR A MINUTE AND VINNIE DRAGGED SOMEMORE CLOTHES ON THE KID, THEN JOEY STARTED YELLING AGAIN, BUT HE WAS ALMOST DRESSED NOW AND MARY WAS STILL UNCON-SCIOUS AND VINNIE WAS STILL MUMBLING TO HIMSELF ABOUT THE KID GOTTA TAKE A HAIR-CUT, HE AINT GONNA LOOK LIKE NO CREEP AND AUGIE WAS GOD-DAMN MAD ROSIE DIDNT MAKE THE KID TAKE A HAIRCUT AND HE AINT GONNA HAVE NO SHIT LIKE THAT AND HE FINALLY GOT ENOUGH CLOTHES ON JOEY AND MARY STARTED TO MOAN AND VINNIE YELLED TA SHU-TUUUUP AND HE DRAGGED JOEY FROM THE ROOM INTO THE OTHER BEDROOM AND VINNIE GOT A JACKET AND PUT IT ON AND THE BABY HAD CRAWLED OVER TO MARY AND WAS SLAP-PING HER ON THE STOMACH AND GIGGLING AND MARY OPENED HER EYES AND VINNIE AND JOEY CAME OUT OF THE ROOM AND SHE TRIED TO GRAB VINNIES LEG AS HE STEPPED OVER HER, BUT HE JUST SHOOK IT LOOSE AND SHE WATCHED THEM LEAVE THE APARTMENT,

SLOWLY GETTING TO HER FEET AND SHE FINAL-
LY MADE IT TO THE LIVING ROOM WINDOW JUST
AS VINNIE AND JOEY WERE LEAVING THE BUILD-
ING, JOEY STILL YELLING, BUT NOT AS LOUD, AS
VINNIE DRAGGED HIM ALONG AND MARY
OPENED THE WINDOW AND YELLED COME BACK
YA FUCKIN SONOFABITCH AND VINNIE SHOOK
HIS HAND AT HER SHUTUUUUUUP, YEAH? AND
HE CONTINUED DOWN THE PATH TO THE
STREET, MARY STILL SCREAMING FROM THE
WINDOW . . .

*　　*　　*　　*　　*　　*　　*　　*　　*　　*　　*

Johnny almost drove Lucy crazy in the supermarket.
Robert sat quietly in the shopping cart, but Johnny skipped
ahead looking at the shelves, stopping to stare at people
and talk with other children. It seemed like every few
minutes she had to drag him away from some child and
he would skip off as soon as she freed his hand and when
she looked around again he would be with some child,
kneeling and looking under shelves or playing with some
kitten or the Lord knows what. And then, of course, he
wanted candy and Lucy finally had to twist his arm and tell
him to behave or she would beat him. O, how she hated the
weekends; having to shop in the crowded stores (Louis was
home for two whole days (sometimes), and he was always
in a hurry to go to bed, but he wouldnt sleep and wanted to
fool around all night), and the laundromat was so
crowded. She finally finished shopping and left the store.
She rushed along the street carrying Robert, dragging her
cart and Johnny, who was running to keep up and turning
every few minutes to look in a store window or to watch
kids play. She was doubly irritated by the people who
strolled along leisurely enjoying the warm weather and the

bright sun. Ada smiled at her when she passed her bench but Lucy ignored her (the filthy jew. Never changes her clothes) and rushed past her. She had to literally drag Johnny away from the children playing in front of the building and slapped his arm when he wanted to know why he couldnt stay down and play. She snarled in his ear and he ran in the building. Of course the elevator was still messed and she had to climb the stairs to the apartment. She couldnt understand why someone didnt clean the mess, after all everyone knew the porter wouldnt be back until Monday. The least someone could do would be to cover it.

Louis was sitting at the table drinking coffee and reading. She let the door slam and plopped in a chair. She took the childrens coats off and they ran yelling to their room and Lucy told them to play quietly. She poured herself a cup of coffee and plopped back in the chair. O, Im exhausted. Louis sipped his coffee (she usually doesnt pull that until we get to bed), continued reading and grunted. Im just worn out. Ive had to climb the stairs twice today with that heavy cart. Uh? Yes, twice. Lucy was slightly peeved at Louis's lack of interest in her discomfort, but reminded herself that he had to study. She waited until he looked at her before continuing. Finally Louis reached the end of a paragraph and turned to her. Whats that? I had to climb the stairs twice, speaking in an exasperated tone. Yeah? Yes. She told him about the mess in the elevator. Louis said he thought it would be easier to wait until you got home than do that. Then he smiled as he imagined how funny the person must have looked as he squatted in the elevator, shitting. Lucy said she didnt think it was so funny, not when you had to climb the stairs, but Louis continued to smile, wondering what would have happened if someone else had walked in the elevator just at that time. They sure wouldve been caught with their pants down. Louis laughed and Lucy frowned. Johnny came rushing out of the room shouting, Robert trailed behind, DA DA. Lucy grabbed Johnny and demanded to know what they were doing. Johnny stared at her and said playing. Well, why cant you play quietly? why must you always make so much noise – just playin cowboys. I dont care. Just play quietly. Do you have to run around like a ragamuffin? Now go in your room and play quietly. The children went back to their room and Lucy sighed. That boy sure can be nerve-racking. Hes under my feet all day long, always arunnin – running around the house yelling. O, it aint so bad as all that. Lucy almost corrected his using – all –, but hesitated knowing Louis would get mad. But I have him all day, everyday. You do not know how it is. Then why dont you just letim go out an play? Lucy cringed. Caus – Because I do not want him playing with any patched pants kids, thats why. Louis squirmed in his chair. He knew what was coming and he was determined to avoid an argument. If we lived somewhere else and had a bigger apartment it wouldnt be so bad. Louis said nothing, but breathed deeply and lit a cigarette – somewheres where I could let him out or where theres enough room so he wouldnt be underfoot all day. Four and a half rooms arent enough. And I dont even have any friends here (you dont have any anywhere). I have no body to talk to – O, what doya mean? Theres plenty a people to talk to around here. Why just look out the window, theres people all ovuh. *I* do not want to talk with those people (the word is *over*). Well, *ah* dont see anything wrong with living here and its goddamn cheap. And ah aint gonna move. But you dont know how it is all day. Already Louis was sorry he had allowed himself to argue, again, with Lucy, but he couldnt stop. Every week-end she starts a argument about something. Look, ah says we stay. This place suits me fine an if we moved we couldnt have no car an ah aint givin up the car. He got up and poured himself another cup of coffee and Lucy argued on.

He sat back at the table and tried to ignore Lucy and wished there was a goddamn baseball game on TV. Lucys voice droned on and he sat smoking and drinking trying not to hear her, not wanting to argue about the same old shit again and have her get pissed off and turn her back on him for a month when they went to bed. It was hard enough as it was to get her in the mood. She always had some kind of excuse and he was too tired to go out looking tonight. But he was damned if he was gonna give up the car – the children started yelling at each other and Lucy ran into their room – and anyway, school was only another few months. And once he got out hed have it made. And when he got himself a good job and a few bucks ahead, then maybe theyd move to a Middle Income Project, but he wasnt going to leave school now (and he wasnt getting rid of the car. If he didnt have that he might never get laid), especially after all the money hed paid them. And it was the best TV/radio repair school in the city – Lucy came back moaning about the kids always fighting over a toy – and hed get a job like *that*, and everybody knew how easy it was to knock down money repairing radio and TV sets. Lucy continued talking and Louis refused to argue, thinking, and having thought all day, of tonight, and wishing to hell there was a ball game on.

* * * * * * * * * * *

WOMENS CHORUS II

The women were still on the bench, looking at a couple who had just sat down on a bench across from them. I wonder how they fuck? The woman was short with braces on both legs, a small hump on her back and she walked with crutches. Her husband had a wooden leg and walked with a twisted limp. May be he unscrews his leg and fuckser with the stump. Laughter. I wonder if she hitsim with her crutches when she comes . . . The *cripples* looked at them and smiled and the women nodded and smiled. Maybe he tapser on the hump when he wants to get humped. Laughter. They smiled again at the cripples, then the smiles left all their faces and they groaned as they saw Mr. Green approach. His wife had had a stroke and was in the hospital and whenever he came out of the apartment he stopped the first one he saw and told them the entire story, and whenever he came in sight everybody ran, but the women were too lethargic to move. It was a funny thing how the stroke happened. We were just sitting in the parlour and all of a sudden she looks funny – you know, very pale like – and she moans and dribbles a little at the mouth and I helped her to the couch and she kind of passed out – I called her and shook her, but she didnt move – and I got one of the chairs from the kitchen and took it over to the couch – I couldnt move a big chair – and I sat there with her – I wouldnt leave her side for anything – I guess I sat there for over 4 hours, then I went next door and asked that nice young girl next door to come in and look at my wife – I dont know what I would have done without her – and she looked at her and said right away to call a doctor – such a nice young girl and smart as a whip too – so I did and they took her to the hospital. They gave her all kinds of examinations and they told me she had a stroke. I couldnt even see her until the next day. Shes been in the hospital 3 weeks now, but shes getting better. She ate very well yesterday, even had a second helping of the stew – she says it was very good – (the women continually looked at each other, giggling and moaning, hoping the old creep would go away and one of the women started looking through anothers hair, scraping off large hunks of dandruff, trying to get the dandruff out of the way so she could look for nits. The large hunks she just flipped away, but the smaller ones she cracked with her finger nail to see if they were just dandruff or a nit. If it snapped she showed it to the woman and told her she got one) she had two helpings of stew and she had a very good bowel movement this morning. It was soft and very dark. I guess the pills they give her make it dark like that. If she keeps improving they may let her come home soon . . . Mr. Green talked on and the women groaned and squirmed (the hunter completely absorbed in her work) and finally he finished and left, stopping someone else as they left the building and telling them the story. The women couldnt understand why he was so upset, the crazy ol bastard, he couldnt get it up for 20 years, or maybe more. Yeah. They cut the bone outta that a long time ago.

*   *   *   *   *   *   *   *   *   *   *   *

Mike got up from the table occasionally, taking his glass of beer with him, and looked out the window. He glanced at the other windows, but not with any real interest or expectation. It was too late to catch some broad walking around in an open bathrobe. He just looked out the window. He noticed the many people walking around and sitting on the benches and remembered that it was Saturday and that his friend Sal would be over. Probably with a bottle. Yeah. Sal would be over and they could get high. Great! He finished his beer then went back to the table and refilled his glass. There was no need to nurse his beer now. Sal should be there by the time he finished the beer and a few shots would set him straight. He turned the radio up and drummed on the table with his fingers. He felt better already. Yeah. Now there was something to do. He cleared the dirty dishes from the table and piled them in the sink. Helen asked again if she could go out and play and Mike almost said yes, but when he looked at her he realised he would have to dress her and he was in no mood to go diggin around looking for shirts, coats and all that shit. No. You can go out tomorrow. What the hell, it wasnt his fault he didnt know where all the clothes were. If Irene would put things out for him in the morning it would be different, but why should he have to go looking around for the kids clothes? Irene could take her out tomorrow. Thank krist Irene was off the next two days. At least he wouldnt have to take care of the kids. And if it was a nice day maybe hed go out somewhere. Take in a show or somethin. Irene usually broke his balls when she was home, always asking him to help her with this or that, and she'd go running around the joint bitchin because she had to wash clothes or clean the house. What did she think he was, a goddamn house maid or somethin. Fuck her. Thats her job. Why should I do it? Its not my fault Im out of work. Maybe he and Sal would go out and pick up some quiff tonight. Yeah. Maybe we'll make the rounds of the bars. I could use a little nookie. Thats what I need, a good piece of ass. He rubbed his cock with the palm of his hand. Thats what he needed. Irene had the rag on for a week and he couldnt even get some of the old stuff. He drank his beer and smiled thinking of picking up a nice lookin head and takin her home and layiner – Helen asked if she could have something to eat. Im hungry. O for krists sake. Why do ya always have ta bother me, trying to still think of the nice head he would pick up, but the image faded quickly and he couldnt bring it back to mind as he looked at Helen and listened to her. He buttered her a piece of bread and slapped some jelly on it and handed it to her. She walked away licking the jelly and when Arthur saw her eating he started whining and Mike got mad as hell. Why dontya stay out here and eat. Why do ya have ta break my balls all the time. Helen stared at him for a minute then slowly started walking back to the kitchen, but Arthur continued to whine. OK, OK goddamn it. Mike took the bottle out of the crib and filled it with milk. Here, goddamn it. Now shut up. Krist, I'll be glad when Irene gets home so I can get you kids off my back.

Irene didnt bother smiling at the customers when they asked her questions. She just told them how much it was; no they didnt have it in green; and that will be 2c tax; and she took money, gave change, dropped articles in bags and handed them over the counter. Saturday was always so busy. If it wasnt for all the crazy crowds on Saturday she wouldnt even think of the days off. There was always so much to do at home. That Mike wouldnt do anything. The bastard. By the time Tuesday came she was glad to go to work. The job wasnt bad. Especially now that she was used to it. It was just getting up in the morning. And she had a few girl friends at work. But Saturdays were terrible. But the day was more than half gone. And at least her period was over. She didnt tell Mike, but she was a week late this time. She was sure she was pregnant. That night the rubber broke. She was really frightened. She didnt want another kid. Not now, anyway. But if she did, whatthell. She supposed Mike would get a job. If he really had to. But that was a good night. The best they had in a long time. Maybe theyd have another one like it tonight. She was always so horny after her period. Mike might be drunk when she got home. He usually was on Saturday. She hoped he wouldnt drink too much. At least not so much he couldnt get it up. She wondered if Mike would get a job if she was pregnant. O well, theyd get by some-how. It didnt make much difference. Theres always Home Relief. But she didnt want to quit her job. It was better than staying home. The kids get on your nerves sometimes. If only she didnt have so much to do at home. She d talk to Mike about it again. When they were in bed tonight. She hoped he wouldnt be too drunk.

*

Sal had been there for a while, having brought a bottle and a bag of potato chips, just in case they got hungry, hahaha. Mike took a couple of quick shots, chasing it with the remainder of the beer, and he was feeling good. Arthur was quietly playing in the crib and Helen didnt bother him anymore about going out and was playing in her room coming out occasionally for a potato chip and Mike smiled at her and patted her head and told her she was a good girl. Sal had a few bucks and they figured theyd hit a few joints tonight and see what they could pick up. After the first few shots they didnt drink too fast, not wanting to get too high, it was too early yet, so they sat at the table sipping their whisky, listening to the radio, waiting for Irene to come home so she could take care of the kids; and waiting for night to come when they would go out and have a ball and get some ass. Yeah!

* * * * * * * * * * *

PROJECT NEWSLETTER
EVICTIONS

The following is a list of evictions from the Project during the last two months:

Morals	7
Dirty Housekeeping	3
Non Payment of Rent	2
Criminal	9
Disturbing the Peace	4
Miscellaneous	8

Be sure you do not break any of the Rules. We want this Project to be a safe and Happy place in which to live. Only you can help.

* * * * * * * * * * *

THE LESSON

A couple of the kids were sparring with each other, the others standing around forming a ring. They hit with open hands and each time one scored all the kids yelled. One of the kids fathers looked out the window and saw them and rushed from the building yelling at the other kids to leave his son alone and yelling at his son for fighting. The kids stared at him for a moment, not moving, then the other kids said they wasnt fighting, they was just foolin around. He was teachin Harold how to fight. The father grabbed his son by the arm and yanked him to his side and slapped his head, telling him he had been warned about fighting and hanging out with those crummy kids. Dont you know we could be evicted if you get in trouble? He pointed his finger at the other kid and told him to leave his son alone, that if he caught him hitting his son again hed take a strap to him. Harold stood pinned to his fathers side afraid to look at him and ashamed to look at his friends. His father continued yelling at the other kid and the kid told him again that they wasnt fightin, that he was just teachin him how to box. The father continued waving his finger in the boys face and told him he didnt have to teach his Harold how to fight. I'll teach him how to fight. I'll teach him how to kill, thats what I'll do. Im not going to have my son hit by lousy kids like you. If he wants to learn how to fight I'll showim. He started shaking Harold by the arm and told him if ever those kids bothered him again to pick up a stick and bash in their heads. Or a rock. The kids just stared at him until he stopped and, dragging Harold by the arm, left. When the door closed behind him another kid took Harolds place and the exhibition continued.

*　　*　　*　　*　　*　　*　　*　　*　　*　　*　　*

Abraham sat through the movies and the cartoons, continually looking at his watch until he got involved in the movie. One of the movies had a real bad cat who was shooting up everybody and Abraham was greatly impressed by the way he had everybody in the town shittin green until that bad bastard from Texas got on his ass and burndim. Ol Abe knew that cat couldnt fuck around with that Texas stud. He chuckled when the guy got his lumps at the end. When he left the theater he walked quickly to the garage to pick up his Cadillac. He looked it all over inside and out and smiled when he saw the big black body shining and the whitewalls gleaming. He paid the bill and gave the stud a buck tip and jumped in and drove off. He drove around for a while, just cruising around the streets, listening to the purr of the motor, feeling the steering wheel in his hands, digging the sounds on the radio. Even while driving he could see the whitewalls and the bigass fins in the back and he felt good. Real great. He drove past MELS BAR and stopped, honked the horn and waved to the guys inside, then slowly drove home. He parked the car, but didnt leave at once. He sat behind the wheel diggin the few cats who were still washing their cars. He stepped forth from his Cadillac and went home to lie down and rest for the night.

＊　　＊　　＊　　＊　　＊　　＊　　＊　　＊　　＊　　＊　　＊

WOMENS CHORUS III

The women finished their shopping, took the beer home and returned to their bench. Mrs. Olson, who had had a stroke 2 years ago when her husband died, came out and as she hobbled by the women watched her and laughed. She leaned forward slightly as she walked and dragged her right foot. She was unable to lower her right arm and it was bent at the elbow and stretched across her chest, her hand partially closed and jerking up and down. The women loved to watch her, wondering if she picked up chewing gum and dog shit with her right foot. She oughtta wear steel toe shoes. She probably got that way from jerking her husband off. Laughter. Maybe thats what killedim. One of the women looked up at a window on the fourth floor then called the others and pointed to a baby that had crawled out the window and was kneeling on the ledge. The women watched the baby as it crawled around on the ledge and window sill. Maybe he thinks hes a bird. Hey, ya gonna fly? Laughter. Others looked up and someone screamed and someone else yelled get back, O my God, O my God. Ada covered her face with her hands. The women continued to laugh and wonder when it would fall. People ran frantically in circles under the window; someone ran up the stairs and banged on the door, but no one answered. They banged again and listened at the door for a sound, hearing something, a murmuring, yet still no answer. They ran back down stairs and people asked if anyone was home? are you sure no one was in? Heard something . . . maybe kids . . . I dont know . . . what can we do . . . O my God . . . Hes moving . . . I cant look . . . call the cops . . . The people continued running in circles, some running to the street looking for a police car; someone else had called the Office and the women stopped laughing now that there were so many people around, but still looked anxiously, waiting for the small body to slowly slip over the edge of the ledge and fall down, down . . . then plop on the ground or in a hedge; and Ada looked at the window with every screech from the crowd, covering her eyes quickly after each peek; and the baby rocked back and forth on the ledge and seemed to be toppling and two men ran under the window to try to catch it and others raised their arms (the women still hoping for a little more excitement) and yelled go back – O my God – go back, and the baby leaned forward a little more and seemed to be looking down at the crowd and hysterical screechings came from them and the baby leaned back and the crowd sighed and someone yelled for the cops, theyre never here when you need them – O why dont they hurry; and someone ran back upstairs and pounded on the door and yelled, still no answer; and someone suggested lowering a rope from the window above and have someone lowered; then 2 Housing Authority Policemen came running up and yelled to the 2 men under the window to stay there and they ran up the stairs and opened the door with a pass key, rushing past the 3 children huddled by the door and into the room where the baby knelt on the ledge, and stopped a few feet from the window, then carefully and silently tiptoed the last few feet trying not to draw the babys attention fearing it might turn and fall, holding their breaths as one inched his arms out the window and grabbed the baby by the arms and quickly jerked him inside . . . held him for a moment . . . closed the window (the crowd still staring (the women annoyed that it was all over and that the kid didnt fall) then slowly lowering their eyes as the window was closed then slowly walked away). Then the policemen carried the baby to the living room and sat down, taking off their hats and wiping their foreheads. Christ, that was a close one, his body starting to tremble. The other nodded. The baby started to cry so they put him on the floor and he crawled over to his brothers and sister. The children stared, frightened, as the cops and the policemen smiled at them and asked them where their mommy was. They continued to stare at the cops and said nothing. Then one tottered over to them and asked if they really was policemen? and they said yes and the boy laughed. They asked him where his mommy was and he said out. Wheres your daddy. The youngster laughed and said mommy says hes drunk and he clapped his hands, laughing, and his sister added quickly that her daddy was gonna get a job on the boats and bring home lots of food and get a TV. The other 2 boys said nothing, continuing to stare at the policemen. I guess we'd better take them down to the office and call Welfare, eh Jim. I guesso. I'll see if I can get some clothes on them. He asked the children where their clothes were and they showed him, saying nothing and remaining silent as they were being dressed. As they were about to leave the oldest boy, about 5 years old, asked them not to tell their mommy what happened. She said not to let nobody in and if she see somebody came in she'll beatus. The cops reassured the children, left a note stating where the children would be, and left.

*　　*　　*　　*　　*　　*　　*　　*　　*　　*　　*

MARY STARED AT JOEYS HEAD WHEN VINNIE TOOK THE BOYS HAT OFF. SEE, NOW HE LOOKS LIKE A BOY. NOT LIKE SOME GODDAMN SISSY. MARY LOOKED AT JOEYS HEAD. YOU SONOFA-BITCH. LOOK WHAT YADID. WHATTA YAMEAN WHAT I DID. I DIDNT DO NOTHIN. I TOOKIM FOR A HAIRCUT. WHATSZAMATTA, YOU DONT LIKE THE HAIRCUT? YA SONOFABITCH, YA CUT ALL HIS HAIR OFF. ALL THE NICE CURLS HE HAD, YA CUTEM ALL OFF. HE LOOKS LIKE HES GOTTA BALDY. AW SHUT YAMOUT. YEAH? HE AINT GON-NA TAKE NO MORE HAIRCUTS. joey went to his room. YA STAY AWAY FROM ME YA SONOFA-BITCH. YA TINK SO, EH? I'LL BREAK YA FUCKIN LEGS. GO AHEAD. GO AHEAD. I'LL KILLYA. MEEE, SHES REALLY ASKIN FORIT. YEAH? YOULL SEE. YOULL SEE. JUST TRY. I'LL CUTCH YA-FUCKIN COCK OFF. WHOSE COCK YOULL CUT OFF, EH? WHOSE? YA CRAZY FUCK I'LL BREAK YA FUCKIN LEGS. VINNIE SHOOK HIS HAND IN MARYS FACE THEN TURNED AWAY AND SLAPPED HIS FORE-

HEAD, MARONE AME, WHATTAIDIOT, AND
WENT OUT TO THE KITCHEN AND HEATED
THE COFFEE. MARY WENT INTO THE KIDS ROOM
AND PICKED JOEY UP, HOLDING HIM AT ARMS
LENGTH FROM HER AND A LITTLE OVER HER
HEAD, TURNING HIM TO LOOK AT ONE SIDE
THEN THE OTHER. WHAT THEY DO TA MY JOEY?
THEY CUT ALL YA PRETTY CURLS OFF JOEY? YA
FATHAS A STUPID. ALL THOSE NICE CURLS AND
YA LOOKED SO CUTE. JOEY STARTED TO SQUIRM
AND SQUINT SO MARY DROPPED HIM TO HIS
FEET. I got a lollypop from the man. WHATTAYA
MEAN LOLLYPOP? WHAT MAN? What cut my hair.
I cried and he gave me a lollypop. SHE STORMED OUT
TO THE KITCHEN. WHATTA YAMEAN GIVIN THE
KID A LOLLYPOP, EH? WHATTA YAMEAN? WHATS
AMATTA WITH A LOLLYPOP? MEEE, YA THINK IT
WAS GONNA KILLIM OR SOMETHIN. I TOLDYA I
DONT WANT THE KID TA HAVE NO LOLLYPOPS.
WHATTA YA MEAN? WHATTA YAMEAN NO LOL-
LYPOPS? ALL THE KIDS GOT LOLLYPOPS. WHY HE
CANT HAVE ONE? I SAID. A KID CAN CHOKE TA
DEAT ON A LOLLYPOP YA STUPID BASTAD. DONT
YAKNOW NOTHIN? EVERYDAY SOME KID DIES
FROM A LOLLYPOP. WHATTA YAWANT FROM
ME? THE KID WAS CRYIN SO THE GUY GIVEIM
A LOLLYPOP. HE DIDNT DIE DID HE? THE KID
CRIED. THE KID CRIED. IF YADIDNT TAKEIM TA
THE BARBAS HE WOULDNTA CRIED. HE DIDNT
WANT NO HAIRCUT. WHY DONT YALEAVE THE
KID ALONE? WHY DONT YASHUT UP, YEAH? THE
KID TOOK A HAIRCUT OK. NOW HE DONT LOOK
LIKE NO CREEP. AND YA GIVEIM A LOLLYPOP
LIKE A REAL JERK. SUPPOSE HE HADDA DIED,
EH? SUPPOSE HE DIED? WHAT KINDDA DIED.

MEEE. THIS FUCKIN BITCH IS CRAZY. HOWS HE GONNA DIE FROM A LOLLYPOP? HE COULD SUCK IT RIGHT DOWN HIS THROAT AND ITD GET CAUGHT, YA FUCKIN STUPID. MARONE AME, SHAKING HIS HAND IN FRONT OF HIM. YA SOME FUCKIN NUT. YEAH? YA TINK SO, EH? JUST DONT COME TA BED THATS ALL. YA STAY OUT HERE TANIGHT. I'LL SLEEP IN THE FUCKIN BED AND DONT YA TRY TA TELL ME NOTHIN. joey and his brother played with plastic trains, tooting and whistling as loud as they wanted. They were having a fine time. YEAH? JUST TRY IT. I'LL BREAK YA LEGS. I SWEAR TA JESUS. I'LL BREAK YA FUCKIN LEGS.

* * * * * * * * * * * *

BABYS BURNED BODY BARED

The burned remains of an infant, judged to be about 10 days old, was found in the incinerator of one of the Citys Housing Projects today. George Hamilton, 27, of 37–08 Lapidary Avenue, a porter in the Project, was cleaning out the ashes of the incinerator when he came across the remains. He immediately notified the authorities. The police investigating the incident think that the body must have been dropped in the incinerator sometime during the night. The Housing Authority expressed the opinion that the baby did not belong to any of the tenants in the Project. The Police are canvassing the nighbourhood and the Project, but as yet no additional information has been released by any of the Authorities involved. This is the second body of a baby found in the Project this month.

* * * * * * * * * * * *

The women sat back on the bench after the baby had been taken safely from the ledge. It was fun while it lasted. Sure was a shame the cops had ta come so soon. Maybe he really woulda flyed. Laughter. Wait till the cops get on *her* ass, leavin the kids alone like that. I guess theyll reporter to Relief. Yeah, itll server right. I hope they kicker off. Boy, theyre really gettin tough on Relief now. We had anotha inspector around yesterday. She looked at the beer bottles and wanted ta know what they was doin here. Yeah, they got some nerve. I toler some friends boughtem. They usually come at the beginnin of the month and I get rid of all those things. Yeah, theyre always nosen around. How come they come back so soon? The inspector said someone had reported Charlie was workin. Thank krist he was off yesterday. Aint he workin steady? What for? 2 days a weeks enough. With Relief we make out good. The guy dont take no social security or nuthin, so they cant check up. Yeah, Henry gets a couple a days a week like that too. I hope no investigator comes around when *hes* workin. Charlie work today? No. Hes upstairs sleepin. Gettin plenty a rest for tanight, eh? Laughter. Yeah I'll give Henry a couple a beers and he'll be good for a while. Try puttin some Geritol in his beer. I hear it puts the bone back in. The women continued talking until they decided to go home and fix supper. They parted at the entrance to the building hoping each other was lucky tonight then went to their apartments and put the beer in the refrigerator, piled the dishes from the day in the sink and started supper.

*   *   *   *   *   *   *   *   *   *   *

Ada remained on the bench as long as it was in the sunshine. There were a few people walking about and a few children still played, but all the other benches were vacant. She sat alone. A few people had said hello and smiled though none had sat and talked with her. Yet it hadnt been too lonely a day. There were people around, and children, and the sun was bright and warm. Sometimes on days like this while the sun was still shining and the cool evening breeze was just starting to blow she and Hymie would stand in front of the store and watch the sun go down behind the building and watch the people rushing home from work . . . and the cars and trucks along the avenue . . . and it used to smell so nice and fresh, like sheets that had been on the line all day, and then she would go inside and fix supper and Hymie would eat his soup and smile . . . God bless poor Hymie.

The sun had gone down behind the building and the street lamps had been turned on. The breeze was cooler. Soon it would be dark. Ada got up and slowly left her bench and climbed the stairs to her apartment. She hung up her coat, closed all the windows then stood by her window. There were still a few children in the playground and she watched them, but soon the entire playground was in shadows and they too left. Cars and trucks passed along the avenue, but she ignored them and just watched the buses stop at the corner and people get off and rush home. She couldnt see the sun set, but she knew what it looked like and she imagined the purples, pinks, reds, laying on each other and mixing, just as she used to see it and as it looked in the picture puzzle she had of a ship on the ocean with the sun setting, the puzzle she put together and took apart, and put together again time after time after time all through the long cold heartless winters . . . and even sometimes in the spring when it rained for days and even looking from her window afforded no comfort. It was getting dark fast now and it seemed very cold outside, the trees barely visible from their shadows, the birds seeming to be jumping for warmth. There was nothing much to see now, just an occasional person rushing home, the cars and trucks which she ignored, and the waving ovals of light cast by the street lamps. She left her window and went to the kitchen. She fixed her supper and sat down at the table, still conscious of the empty chair opposite her. So long hes dead now and still it seems like yesterday we would sit and Hymie would put a big piece of sweet butter on an onion roll. She smiled remembering how much Hymie had loved onion rolls, and the way he would spread the butter. God bless him, hes happy now. No more suffering for him . . . only for me. She ate slowly and lightly then sat for a few minutes remembering how Hymie and Ira used to kid her because she took so long to eat. I could eat two times before youre finished Momma. Thats what Ira would say. I could eat two times. And all the cookies they sent Ira while he was in the Army. So many cookies. How many did he ever eat? Maybe he was dead a long time and we sent cookies. And he always wrote and said thanks Momma for the cookies . . . Such a good boy, God bless my Ira . . . She went into the bedroom, turned down the bed cover, laid out her nightgown and Hymies pajamas and went into the living room to listen to the radio for just a little while before going to bed.

*　　*　　*　　*　　*　　*　　*　　*　　*　　*　　*

Irene came home from work glad Saturday and her period were over. She was hoping maybe Mike would go to the store for supper, but she didnt expect it. But she didnt mind because she was in a good mood and it was nice out. Especially after being in the store all day. Before she opened the door she could hear the radio and wasnt surprised when she did open the door to see Mike and Sal sitting at the table drinking. She said hello and went straight to the bedroom and threw her jacket on the bed, then picked up Helen who had run after her. Helen told her everything she did and Irene ooooed and aaaaad and they both went in to see Arthur. She stayed with the children a few minutes then came out and, smiling, asked Mike how he was doing. Pretty good babe. Sal came over a little while ago and weve had a few drinks, hahahaha. She smiled again and wondered if she should ask him if Helen had been out. You want something to eat Sal? Of course he does. Ya think he dont eat? Irene shrugged her shoulders. I was just askin. How about gettin us a steak, handing her some money and smiling at Sal, making sure he understood that he was the boss in his house and just because Irene worked didnt mean he had to take any shit. Go getus a steak babe. Irene went to get her jacket, her good humor leaving her, feeling at that exact moment, humorless, and ready any second to lose her temper. He could have at least asked and not show off so damn much. She stopped in front of the table and asked him, attempting a slight nonchalance, how come Helen didnt have her overalls on? Didnt she go out today? No, she didnt go out today. Why not? It was a beautiful day. Because I didnt feel like trying ta find where ya hid her clothes. So what? not able to return her stare and turning his head to look at Sal, increasing the scowl on his face. Irene clenched her teeth and left the apartment. The bastard. Wont go to the store; wont clean the house (probably get too drunk tonight); wont even let the kid out. She hustled from one store to the other, buying what she needed; rushing home; prepared and served the meal in silence; Mike ignoring her, feeling he had made his point with Sal; he and Sal leaving as soon as the meal was over.

* * * * * * * * * * *

THE DASHER

A young girl was waiting alone for a bus. She stood smoking and looking down the street for the bus. She had to meet her friends in a few minutes and she was late. She kept stepping off the curb to look down the street. A car stopped a few feet from the curb and the guy in the car yelled, can I takeya somewhere baby? The girl looked at the car, then down the street, but no bus was coming. Comeon, I'll takeya where ya wanna go. She looked at the guy for a minute wondering if he would take her to 5th avenue or if hed start fuckin around. She thought she'd take a chance, hoping the guy wouldnt kick her out when she said no. He yelled again and she started to walk to the car when she saw the bus turn a corner 2 blocks away. She stepped back on the curb and turned her head. He yelled again and she said, go on, beat it. He mumbled something and she flipped her cigarette at the car and told him ta get the fuck outtahere. The guy started the car and drove away, but stopped a few hundred feet up the street and got out of the car. He whistled and yelled at the girl and when she turned and yelled at him ta go screw he opened his fly and took his cock out and waved it at her, still yelling and whistling. She told him ta shove it up his ass and he finally got back in his car and drove away. The young girl watched the car go up the street then turned as the bus approached. What a fuckin creep.

*   *   *   *   *   *   *   *   *   *   *

Nancy and the kids were still eating when Abraham got up. She asked him did he want some supper and he said hell no. He didnt want to eat none a her slop. He filled the tub and sat in the water smoking a cigarette, gently rubbing himself with the soap with his free hand, thinking of the brownskin gal and contemplating his stiffened dick. After he finished his cigarette he lathered himself up good, carefully and gently lathering his crotch so it would be sure to smell sweet (kissen sweet, hehehe), then rinsed and dried himself. Then he put deodorant under his arms and balls; massaged skin cream into his face; splashed after shave lotion on his face, neck and chest; rubbed pomade between the palms off his hands and rubbed it on his hair, then spent 20 minutes combing it carefully and adjusting his waves. Ghuddamn if he wasnt a sharp lookin stud. He checked the back of his head with the small mirror then satisfied that each wave was in its proper place he washed his hands and went back to the bedroom to dress. He put on his new white on white shirt with the Hollywood Roll collar and tied his silk lavender and purple tie in a large windsor knot. He selected his brown suit, the one he had made last year, and man its a sharpass suit. Put me back a 100 clams. He carefully adjusted the waist of his shirt before pulling the thin belt tight. He put on the jacket, buttoned it and rolled the lapels, fixed the handkerchief, and straightened out the things in his pockets. Then he took down the cool tan top coat, checked his shoes, put the coat on, then carefully placed his hat on his head. Man, he was ready. He left the house and didnt stop till he opened the door of his bigass Cadillac. He sat behind the wheel and pulled the door closed, smiling as he heard the heavy thud of the door. Sheeit. This is gonna be a night. I mean a *night* Jim . . .

* * * * * * * * * * *

WHATTA YAMEAN THE SAUCES NO GOOD? THATS WHAT I SAID, THE SAUCES NO GOOD. WHATS THE MATTA, YA DONT UNDERSTAND ENGLISH? ITS NO GOOD. NO GOOD. NO GOOD. WHATTA YAKNOW ABOUT SAUCE? MEEEE, WHATTA I KNOW? I KNOW IT STINKS. NOT EN-

OUGH GARLIC. ITS GOT THE SAME GARLIC. JUST
LIKE ALWAYS. THE SAME 8 CLOVES OF GARLIC
AND YA SAY NOT ENOUGH GARLIC. YUR A FUCK-
IN DUMMY. ITS GOOD SAUCE. DONT TELL ME ITS
NO GOOD. WHOSE A FUCKIN DUMMY? EH? WHO?
I'LL GIVEYA A RAP IN THE MOUT IM A DUMMY.
YA CANT EVEN MAKE A SAUCE. WHY DONTCHA
EAT AND SHUT UP, YEAH? I DONT LIKE THE
SAUCE, BANGING HIS FORK DOWN ON THE TA-
BLE AND SHAKING HIS HAND IN MARYS FACE. ITS
A FUCKIN IRISH SAUCE. NO GARLIC. NO GARLIC.
little ralphy picked up a string of spaghetti and dropped it
on the floor. joey picked it up and put it back on his plate.
ralphy threw another string down and joey picked it up.
DONT TELL ME. THERES NOT ENOUGH GARLIC. I
LIKE GARLIC IN MY SAUCE. SO SHUT UP OR I'LL
RAPYA OVA THE HEAD. AAAA, WHATTAYA-
KNOW, EH? WHATTAYAKNOW? little ralphy picked
up a handful of spaghetti and threw it hitting joey in the
face. joey yelled to stop and slapped ralphys hand. ralphy
yelled and threw another handful in his face. joey hit
ralphy with a handful . . . GET ME ANOTHA MEAT-
BALL. I CANT EAT THE MACARONI. YA CANT EAT,
YA CANT EAT? WHATTAYA, A KING OR SOME-
THIN? YA CANT EAT. GET ME ANOTHA MEAT
BALL AND SHUTUP. WHATTSAMATTA YA CANT
GET THE MEATBALL YASELF, EH? WHATTA YA-
MEAN GET IT MYSELF? GET ME ANOTHA MEAT
BALL OR I'LL BREAK YALEG. AAAA, GETTING UP
AND LADLING ANOTHER MEATBALL OUT OF THE
POT AND PLOPPING IT ON VINNIES PLATE. MAYBE
I CAN EAT THIS. CANT EVEN MAKE A SAUCE.

*　　*　　*　　*　　*　　*　　*　　*　　*　　*　　*

Lucy said little during the meal, just reminding Johnny to eat from time to time and asking Louis to pass something. Half way through the meal Robert decided he didnt want to eat any more and Lucy forced food into his mouth in between feeding herself and telling Johnny to eat. When she had finished she started clearing the table, forcing the last bit of food on Roberts plate into his mouth. Louis just left the table and turned on the TV. Johnny started playing with his food and Lucy yelled at him sharply and Johnny whined and started eating and Lucy told him to hushup and eat. Louis felt like telling her to stop yellin, ghuddamn it, and rap her side the head. Seemed like she was always yellin about somethin. Especially on the weekends. He just stared at the TV thinking about goin for a drive tomorrow (maybe alone), and hoping the next few hours would pass fast. Lucy finally shoved the last spoonful of food in Johnny's mouth then did the dishes, leaving the kitchen occasionally to tell the children to be quiet (Louis squirming in his chair), then finishing the dishes she put the children to bed and sat in the living room, saying nothing, and watched TV. Louis turned to her once in a while and made a comment about the show hoping to get her in a good mood before they went to bed, but Lucy only grunted, thinking how soon she would have to go to bed with him and it would start like every weekend (and many week nights too) and just the thought made her muscles tighten and her flesh get clammy. Lucy just grunted so Louis figured the hell with it. Theyd be going to bed soon and maybe tonight will be different.

* * * * * * * * * * *

THE QUEUE

The Welfare checks were cashed and there were long lines outside the Liquor Store across the street from the Project.

The owner had his 2 sons and a brother helping him as he did every Saturday night. The store was in the middle of the street and the two lines went out of sight around each corner, and the cop on the beat stood near the entrance so a fight wouldnt start as people pushed their way into the store. Yet even with the cop there there was much pushing and cursing. The clerks in the store worked as fast as they could and wrapped the bottles quickly, but still the lines were out of sight around both corners. Those at the end of the line would step out occasionally and look to the front wondering how much longer they would have to wait and then finally they would turn the corner and eventually they would come in sight of the lighted window and then they could at least look at all the bottles on display and then the time seemed to pass faster with their goal in sight. Someone tried to get in ahead of time, but someone else pulled him out of the doorway and an argument started and everyone yelled for them to clear the front of the store so they could get in and the owner came out and frantically yelled at them to stop (the people in the store fearing something would happen to prevent them from getting their bottles after having waited on line for so many hours) and finally the cop came over and yanked them both out and told them to beat it. They pleaded to be allowed to get their bottles or at least to get on the end of the line (offering the cop money), but the cop refused (not wanting to louse up the beautiful deal he had with the owner) and they finally walked off, sneaking back and giving money to friends to get them a bottle. Before the last customer was taken care of the clerks were soaked with perspiration and completely knocked out, but soon the last few customers were in the store. Many parties had already started and as the last customers bought their bottles and walked happily toward home the bells in a nearby church tolled midnight.

*   *   *   *   *   *   *   *   *   *   *

Abraham stepped into MELS and stood by the door for a moment digging the scene, his hands in his coat pockets, a coolass stud man, and every cat in the joint knew it. He waved to his boys, hung up his hat and coat and went to the bar, ordered a scotch and tossed a bill on the bar. He leaned sideways against the bar and dug the scene. The bar was not too crowded and the brownskinned gal wasnt there yet. He went in the back and sat at a table and ordered some of those fine ribs that were so great at MELS and sucked each rib dry then sat back sucking his teeth and smoking. Man he felt great. He paid the check and went to the bar, saw the brownskinned gal and went up to a cat he knew who was standing near her. He patted the cat on the back, called the bartender, give my man here a drink, ordered another scotch and tossed a 20 dollar bill on the bar. Man that chickll have big eyes now. He knew how to play it cool. Yeah, ol Abe was a cool ass stud. He let his change lay on the bar and when he finished his drink he ordered another and told the bartender to give the young lady a drink. He smiled at her and when they got their drinks he slid over next to her and told her his name was Abe. Ol honest Abe, hahaha. Mahns Lucy. He asked her to dance and he winked at the cats at the bar as they walked to the dance floor. Sheeit, nothin to it when you operate like ol Abe. They danced and he told her she danced real great and she must be new around here, he comes here all the time and he never seen her before and she smiled and said yes she'd only been here a few times before and they danced and drank and Ol Abe smoothed talked her and he was in and he told her he had a Cadillac, with whitewalls and would she like something to eat and when you with ol Abe you move and he knew this would be a great night and hed fuck the ass of this bitch.

*

Nancy put the kids to bed and got out the bottle of wine she stashed in the closet. She sat down and watched TV for a while, taking slugs from the bottle, then went to bed and lay there drinking, smoking and playing with her crotch. She wisht the fuckin Abe would come home and lay her. The sonofabitch aint fucked me but once in the last month and nobody else ever come around this house. If she could get somebody to sit with the kids she could go out, but she couldnt get nobody. Sheeit. She was tired. Almost felt like going to sleep. But it was too early yet. Still almost half a bottle left too. She'd drink that first. Somebody might come around looking for Abe. No sense in waiting for him though. He'll be gone all night. Sheeit. Ah need me some cock. She finished the bottle and threw it down the incinerator then went back to bed and lay down, remembering how big and hard Abes cock was and how it felt going in.

* * * * * * * * * *

THE WORSHIPPERS

A woman screeched hysterically, AH LOVESSIM, AH LOVESIM and she rolled on the floor, beating the floor with her fists. The people in the adjoining apartments listened, laughing. COME DOWN! COME DOWN! and someone beat a drum, someone else pounded on a table, OOOOOOO AH LOVESIM! AH *DIE* FORIM! and other voices screeched and a roar came through the walls, the people on the other side listening and laughing. OOOOO JESUS! JESUS! OOOOOO JESUS! and the other voices roared a HAAAAL LAY LOOOOOO YAAAA! WE *LOVESYA*! O *JESUS*! WE *LOVESYA*! and the beating of drums and table grew louder and a voice moaned AH SINNED! AH SINNED! OOOOO

282

LORD, AH SINNED! FORGIVE ME LORD! another body fell to the floor and grovelled and beat its fists and the drummer beat frantically and the clanging of a pot joined the drum and table and other bodies fell to the floor and they rolled and beat and kicked and the voices screeched and boomed and roared AH LOVE-SIM! AH LOVESIM! HAAAAL LAY LOOOOO YAAAA! OOOOO LORD! LORD! HAAAAL LAY LOOOOO YAAAA-DA-DUMDADUM-DADUMDA-DUMDADUMDADUM-WEES YO CHILLEN LORD! O BLESS US LORD-AH SINNED! AH SINNED! FO-GIVE ME LORD! OOOOOOO LORD FOGIVE A MISERABLE SINNER! (ears pressed against the wall, hands raised for silence, laughter) – AN JOSHYA TUMBLED THE WALLS! OOOO *JERICHO*! O *JER*-ICHO! – BABUMBABUMBABUMBABUMBABUMBA-BUMBABUM – EEEEEEEEEEEAAAAAAAAA – OO OO MERCY! OOOOO MERCY! FORGIVE YO CHIL-REN LORD! FOGIVE WE SINNERS! – COME DOWN! COME DOWN *JESUS*! – HAAAAL LAY LOOOOO YAAAA (a door was opened slightly to hear better) – AH *LOVESIM*! AH *LOVESIM* – HAAAAL LAY *LOOOOO* YAAAA – A MISERABLE SINNER – COME DOWN – OOOOOOOO – IN THE FIERY FURNACE – O LORD! LORD! – DRRRRRR – COME DOWN – BLESSUS! BLESSUS! – *JESUS! JESUS! JESUS! JESUS! JESUS! JESUS!* – HAL LAY LOOOOOOO YAAA! LORD – THE PEARLY GATES – WE *LOVE-SYA* – COME DOWN – EEEEEE-AAAAAA – O *JESUS* – BLESSUS – AH LOVESIM – YO CHILREN – SIN-NERS – FOGIVE – AMEN! – AMEN! LORD! AMEN! and the door was closed.

*   *   *   *   *   *   *   *   *   *   *

THE CONTEST

The street was quiet and a gang of young spades on one corner started walking toward a gang of spicks on the other, each gang ripping the aerials off the parked cars; some carrying rocks, bottles, pipes, clubs. They stood a few feet apart in the middle of the street calling each other black bastards and monkey mothafuckas. A car came along the street, horn blowing, trying to pass, but they didnt move and finally the car had to back out of the street. The few people on the street ran. The gangs remained in the middle of the street. Then someone threw a rock, then another was thrown and 30 or 40 kids were screaming, throwing bottles and rocks until there were none left, then they ran at each other swinging clubs and whipping the car aerials, cursing, screaming, someone crying in pain, a zip gun being fired and a window breaking and people yelled from windows and one of the kids went down and was kicked and stomped and knots of kids formed, swinging, clubbing, kicking, yelling and a knife was stuck in a back and another went down and a cheek was cut to the mouth with an aerial and the ragged flesh of the cut cheek flapped against the bloodied teeth and a skull was opened with a club and another window was broken with a rock and a few tried to drag another away as three pairs of feet kicked at his head and a nose was smashed with a pair of brass knuckles and then a siren was heard above the yelling and suddenly, for a fraction of a second, everyone stood still then turned and ran, leaving three lying on the street. The cops came and people came back to the street and the cops kept them back, asking questions and finally the ambulance came and two were helped in the ambulance the third being carried. Then the ambulance left, the cops left, and it was quiet once again.

*　　*　　*　　*　　*　　*　　*　　*　　*　　*　　*

As soon as they got in the door the guy grabbed her ass. Goddamnit, cant yawait, pushing him away. She staggered and leaned against the wall, the guy leaning over her kissing her neck as she yanked open a closet door looking for a bottle, then slammed it shut when no bottle could be found. She looked around trying to figure out what was wrong. Somethin was wrong. Maybe her husband came home. She called. Called again and still no answer. She pushed the guy away and staggered into the bedroom to see if he was there, but he wasnt. Guess he aint here. Somethin sure as hells wrong. Then she remembered her kids. They should be here. She looked in their room and called, but they were gone. Shit, whered them little bastads go. I toldem ta stay put. She went back to the kitchen, the guy still behind her pulling her coat off and grabbing her ass. She looked around the kitchen and the living room, reaching behind her and bouncing the guys balls with her fingertips, the guy slobbering over her, groping and mumbling. Finally she saw the note left by the Police. Well, fuckem then. They can stay the night. She went back to the bedroom, the guy behind her. They undressed, fell onto the bed and fucked.

* * * * * * * * * * *

Mike and Sal made the rounds of a few joints, but couldnt score. They had danced with a couple a broads, but nothing else. Not even a phone number or a date for the next weekend. Sal wanted to try a spick joint on Columbia street, but Mike didnt feel like walking that far and anyway he didnt trust the spicks. So they stood at the bar drinking, hoping something might come in that they could latch on to, getting drunker. Mike laughed at Sal and toldim he could go home and get laid and Sal had to pull his prick. Sal laughed and said that was OK, hed rather pull his prick than take care of a couple a kids all day. Thats OK man, at least I get mine. They had another drink and Mike was getting tired of hanging around, and was too goddamn horny to wait any longer. He told Sal he was gonna leave and asked him if he was goin. No, I think I'll hang around a while. Nothin ta do home. Mike told him not ta pull it too much, he was goin home ta get laid (and by krist he was, rag or no rag). The apartment was dark and Mike let the door bang then stumbled toward the bedroom, cursing the fuckin chairs for bein in his way. Irene woke when Mike came in and listened for a moment to hear if the kids woke up, then waited for Mike. She said hello and he flopped on the bed and started undressing, throwing his clothes onto a chair. You still awake? You woke me up when you came in. Whatid ya want me ta do, crawl through the key hole, determined he wouldnt take any shit off her tonight and if she said a word hed knocker teeth in. I didnt say anything Mike. Comeon, come to bed. He finished undressing and flopped over toward her and she put her arms around him. He tried to kiss her, but he missed her mouth and kissed her nose and mumbled something about her staying still and she finally directed him properly and she kissed him and Mike fumbled around for her crotch and they kissed and Irene ran her hand along the inside of his thigh and Mike squirmed and grabbed her crotch and they continued kissing and squirming and Irene worked steadily and expertly with her hands and tongue, but after 15 minutes Mike still couldnt get a hardon so he cursed and rolled over on her and tried to get it in anyway, but it kept bending and flopping out and he tried to stuff it in with his finger but it was useless and Mike cursed her for a useless bitch, still trying, still stuffing, until he eventually passed out and rolled off her. Irene pulled her arm from around him and sat up looking at him, listening to him breathe, smelling his breath . . . Then she laid down and stared at the ceiling.

*   *   *   *   *   *   *   *   *   *   *

Naturally Lucy smiled demurely when Abe asked her if she'd like to cut and asked where theyd go and ol Abe said theyd make a party of their own and Lucy hesitated and ol Abe turned the sweet talk on that chick and told her, comeon baby, we'll have a time and he giver the *BIG* smile and she started to waver and ol Abe knew, as he had known all along, that he would make another conquest. Sheeeit, theres no bitch livin that ol Abe couldnt fuck. They left MELS and Abe let her look his Cadillac over before he opened the door. He wanted to be sure she saw those bigass fins and the whitewalls. Abe flipped on the radio and handed her a cigarette and they took off. They drove downtown and stopped at a hotel and when they got up to the room ol Abe tipped the boy big and asked for a bottle of whisky and some ice. He came back with it in a few minutes and by the time Abe poured the drinks Lucy was undressed and in bed. Ol Abe stared at those fine tits and set the drinks down and undressed. As he rolled over on her the first time he smiled thinking how hed have that bitch callin him DADDYO before that night was ovuh. After fucking her once Abe wanted to have a drink and a smoke, but Lucy wasnt the type of girl who believed in rest periods so ol Abe sunk it again and this time he really concentrated on his work, but he didnt have his drink and smoke until he had fucked her 3 times and by then ol Abe was even thinking of a little sleep. Not much, just a little. Lucy finally gulped her drink down and put out her cigarette and rolled over on Abe and though he was a little beat he did justice to the girl, but he was thinking hed have to stop for a while. After the fourth piece they did stop for a while, but Lucy wouldnt let him sleep, continually playing with his ear, kissing his neck, caressing his balls, playing with his cock until it was hard and then she pulled him over again an ol Abe fucked, but he wasnt concentrating too hard and was thinking that the ghuddamn bitched fuckim ta death.

* * * * * * * * * *

Most of the parties in the Project were over and the only lights lit were in those apartments where pay-parties were being thrown where the guests played cards and dice and the host cut the game and supplied beer at 35c a can, gin at 6oc a shot, wine at 3oc a glass, sandwiches 5oc each and a real fine chicken dinner with rice and yams for a buck and a half. Occasionally someone got too drunk and accused someone else of cheating and started an argument or pulled a knife, but the host was always fast and cooled the scene with a quick rap on the head with a small club and so no real disturbances occurred. The rest of the Project was dark and quiet, the only noise caused by a passing drunk or someone being mugged, the victim, when regaining consciousness, usually yelling like hell for the cops, but this didnt happen more than once or twice on a weekend night and bothered no one. VINNIE AND MARY HAD STOPPED ARGUING, VINNIE FINALLY PULLING HER LEGS APART AND GETTING A PIECE BEFORE GOING TO SLEEP, AND THEY ROLLED NOISILY IN THE BED, THE SPRINGS SQUEAKING AS THEY SLEPT UNDER THE PICTURE OF THE BLESSED MOTHER; Lucy and Louis had been asleep for hours, their backs to each other, her body still stiff and tense, Louis grumbling in his sleep; Mike rolled and grumbled drunkenly, but Irene eventually fell asleep; Ada slept, after kissing Hymies and Iras pictures, with one hand touching the pajamas on the other side of the bed; and Nancy dropped off with her clothes still on and her hand still on her crotch; and even ol Abe was eventually allowed to sleep for a while.

* * * * * * * * * * *

Abe was dragged from sleep with the hardening of his prick. He had trouble focusing his eyes and could feel something brushing lightly against his thighs and stomach. He raised his head slightly and could see the fine nipples of Lucys tits caressing him as she sucked his cock. When she saw his head move she got up and sat on his dick and rotated, smiling at Abe, his eyes opening wider with each gyration. She sat on it grinding away and leaned over and took two cigarettes from the table, stuck one in her mouth and one in Abes, then lit them. You want a drink daddyo. Abe shook his head, moving automatically in perfect time and rhythm with her grinding. He took a few drags of the cigarette then put it out and started to fuck with concentration . . .

* * * * * * * * * * *

The sun rose behind the Gowanus Parkway lighting the oil filmed water of the Gowanus Canal and the red bricks of the Project. Church bells announced the beginning of services. Ada looked out her window for a while before starting breakfast; Louis got up planning on getting out as early as possible, alone, and going for a ride; Irene woke up before Mike and laid in bed listening to him grumble and wondering how he would feel when he woke up; VINNIE GOT UP FIRST AND YELLED FOR THE KIDS TA KEEP QUIET, YEAH? AND DRAGGED MARY BY THE ARM ACROSS THE BED AND TOLDER TA GET

UP: Nancy woke, scratched her crotch then smelled her finger and yelled for the kids to shutup. When ol Abe got home the kids were sitting at the table yelling and eating and he told them to be quiet, he wanted to sleep and went into the bedroom, staggering slightly, his eyes red and barely open. He carefully took off his clothes and hung them up, put on his hairnet and went to bed. Nancy came in and lay down beside him and started tickling his asshole. He shoved her away, laughing at her, and told her to get the fuck out and leave him alone. She told him she werent goin, that she was gonna have some cock and he backhanded her across the face and toler ta go get a banana and she called him a noaccountblackniggabastard and he punched her in the motherfuckin face, knocking her off the bed, and toler ta get her ass outta there or I'll bust ya apart woman, and rolled her out of the room. She crawled out to the kitchen and pulled herself up, holding onto the edge of the sink, still yelling he was a blackniggabastard, then let cold water run over her head. Her daughter came over to help her and Nancy continued yelling and then the frustration started her crying and her daughter told her not to cry, Jesus loves us Mommy. Nancy told her to get the fuck away from her.

Abraham slept.

A NOTE ON THE AUTHOR

Hubert Selby Jr was born in Brooklyn, New York. After leaving school he went to sea until illness forced him to leave the Merchant Marines. He began publishing stories in the 1950s, but it was the appearance of *Last Exit to Brooklyn* in the mid-1960s that brought him widespread recognition. On British publication the book was prosecuted for obscenity, but won its protracted court case on appeal. Hubert Selby's other works are *The Room* (1971), *The Demon* (1973), *Requiem for a Dream* (1978), *Song of the Silent Snow* (1986) and *The Willow Tree* (1998). He died in Los Angeles, California in 2004.

A NOTE ON THE TYPE

The text of this book is set in Linotype Sabon,
named after the type founder, Jacques Sabon. It
was designed by Jan Tschichold and jointly
developed by Linotype, Monotype and Stempel,
in response to a need for a typeface to be
available in identical form for mechanical hot
metal composition and hand composition using
foundry type.

Tschichold based his design for Sabon roman on
a fount engraved by Garamond, and Sabon italic
on a fount by Granjon. It was first used in 1966
and has proved an enduring modern classic.